FLIRTING WITH THE ROCK STAR NEXT DOOR

NADIA LEE

Flirting with the Rock Star Next Door

CHAPTER 1

Emily

I stared at the blank screen and huffed out a frustrated breath. I'd already floundered around for a week, writing nothing because I'd been blocked worse than a sinus during hay fever season. Fear was pounding at me, my veins throbbing in my head.

One star, this book sucks.

One star, I can't believe anybody with a brain would read this.

One star, quite possibly the worst book ever.

The actual reviews left on my last book. Mom had told me to ignore them and cheer up because the book had also received over six hundred five-star reviews. But of course the crappy ones always hit the hardest.

And now they were hanging over me like a dark miasma, sucking up all my creative energy. Just what the hell was so terrible about the last book? And how could those reviews have appeared so fast after the book went up on Amazon? They were like a freakin' guerilla hit squad.

Now I had two weeks to hammer out the last fifty thousand words. It was already seven in the evening. Another day almost wasted.

Crap.

My phone started ringing, distracting me from my mental diatribe against my creativity—or lack thereof.

It wasn't one of my writing pals, because they knew better than to call when I was working to meet a deadline. So it could only be...

Mom.

Dread curdled in my belly. We chatted once a month to discuss my social media stuff because she managed my accounts for me. I paid her a set amount every month so she'd feel more financially independent and assertive. She needed that, living with my dad, who, well... Calling him a control freak would be kind. "Asshole" was starker, but much closer to the truth.

But this wasn't a scheduled call. And if Mom wanted to show off some nice stuff she got while out shopping, she usually just texted pictures.

So this could only be about the longstanding marital drama. I wished I could ignore it, but it was likely an emergency that would give me one more reason to hate Dad.

"Hi, Mom," I said, keeping my voice sympathetic despite the impatience and annoyance for being write-blocked bubbling inside me. I told myself I wasn't doing anything productive anyway, so what would be the harm in spending some time to console her?

"Hello, baby! Am I interrupting anything? What am I saying? Of course I am. But I had to call." Mom sounded breathless, but not with rage over discovering that Dad was cheating on her again. She seemed to be brimming with something akin to excitement plus indignation.

"Is something wrong?" I started praying for the miracle of divorce. That would be the happiest ending for Mom. I'd have to buy her a membership to some dating app to celebrate. Hook her up with some hot young men she could flaunt in Dad's face.

"No! I figured out who's behind the One-Star Hit Squad!"

The angst over my deadline vanished, and I nearly jumped to my feet. The One-Star Hit Squad was the name Mom had given to a group of about fifty or so reviewers who left me one-star reviews as soon as my book was published. They'd started to target me immediately after one of my books made the *Wall*

Street Journal bestseller list for the first time. *Why* was anybody's guess. They weren't the people I'd given early review copies to, so they couldn't possibly have read the book so fast, unless they'd quit after a couple of chapters. And they certainly weren't leaving reviews that meant anything, objectively speaking. "One Star, This book is stupid" was as meaningless as a review could get, but it hurt my release week to have all those terrible ratings. And it hurt me creatively when I was trying to write, because those comments stayed in the back of my mind. I'd been countering them by having more people on my own review team, people who loved my books. But it had never occurred to me that there might be someone orchestrating the haters.

"Who?" I demanded.

"Your father!"

My head started to spin while I grappled with this bombshell. Of all the possibilities, this one had never crossed my mind.

"I was looking at the credit card statements, and he hired a virtual assistant to do some contract work," Mom continued, correctly interpreting my silence as incredulity. "That's not like him at all."

Not at all. He liked to hire hot women he wanted to fuck. You can't really leer at a virtual assistant.

"So I was going through his tablet," Mom said, her voice vibrant with petty pride. "He forgot to take it with him today, and his password is his birthday." She laughed a *what a dumbass* laugh. "He hired her to gather up reviewers to post fake reviews on Amazon for your books. I read their emails."

He'd left an electronic trail. But then, of course he would. He was that arrogant. Shock began to turn to fury. "Can you screencap them all?" I needed the evidence so I could use it to have my revenge. I didn't know exactly how yet, but something would present itself.

"Already done. I emailed them to you before I called."

"Thanks." If he'd been here, I would've punched him. Then run him over with my car a couple of times.

"He wants to win."

The damned bet. I ground my teeth as the fury spiked and made the veins in my head throb. He'd wagered I'd fail, and I'd wagered I would top the Amazon Kindle chart. I had until the fifth of May to do it or admit failure and suffer public humiliation. So he was determined to see me beaten...apparently by any means necessary.

"Even if it means destroying my career." *And hurting me.* I swallowed the bitter thought. "Is he home now?"

"No. He's working overtime."

Yeah, sure. If I believed that, I was some alien slug from outer space with nothing but air for a brain. A real pneumo-cephaloid. "Okay, I'll deal with him later. Look, I have to go. I'll have more time to chat after I turn in this book."

"Sure. You go *win*, sweetie! I know you can do it!" Mom hung up.

I glared at the phone for a moment, breathing slowly to try to control the raging fury in my chest. It didn't help. I wanted to wrap my hands around my father's neck and strangle him, force him to his knees and make him say he was sorry. But since that wasn't a viable course of action, I decided to call.

He answered on the fourth or fifth ring, sounding slightly out of breath. "Hello?"

A female murmured in the background and disgust twisted around my belly like a thorny vine. Who was he screwing now? His assistant? A client? Some random woman he'd picked up at a bar?

"Did you hire fake reviewers to trash my books?" I demanded.

"Oh. It's you." He sounded completely unconcerned.

What I wouldn't do to wipe that irritatingly smug dismissiveness away! "Did you? And don't even think about lying! I have evidence!" I quickly checked my email. Mom's message with screencaps sat on the top of my inbox. The sight of it caused an internal tug of war between confidence and anger.

"Calm down."

"How am I supposed to calm down?!"

"Jesus. Are you PMSing?"

I inhaled as another surge of fury swelled within me. He did *not* just say that! "You're cheating to win the bet!"

"What 'cheating'? We never agreed I couldn't do that. If you don't remember, call Holly Stein to explain the details of our contract."

Holly, the attorney we'd hired to make sure everyone kept their word, had copies of the ads that would go out the weekend after the fifth of May. She was also in charge of an escrow account with enough money to cover the bills from the newspapers. Neither Dad nor I trusted each other.

He added, "Or—if it's hard to think from all the hormones—ask your lawyer. He vetted it. And it isn't like the reviews said anything that isn't true. Romance is the dumbest thing to waste your life on, and its so-called readers are so illiterate and stupid that they can't see what they're reading is trash."

Oh my God. Grandma's egg had to have been expired when this man was conceived. "Romance is not trash!"

"Well, what's the word for something that's unrealistic, badly written and basically just porn for bored women who have nothing better to do with themselves? I think 'trash' is good."

"At least they aren't fucking other people while they're married!" I yelled as my vision went hazy red.

He laughed. He didn't feel a smidgen of guilt that he wasn't faithful to Mom. Nor did he care that the woman he'd just screwed might hear my shriek. "If they read less, maybe they'd have more time to screw around. I can't wait to see the ads you're gonna have to take out, admitting I was right. What papers did we agree on again? Oh yeah... the *Wall Street Journal*, *New York Times*, *USA Today* and *L.A. Times*. It's not gonna be cheap! But if you don't want to fork over your hard-earned money, you can always just tell me I'm right and post what you're supposed to say in the ads on your author website. I'll be nice and tell Holly we can cancel the whole deal. Get our escrow back."

My hand was wrapped around my phone so tightly that my whole arm was shaking. "Over my *dead body*."

"I'm only doing this because I'm your father and I care about you. I don't want to see you waste your money like that. All the good things that have happened in your life are because of me—because I made it so."

My ass, he cared about me! He only cared about himself. And he was pissed off that I wasn't doing something he approved of—

being a respectable corporate drone he could proudly bring up in public. Everything was about his self-image and selfish desires. It had gratified him to brag to everyone that I'd graduated at the top of my class at UVA...and that I'd gone to Harvard. But he told me the only reason I'd been able to attend those universities was because he'd hired tutors—which I hadn't needed—to prep me for the SAT and GMAT.

And that was just a sliver of what he took credit for. As far as he was concerned, all my accomplishments were due to him, and it enraged him that I'd chosen a path he disapproved of.

"It's going to be absolutely *delicious,*" I said between clenched teeth, "seeing you spend money to take out full-page ads admitting you were wrong—and that romance is the most wonderful, smartest reading choice for the most intelligent and discerning women. I'm going to frame those ads, take pictures of them and run a social media ad campaign targeting all your buddies and clients!"

He laughed. "Big talk, but you have to win first. Your last three books peaked at four, five and seven on the chart. The trend doesn't look good...for you." He hung up.

I struggled to suck air in around the iron ball of anger lodged in my chest and ignore the hot tears gathering in my eyes. It wasn't that I was hurt; Dad was always like this. I was simply furious. Determined. Ready to show him he was wrong.

Shaking, I stared at the half-finished manuscript. Staying home and trying to type something up wouldn't work. I needed to put on my big-girl panties and use the thermonuclear option.

I took off my glasses and put in contacts. Then I grabbed my keys, slipped on some running shoes and left. There was work to do.

CHAPTER 2

Emily

I ran along the only trail in my small town, which, naturally, was located at the opposite end from my house. Well, "ran"... What I was doing was more like a jog. A very slow jog because, like most writers, I wasn't an athlete. And I was a clumsy writer at that—ten minutes in I'd snagged my pants on a bush and heard something rip. Plus I'd lost a contact lens somewhere on the dirt trail and hadn't been able to find it, even with my phone light. Maybe I shouldn't have switched from glasses to contacts before leaving the house, but I hated how the frames slid down my nose when my face got sweaty. I told myself it was okay to lose the contact because I still had my left one. It was enough to see with, especially if I squinted a little.

I pushed my body even though it wasn't designed for anything more strenuous than speed-walking toward beer. I wasn't stopping until my head was full of ideas. And not just any ideas, but good, usable ideas that would ensure I could finish my book in the next two weeks, then edit and publish it by May fifth.

Without a book to promote, I couldn't win that bet with Dad. And the idea of losing was just... I shuddered.

I'd rather jump headfirst into some medieval torturer's largest and most disgusting pit of vipers.

My head works in mysterious ways. When I push my body to its limit, my mind finally gives up being blocked. Probably my subconscious knew I'd jog until I collapsed if it didn't do what I wanted. As I jogged, snippets of dialog and scenarios and scenes swirled in my head like a confetti storm, enough to make me slightly dizzy. Or maybe the lightheadedness was due to the fact that I couldn't suck in enough air to sustain my out-of-shape body's sad attempt to run.

Also, I hadn't had much to eat. And my refrigerator didn't have much to live on while I holed up to work on my book.

Not good.

Wars aren't won based on which general is the smartest. They're won based on who has the best supply lines and provisions. I had two weeks to go to finish my book and send it to my editor, and nobody can fight on an empty stomach.

I drove my car from the trail to Sunny's Mart, parked and marched inside, snagging a huge cart along the way. I knew exactly what I needed and where to find it.

First, white wines from Virginia. The store had blended whites from Jefferson Vineyards, and I loved them, having discovered the brand while attending the University of Virginia. I took all seven bottles, then moved on to the section with flavored beers from the local brewery, Hop Hop Hooray. They made the most amazing raspberry and Virginia apple beer. The only problem was that their stock was limited. They usually sold them at their own bar and restaurant in Kingstree. I almost never went, because going out meant I had to people. (*People* was most certainly a verb.) Kingstree was a lovely, sleepy little town in Central Virginia, but people could be so...friendly and overly talkative, to put it kindly.

That fact should've been in the real estate brochures, I thought morosely. It might've made a difference in my decision to move here. I'd only wanted to settle down in a small town after living in D.C. because a tiny population meant very little human interaction, a delight to my small hermit heart. Or so I'd assumed.

I told myself the town had a well-stocked grocery store, so I should be happy. And I would be, as long as it had... I scanned the beer section, and—*yes!*—Hop Hop Hooray sat on the shelves.

Woohoo! Doing a little victory shimmy, I grabbed the entire stock of Triple-H beer and placed it in my cart. Along with two bottles of decent whiskey, just in case. Then I went down the snack aisle and cleaned out the Animal Crackers section, too.

Now for some ice cream...

I prayed that Sunny's had just gotten a shipment from Bouncing Cows. It was a local dairy that only used organic milk from grass-fed cows to make ice cream. Once you had it, you could never go back to eating the mass-produced stuff. And out of all the flavors they offered, my absolute favorite was Bouncy Bare Monkeys. It had dark chocolate chunks and mini-marshmallows in the smoothest, richest chocolate ice cream ever. It was a kind of crack that the rest of the country hadn't discovered yet. It tasted like a fever dream of tiny little angels copulating on your tongue.

Saliva pooled in my mouth. Just like Hop Hop Hooray, Bouncing Cows never made enough for my taste. If they did, I would've started every day with a big bowl of their Bouncy Bare Monkeys.

I maneuvered my cart around the corner, and *Ah-ha!* There it was.

I inhaled, feeling an almost Tantric bliss. It seemed like an incandescent shaft of heavenly sunlight was illuminating the freezer in front of me. *The special jumbo tub!* And there was only one left!

Closing my eyes in silent thanks, I opened the door, wrapped my hand around the tub and pulled.

It didn't budge.

I scowled and opened my eyes. Another hand was on the carton, the long, strong fingers latched around the lip of the lid like demon claws from the darkest depths of hell.

Snarling, I turned around, then closed my right eye and squinted so I could see the would-be thief better.

Holy shit. What the...

My mind went blank for a second as I took him in. Hot shivers skittered along my spine. What a face... And what a waste.

Longish black hair that reached a little below his ears. Strong, bold lines. Brilliant, piercing blue eyes and a thin, straight nose. His lips were a little puffy, like he'd gotten really lucky in the genetics lottery or lightly cuffed in the mouth. Probably the latter. Anyone who'd snatch someone else's ice cream...

Regardless, I couldn't help but acknowledge—only to myself—that he'd be amazing on the cover of a romance novel. Dress him in a wet white button-down shirt (unbuttoned, of course) that clung to his torso...a pair of dark jeans that hung a little low on his hips... *Mmm.* Maybe put him in a meadow and have him stick a thumb into his waistband and look at the camera like "I want to have my way with you, you sultry vixen..."

Oh yeah. That would make readers one-click, just to own the damned shot of him.

Better yet, have him in my bed, naked and ready. He seemed fit and looked like he could screw until I saw stars and turned into a puddle of flesh. A strong orgasm usually helped with insomnia. And I hadn't had any—orgasms, not insomnia—in a while.

Still, I reminded myself he was likely a terrible human being I shouldn't fantasize about. Why else would he be holding on to *my* ice cream?

"Let go," I said in my no-nonsense tone, the one that used to put fear into people before I'd quit my corporate job to be a writer.

He cocked an eyebrow. "*You* let go. I touched it first."

His voice was low and a little husky, reminding me of aged whiskey with a smoky finish. I liked it, which was annoying. Actually, more than liked it. It made my insides hot, and I noted the flesh between my legs felt a little wet.

Probably just sweat, I told myself. I was not attracted to this guy, no matter how stunning he looked. Men this gorgeous were always trouble.

Just look at my dad. Pretty on the outside, completely rotten inside.

I narrowed my eyes and tightened my mouth into a flat line. This bozo knew he was good-looking and sexy-sounding. And he wasn't above using his charms to his advantage.

"In your dreams." I tried to hiss it at him.

He ran his tongue over a row of perfectly straight white teeth and squinted at me. "Do you know who I am?"

Was he serious? I let my gaze roam over him. It took a while because he was so damn tall. But I wanted to be thorough...from his head to the broad shoulders and lean frame with ropey muscles, the nicely formed chest peeking through the V of a slate-gray shirt, narrow hips and nice pair of legs encased in black jeans...then back up. He had tattooed forearms and one of those huge wallets on a chain attached to his belt.

He looked at me like he was waiting for me to fall at his feet.

Puh-*leeeze.*

I, Emily Katarina Breckenridge, did not fall at any man's feet. Seeing how Dad treated Mom was a one hundred percent fool-proof vaccine against pretty men's charms. Yes, it was true—my mom had married my dad for his face. Look how that had worked out. Dad was with another woman, and Mom was waiting for him in that huge, echoing house back in McLean. If he was feeling especially considerate, he'd shower at the hotel before heading home.

"As it happens, I don't know who you are. Do you know who *I* am?"

The man pulled back a little, eyebrows rising. It was his turn to run his gaze over me. Slowly. Insolently. And the skin along my spine and chest felt weird, somewhere between a hot tingle and an itch. I grimaced. Probably dried sweat from the exercise. Back sweat and boob sweat were the worst.

I was most definitely not thinking about him naked. Or in my bed. Or in me.

His mouth started to purse. And almost immediately after that, his nose wrinkled. I recognized the evaluating, assessing look in his eyes. I'd seen it plenty of times in my dad's, most recently when I became a romance novelist.

How dare this ice cream thief *judge me*?

"No," he said finally.

I gave him a fake smile. "So we're even." I tugged at the tub, but he still wasn't letting go.

I didn't have all night to fight this guy. I needed to shower for the first time in four days, take a short nap and get back to work.

How to make him back off...?

I flicked my eyes down. "Oh my God!" I screeched, infusing

the high-pitched yell with all the disgust I could muster. "There's a *cockroach* on your foot!"

"What?" He looked down, flinching.

And his grip on the ice cream relaxed. I yanked it out of the fridge and placed it firmly in my cart.

"Hey!" he protested.

"What?" I put a hand on my chest with all the innocence I could muster. "You're the one who let go."

"That was cheating!"

Cheating? He wanted to talk about *cheating*? All the frustration with my dad resurfaced, aggression boiling in my blood. "What are you going to do? Fight me for it?" I snarled, letting him see my teeth, and raised my clenched hands to signal that I was willing to bloody that pretty face to keep the ice cream I'd just earned. Hopefully he'd be intimidated.

His expression twisted in distaste. "Fight some homeless alcoholic? No thanks."

"Ha. Call me whatever you like. I still won!" I fist-pumped the air.

He was looking like he couldn't believe what had just happened. It was obvious he'd expected me to hand over the tub of ice cream ambrosia.

Over. My. Dead. Body.

Triumphant, I sashayed up to the cashier to pay for my writing supplies. No asshole was going to get between me and my provisions...even if he was the hottest asshole I'd ever laid eyes on.

CHAPTER 3

Killian

The ice cream bandit walked away, hips swinging to a rhythm only she could hear, blond hair bobbing. Her yoga pants had at least two holes, and some of the seams were coming apart. They had to be older than the oak in Grandma's front yard. And her shirt wasn't any better. Dingy white, wet with what I hoped was sweat...and it sported three holes, one of them right below her armpit.

She was also muttering to herself again. I was sure she wasn't aware of it, especially given all her weird tics. She'd gone on and on about Molly and Ryan while approaching the ice cream section—about how Molly owned a cat, and she and Ryan were going to hook up. But Molly Patterson was allergic to cats, and Ryan Johnson was sixty-eight years old—in addition to having been happily married for forty-seven years. Molly and Ryan were definitely not hooking up, no matter what this loon thought.

But that wasn't all that was weird about her. The entire time she'd been checking me out in front of the freezer, her right eye kept winking. It was unsettling, like some kind of alien Morse code.

And that was too bad, because she had gorgeous green eyes with flecks of bright gold in them.

I watched her make off with the last of the ice cream I'd been craving for the past three years. The temptation to grab it out of her cart had been hard to resist, but somehow I'd managed.

Those fists she'd raised weren't much of a threat. But the teeth she'd kept baring? Definitely dangerous. And who knew what she might be carrying? Her cart didn't have anything except crackers and alcohol, plus the Bouncy Bare Monkeys I rightfully should've been enjoying tonight to celebrate surviving my twenty-hour flight.

It'd been three years since I'd last visited my grandmother in Kingstree. *What the hell had happened to the nice, quaint little town since then to have* that? I asked myself as I watched her check out. At least she had some money, even if it was probably from panhandling. The folks in Kingstree were generous. And when she batted those eyes—or not, since she had that weird winking tic—and pouted that soft rosebud mouth, I bet people gave her whatever change they could scrounge from their pockets and car seats.

An unsettling feeling came over me as she left. I shook my head and headed to the liquor section to grab a consolation prize—some of Hop Hop Hooray's specialty beer. Why did I feel so... perturbed? It wasn't like I'd never seen a wack-case before. Being out on tour was like a magnet for them.

But you've never felt a spark for one before.

I pulled myself up short. *A spark? For* her?

I mean, there was definitely a weird sensation. The hair on the back of my neck stood up and my skin prickled. But that had been annoyance and disbelief, not a spark. I hadn't felt a spark in...

Too damn long.

My mood deflated further. My sister Miriam said I was burned out, and that was why everything felt about as exciting as a wet blanket in a rainforest. She would know—she was the queen of burnout, having gone through it three times already. I'd been busy, working nonstop for over a decade. And although my band had made a big splash five years ago, and the media still called us "an overnight sensation," the actual work to get ready for our debut had taken years of dedication, day and night.

Recently, I hadn't been able to muster the energy or creativity to write songs or play music. And it had been scary as hell backstage after our final concert when my vision went blurry...then turned black. Since then, I hadn't come up with a single new lyric or idea for where the band should go next, creatively and musically. And that was more terrifying than passing out. My brain had never been such a black hole of nothingness when it came to music.

Granted, my band mates had their own ideas, but I'd never failed to provide some kind of opinion—some meaningful contribution.

Being back in Kingstree should help, though. This was my true home, with friendly folks treating me like a person rather than some celebrity to hassle. They were too familiar with my teenage shenanigans to be awed by my current fame.

I stopped abruptly in front of the beer section, my jaw slack. Not a single bottle of Hop Hop Hooray beer. *Are you kidding me?*

I spun around and marched to the cashier, Jenny. I tried to remember how old she was now...fourteen? Fifteen? She was the daughter of my junior prom date, who'd married the captain of the high school football team the next year when she found out she was pregnant. Because Jenny hadn't witnessed my colorful history of teenage pranks and dares, she looked at me with half awe and half shyness. But unlike the people I encountered outside of Kingstree, she implicitly understood the proper boundaries, just like everyone in this town. She'd never take a photo and upload it on whatever junky social media kids these days liked to be on.

"Hi, Mr. Axelrod," she squeaked. "Or should I call you Killian?"

"Killian's fine. Do you have any more Hop Hop Hooray in the back?"

She shook her head, her young face falling. "I'm so sorry. Gerry put everything out before heading home." She cleared her throat. "I think Emily bought it all."

"Emily?" I didn't remember any vagrant named Emily in

Kingstree. And even though I'd been away, Grandma had kept me in the loop.

"You know, the lady who checked out a few minutes ago?"

"That cra—" I caught myself before I called her a "crazy hobo." It probably wasn't an appropriate thing to say in front of Jenny.

"Yeah. Have you met her?" She blinked her big, owlish brown eyes, then continued without waiting for a response. "I'm sure you will soon. Sometimes she doesn't leave the house for, like, forever. But she's your next-door neighbor."

"My *what*?" I asked, stunned.

"Next-door neighbor. She bought the old Thompson place. You know."

"Yeah," I said slowly.

She grinned, then leaned closer with an eager light in her eyes. "When she bought it last year, the roof needed to be replaced. And she chose *pink*! I heard it was a custom job. Cool, huh? Told Mom we should do the same to our house, but she's totally not into spending that kind of money, which seems crazy to me. Pink is such a cool color!"

I nodded, not paying attention to the rest of the gossip pouring out of her eager mouth. I left the store dazed and empty-handed as my brain tried to work overtime to find a way to digest what Jenny had just shared.

Grandma had mentioned the neighbor who'd moved to Kingstree a year and a half ago several times.

A nice, sweet girl. A true Virginia lady.

Her job must be important. She's always working. It's impossible to catch her for tea or even a neighborly chat. Since she moved next door three months ago, I think I've run into her twice. Exceptionally polite. Such lovely bearing.

Oh, did you know she attended UVA? And Harvard for some kind of master's degree. A smart child. Wonderful, isn't it?

She has the most elegant name. Emily. I always wanted to name my daughter that if I'd ever had one. I wish you could meet her. You would love her.

I invited her to dinner. She's all alone, and she could use some company.

My mental picture of "Emily" had consisted of a *lady* because Grandma had said so. Elegant, too. Maybe in a pale dress and slim-heeled shoes, her hair perfectly done, nails flawlessly shaped and lacquered. Speaking with precise, proper diction. And her manners impeccable.

Not some ice-cream-thieving maniac in dumpster couture who walked around muttering to herself.

I drove to the house Grandma left me when she passed away last September, then slowed down as its pink-roofed neighbor came into view. The same neatly trimmed lawn and small pine tree in front. But the walls were buttercream-colored now, and colorful gnomes held giant lollipops.

It was...pretty. Like the candy house of the old witch from "Hansel and Gretel."

You should never judge a person by their home. It was the moral I must've missed when my mom read me and Mir the fairy tale when we were young.

I had no idea what Emily had done to con my grandmother into thinking she was a respectable lady. Even gotten invited for free food a few times.

But I knew her true colors. And I was going to teach her a lesson as payback for the ice cream, beer...and lying to an elderly woman.

CHAPTER 4

Emily

I rolled out of bed the moment my eyes opened. Unfortunately, the bedside clock informed me it was four in the morning. *Damn it, overslept.* I'd meant to get a four-hour nap, not five.

After splashing some cold water on my face, I put a pair of pink-rimmed glasses on and headed downstairs. Crunch time meant glasses, since I needed to write as much as I could, then nap whenever I absolutely had to rest. Contacts got in the way of naps. Besides, it was a pain if I forgot to take them out every so often. I'd gotten an eye infection from that last year, and never would I put myself through that suffering again.

I got the coffeemaker going, then scooped two big mounds of Bouncy Bare Monkeys into a bowl. Nothing could beat that combo for breakfast. The cold and creamy sensation mingled with the hot coffee in my mouth and somehow produced a repast for the gods. The gears in my head started churning faster and more smoothly.

Once that was done, I took some water and a raspberry beer from the fridge and sat down in front of my laptop. The moment I flipped the lid open, the cursor blinked on the Word doc.

Write, write, baby.

I popped open the beer and took a long swallow. Then, after

linking my fingers and stretching them, I started to type up the scenes that had come to me yesterday.

"You go, girl," I muttered to myself as my heroine Molly sassed the hero. I loved Ryan, but he needed to learn his lesson. He was a bit of an ass.

It's unfair. I never wanted to be an ass. You made *me an ass!* Ryan whined in my head.

"Yeah, yeah. If you don't like it, write your own book," I whispered as my fingers moved across the keyboard. The tapping clicks sounded a little like rain on a roof...

The only break I took was to go to the bathroom. And to grab more beer and water because I needed to lubricate my brain and hydrate myself.

After about five thousand words, finally Molly and Ryan were about to have sex for the first time, and I needed to make it not only scorching, but funny and emotional. No mere "his penis drove into her vagina" sex for my couple.

Let's see... "His tongue stroked mine," I murmured as I typed. "An urgent, irresistible heat began in my—"

A loud banging shattered my train of thought. *What the hell?* I jumped up, knocking over the bag of Animal Crackers. Shit! Two lions and a lot of crumbs ended up on the floor under the table, rather than—thankfully—on my laptop. Getting my keyboard gunked up would *not* be good.

After putting the lions next to my beer, I looked up, wondering where the noise was coming from. I'd bought a detached single home for a very specific reason: to not hear noise from my neighbors. Mrs. Axelrod had been quiet. And not overly nosy compared to others in town.

But the silence returned. I shook my head. Part of me was curious what it was about, but I slapped myself mentally. *No time to procrastinate! Got to refocus.* Molly and Ryan had some banging of their own to do.

Bang bang clang!

There it was again! The muscles in my shoulders and neck tightened up, and I growled under my breath. How could my couple have hot, funny, emotional sex when there was this clanging ruckus outside?

Not just clanging, I thought as I jumped to my feet. Some asshole was banging on a drum set. Didn't they know what time it was?

I glared at the clock on my laptop. Ten thirty. Early enough for this to be noise pollution. What if somebody wanted to sleep in?

Actually, this was a cul-de-sac with only two homes. Mine and Mrs. Axelrod's, and she'd passed away last year. So, okay, nobody wanted to sleep in, but somebody—*me!*—wanted to work!

The mannerless jerk was banging around like he was a drummer at a rock concert. I had to admit—grudgingly—that he was pretty good. Okay, *really* good. But that didn't mean the noise was any less irritating.

I shoved my feet into flip-flops and marched out, determined to get the noise polluter to stop. The racket was coming from the late Mrs. Axelrod's home. I stormed over, hands in tight fists. As I got closer, I noted the windows were all open. Totally inconsiderate. *Just who the hell bought this house?* I hadn't seen a For Sale sign outside. If I had...and if I'd known some drum-banging jerk would be moving in, I would've bought the damn place myself!

I beat on the door. The drumming continued. The turd-brain was either ignoring me or couldn't hear over his own ear-destroying sound. I beat harder, using both fists. I imagined the door was actually an extension of the drummer. I should've put on boots so I could kick it, too!

The noise finally stopped. A moment later, the door opened.

I glared up at the offending man. Wait... Was this...? Yes, it was! That sexy-looking, sexy-sounding asshole who'd tried to steal my ice cream the night before.

"You!" I gasped.

He was still sexy-looking, his dark hair slightly messy, and a night's worth of stubble shadowing his jaw, adding to his masculine good looks. His blue shirt brought out his eyes, and he'd pulled the sleeves up, showing off those lean, tattooed forearms.

The sight of them was hot. And it annoyed me that I found any part of him hot. I was too smart and levelheaded to think anybody who wasn't a perfect gentleman was hot.

"Yes, it's me." He gave me a slow once-over. "So you do own clothes without holes."

"What?" I looked down. I was in a pink T-shirt and white boxer shorts with red hearts.

"Interesting shirt." His voice was dry.

So the Neanderthal could read. The front of the T-shirt said, CUN CRUD IS REAL, across the chest. On the back it said, SO DRINK MORE ALCOHOL, which this jerk couldn't see. It was a custom shirt my friends and I had made when we'd all come down with a hellish flu after a writers' conference two years ago. We'd been so sick that we'd misspelled "CON," and none of us had caught it until the shirts had been delivered. We'd all laughed about it, though, and worn our shirts proudly, especially at conferences.

I put my hands on my hips. The first thing out of his mouth *should* have been "I'm sorry for being a loud dick."

"I like the placement of the heart right there, too." He pointed.

Huh? I checked, then rolled my eyes. Of course he was referring to the lopsided heart over my crotch. *Pig.*

"Look, can you keep the noise down? I'm trying to work here," I said.

"You are?"

"Yes. Is that so hard to imagine?"

"You smell like beer."

I guessed he thought that would shame me. "So? I do my best work when I'm drinking."

That wasn't actually true. I did my best work when I was inspired and ready to go. But a little bit of alcohol was the muse's great helper, especially when it was Hop Hop Hooray's raspberry brew.

Then I realized I'd gotten off track. Must not let him distract me. "Anyway, as I was saying, I'm trying to work, and I'd appreciate it if you could cut it out."

"Well, see, we kind of have a problem."

"Problem? You stop drumming. No problem."

"Yeah, but I'm trying to work, too," he said with a smile more fake than my dad's promise never to screw around again.

"Huh?"

"Work. I'm trying to do some."

I scowled. "That isn't work. That's just being loud and obnoxious."

He gave me a funny look, like he couldn't believe I was being this stubborn. Ha! If he thought *this* was stubborn, he was in for a lot of surprises. "I'm a private citizen in my own home," he said. "And I do have to make a living."

"By being loud? With your windows open?" I pointed at one of them. The soft pastel green and white curtains billowed in the breeze. The sight would normally make me smile with appreciation for understated good taste. Like when Mrs. Axelrod had been alive. But this guy? No.

"It's hot," he said.

"It's only seventy degrees!" I'd caught that on the car radio yesterday.

His lips quirked into something halfway between a smirk and a smile. "Yes, but drumming is sweaty work."

Then he winked! The nerve!

"Turn on the A/C, then!"

"I'm trying to reduce my carbon footprint."

"Your very existence is a waste of carbon!" I said, irritated beyond measure. Then another possibility occurred to me. "Did my father hire you?"

He laughed. "I have no idea who your daddy is. Don't much care, either."

He didn't look like he was lying. Besides, Dad wouldn't have hidden it. He would've flaunted it and mocked me like when I confronted him about the One-Star Hit Squad.

The jerk added, "Don't you care about the planet? Organic cows might not produce enough organic milk to make Bouncing Cows ice cream at the rate things are going."

I crossed my arms. "Oh, I see. This is about the ice cream."

"And stealing all of Hop Hop Hooray's raspberry beer. *And* their Virginia apple, too."

My jaw slackened. "Was I supposed to leave a bottle behind just in case somebody might want some?"

"Yeah, it woulda been nice. Didn't anybody teach you to share?"

"First come, first served. Didn't anybody teach you *that*? Or are you so good-looking that the rules of polite society simply don't apply?"

He smiled. It was genuine this time. And he had a dimple by his mouth. It was totally unexpected and cute. Like a maxed-out *ten* cute.

Oh my freakin' God! What the hell was wrong with me that I was rating the cuteness of his dimple? I was never this stupid, regardless of who I was dealing with! I must be too pissed off to think clearly. I'd been playing into his evil tactic all along.

"You think I'm good-looking?" he asked, his eyes sparkling. They reminded me of sunlight glittering on a lake in summer—

Argh! I clenched my hands into fists, wishing I could punch him until he looked like a panda with a case of incurable botulism. "Petty asshole!"

His smile widened. "Nah. Just a reminder that karma is a bitch."

Every inch of my skin heated with rage. I should've known rational discussion would be impossible with this guy. I spun around and marched back across his lawn toward my home.

"Hey," he called out from behind me. "That's a nice ass."

Fuming, I got back inside my living room and snatched my phone up from the coffee table. Kingstree had a functioning sheriff's department. As a taxpaying citizen, I should avail myself of their service. There was more than one way to peel an orange.

I called 911 and waited for the dispatcher to ask me about my emergency. Her voice was reedy with age and slightly gravelly. Probably a long-term smoker.

"Would you mind sending somebody out to ask my next-door neighbor to keep his drumming down? It's really loud and disruptive. I'm sure it's a violation of some noise pollution ordinance or other." Every civilized community had them. And Kingstree was very, very civilized.

"You're calling from...250 Oak Court?" she asked like she couldn't believe it.

"Yes."

She sighed as though I were an unreasonable toddler asking for more candy. "Honey, just enjoy the free concert."

"Free *concert*? Someone would have to pay *me* to listen to this, this...cacophony!"

"He charges a lot of money to perform, you know." She spoke in a tone an exhausted grandmother might use to explain to her grandchildren that it was never okay to pee in their pants.

It was all I could do to keep calm. "I don't care if he charges a million bucks!"

"He isn't breaking any laws," she said. "We really can't help you here. You need to work it out with him directly."

"I tried that option. If it had worked, I wouldn't be calling you now, would I?" I said, doing my best not to sound *too* sarcastic. Kingstree was a small town. Everyone knew everyone. Well... except me. I'd made it a point to keep to myself, especially after some nosy woman had tried to volunteer me for activities I didn't want to do.

"Killian is such a sweet, reasonable child. Just talk to him." She hung up.

Ack! I clenched my phone hard, doing my best not to give in to the urge to throw it against the wall. It'd hurt me more than the pest next door.

Killian, huh? The name probably meant "asshole" in Latin.

I glared in his direction even though he couldn't see me through the walls. A sweet, reasonable child. Ha! There was nothing childlike about him. And sweet and reasonable? When did their meanings change? I was a writer. I would've heard about such a thing.

I went on Amazon and placed an order for two noise-canceling headsets. Then, as he was being quiet for the moment—maybe he needed to cool off, since drumming was such sweaty work—I started typing as fast as I could to give Molly and Ryan the hump of their lives.

CHAPTER 5

Killian

I smirked as Emily stormed off. When she vanished into her house, I shut my door and stood there in the living room for a moment.

Normally, I wouldn't be drumming with all the windows open, but whatever. America was a free country, and the only person close enough to hear me play was her.

She'd claimed she was working, but that was doubtful. Unless she was a professional alcoholic, chances were she was unemployed. Probably couldn't hold down a job. Folks here were nice, but they weren't soft enough to put up with workers showing up drunk. Not to mention she hadn't bought any food except Animal Crackers. Gainfully employed people could usually afford to eat a little better than that. They for sure didn't use their real food money to buy alcohol and ice cream.

My first impression of her was dead-on. There was something seriously wrong with this chick.

Only problem was that I liked what I'd seen when she came over. She'd cleaned up some, not that it had required a lot of effort, since our previous encounter had set the bar so damned low. But she'd showered and her clothes were intact. No sweat stains. And she wasn't doing that weird squinty winking thing. Maybe it was a withdrawal symptom and now that she'd had some beer she was fine.

But best of all...she hadn't been wearing a bra. I had no clue if she knew...or if she'd shown up braless on purpose. She wouldn't be the first. But those nipples had been pointed dead at me. Headlights on *high*. And they'd stayed pointed even when she got heated up. If she could, she might've fired bullets through them.

Weirdly enough, I wanted to continue teasing her. The fury in her eyes and the color in her cheeks had sparked something in my gut, and I hadn't felt so hot and alive in years.

I didn't understand it. Out on tour I'd had my absolute fill of crazy, delusional women who thrived on drama, and I avoided them the way Superman avoids kryptonite. But somehow I was drawn to Emily.

My burnout must be worse than I thought.

I started back toward the drums, but my phone went off, playing Darth Vader's theme from *Star Wars*. Miriam's ringtone, chosen because Vader was her favorite character.

"Hey, Mir," I said, and parked my butt in a lounger. I'd bought it for Grandma, and she'd told me it was the best thing ever. As the soft cushions molded to my body, I couldn't bring myself to disagree.

"Hey, just calling to see how you're doing. All settled in?" Her voice was chirpy.

"Sort of. A little tired. Just got here yesterday."

She made a small sympathetic noise. "The tour must've been exhausting."

"God, yes. You have no idea."

I couldn't shake off how I'd just...*collapsed* after my last concert. Like a puppet with its strings cut. I'd gotten an IV at a local hospital and braved a long, horrific flight, trapped in a death tube thirty thousand feet above ground, to spent two weeks in an overwater bungalow in Bora Bora at my band mate Max's suggestion.

"Nothing clears your head and recharges your soul like sea and solitude," he'd said. It was an amazing show of love, since he generally avoided that many syllables if he could. Except it hadn't helped, which was why I was now in Kingstree to recover.

"So you gonna take it easy there for a while?" Mir asked.

"Yeah. Relax. Recharge." I needed it badly. My creative well was drier than a handful of Saharan sand. Not even drumming had helped.

"And enjoy the local delicacies," she said wistfully. She lived in Alexandria and worked in D.C. Too far to drive for ice cream and beer.

"I wish," I said morosely.

"You wish? Why? You were grumbling about missing them while on tour."

"Some witch cleaned the store out. You might've met her. Emily, Grandma's next-door neighbor?"

I hadn't run into her the last time I was in town, to bury Grandma. Even if I had, I probably wouldn't remember. Everything was such a haze. And I'd started the new tour soon after. My band mates had told me to take it easy, even cancel the tour. The fans would understand. They knew we weren't machines, but people with hearts and souls.

And they were right. I'd received an outpouring of support and love from our fans. They'd posted countless messages on social media, expressing condolences. And many of them had sent letters and email.

I'd chosen not to cancel and done the tour. The decision had nothing to do with my sense of obligation to our fans or greed or whatever else the media had said. It was that Grandma had been so proud of what I'd accomplished on my own. I wasn't living off the trust my parents left me and Mir. She'd said I was bringing joy to people with my music...that what I was doing was *worth* something. She wouldn't have wanted me to stop, especially not on her account. The tour had been my farewell to her—my pillar of strength, my guiding light, always giving a loving hug when I needed it and the whupping I deserved every time I acted like a dick.

"Doesn't ring a bell," Mir said. "I don't think she was in town when we were in Kingstree after Grandma passed away." She hadn't been back since. She'd been busy cleaning up and going through things in the Virginia Beach cottage Grandma had left her. Once that was done, Mir didn't want to intrude on the house in Kingstree that Grandma had willed to me.

"Grandma said she was a lady," I said. "Remember that?"

"Um...yeah. She was really complimentary."

I told Mir all about what had happened at Sunny's. The weird tic and the sweaty, filthy clothes and the teeth baring and the wild mutterings about Molly and Ryan.

"Molly and *Ryan*? Banging each other? Whaaaat?" Mir said. "That's crazy." She paused. "And kind of disgusting."

"Right? That woman isn't a lady. She's a loon."

"Then why was Grandma so taken with her?"

"Probably *got* taken," I said, still peeved about the ice cream. And the beer. Emily had some nerve coming over smelling like Hop Hop Hooray.

"Yeah, but she was such a great judge of character. I just can't believe she got this one wrong."

"Everyone makes the occasional mistake." I sighed. Damn, I missed Grandma, no matter what she thought of my neighbor.

Mir made a small sympathetic noise in her throat. "I miss her too, Killian."

"Yeah."

"I hate to cut this short, but I have a meeting in five and need to get going. Chat later?"

"Sure."

"Welcome back to the States. And Kingstree."

"Thanks."

We hung up, and I looked around the living room. The soft white and green muslin curtains. The worn but comfortable fabric sofa with the sage and gold floral pattern Grandma had loved so much. Purple and pink butterflies fluttering away as a black cat chased them—all carefully and lovingly stenciled on white walls.

I should change things up at some point, I thought. This was all Grandma, not me. But right now, I didn't want to touch anything. This place looked and felt more like home than any of the swanky hotels I'd stayed in.

I went back to the drums and start banging away at Axelrod's top hits, while praying something new would pop up and inspire me.

CHAPTER 6

Killian

The next three days passed peacefully. The loony ice cream and beer bandit next door didn't bother me again, and I drummed away to my heart's content, even though it didn't do a thing to get my creative juices flowing again. I didn't understand how that could be. When the stunning vistas of Bora Bora had failed, I chalked it up to not having my instruments. Wouldn't I be more inspired with some well-worn drumsticks in my hands?

Of course, I didn't just drum. I was Axelrod's lead vocalist and guitarist, as well as occasional keyboardist when our songs called for it. So I also played electric guitar and Grandma's old piano, just for variety. And to keep my skills up.

But I always went back to the drums. I loved drumming. If Dev wasn't better at it than me, I would've been the band's drummer. There was an explosive, physical satisfaction to percussion I couldn't get from other instruments.

Unfortunately, Bouncing Cows and Hop Hop Hooray didn't produce any more ice cream and beer during those three days. Not even Sunny Zimmerman, the owner of Sunny's Mart, knew when there would be more.

"Sorry, Killian, I wish I did. You aren't the only one asking," Sunny said, her slight drawl a vestige of her Houston roots.

"Can you call me when they get here?" I gave her my best sad, needy puppy face.

She let out a sound that was halfway between sigh and laugh. "No can do. I'm not calling anybody because I don't have the time to make over a hundred calls."

"That's fair." I nodded, although I was slightly disappointed that she wouldn't make an exception for me. Wasn't I her favorite rocker? "Thanks anyway."

At least the store had wine and whiskey. But it wasn't the same. I could drink regular wine and whiskey anywhere. I could only have Bouncing Cows and Hop Hop Hooray in Kingstree.

Fortunately, I'd run into Jenny at the cash register again. She offered to make an exception and call or text me, while looking around to make sure nobody else would catch her doing me this illicit favor. So I gave her my public number, the one that I gave out to people who weren't in my closest circle of friends and family. Now all I had to do was wait.

But I should've known that three days of peace was all I would get. The trouble started on the fourth day.

I rolled out of bed at six. Went out to run for an hour, since the town didn't have a gym and I'd go stir crazy if I didn't exercise several times a week. It was peaceful outside, and the sky was beautiful as the sun rose and changed it from black to deep navy to the gold-infused blue of early morning.

I went home, chugged a cup of black coffee—real men didn't do cream and sugar—and ate a bowl of cereal. Then I dragged myself into the shower, luxuriating under the hot water spewing out of the faucet with the perfect pressure. Aaaah. Heaven. I considered myself a tough guy, but I'd also accepted a long time ago that I'd prefer to die if there was some dystopian apocalypse. Not because I couldn't hunt or cook or fix cars. But because I couldn't stand a cold shower. Cold showers were right up there with sociopathic groupies and fame-hungry exes.

I shampooed my hair, lathering it until there was a huge mushroom of suds. I moved, positioning myself under the shower head.

Was it me...or did the water actually feel a little cool?

I moved away from the spray and stuck my hand out. Shit.

Now it was outright cold. I twisted the faucet to the point where the cold-water tap was cut off. But it remained frigid.

Fuck.

Me.

I stepped out, suds still clinging to my hair. Some were sliding down my body, making a mess. After wrapping a towel around my waist, I went over to the bedroom, grabbed my phone and strode to the kitchen. Grandma's emergency phone number list was on the fridge.

"Come on. Water heater... Water heater..." I muttered, going down the list.

There. Billy's Plumbing and All Things Water.

I called. It should be open. Today was only Thursday. This Billy person—or his minion—should be able to fix it today. Preferably within the next hour. This was an emergency!

"Billy's Plumbing and All Things Water," a bored female said. "How can I help you?"

"My water heater isn't working anymore."

"Oh, that's too bad. What seems to be the problem?"

Could she sound any more uninterested? "Water heaters have only one job."

"Right. So..."

I sighed, running my hand impatiently over my forehead to get the water off. It ended up covered in white, foamy froth, which I wiped off on the towel. "The water. It's cold."

"Oh, that's too bad."

You think? Also couldn't she come up with something better than "Oh, that's too bad"?

"Where are you?"

"Two fifty-two Oak Street, Kingstree. Can you come now?" I decided to make the direness of the situation crystal clear. "I'm not getting any hot water at all. Nada. Zip. Can't even shower."

"Oh, that's too bad. But it's going to be two weeks."

No way I'd heard that right. "*How* long?"

"Two weeks," she repeated in a tone a high school senior must use to read *Moby-Dick* out loud in class.

"Two weeks! Didn't you hear what I said?"

She didn't bother to answer my question. She probably hadn't heard anything. "Billy's busy, and so is Junior. They're booked solid."

"I'll pay extra."

"All the after-hour slots are booked, too."

Fuck this. "Can you tell me if there's another company I can call?"

"Far as I know, we're the only one serving Kingstree. You want to set up an appointment?"

Jesus. She was droning like she was fighting to stay awake. Or couldn't even bother to fake some interest. This was what happened when you let an evil monopoly dominate an entire local area. But I needed them more than they needed me, so I kept that to myself. "Yes!"

"Okay. Thursday the twenty-first good?"

"I guess."

"You're all set."

"Wait, what time are you coming?"

She paused, then sighed. "Whenever Billy gets over to you. Just be home." She hung up.

"You gotta be shitting me!" I yelled at the phone like she was still on the line. "I'm not doing cold showers for two freakin' weeks!"

Nor was I going to forgo showering for two weeks. That would be disgusting.

And what was I going to do about my current shower interruptus? I still hadn't washed my body. And I could feel the suds fizzing in my hair.

There was a simple solution to my problem. If you could borrow sugar from a neighbor—I'd never done that, but it happens all the time on TV shows and in porn—surely you could borrow a little hot water as well. And luckily, my neighbor lived within walking distance.

My mind made up, I strode out of Grandma's and walked over to Emily's pink-roofed buttercream house, one hand on the towel around my waist.

CHAPTER 7

Emily

Killian wasn't just an asshole, I decided as I glared at the Word document. Its cursor blinked mutely. He was a Class A asshole. If he were a romance hero, he would've been beyond redemption—the type of hero who would earn your book half a million one-star reviews.

I hadn't been able to finish writing the dirty sex scene for Molly and Ryan. Not when Killian started banging on the damned drums and cymbals again like the fate of the galaxy depended on it. Then he also spent some time on an electric guitar and a piano that badly needed tuning. I hadn't realized until then that music could actually induce a person to want to commit murder. If I thought I could get away with it, I would have. But I knew the cops were too damned good at catching half-assed amateur murderers, based on numerous late-night chats with romantic suspense writers at bars in conference hotels. Goddamn advances in forensic science...

I hadn't been able to escape to a café to write, either. There was only one café in town, and the owner had refused to let me monopolize one of its four tables. Said it wouldn't be fair. I even offered to buy a latte every hour, but that hadn't persuaded her.

"Other people have the right to sit and enjoy our café, too."

She hadn't cared that other people didn't have to endure excruciating noise pollution from Killian Axelrod. Just like the dispatcher lady, everyone I encountered seemed to think I was lucky—*lucky!*—to listen to an obnoxious ruckus that not even a noise-canceling headset could block out for the entire day.

I picked up my phone and texted my writer friends, Lucy and Skye. I needed some genuine sympathy and understanding.

–Me: Are you sure there's no way to get away with murdering an obnoxious neighbor?

–Skye: Nope. Trust me on this. There is no perfect crime.

I glared at the text. What did Skye know? Her genre of choice was heartwarming contemporary romance.

–Lucy: Exactly. Especially in a town that small. People are gonna know if somebody's missing.

Damn it. Lucy wrote gritty romantic thrillers and suspense. If anybody was creative enough to come up with a plan to pull off an unsolvable murder, it'd be her.

–Me: I just can't write the sex scene with all this noise!

–Lucy: Just put SEX in there as a placeholder and write the other scenes.

I wanted to bang my head against the table. Better yet, I wanted to bang Killian's head against it.

–Me: I'm a linear writer. I can't skip around like you do.

–Skye: But it's just one sex scene, right? You can skip it for now and come back later. I promise. I do that when my kids are home and won't leave me alone. Trying to write sex with kids around? IMPOSSIBLE!

Point. Her kids were rambunctious. Still, I wanted to whine, because if I couldn't whine to my friends, who could I whine to?

–Me: I can't write anything romantic with all that damn drumming. And it's hard to intuit how the relationship should morph and evolve when I haven't written out the first sex scene! It has a big impact on the rest of the story, you know.

I added a sobbing emoji.

–Lucy: Why don't you check into a hotel?

–Me: There aren't any in this town.

–Skye: Drive to a bigger town, maybe? You only need a few

days of quiet to finish the book. Hotels are nice. You can order room service.

True. And I could take my Hop Hop Hoorays with me. Leaving the ice cream behind was sad, but it'd be waiting for me when I came home with the completed manuscript.

–Me: That sounds like a fantastic idea. Thanks, girls. I knew I could count on you.

–Skye: Anytime.

–Lucy: Yup. Sorry we don't live closer. If we did, I'd let you stay at my place.

I smiled at her offer. Lucy lived in Colorado. A little too far for a sleepover.

–Me: Thanks. But the hotel idea is fantastic. I'm going to look for one right now. Ciao!

Filled with renewed determination and hope, I opened my laptop and looked for a decently priced hotel not too far away. *Oh, look at those.* There were several within a hundred-mile radius. Not that I really wanted to travel, but it was a workable distance. I could drop by any one of them and get to work in peace and quiet.

Someone knocked on my door.

I frowned. One of many good things about Kingstree was that the town didn't have door-to-door salespeople. Nor did it have anyone concerned about saving my soul. So unless I was getting a package, there shouldn't be any knocks on the door...and I hadn't ordered anything since getting the headsets.

Screw it. I wasn't going to answer. Who cared if some clueless travelling salesperson had decided to grace my doorstep?

I turned my attention back to the search results. Marriott had a property about an hour away that looked promising. Good price on the room, too. *Still, an hour away...*

A fist slammed my door with enough force to shake it. "Hey, Emily, I know you're in there!"

I froze. That husky baritone... It sounded just like Killian, number one on my personal hit list—which I would never be able to act on. What the hell did he want?

Actually, so what if he wanted something? I leaped to my feet, rage boiling over. Wasn't it enough for him to endlessly bang on drums and other instruments with the damned windows open? Now he had to bang on my *door*?

Hands clenched, I marched to the door and yanked it open. "What the hell is your problem?" I yelled in my meanest voice, then promptly ruined the effect by letting my jaw go slack.

Oh my God.

Killian was standing there in nothing but a towel wrapped loosely around his waist. It hung so low that I was afraid it might slip and show me an accidental Full Monty. He was also wet. His hair stuck to his skull, and water droplets beaded and sparked all over his sinful face...not to mention the most gorgeous torso I'd ever laid eyes on.

Forget the wet shirt and low-slung jeans I'd considered earlier. This shot would totally make the most sellable romance cover ever...and push the book to number one in the entire Amazon Kindle store.

For a moment, I wondered if I should ask him to model. Then I decided no...it would only inflate his ego. And I had already bought a photo I liked for my cover.

Regardless of my personal feelings for the man's personality, my mouth dried. He was sex personified. For a moment, I couldn't even recall why I was so mad at him.

"Trying to trap flies with your mouth?" Bright laughter twinkled in his blue eyes.

I snapped my mouth shut so fast that my teeth clacked. *Now* I remembered why I was pissed off at him. All he'd had to do was to say something.

"What the hell are you doing here?" My tone bristled with aggression because that was what he deserved. Based on the smug expression on his *too handsome for everyone's own good* face, he knew the effect his almost naked body had and was enjoying it. Son of a bitch.

"Can I borrow some hot water?" he asked.

What kind of question was this? Was he trying to prank me? "What's wrong with your stove?" I demanded, my hand still on my door. He couldn't possibly expect me to give him anything, not after what he'd pulled.

"Stove's fine, but the water heater's broken. I can't get any hot water."

Aaah, I thought with petty satisfaction. *Karma got him.* I smirked.

"Billy's Plumbing can't come for two weeks, so I was thinking I could shower here until then." He smiled and stepped forward as though it was a foregone conclusion that I'd agree to this lunacy.

It was already bad enough he was harassing me with his so-called music. Now he wanted to "borrow" my hot water? Ha! I blocked him by moving into his path. "Hold it, buster." His smile slipped a little, and I shot him a bland look. "Why should I let you in? You could be a serial killer."

Both of his eyebrows went up. "You're worried about that *now*?"

"Of course I'm worried about it *now*. You're here *now*. It's a legitimate concern."

"Yeah, but...you already opened your door. So it's kinda too late."

He had a point. But all the reasons I shouldn't kill him also applied to him, and he probably didn't like going to jail either.

"I have a gun," I said finally. Mom had bought me a handgun, saying a woman living alone needed protection. She hated it that Kingstree was a small town, and the cul-de-sac my house was on was at the outskirts.

"But not on you." He gave me a *why don't we compromise and be nice* smile. "Look, I'm not a serial killer. You can ask the sheriff."

My teeth clenched. Kingstree's most *un*helpful sheriff's department. If they'd been more useful, I would've already been done with the sex scene and more. "Then borrow hot water from him. I'm not letting you use my shower. It's a free country."

"But it's also a *kind* country. Neighbors let neighbors borrow water and stuff all the time."

"Not this neighbor." I gave him a fake smile, deriving petty enjoyment from saying no. "Why should I? Maybe if you can't wash for two weeks, you'll quit trying to make me deaf with your drumming. What was it you said? Drumming is sweaty work?

Maybe you could take up something less sweaty. Like reading. Or meditation. Or going comatose."

He threw up a hand in the air like he couldn't believe my reaction. It made his abs stand out more. "I'm a professional musician. People pay to listen to me play. I really do have to practice."

"Do you expect me to believe that? Delusions aren't meant to be shared, you know."

His face fell. He looked like an author discovering the first one-star review on his precious debut novel.

I felt slightly bad at how upset he seemed, even though I was annoyed that I felt bad, since he was the one who'd made it impossible for me to write. But he seemed sincere in his reaction. Maybe he really *was* a musician. I remembered how much I resented my dad and strangers putting my writing down because I wrote romance. The arts were hard, and maybe I shouldn't have been so harsh.

On the other hand, he was the one sabotaging my effort to finish my work in progress. I had a deadline, not only on the manuscript but also on the bet with my dad.

"Look, why don't we compromise?" I said, as a genius idea struck me. "Why don't you refrain from making any noise for the entire month? You can at least do that, right?"

He looked at me like I was showing him an email from a Nigerian prince. "Oooo-kay... What do I get?"

"You can use my shower until your water heater's fixed, assuming it doesn't take more than a couple of weeks." Killian was a man, which meant it shouldn't take more than ten minutes for him to do his thing. Ten minutes *max*. And that was a small tradeoff for a month of silence. Much as I liked the idea of room service, I would prefer to be home with access to my favorite ice cream and beer.

"Well." He pulled his lips in and considered for a moment. "That seems unfair. I only get to use the shower for two weeks."

Oh, so you want to play hardball? "Well, if you don't like the terms, you're welcome to man up and take a cold shower every day." I made sure to add my sweetest, brightest smile. If he didn't care about cold showers, he wouldn't have trekked all the way over here in nothing but a towel.

He stared at me, his eyes slightly glazed. Then he shook his head. "So...no noise at all?"

I nodded. "I need my peace and quiet."

"That seems kind of impossible. I mean, can I watch TV?"

I frowned a little at the ridiculous question. "As long as the volume's low."

"How about cooking?"

I gave him a long-suffering look at his pathetic attempt to find loopholes. He was an amateur compared to my dad. "Of course you can cook. I mean annoying noises."

"How about snoring? Can I snore? It isn't annoying?"

I gritted my teeth. "You know what I mean! Obnoxious, loud noise I can hear from my home! I don't care if you snore, belch or fart, as long as I don't hear it!"

"Just wanted to make things clear. Keeping one's word is important," he said, his eyes innocently wide.

"Don't even try," I said.

"Try what?" This time he batted his ridiculously long eyelashes, which were gorgeous.

And the fact that I noticed their gorgeousness annoyed me to no end. I was above being stupid over a pretty face and a hard body. I had brain that didn't reside in my loins.

I narrowed my eyes. "I'll bet there isn't an innocent bone in your body."

He gave me an enigmatic smile. "So. The shower?"

"Fine. Upstairs." I moved away from the door, permitting him into my home and praying I didn't end up regretting it.

CHAPTER 8

Emily

While Killian was availing himself of my shower, I quickly texted my friends again.

–Me: Don't need to check into a hotel. The noise polluter caved.

–Skye: Really? I thought he was uncooperative.

–Me: He was, but karma is on my side.

–Lucy: What happened?

I summarized Killian and my bargain.

–Lucy: Oooh. Is he hot?

–Me: Is that what you got out of the story?

–Lucy: Yes because you're lending him your shower. You wouldn't have done that if he was some gross old orangutan-looking guy.

Ew.

–Skye: Cosigned.

–Me: You're both being ridiculous.

–Skye: She didn't deny the hotness.

–Lucy: Nope.

I rolled my eyes. They knew me too well.

–Me: Okay, he isn't too bad. Didn't max out the orangutan meter.

And my text just became the most flagrant understatement of the year. But it wasn't like Lucy and Skye were going to meet Killian.

–Lucy: I want pictures.

Oh come on!

–Skye: Yep. Photographic evidence, please.

–Me: Take my word for it, ladies. He's not worth the data.

–Skye: I'm on wifi.

–Lucy: Me too.

–Me: I'm not taking a picture of him in the shower!

–Skye: Of course not.

–Lucy: That would be porn.

–Skye: Do it after he's out.

I gave up. My friends were acting like pigs, but I grudgingly admitted they were right to be skeptical. I was known to disparage good-looking men. It wasn't because I had anything against attractiveness. It was just that... Men who were too hot for their own good reminded me of my dad. And I wasn't too crazy about how I looked, either, because I'd taken after him in every way except for my hair, which was blond like my mother's.

"Hey, Emily! Can I borrow a towel?" came a shout from upstairs.

I glared up at the ceiling. Now he wanted a towel, too? "What's wrong with the one you brought with you?" I yelled back from my couch.

"It's wet!"

Oh, for God's sake! "Hold on a minute! Don't drip water everywhere or I'm making you mop the floor! On your hands and knees!"

Ooh, and you should totally watch while he's doing that, a voice that sounded suspiciously like a chorus of Lucy and Skye said. *Men who clean are extra hot.*

No, I did not need to see that or think about it...or imagine his back and arm muscles flexing while he cleaned my floor.

Don't forget those wide shoulders...

No, no, no. What I needed was to kick the sexy pest out of the house as soon as possible. And I most certainly would not wonder why my face felt so warm at the moment.

I got off the couch and went upstairs, grumbling under my breath about men who wanted more than what they'd agreed to. I wasn't a hotel! On the other hand, Killian was shameless enough to parade around naked if he got a chance. Otherwise, he wouldn't have shown up on my doorstep draped in a towel in the first place. Hell, if I screamed at him to cover himself, something in his brain might break from the overexertion of trying to figure out why a woman wouldn't want to see his naked body.

Okay. Maybe some women would want to see him nude. Well...not just some, but a lot of women. But I wasn't one of them. I just thought he'd make a great cover model because photography hadn't advanced enough to capture a subject's personality.

I looked through the linen closet's neatly folded stacks of towels. My gaze fell on the blue one first, but then I noticed the pink one right under it. *Well, well, well.* Feeling spiteful, I pulled that one from the stack, then, making sure to turn my head away, I threw the towel into the guest bathroom. "Here!"

"Thank you!" His response was so cheery that I could almost picture him waving as well.

Okay, this was still a small price to pay for a month of peace and quiet. I clamped down on the terrible urge to sneak a peek at his bare body and took firm, purposeful steps back to the living room. I should get back to the story—and finally finish the first sex scene between Molly and Ryan. I felt awful about stopping in mid-kiss and leaving the characters there for more than twenty-four hours. My couple deserved better treatment. Maybe I should add an extra sex scene. And a baby epilogue. My readers loved babies.

I sat down on the couch with the computer on my lap. I found the spot I'd marked for a full sex scene toward the end of the document.

"Oh yeah, baby," I murmured. "You're going to get laid today. Woohoo!"

"Who's getting laid?"

I almost jumped. My laptop tilted and I grabbed it fast. After placing it on the table, I spun around to face Killian. Who was standing behind me in nothing but the pink towel. *Holy shit.*

He smelled fresh with a hint of soap, and looked as good as he smelled. His skin gleamed as a couple drops of water fell from his still-damp hair and slid down his naked shoulder and ropey arm, tracing an irregular path of the crevasses between the lean muscles. Those eyelashes were incredibly thick, and his eyes so, so blue. Regardless of what I thought of his personality, he was scrumptious. I felt an urge to lick all the water off him that the towel had missed.

And as soon as I realized that, I blinked and wanted to smack myself for thinking with my hormones. Since I couldn't do that without appearing weird, I opted for a *you're not welcome here anymore* expression instead.

"Shouldn't you be going home now?" I said coolly.

"Don't worry, I will. Soon as I finish air-drying my chest hair."

It was the most ludicrous thing I'd ever heard coming out of a man's mouth. For one thing, he didn't have enough chest hair to dry.

I caught myself before I asked whether he had to air-dry his pubic hair as well. Killian wouldn't be scandalized. Or become self-aware enough to realize how ridiculous his explanation about air-drying chest hair was. No, he'd just laugh, say, "Now that you mention it..." and whip the towel from around his waist.

I did not need to see his cock. Ever. No matter how big it might be. And I could tell it'd be big and impressive. God had been unfair when he'd created Killian. Why stop at a pretty face and a hard body?

"Hey, you got a beer?" Killian asked.

"Are you kidding? I'm not a grocery store." Besides, he owed me a favor, not the other way around. I'd even lent him my good pink towel.

"You took all the Hop Hop Hooray. Sunny told me the store has no clue when there'll be more." He raised a finger. "Just one. I promise I won't bother you again."

The man was utterly shameless. "You promised to be quiet," I reminded him. "And yet I can hear you."

"Is my voice annoying you?" he asked incredulously.

"Yes," I lied.

He sounded hot as hell, a baritone that stroked my nerve endings and lit them up until my mouth felt dry. And that made him extra irritating. On the other hand, I wanted a beer now that he mentioned it, and I didn't feel like getting off the couch.

"Fine. *One*," I said finally. I made sure I sounded super grudging. He needed to know I wasn't doing it because I wanted him to do something for me, and I knew he wouldn't lift a finger without getting something back. "And *you* can go get me one from the fridge as well, since I'm out of my work drink."

"Awesome. Thanks." He smiled.

My breath stilled, and my brain froze. It was a genuine smile, one without a hint of mockery or ego. It seemed like the sun, brilliant and mesmerizing, but utterly out of my reach. All coherent thought drained from my mind, and the only thing left was potent admiration.

He didn't seem to notice my reaction, though. As he walked over to the fridge, the light coming in through the windows created a hazy halo effect around him. My fingers curled with the desire to touch him, just to see if he felt as fine as he looked.

The sound of the fridge door opening and closing jerked me back to reality.

Holy hell. How could I have been so juvenile, like some high school girl around a hot quarterback? I was much too old and sensible for that.

He brought over two beers. I accepted one, trying not to notice—again—how wide his shoulders were. Or how hard his chest looked. He sat down next to me on the couch, and suddenly the couch seemed to shrink. Killian smelled so freaking good.

I wanted to ask him to get off the couch, but that would make me an ungracious bitch, considering there wasn't any other good place for him to sit, so I bit my tongue. Then prayed the beer would lessen his attraction. Men who drank said stupid things.

"So. You didn't answer my question. Who's getting laid?" he asked again.

One-track mind. But if I ignored him, he would continue to pester me—if not today, then tomorrow and the day after—because he was a man and, as such, wouldn't just forget about sex. "Nobody you know."

He leaned closer and tilted his head. "Do you still think Molly and Ryan are hooking up?"

I choked on my beer, dripping a mouthful on my shirt. "Shit!" I coughed to clear my throat and nose. "How did you—*agah!*—know?" Had he managed to read a snippet off the screen earlier?

"You were talking about them in the store."

I stared at him. "I was?"

"Yeah." He gave me a long, evaluating look. "Just so you know, that's how rumors start."

I bristled. How dare he sit in *my* home, drink *my* beer and judge me? I could write whatever the hell I wanted! I wasn't creating or spreading rumors! It wasn't my fault some people couldn't tell the difference between fact and fiction. "It's none of your business what I do or don't do," I said stiffly, regretting wasting a good beer on this ungrateful, sexy piece of shit.

"Yeah, but Molly and Ryan are good people. Molly has a couple of kids, and Ryan's been married for forty years. Don't you think you should be more considerate?" Now even his tone was judging.

"What are you talking about?" Molly was in her twenties, Ryan in his thirties. Neither had ever been married.

Killian's eyebrows pulled together until lines formed between them. "You know, Molly Patterson and Ryan Johnson?"

I sat back, my body sagging as the indignation subsided. He thought I was talking about real people in town. I didn't know who Ryan Johnson was, but I'd run into Molly Patterson at a farmers' market once or twice when I first moved in. An okay but kind of pushy lady. Overly chatty, too. She'd wanted me to join the local PTA despite the fact that I was single and childfree.

"Oh Lord, nobody cares if you're single!" She'd laughed as she said it, waving a hand like my reply was the silliest thing ever. "Kids or no kids, we'd love to have you chip in and help out. There are so many things to be done. I mean, you're home all the time, aren't you?"

The unspoken message being: *You can't possibly be doing anything worthwhile—you're home all day.*

She'd continued, oblivious to my rising annoyance. "It'd be a fantastic opportunity to meet the people around here and use your time productively."

"I'd rather eat bull—" I'd caught myself in time because her kids were listening. "I'd rather stick my face into a wasp nest."

It was like I'd confessed to burning books and streaking naked under the full moon, drenched in Satan's blood. "Why, I never...!"

Chin held high, she'd stormed away in a huff, herding her children like little sheep, before I was able to point out that it was rude to presume I had nothing better to do with my time. Readers were waiting for my next book. Just imagine what they'd say if I told them I had to delay the release because I'd been too busy helping out with a local PTA that had nothing to do with me.

"Are you friends with Molly?" I asked. He might've hung out with her when he came to visit his late grandmother. That could explain his defense of her and this Ryan Johnson guy.

Killian's expression turned mildly annoyed. Was he upset that I asking about his relationship with Molly? Or was he just annoyed that I wasn't saying, "Yes, you're right, of course. I'm so sorry I said things you thought were objectionable even though I wasn't talking about your Molly and Ryan."

"No," Killian said. "But I know who she is. Everyone in town does."

"So do I, unfortunately. And don't worry. I wasn't talking about her. Or your buddy Ryan. There *are* Mollys and Ryans other than the ones in this town, in case that's never occurred to you."

He blinked. Something crossed his intensely blue eyes, but he was probably just processing the shocking factoid.

"Isn't your chest hair sufficiently dry now?" I asked, leaning back. "Maybe you should get going."

"Just trying to finish my beer." He lifted his bottle, and his Adam's apple bobbed as he swallowed. The movement was mesmerizingly sexy. I needed to make an appointment to see a therapist, because a man's throat shouldn't be this hot. Thankfully, Killian was almost done. His gaze flicked to something behind me. "You must really love Emma Grant."

Huh? How did he know my pen name? I hadn't mentioned it in a haze of sexual fascination or something... Had I?

"You have a *lot* of copies of her stuff," he said, as though he'd sensed my unspoken question. Then he spotted my latest book on the coffee table and picked it up. "A *Wall Street Journal* bestselling author, huh?"

"Yup. Hit the list four times," I said proudly. I'd texted the screenshots to Dad every single time, too. It was an extra pleasure in life, since cutting him and dousing the wound with salt was likely illegal.

Killian gave me an oddly guarded look. "You follow her career pretty closely?"

Geez, did he think I was a stalker fan? "I should hope so, since I *am* her," I said. I didn't necessarily advertise the fact that I wrote, but I didn't hide it, either, especially when somebody was in my home. And I had no reason to hide it with Killian. As a matter of fact, it would be a great chance to figure out what level of asshole he was.

Killian did a double take. "*You*'re Emma Grant?"

I nodded, then braced myself for a light dismissal—"Oh that's so cute!" or "I always wanted to knock out a romance novel in my spare time!"—or mockery—"Mommy porn paying the bills?" or "I didn't know people still read trashy smut!" That was the general reaction when people found out what I did, and there was no reason to think Killian would be any different. I decided to consider him a civilized asshole if he wasn't as obnoxious and offensive as my dad, which was setting the bar pretty low. But since Killian would be coming over for half a month to borrow my shower, I wanted to avoid feeling homicidal rage at the sight of him. I still didn't know how to execute a perfect murder.

"Huh." Killian looked at the cover again, then back at me before placing the book back on the table. "If you're such a famous bestselling author, how come I've never heard of you?"

I rolled my eyes. Lots of people said that when they found out that I'd hit the bestseller lists a few times. So I gave him the clichéd response I always handed out when I was dealing with them.

"Maybe because you don't read anything except utility bills?" Which was most likely true. According to statistics, most people didn't read for pleasure, and therefore didn't know that many authors. And even those who read a lot usually only knew writers who released books they liked to read. Sort of like me—I didn't know any musicians. I didn't listen to music because I found it distracting to my creative process. The only band I really knew was Queen, because Skye and Lucy had said I had to listen to Freddie Mercury sing or I was missing out. And the Beatles, only because I'd studied them in modern American pop culture class in college.

"I read," Killian protested, as though I'd accused him of not brushing his teeth every day.

I crossed my arms. "Like what?"

He started to tick titles off on his fingers. "*Jurassic Park*. *The Martian*. *The Firm*. *Minority Report*. *Interview with the Vampire*. *Twilight*...but that was only because my sister made me. *Game of Thrones*." He gave me a triumphant smile. "That's just a small sample."

Huh. Surprisingly eclectic. Science fiction to high fantasy to young adult paranormal romance and a legal thriller... Then I noticed something. *Game of Thrones* was the title of an HBO drama. *A Song of Ice and Fire*, George R. R. Martin's series that the drama was based on, kicked off with *A Game of Thrones*.

I snorted with amusement as I realized what Killian had done. "You mean you watched movies and dramas *based on* books."

"So?" He shrugged and took a swig of the beer. "It's like reading, but better."

"Books are ten thousand times better," I countered. "Trust me. Adaptations are pale shadows at best."

"Says you."

"That's right. And I'm the authority because I actually read, unlike you. Also, I'm an *author*."

"Being an author doesn't mean you read."

I sighed. "It was a joke."

"I don't get it."

"*Author*. It's the same root as *authority*— Oh, never mind! Are you done with that?"

Killian stood, put his empty beer bottle in the kitchen recycling bin and came back to the living room. He started to leave, stopped and returned to the coffee table, where he picked up my book and looked at it for a moment. "Mind if I borrow this?"

Mr. I Watch My Novels wanted to read *my* book? Seriously? He didn't even like romance. He'd said he'd only seen *Twilight* because of his sister.

"No," I said. "You'll probably use it as a paperweight."

"Oh, come on. I have nothing to do, since I can't make any 'obnoxious'"—he made air quotes—"noises. Assuming you'll forgive the sound of me turning the pages of your masterpiece, of course."

"Argh. I told you it was fine as long as I can't hear it."

He laughed. "You're cute when you fume. You look like an overheated teakettle with steam and a whistle. Grandma owned one that turned red when it got hot. Like in a cartoon."

I pointed at the door. "Out."

"Okay, okay." He kept holding the book, and I decided to let him try to read it. He'd give up after a page or two. Men hardly ever read and liked romance because most of them were narrow-minded about books written by women for women. Just look at my dad.

Killian started to walk off.

"And give me back my towel!"

"You really want it?" He smiled, flashing his dimple again and hooking a thumb under the edge.

Dammit, he was naked underneath. And easily shameless enough to give me the towel this instant.

"I mean *tomorrow*!" I shrieked. "Now out! I have to work."

CHAPTER 9

Killian

I chuckled and occasionally laughed out loud as I read Emma Grant's, a.k.a. Emily-next-door's, book. Out of self-preservation, I quit drinking anything while reading. Snorting whiskey up my nose hurt.

Darth Vader's theme played on my phone. *Not now!* I thought. I wanted to let it go to voicemail, as there were only forty-some pages left to read. But it was Mir, and I didn't want to do that to my baby sister.

"Hey," I said. "Make it quick."

"Well, hello to you, too," Mir said. "How's everything? Life treating you better now? Writing any new songs?"

I was too engrossed in Emily's story to react very strongly. "I'm fine. Could be better if I could finish this book without getting interrupted." Hint, hint.

"A 'book'? Is that what we call Netflix adaptations these days?" she asked with a laugh. "Oh, wait. Are you watching a foreign film and need to read the subtitles?"

"No, I—"

"No, probably not. Italian porn doesn't have a lot of dialogue."

I sighed. She knew my motto was that if a book was any good, it'd be made into a movie or show. I didn't actually have to read clusters of letters.

"I'm *reading*, Mir. A novel. Emma Grant's *Holiday with a Grumpy Boss*. It's hilarious, and I'm almost finished with it."

Silence. Mir finally said, "Okay, so you really are *reading* reading. What's happened to you? Should I call a lawyer to help you get started on a will?"

"I *do* actually read more than utility invoices, you know."

"I'm shocked. I thought your assistant took care of your invoices."

"Fine, but I'm just saying I do read, and I'm liking this Emma Grant book. Have you read it? It's a chick story."

"It's called romance. And yes, I read it the day it came out. Emma Grant is one of my absolute faves. I one-click every time she puts out a new book."

"Huh. I didn't know you had time to read." Mir lived to work, or so I'd presumed based on the number of hours she claimed to spend at the office. "I'll let her know. Maybe that'll make her more agreeable."

"Wait, what? Are you hanging out with *Emma Grant*?"

Hanging out would be fudging it. I mean, Emily had glared at me like I was a fly she couldn't wait to get rid of. But something about her really got to me. Maybe it was her smile. Her *I'm not letting you get away with shit* attitude. Whatever it was, she made me curious, hot and interested. Emotions I hadn't felt since my last breakup a year ago. "Yup. Just so happens she's the next-door neighbor Grandma liked so much. Remember Emily?"

Mir let out a shriek loud enough to pop my eardrum. I pulled the phone away to save my hearing and career. "*Oh my God!* Grandma's Emily is *Emma Grant*? Oh my... Holy *shit*!" She started panting.

"Breathe, Mir, breathe. Don't want you fainting and hitting your head. Concussions hurt." The intensity of Mir's fangirling was weird. Emily was wasn't a secret pop star, was she? Or a minor Instagram celebrity? Were authors famous enough to get this kind of reaction?

"Fine, fine. But oh my God. *Emma fucking Grant!*" Mir let

out more shrieks. "Can you ask her to autograph a book for me? Wait. I'm going to order a copy of each of her books off Amazon right now and have them shipped to Kingstree. When they get there, have them autographed. Tell her to make them out to Miriam. Oh, and let her know I am her *big*gest fan! Oh my God. If I show up, you think she'll autograph my boobs with a Sharpie?"

I shook my head at the way my sister was going on. Boob autograph, really? Mir was acting like she was about to get a hug from Captain America.

A naked Captain America.

"I don't know. She'll probably think you're a psycho stalker if I tell her about this interaction. Hell, she might flee the country. Who wants a Kathy Bates type coming after them?

"Ha ha, very amusing. I'm a normal, sane fan, thank you very much, although I wouldn't mind her spending all her time writing, since food and sleep are overrated. Besides, do you think your fans are insane when they scream your name? When they start crying because you looked at them at a concert?"

"That's different. None of them ever tried to kidnap me and imprison me in a basement. And honestly, you know, I'm flattered that they love my music, but it makes me uncomfortable that they react that way to somebody they don't even know." It was something that'd always bothered me. "Anyway, I gotta go. Don't send any books. She has tons of them lying around. I'll just buy a copy of each and send them to you for your birthday." That would take care of birthday gifts for Mir. She was a hard person to buy stuff for.

"You're the best."

I laughed, warmth filling me at her bright happiness. As annoying as my baby sister could be, I loved her and liked to do things for her. "I know. Now unless you have something really important to tell me, I want to finish this book."

"Okay. What little gossip I have can wait. I can't believe you even answered my call in the first place. I don't when I'm reading her books." Mir hung up.

I flipped the book open and read the rest. Emily's characters were over-the-top funny. Reading the book was an ab workout all by itself.

I wiped the tears beading in the corners of my eyes. I had no idea Emily had such a killer sense of humor. And the three sex scenes were hot as hell, too. I was sad she hadn't written another one in an epilogue. Every fictional couple deserved to have more sex, especially if I got to read it in explicit detail.

My annoyance with Billy's Plumbing and All Things Water had completely vanished. I had discovered a new side of my adorably irascible neighbor and scored a free Hop Hop Hooray beer.

I flipped some more pages until I hit her bio. From McLean, Virginia. Graduated from the University of Virginia. Held a corporate job until she went off to Harvard to get an MBA. Upon graduation, she started writing romance. At the end was her website and a list of her social media sites.

Normally, I'd put the book down the second I got to the end of the story. I'd never read beyond the last page of a boring English lit book in high school, that was for sure. But I wanted more. Emily fascinated me. Her sharp tongue, her take-no-prisoners attitude, her *I don't care what you think* sense of fashion and behavior.

I still couldn't quite believe she had no clue who I was. She claimed she didn't at the supermarket, but I'd eventually decided she only said that to take the ice cream. But when I was drumming, she'd glared at me like she wanted to put a bullet between my eyebrows. And earlier today, she'd been more annoyed than fangirling when I showed up on her doorstep in nothing but a towel.

I'd never had a woman behave that way around me. Even before I'd become famous—much less after—women tended to smile dreamily and let me do whatever I wanted. What would Emily do when she found out who I was?

My gut said, *Don't count on her squealing and fawning all over you.*

I picked up my phone and checked out her social media accounts. There were quotes from her books. Several selfies. I squinted. Those couldn't be her, even though they'd been tagged with her pen name. Where was the messy mane? The glasses? The bare face and annoyed scowl?

Her face was flawlessly made up in the selfies, her hair lying sleek and tidy around it. The eyelashes framing her wide eyes were so curled and thick that I knew they had to be from mascara. Emily had gorgeous green eyes that reminded me of a summer forest, but her lashes weren't as long as in the picture. And whatever she'd done to her lips made them look fuller, although I liked her nude lips better. That way they'd only taste like her, not lipstick.

And her clothes actually looked *nice,* like something Mir would wear to work or a nice restaurant. So weird to see Emily with such a public façade.

As put together as she was in these photos, I liked her better all private and casually disheveled. She would've never forgotten a bra when she was dressed to face the world. And she was cuter when she wasn't wearing makeup. More real. Bet she smelled like herself rather than perfume and cosmetics. I should probably check. Just to establish the truth, not because I harbored an unhealthy fixation with my neighbor who didn't know who I was and hated my drumming.

I scrolled down. There were more pictures of Emily at some signing event. She still looked virtually unrecognizable in the photos. Too polished. Too dressed up.

Something about them reminded me of my ex, Caitlyn Shaw. Caitlyn wasn't a writer. She was a social media influencer with half a million followers worldwide. She both recognized me and treated me well...unlike Emily. But everything else had been a lie, a carefully cultivated image and brand. The real Caitlyn was nothing like social media Caitlyn, and I'd been fooled. I'd thought she cared about me and wanted to be with *me.* But she only wanted what being with me could do for her career.

I'd been such an idiot. Devlin had told me that shit like that happened all the time. Said it'd get better. But even now, the memory of that shit-tastic relationship embarrassed me and pissed me off. Made me more cautious and standoffish because I didn't want to repeat the experience, even though I knew not every woman in the world was like Caitlyn.

The more photos I saw of Emily as Emma Grant, the more a bitter taste filled my mouth—the same taste as when I'd found out Caitlyn was livestreaming our dinner. My manager had texted me to let me know because he wasn't sure if it was something I wanted.

It wasn't. I'd been planning on proposing to her that night. Instead, I broke up with her while her audience watched live. I hoped she'd received thousands of the likes she loved so much. And I'd made sure to like that video myself to show "support," since that had been what she wanted more than anything else in the world.

Still... It didn't look like Emily was trying to be an influencer. She only talked about her books and engaged her fans. I shouldn't judge her for being so different in person. She wasn't like Caitlyn, who had been image-conscious all the time and puked after meals when she thought I wouldn't notice, then lied about it when I asked her to seek help. (I'd learned after the breakup that she wanted to tell her followers about all the rich, sumptuous meals she was enjoying while "effortlessly" maintaining a size-two body.) Emily ate ice cream, drank beer, crunched on crackers full of carbs and obviously didn't care that her body wasn't anywhere close to a size two. A decent publicist would've advised her to clean up before appearing in public so she wouldn't scare away potential readers.

My eyes landed on framed photos of the family on the fireplace mantel. Grandma was smiling in many of them, looking happy and proud, her arms looped around the younger me and Mir. I was smiling in one, showing my braces and looking slightly dorky, even though I was doing my best to hide that from the world with a confident grin.

Nowadays, that same grin on stage made women scream and throw themselves at me. I was still me—Killian Axelrod—but Killian the Rock Star was very different from Killian the Teenager or Killian the Private Citizen.

I looked back at the photos, at my grandmother. She'd always known I'd make it big, even though some of the more pessimistic people in Kingstree told her most artists never make enough to pay phone bills. "Don't judge my grandson's future based on what happened to other people. He's different. He'll be a success," she'd said all the time, in an indomitable tone that told everyone she knew she was right.

I should follow her advice. I shouldn't judge Emily based on what Caitlyn did. They were different people.

CHAPTER 10

Emily

"Oh yeah, oh yeah, oh yeah."

I did a little shoulder dance as I hit six thousand words for the day. I could finally hear myself think now that the annoying noise had stopped. I blew on my fingers, 'cause they were smokin'!

I checked the time. Nine thirty p.m. My stomach let out a growl, begging for food. I realized I hadn't eaten anything except some crackers in the morning. But it was hard to remember to get off the couch when I was busy with scenes pouring out of me. I never interrupted my flow when I was on fire.

But now that my belly had gotten my attention, I couldn't ignore it. I opened the fridge. Beer. More beer. Wine coolers. *Ooh, a strawberry one*! I pulled it out and put it on the counter. A tub of peach yogurt...*ugh*. Expired a month earlier and undoubtedly toxic by now.

I rummaged through the freezer. I didn't even have any Bouncy Bare Monkeys, having consumed the last of it for breakfast yesterday. An unopened bag of frozen halibut filets lay on the bottom. I couldn't recall why I'd purchased them. I liked seafood but almost never cooked it, generally for lack of time. When I did have time for a relaxing meal after meeting a deadline, I ordered takeout or delivery because usually I couldn't bother to exert the effort, especially when it was just for one person and I loathed cleaning up afterward.

The two or three diners and takeout places that existed in Kingstree were closed now. That was one disadvantage of living in a small town. But I still had Animal Crackers. They were nutritious enough. They'd sustained me in college and business school, and they could sustain me now.

I opened a new bag and grabbed a few. I bit off the head of a lion first, then washed it down with the wine cooler. After several bites, my stomach quit grumbling so much. I let out a soft sigh of satisfaction. Couldn't do better than the current combo for a quickie dinner while on a tight deadline.

I'd polished off at least two fistfuls of crackers when my phone rang. Shit. It was Mom. She understood I shouldn't be bothered when I was on deadline, but she didn't care when she desperately needed somebody to talk to about family drama, a.k.a. "What did Dad do now?"

It couldn't be about anything underhanded he was doing to sabotage my career, because we'd already figured out the One-Star Hit Squad. So...was he "working late" again? Did he go home without showering first at a hotel?

Mom wasn't stupid, just in terrible denial about her marriage. I took another big swig of the wine cooler because it wasn't the kind of conversation anybody could have while sober.

"Hey, Mom," I said. My voice sounded flat, even though I was aiming for friendly. Shit.

Instead of saying hello, Mom sobbed. "Oh my God, Emily!"

"What's wrong?" I asked with all the sympathy I could scrape up, although I already knew. This was her standard greeting every time she caught Dad cheating.

"Your father. His shirt smells like perfume!" She sobbed harder.

All the jubilation at having written six thousand words vanished, and the familiar feeling of resignation and pity settled over me. She just noticed that today? Didn't he always smell like perfume?

"I was going to do a load of laundry, and...and... It was so *strong*. I'm devastated," she continued. The sound of her blowing her nose came through the line.

This was going to be a looong call. "Mom..."

"It wasn't my perfume!" she yelled like a wounded animal, then cried again.

"Why do you put up with this? With him?" It was the same question I always asked. Futile, of course. She'd only ever given me one answer. But I hoped she would finally open her eyes and see the light, because it was frustrating as hell that she was calling me instead of kicking him out, dumping all his stuff in the front yard and setting it on fire. It was the least he deserved.

"Where would I go? What would I do?" she wailed.

Annoyance welled like poison. It was the same answer she always gave. And I knew exactly what she'd say next.

"A woman's place in life is next to her husband," she added, at the same time I muttered it. "Wait, what did you say?"

"Nothing." It'd only add to her angst if she thought I wasn't one hundred percent on her side, even though I was. To her, unless I agreed with everything she said, gave her unconditional, boundless sympathy and a shoulder to cry on, I was against her.

If I'd had a decent meal, I might've been more sympathetic. But some Animal Crackers and a wine cooler weren't enough to fortify me for the endless understanding she wanted when she continued to reject my solution—*Divorce Dad. Boom! Problem solved.*

So maybe that was why I said, "You forgot to add faithful."

"What?" Mom said, more confused than ever before.

"A woman's place in life is next to her *faithful* husband."

"You are *so* judgmental." Rage vibrated in every syllable, a predictable turn. This was what I called the "Incomprehensible Tantrum" phase, because she was angry with the wrong people. She could criticize Dad for being a cheating asshole, but nobody else could, including me, even when she was the one who'd called to complain about him being a cheating asshole in the first place. "You think everything in the world is like your books."

"I actually don't," I said dryly. I wrote romance because I knew how crappy real-life relationships could be. "If he's coming home with another woman's perfume all over him, leave him." *But don't come here,* I added—silently, in case that hadn't occurred to her yet. I didn't want to give her any ideas. Staying with me was her typical "revenge" for Dad's cheating. Usually, I let her, because I couldn't exactly flee the country to avoid it, even though she drove me crazy by insisting on remaining with Dad. But right now, I couldn't afford several days of babysitting her hurt feelings. I had a book to finish.

I wondered vaguely if this had been his plan all along—to get caught so Mom would drive down to Kingstree and disrupt my writing. It wouldn't surprise me a bit.

"I can't do that!" Mom wailed. "We love each other, even if he strays from time to time."

My jaw slackened with shock. *Time to time*? Dad "strayed" at least every other month. And that was only the times he'd gotten caught. There probably had been a lot more. How could Mom be so blind?

"Besides, he needs me." She sniffled. "He always comes back."

"He just doesn't want to pay alimony." He had a law degree. Even though he didn't practice, he had to know exactly how much he'd pay in a divorce settlement.

"That's so cold," Mom said, her voice hard.

Oh, for God's sake. "You don't have to leave permanently," I clarified quickly before she started accusing me of being insensitive. I still thought she should divorce his sorry ass. But if she hadn't done it in the last twenty-some years, she wasn't going to do it now. "Just long enough for him to learn his lesson. Don't you want to see him groveling on his knees to get you to come back?" I laid it on thick. I couldn't imagine Dad doing that. He was a proud man. Just not proud enough to keep his wedding vows. Or play fair to win a bet.

But he was clever enough to understand that some flowers and silly gifts would soften Mom. That was how he'd gotten her to come back every time she came over to stay with me after discovering some new infidelity.

"Huh." I could hear the gears in my mom's head turning.

"That does sound...doable. And fun, too. I'd love for him to grovel."

"Exactly," I said, warming to the most critical point in all this. "Go to New York, check into a hotel for a week or so and don't answer his texts or emails or calls. Go shopping. Have fun. Post lots of happy selfies on Instagram. He'll get the hint." The issue was that they were terrible enablers of each other's vices. Dad needed to cheat to feel smart and powerful, and Mom needed a financially well-off husband to feel secure and wanted.

"That's not a bad idea. I'll do that next time," Mom said.

"Do it *now,*" I said, trying not to sound desperate. I couldn't have her come here. *Go to New York City! Please!* "I'll pay for your hotel."

"I can't do that, not when I have to plan and strategize your next release launch."

That meant she wasn't coming to Kingstree. I took a relieved swig.

"By the way, are you on target with the next book?" Mom asked, finally on another track.

"Yes." Now that my asshole neighbor was quiet... "As long as I'm not interrupted, I should be fine." I tried to subtly emphasize "not interrupted," so she got an extra-heavy hint not to come.

"We have to make sure to push it to number one in the entire Amazon store. I'd love to see your dad eat his words." Vengeful malice laced her words. She might believe her place was by her philandering husband, but she could be surprisingly vindictive when she wanted. She just wasn't vindictive enough to divorce him and take all his money.

"I do too, especially since it's my last chance." The book was coming out on the fourth anniversary of me going pro with writing. And that was the deadline for the bet between me and Dad.

"Don't worry, hon," Mom said. "You'll hit it. I have faith in you, and I'm going to make sure it happens, too! I've already made a ton of graphics and brainstormed some ideas to help."

I smiled at her enthusiasm, even if it was mainly motivated by her desire to see me win and humiliate Dad. I wanted to see him humiliated too, but mainly, I wanted to see him admit he was wrong—wrong to mock me and other women for enjoying romance, wrong to belittle my choices and desires.

"Thanks, Mom." I took the last swig. "I gotta go and finish the scene I was working on."

"Okay! You go make me proud."

CHAPTER 11

Killian

The next morning, I puttered around in my kitchen, intending to make myself an omelet. I'd decided to make it a habit to eat better, especially when I wasn't touring. Things could be hectic on the road. My recent collapse had reminded me I needed to take care of myself if I wanted to be singing and performing for decades to come, even though the specialists who'd examined me had said I was healthy enough. I didn't plan on fading away after only a few years like so many others. I wanted longevity.

Probably should get the other guys to start eating better, too. We could be like the Stones, or Aerosmith...

Besides, I did my best work when I was well rested and well fed. There was a myth of suffering, cocaine-snorting musicians pouring out amazing work in a drug-induced haze. Might be true for some, but not me. It was a terrible way to work, more self-destructive than creative.

But in the last several years, I'd pushed anyway because I wanted to see how far I could go. And my body had punished me for it, so now it was recovery time. Recharge the batteries. Sleep. Rest. Take it easy. I was certain if I could get over this burnout, I'd go back to writing brilliant songs again, with the kind of lyrics that resonated with millions of listeners.

Not doing that was...

My mouth dried, and a chill crept into my body. Not write songs and perform them? It was the thing that made me matter—the vehicle through which I made a difference in the world and touched people's hearts. Grandma's proud expression fleeted through my mind. I didn't want to disappoint her, even if she was gone now. I couldn't let my band mates down...or my fans.

And it wasn't about money or fame. My parents had left me and Mir a huge trust worth billions. I could live like a king even if I never did anything productive for the rest of my life. But that wasn't what I wanted. Not what Grandma would've wished for. I only had one life, and it should be meaningful. Make an impact.

As I pulled out eggs and cheese from the fridge, I paused. Emily's refrigerator had looked pretty barren yesterday. And she'd only bought alcohol, ice cream and Animal Crackers at Sunny's Mart. I doubted she'd gone back later to get something more nutritious.

Her eating habits irked me, probably because they reminded me of Mir's. My baby sister liked to subsist on mainly junk food because it was quick and easy, and she hated wasting time with something as "mundane" as eating when she was working. Thankfully, she was now dating a nutritionist, who was making her eat more like an adult.

I turned my head toward Emily's house. Left to her own devices, she'd probably have potato chips and beer for breakfast. Maybe a cup of coffee if she was feeling particularly mature.

You're not her mother.

Yeah, but I have to go over there to shower anyway, so...

My mind made up, I picked up a carton of dozen eggs and some shredded cheese and put them in a plastic bag I grabbed from under the kitchen sink. Grandma had always kept a few there just in case. I tucked a bath towel in, plus the pink towel I'd laundered last night. I put the book Emily had lent me under my arm, picked up the bag and walked over to her place.

When I knocked on the door, Emily opened it. She was in a ragged T-shirt that I was certain had been blue at some point, but had faded into some odd shade between a bruise and dirty dish-water. It hung over her, the fabric tired and droopy. Her yoga pants were frayed around the ankles. No makeup. Her hair was so messy that it was hard to tell if she just hadn't bothered to brush it or if her hair was the type that couldn't be tamed without a team of professionals armed with a cabinet full of product. Then I remembered her photos and decided she couldn't be bothered.

Normally, I wouldn't feel anything in a situation like this. Hell, I didn't always feel anything even when a half-naked groupie rubbed her tits along my arm. But with Emily, my curiosity intensified. She was probably decently successful enough in her career. She was a bestselling author, so she must've made some money from her writing. So why did she look like she went dumpster diving for her wardrobe? I knew she had nicer clothes, the ones she'd worn to conferences and book signings. Part of me wanted to tease her a little, play with her hair—not because I wanted to touch her hair necessarily... Okay, who was I kidding—I wanted to touch her hair. But it wasn't just about fulfilling some lurid desire. I could run my fingers through the cool strands until it was neater, close to the way it had been in her social media photos.

Then there was something else, too, underneath the curiosity. The same spark that had gone through me at Sunny's Mart. It sizzled through my system, made the base of my spine tingle.

Was Emily was feeling it too? Looking at her narrowed green eyes, I decided...maybe not. The notion was vaguely disappointing but also stirred my sense of challenge. This must have been how mountain climbers felt at the base of Mount Everest.

"You're here early," she said. "It isn't natural."

I smiled. "I'm an early bird."

"I thought music people stayed up all night."

"I might've, if you'd let me practice my drums," I said. "But in general, I like to get up when the sun is up."

"Like I said, not natural." Her face contorted with distaste, and she shuddered in an exaggerated fashion then moved back into the house. "Come on in."

I followed her in, gently kicking the door shut after me. Several empty beer and water bottles stood around the living room along with a few empty bags of Animal Crackers and M&M's. Her laptop was on the coffee table. A purple blanket and a pillow lay on the sofa, a prone-body-shaped impression in the cushions.

"Did you sleep on the sofa?" I asked, stunned. Her bedroom was just upstairs.

"Yeah. I was working, then sort of fell asleep there." Wincing, she rolled her shoulders and neck.

Exasperation tugged at me. She should've known better. Sleeping on couches was overrated for creative types, unless you had the spine of a teenager. Working with tight muscles the next day was a bitch, and all your brain could think about was how much you wanted a massage. "You might need to stretch."

"Yeah. If I can find the time." She dug her fingers into the back of her neck.

That half-assed attempt wouldn't do anything. And I'd hate to see her suffer for the rest of the day, since I could tell she wasn't going to stretch or get a proper massage.

"Let me."

I put my stuff on the couch and went over to her. As I placed my hands on the muscles of her neck, a prickly sensation traveled up my arms, then settled in my lower gut, close to my dick. Jesus, it was just the back of a neck, I reminded myself, even though it didn't feel like "just" anything. I couldn't quite figure out what was so different about it. Or why I liked touching her so much. Or why my body was reacting like minor fireworks had just gone off inside me, spelling *YOU WANT HER*.

I shoved all that aside for the moment and brushed my thumb against the base of her skull, where the hairline started. But her bare skin was so warm and soft. I liked the way it felt against my fingertips entirely too much as I worked on the tight little knots.

She inhaled sharply, then let out a whimper. More prickling waves went through me, drying my mouth and constricting my lungs until it required some effort to drag in air.

"That feels really good," she said softly.

"Mm-hmm." Modulating my breathing so I didn't end up sounding like some panting pervert, I kept it up because it just felt so good to continue touching her. She smelled great this close —pretty and female, with a hint of something fresh and citrussy. I ran my fingers along the delicate neck bones as she bent her head forward to give me better access.

What would it be like to press my lips there? How sensitive was that spot? How would she react?

She shivered a little, then cleared her throat. "I'm not as young as I used to be," she said, her voice slightly off—either from the pleasure of the massage or something else. With a long sigh, she pulled away from my ministrations. "Life is unfair," she added, like she needed to fill the silence with words—any words.

I opened and closed my hands, missing the feel of her skin underneath them. She continued, "I could pull all-nighters three or four days in a row when I was in college and working corporate. I gave away my best years to soul-sucking suits, and they never gave a damn about anybody but themselves."

An interesting and sad observation from a woman who'd studied finance and economics. Didn't those disciplines teach how to rape and pillage...er...extract the value out of everything and toss away the reamed-out carcasses? Mir had complained about it in college while studying accounting. But unlike my sister, Emily had quit and moved on to something different. And for that, I gave her credit and respect. It wasn't always easy to shake up your life to pursue what you want.

Emily's gaze fell on the bag. "Did you bring your toiletries?"

"No. Something better." I shot her a generous smile. I was the kind of man who knew how to do give-and-take well. "Food, actually."

"Food?" She twisted around and faced me, scowling. "Our deal was for showers, not hanging out and eating. I have work to do."

She looked like an adorably annoyed kid. I wanted to reach over and pull those tightened eyebrows apart, but refrained. "It's a little thank-you for the book you lent me yesterday."

The hostility slipped as surprise spread over her pretty bare face like pancake batter poured into a skillet. "Are you serious?"

"Yup. I make a fantastic breakfast," I said, doing my best not to smirk smugly. Karma wasn't just a bitch, but it was also nice, when it had my face. "But let me shower first."

I couldn't tell if she'd actually consumed any real food since yesterday. Based on the beer bottles and cracker and candy wrappers on the floor around her laptop, the answer was no. She'd said she fell asleep on the couch. She might've never left the spot. And that wouldn't do. I wanted her well fed...and...

Why? You like her?

No, not *like*, I thought. But because I was a nice guy. And she could use the fuel. Besides, I wanted her to write more funny books, and she couldn't do that if she was hungry or malnourished...or collapsed in a heap, like me when I burned the candle at both ends a little too long.

I placed the bag on the kitchen counter and walked up the stairs, convinced that Emily was looking at my ass.

CHAPTER 12

Emily

I watched Killian walk up to the shower after announcing his intention to feed me breakfast. He had a *great* ass, but of course I thought that only as a firm believer of appreciating exceptional assets. The way his butt muscles flexed as he walked...it was like a kind of performance art.

Then I thought about his fingers on my neck and shoulders. They'd felt *good*. Of course, he'd probably practiced on thousands of other women.

The thought annoyed me for some bizarre reason. Why should I care how many women he'd massaged? It was none of my business.

I shook myself mentally, then went into the kitchen. There was no way Killian was actually planning on making me breakfast. Didn't I annoy him by telling him not to play his drums? And he'd been definitely less than happy that I grabbed the last tub of Bouncy Bare Monkeys.

Arsenic. He was planning on feeding me arsenic. Then he could have my shower to himself and drum until his head exploded.

I looked into the plastic bag he'd brought. A dozen brown organic eggs. A Ziploc bag with some kind of brittle-looking shredded cheese in orange, pale yellow and off-white. Probably cheddar, Gouda and Parmesan. I stuck my head closer and sniffed.

Smelled okay... But then, what did I know? I'd never smelled arsenic before. And it might not even be arsenic. There were thousands of poisons in the world.

I went to the sofa and picked up the phone I'd stuck under the pillow.

–Me: Help. How do you know if somebody's trying to poison you?

–Skye: What kind of research is this? I thought your book was rom-com?

–Lucy: Is this slow poisoning? Feeling sicker than normal? Hair falling out in clumps?

–Me: No. It's just that my next-door drummer brought stuff to make breakfast.

–Lucy: Is he going to eat with you?

I thought back on what I'd seen. He probably knew I couldn't eat a dozen eggs on my own.

–Me: I guess?

–Skye: Then obviously he's not going to poison you.

–Me: He could've taken an antidote beforehand.

–Lucy: You sure you don't want to write romantic suspense?

I rolled my eyes. Lucy was convinced I'd be really good at romantic suspense because I could be a bit paranoid. But that was why I wrote rom-com. I wanted to immerse my mind in a fun, awesome fictional world because the real one sucked cow poop.

–Me: I'm sure.

–Skye: Didn't you say he was hot?

–Me: I said he passed the minimum requirement.

–Lucy: Definitely hot. She didn't deny it.

I quirked my eyebrows in annoyance and affection. They could be so single-minded.

–Me: How is that relevant?

–Skye: Because if a hot guy uses your shower and makes you breakfast, you should just lie back—metaphorically, of course—and enjoy it.

Et tu, Skye? She was saying what that 911 dispatcher had told me when I called to report Killian for noise pollution. Neither Skye nor Lucy seemed to understand I didn't want to enjoy it.

Killian was *too* hot. And he knew it, which always meant trouble. Just ask my mom.

–Lucy: What she said. The world isn't full of nefarious people. I don't know why you think that when I'm the one writing about horrible serial killers and you write about nice guys who do nice, sexy things.

–Skye: If it makes you feel better, if you don't text us in the next three hours, we'll call the police and tell them who killed you.

I laughed because I could imagine Skye looking eager. Her main complaint about life was that it was too ordinary. Nothing exciting ever happened.

–Me: Fine. I'll hold you to that.

The floor above me creaked, which meant Killian was out of the shower.

–Me: OK, he's done showering. Gotta go.

Unlike yesterday, Killian had put back on the pair of dark shorts he'd worn to my house, like a decent, civilized human being. Somehow, part of me was vaguely displeased.

He looked better without the pants.

The thought just popped into my head suddenly, like all my best story ideas. Except this wasn't a story idea...and definitely wasn't the *best* idea. I wasn't feeling mildly annoyed because of his clothes. My gaze jumped up to his torso. I was annoyed because...

"Where's your shirt?" I demanded, doing my best to ignore the fact that my face and neck were heating up for no good reason. I'd seen topless men before, even if none of them had looked as sexy as Killian.

"What, you forgot already? My chest hair." His expression was positively shameless.

I crossed my arms. "You don't have enough hair on your chest to need to air-dry it."

"Didn't realize you were looking so closely."

I did my best to ensure my face didn't go red, but that turned out to be as feasible as a teenaged boy trying to control an erection, so I gave up. Of course I'd looked at his chest. It was a damned fine chest. Bet he knew that, too. He was much too smug for his own good.

"Did you use my shampoo and body wash?" I asked, getting a whiff of minty scent from him.

Yay, you guys are like a couple living together. That's so cute and sexy!

Shut up, hormones!

"Yup," he said. "They weren't floral. I like 'em."

Floral perfumes generally gave me a headache, so I didn't use them. I always ordered the same mint and lime toiletries from a specialty store in San Francisco after Lucy had recommended them to me. But I'd never noticed their scent could be so mesmerizing—clean like a gust on the night of the first snow of the year—or so starkly masculine. Maybe I should look for something different. I didn't want to smell like a man...

Or think about how awesome Killian smelled after using my shampoo and body wash every time I showered, which would then make me think about him standing naked under the water spray. *Holy shit, stop!* I told myself. My brain did not need to go there.

Killian chose that moment to step forward, dramatically reducing the distance between us. I inhaled sharply, my whole body frozen. He lowered his head near my neck, close enough that his breath tickled my bare skin.

My pulse went erratic. Goosebumps broke out, sending shivers down my back and ending between my thighs.

I stiffened, trying to ignore the sensations, which had to have been from shock. Shock could end between the legs, right?

"What are you doing?" I demanded, attempting an affronted tone. But it came out in a squeak. *Shit.* Talk about a cut to my dignity and self-respect.

Killian straightened, taking a step back. Was it my imagination, or did those blue eyes look a bit darker? "Just wanted to know if it smelled as unisex as I thought. But it's actually kind of feminine." He frowned a little, but it didn't feel genuine. No, he seemed like he was acting, except I didn't know what the hell it was all about. "Maybe I should bring my own body wash."

"You should," I said, the picture of ungraciousness. My pulse was still jumping. I didn't like it one bit, because if I hadn't known better, I might've thought it was from attraction. But how could I be attracted to a guy who annoyed me so much?

Acting like he hadn't heard me, Killian moved to the kitchen, pulled out the eggs and cheese and set them on the counter. "Hey, where's the frying pan?" he asked.

"Behind you," I said quickly, glad I wasn't within smelling range anymore. I needed some distance to get myself under control again. This was what happened when you hadn't dated in over a year. Actually, my last boyfriend had been a year and a half earlier, a nice but boring doctor who had a practice near Arlington National Cemetery. I probably just needed a quick orgasm or three. I made a mental note to take care of that later when I could find some free time.

Killian turned around and grabbed a Teflon pan. "Perfect. Oil?"

"In that cabinet. Anything else you need?"

"Salt and pepper?"

I pointed to the ceramic shakers, which were on the counter in plain sight. To be fair, they looked like Sydney Opera House.

"Those are cool." Killian picked up the salt shaker and looked at it more closely. "Where'd you get them?"

"They aren't for sale, as far as I know," I said, torn between pleasure and guilt.

"How come? Discontinued?"

"Uh...no."

"Then?" His gaze took on a stubborn gleam. The bastard wasn't going to give up until I answered him.

I sighed, feeling my face heat again. Maybe I should lie, but that'd be doubling the shame.

"Because I got them from Virgin Australia," I said super fast.

He stared at me like he couldn't believe it. "You *stole* these from an airline?"

My spine prickled with embarrassment. I wasn't exactly proud of what I'd done, but they had been just too damned cool to ignore. And the part of me that loved fun and funky things patted myself on the back every time I used them.

"Hey, I sent them a check for twenty bucks after I got home. And given how much I paid for the business-class ticket, they could've given them to me for free." But okay, I probably shouldn't have done that. It had been an impulse, especially when they popped up with every meal. There had been a lot of meals between Sydney and the States.

Still, Killian was looking at me like my hair color had suddenly changed right before his eyes. "I didn't know you traveled."

That was what he got out of the story? Well, at least we wouldn't have to talk about the shakers anymore.

"I also drive from time to time. I'm not a complete hermit," I said. Mom still wailed about my refusal to leave my house unless I had to, saying I'd never meet the perfect guy if I didn't get out more. She refused to accept that that was the absolute *last* thing I was worried about. Killian's reaction reminded me of the call I'd had with her the month before. She'd wanted to discuss how her friend's daughter was getting married, like I should do something about the fact that I wasn't even dating, much less getting engaged. She didn't understand I'd moved to Kingstree to avoid the meat-market scene. "I travel for conferences and book signings."

"Huh." He turned his attention back to the salt and pepper shakers. "Don't feel bad. I might've done the same. These are really cool."

That made me feel better...until I realized I was giving his opinion of me way too much weight. It was irksome. I never cared much about what strangers thought of me. The only thing that mattered was how my readers felt about my books. And my friendship with Lucy and Skye.

But apparently, Killian was finished admiring—or judging—my salt and pepper shakers. While I stood there with my arms crossed, watching him—to make sure he didn't do anything funny to the food—he cracked eggs into a huge bowl I'd left in the dish rack days ago and forgotten to put away, then whisked them with a fork. He turned on the stove and poured some oil into the pan. He looked at home in my kitchen.

I couldn't decide if I liked that or not. I also couldn't decide if

I should let him continue to parade around topless. The morning sun shone over his body, making him glow like an angel...except I knew he was no angel. Maybe one of the fallen variety at best. And his forearm tats shifted as he moved. The entire effect wasn't exactly giving me the calmness I wanted to achieve.

"You should put on a shirt," I said.

"Why?"

"That oil might spatter and burn you." And what a shame would that be on such a fine torso. Not that I'd ever say it out loud.

"Still drying my chest hair, remember? Oil and water don't mix. It can't hurt me."

Must be some type of man logic, because it made zero sense. Probably the same sort of thinking that made men do stupid stuff. "Don't sue me if you get hurt."

"I won't. Now go away and let me work my magic. I'm a pretty decent cook."

That remained to be seen, although if it tasted half as good as it smelled, it'd be all right. I sat at the island and pretended to fiddle with my phone, although I watched him surreptitiously. I told myself it was for self-preservation, because my presence might discourage him from sprinkling arsenic all over my eggs. The fact that I noticed how broad his shoulders were...how hot it was to see his back muscles flex... Well, all that was just going to be there, no matter what. Very much like the irritating side effects you had to put up with while taking a life-preserving drug.

As he started to place omelets on plates, I took out a couple of icy lemon-flavored sweet teas from the fridge, because first, I needed one, and second, he probably wouldn't complain, since it was that or water. Even I thought it was too early for beer, even if it was Hop Hop Hooray. When he brought the omelets and forks to the dining table, I quietly switched our plates.

"What's that about?" he asked, sitting down.

"Yours looked bigger," I lied, not wanting to tell him about my suspicions. I'd been watching him, but there was that distracting bare torso. I might've missed something.

"I made them the same size."

"Why?" Didn't guys usually want to have more food?

"Because you don't seem like the type who'll stop to eat lunch or dinner."

"You don't know that."

He gave me a look. "I've seen your fridge. And your cart at Sunny's."

I shrugged. "Eating is overrated."

"It's essential for survival, but go ahead and humor me. Do the overrated activity." He gestured with his fork.

Ha! Sarcastic bastard. I bit into the omelet. *Holy cow*. It was good—fluffy and gooey, with melted cheese in the center. The man knew how to cook. And with the first bite in my mouth, I suddenly realized I was starving.

"How'd that taste? Overrated?" he asked after I'd swallowed.

"Good," I said. The man already knew it. There was no point in lying.

"So. Mind if I borrow the rest of your books?"

I regarded him, wondering what he was *really* getting at. "Why?"

"I liked the one I read."

I looked at him, stunned. Since he'd brought the one from yesterday back so fast, I assumed he hadn't been able to read more than a few pages. "You did?"

"Yeah," he said, shoveling down food.

"What did you like about it?" Men sometimes said that they liked my books after they'd found out what I did for living in order to hook up. Killian could avail himself of my shower, but he wasn't availing himself of my vagina.

"The humor, mainly. And the emphasis on community and people just being decent and good to each other. Oh, and the glitter bomb Erika sent her boss at the end." Killian grinned. "That was hilarious."

"So you really did read it," I said, surprised and pleased. Those were the reasons I loved that book, too. And I appreciated that here was the first man I'd met who not only read one of my books but understood what I wanted to convey in my writing world: good people finishing first and living happily ever after. Maybe he wasn't so bad after all.

"Of course. I wouldn't lie about it, not when I'd get found out in a second." He washed down his latest bite with the tea. "Could've used more sex, though."

I almost choked on my eggs. *Should've known he'd go there.*

"But the three sex scenes it did have were hot as hell. Erika came 'over five times'"—he was making air quotes with his fingers—"in the first one. How many times did she *really* come, though? It wasn't clear from the text."

I bit my lip to contain a laugh. Of course he remembered *that* detail and wanted to know more. It was such a guy thing!

"If the book didn't say, it means you don't need to know." I tried to say it with a touch of prim asperity but the truth was that I didn't recall every detail of the story. It'd been months since I'd finished it, and right now, my mind was focused on Molly and Ryan's romance.

He grunted. "Too bad. Your readers would definitely want to know that level of detail. So tell me, do you write the kind of sex you want to have?"

Here we go. I inhaled deeply so as not to lose patience. For some reason, every time people learned I wrote sex scenes, they considered it completely acceptable to ask personal, sex-related questions. Even my now-former dentist had asked me how much "research" I did while getting his tools ready and having me inhale laughing gas.

At least Killian had cooked me an excellent breakfast. And he wasn't being overtly condescending—or asking with an unhealthy leer, like the dentist. "Are you going to ask me if I research them in person, too?"

"Do you?" His blue eyes sparked, a smile curving his lips. The dimple popped on his cheek, and he looked more tempting than a ripe strawberry dipped in chocolate. "If so"—he raised a hand—"I volunteer as tribute!"

I burst out laughing at his homage to *The Hunger Games*. His questions were predictable, but he just seemed curious. And I liked the way he'd made a joke with my question.

"Tribute? As in the Roman sense? Like a slave?"

"Hey, whatever you're into. I'm an equal-opportunity kind of guy." The smile went up about two thousand kilowatts.

I laughed again, the exchange lightening my mood. I took a

swig of tea and looked at him speculatively. The sex scenes in my books weren't necessarily my fantasy. The kind of sex my characters had largely depended on their personalities and the couple's dynamics. But that didn't mean it wouldn't be fun to research some of them in person for the first time in my life, especially if the partner was as fine as Killian.

On the other hand, he was very aware he was just oozing sex appeal, and men like that were bad bets for relationships. Exhibit one: my father. He charmed the panties off every pretty twenty-something he ran into. It was gross and humiliating.

But...why was I thinking about relationships in conjunction with Killian? I wasn't in the market for a boyfriend, long-term or otherwise. If I needed to scratch an itch, a collection of nice sex toys that had never let me down was waiting in a drawer next to my bed.

"I don't do research," I said finally. "And you can borrow my books if you'll keep cooking me breakfast." If I wasn't going to bother with lunch and dinner—he was right about that point—so I should have a decent breakfast every day.

The dimple appeared again. "That's a deal. Oh, and my sister is a huge fan and wants to buy all your books. Autographed. Can I buy them from you directly?"

I nodded, happy he wanted to talk about more harmless things. I told myself the heavy, languid feeling settling in my gut was something other than longing.

CHAPTER 13

Emily

When breakfast was over, Killian put the plates in the dishwasher. He was surprisingly capable in the kitchen when it came to cleanup, too. It was a bit of a shock, since he'd acted like he was somebody famous in Sunny's Mart when we'd first met. Maybe he wasn't *that* famous, because...did really famous people even know how to open dishwashers? Didn't they have maids and people who took care of everything like that for them?

While he was cleaning up, I signed my backlist for him. He left with the autographed books and a second copy of *Working for the Filthy Billionaire*—the one he wanted to read today.

Once I was alone, I threw myself into work. After about an hour, I got a text.

–Skye: So, are you dead?

I laughed and texted back, *No*.

–Lucy: I knew it.

Both of my friends seemed entirely too pleased with themselves. So I decided I should tease them.

–Me: How can you be sure it's not the killer responding to your text?

–Skye: Because you only said no.

–Lucy: Exactly. The killer would've added something like

how the guy was nice or hot or the food was amazing, etc. to reassure us. That's usually how bad guys get caught. They try too hard to cover up the crime.

They knew me too well.

–Skye: Was the food good?

–Me: Yes.

Then—since I knew they would continue to question me until all their curiosity was satisfied—I sent another text.

–Me: I love you girls, but I really have to go back to writing. I gotta get at least four more chapters done today.

–Lucy: Got it! You go, girl!

–Skye: You can do it!

Smiling, I went back to my manuscript. As long as I could maintain my production quota for each day, I'd hit the deadline. Molly and Ryan were fantastic characters, and I knew they would resonate with my readers.

They had to.

Ryan wooed Molly by making her breakfast and giving her a massage. I paused as I ended the chapter, realizing that Killian had been exceptionally sweet, and my subconscious probably recognized that even if I hadn't wanted to admit it.

Wonder what he would do next if he were in Ryan's shoes...

Stop thinking about Killian. The book is about Ryan and Molly!

Shit. I gently slapped myself to pull out of the ridiculous daydream. Ryan wasn't anything like my neighbor, and I shouldn't confuse the two.

Must. Focus. On. My. Couple!

When I was finally done, I closed the laptop and placed it on the coffee table. I tried to get up, then plopped back on the sofa with a soft groan. *Ow...* My damned back. My vertebrae seemed to be permanently set in the slightly rounded position I'd been in for hours, and they *did not* want to move.

I checked the time. Five thirty. Since I'd finished the day's word count, I needed to give myself a break and recharge. In case tomorrow didn't go as well as today and required pulling an all-nighter.

I slowly rose to my feet, bones creaking and popping. *Damn. I should book a celebratory massage session for after I send the manuscript off to my editor.* Since I was starving, I opened the fridge, then paused.

Nothing to eat. And after the delicious, real food Killian had made in the morning, I didn't want to settle for crackers again.

For a split second, I didn't feel like eating alone. My head swiveled toward Killian's house, but I caught myself before I did something stupid. Like going over and asking him to eat with me. We'd only agreed on breakfast. Dinner was too much. Too much like a real couple or something. Although he was easily the most eligible bachelor in town, I wasn't in Kingstree to date.

Okay, I was being ridiculous. I was hungry and my brain didn't function well on low blood sugar. Once I had some decent food in my belly, I wouldn't be thinking about Killian that way—I was certain of it.

Okay, put on your big-girl panties and adult, I decided. Eat more than the junk I used to live on in college and my first job. Just look at Killian. There was a reason he looked so hot and healthy every time he came by. The man fed himself actual food.

Hmm... Wonder what he was having for dinner. Probably he was planning on making himself something delicious. Did he cook dinner topless, too? Flex those forearms while he was shifting pots and pans? Maybe even admire his own tats?

I would if I had arms like his.

My stomach growled. The sound probably meant, *Less fantasizing, more food!*

I grabbed my keys and went outside. The air was getting warmer, typical of this time of year, when spring was transitioning to summer. The breeze was refreshing, carrying the scents of grass and new leaves on the trees, and I inhaled it deeply. I didn't know air could smell like this. I needed to open windows in my home and let some of it in.

Deliberately not looking toward Killian's house, I drove to Sunny's Mart. Grabbed a big cart and pushed it into the store like a responsible adult who intended to eat healthily.

But the piles of vegetables just weren't enticing. Washing, peeling and prepping everything... Simply imagining the amount of work made me feel exhausted. I grabbed some strawberries and oranges. They required the least amount of effort. Since I was being so good, I went to the beer section, spotted two cases of Hop Hop Hooray raspberry beer lying in the aisle that nobody from Sunny's Mart had put on the shelves yet and seized them. The raspberries used in the beer must count. Nobody ever said you had to chew your fruit.

I went to the frozen food section to get some TV dinners. A few looked decent. Then I spotted the ultimate prize: a guy in a purple Sunny's Mart apron stocking ice cream. And not just any ice cream, but Bouncy Bare Monkeys.

Jackpot! This must be how Neolithic hunter-gatherers had felt when they discovered a giant mammoth stuck in a crevasse.

He shut the clear freezer door and moved off. Excitement sparking through me, I hurried over to get the ice cream. But a loud scream rang through the otherwise quiet supermarket.

Molly—not my Molly, but Kingstree's Molly—was coming around the corner, while her son bellowed, "I said I want cookies, not stupid ice cream!" He was disheveled and his eyes were wild, like a cat being pushed into a bathtub full of water.

What kid doesn't want ice cream? Maybe he was lactose intolerant. My dad was, and he couldn't have any ice cream, which was karmic justice.

Instead of shushing her son, Molly was texting, her thumbs moving busily. He threw himself on the floor and started kicking like a toddler, even though he had to be at least eight.

"We're getting ice cream," she said finally, not even looking up, which only seemed to make her kid's face redder. Now he looked like an overripe tomato. Tears and snot covered his cheeks, nose and chin.

I shot her my meanest look. *Lady, rein in your out-of-control kid!*

She looked up from her phone as though she'd sensed my evil laser glare. "What are you looking at?" she demanded, moving toward me.

"I'm looking at what I'm being forced to listen to," I said, then snapped up every tub of Bouncy Bare Monkey. Partly to spite her and partly because who knew when the store would get more?

All six tubs sat in my cart. I'd give one or two to Killian

tomorrow morning. That seemed fair, since he was paying for the eggs and cheese for my portion of the breakfast.

"Wait, are those Bouncy Bare Monkeys?" Molly said, coming rapidly toward me in her heels. She hadn't looked at her kid, not even once.

He was still throwing a fit, although he'd somehow rolled around in the aisle to follow her. It looked like he had a lot of experience sticking close to his mom and pitching a fit at the same time.

"Give me that!" she said, reaching into my cart with both hands, each on one tub. "George, stop hollering and come help me!"

Rude, much? "Don't even think about it." I shoved my cart away, while her son completely ignored her.

Red mottled her face. "Don't be a selfish bitch!"

"Selfish? At least I'm not imposing my kid on everyone in the store. Buy your son the damn cookies."

She nodded, somehow making the movement sarcastic. "Oh, I see. A lot of experience with kids?"

"None at all. But I'm certainly not going to have one and let him roll all over a grocery store while screaming."

She tried to stick her hands into my cart again, and I quickly turned it so she couldn't grab the ice cream.

"I'm buying these for a neighbor," I said. Only a couple were for Killian, but she didn't need to know such an inconsequential detail. "Now cut it out or I'm calling the manager."

Before she could stop me or try to steal my ice cream again, I went over to the checkout. A cashier who I'd seen a couple of times sighed and shook his head at the antics of Molly's kid.

"Does he do that often?" I asked, despite my firm resolution not to gossip with the townsfolk.

"Yeah. We have special cookies for seriously lactose-intolerant people, so that's what he gets when he gets an A on a test. But every time he doesn't get an A, she buys ice cream, knowing he can't have any." He frowned.

"That is *shameful*," I said, hating Molly even more. What she was doing to her kid reminded me of my dad. He'd used his affection as a weapon when I was growing up. When I did well in school or made choices that he wanted me to make, he'd praise me and shower me with attention and love. Otherwise, he'd be a complete bastard. I'd wasted so much of my life trying to please that son of a bitch.

Shaking off the memory, I went home and made myself an extra-healthy TV dinner. Extra-healthy because I added a small salad with extra ranch dressing to it. Afterward, to reward my adulting effort, I had two scoops of Bouncy Bare Monkeys. Then I told myself I was happy I'd seen the light and was living a life of my choice, not anybody else's.

CHAPTER 14

Killian

–Jenny: New deliveries of Bouncy Bare Monkeys and Hop Hop Hooray just got here. Just letting you know.

Shit. The text had hit my non-family-and-friends phone yesterday at five. I'd been engrossed in Emily's book and missed it.

I checked the time. A quarter to seven, and the sun was barely coming up. There should be still some left. It hadn't been twenty-four hours.

I rushed over to Sunny's and into the store to the ice cream freezer. And shoved my fingers into my hair in dismay and outrage.

What the hell? Not a *single tub* of Bouncy Bare Monkeys. I went over to the beer aisle. No Hop Hop Hooray, either.

Argh!

I spotted Sunny and went over. "Hey, Killian. Find everything you need?" she asked with a friendly smile.

"That's the problem. I thought you had some Bouncing Cows in, but..." Then a thought struck me. "Maybe in the back?"

She shook her head. "Sorry. Benny put out everything before he left last night."

"You gotta be shi—uh, kidding me." Sunny was old enough to be my mother, and she'd taken soap to my mouth once when she heard me cuss as a kid. I hadn't said a bad word in front of her since.

Sunny gave me a sharp look, then shook her head with a small laugh. "You're too old for that these days. And before you ask, no, I don't know when we'll get more."

My shoulders slumped. Damn it. If I told my band mates I was this hung up on ice cream, they'd give me a huge ration of shit. But it really was the best. If Bouncing Cows could mass-produce its Bouncy Bare Monkeys, nobody would be doing drugs. It was that amazing.

Since I was there anyway, I did a quick grocery run, buying some eggs, cheese, spring veggies and meat. I got extra because Emily seemed to enjoy my eggs, and the woman needed some protein in her diet. Then, on sheer impulse, I also paid for a bottle of tequila and a bag of limes. Why not?

I was still morose when I went over to Emily's for a shower, breakfast and the next book to read. Maybe I should've hired a teenager to watch the freezer for Bouncy Bare Monkeys...

I was so preoccupied that I almost didn't see the pink sticky note on her door:

Killian,

Don't knock. Just come in quietly without disturbing me. I'm too inspired.

–E

Good for her. That meant more stories for me to read, since, at the rate I was going, I'd be done with her whole backlist before the year was over. But at the same time, a pang of despair lanced my heart, because my own creative well was drier than Mir's so-called home-baked cookies.

If I could just drum again... But then, maybe not. I'd held the drumsticks, run my hands over their smooth length...but felt nothing. No excitement. No flash of insight. It was like I'd lost something inside. Whatever fire had been burning had gotten doused somehow.

And I had no clue how to get it going again.

Emily had been right to call my drumming noise. Because that was the only thing uninspired music could be.

Feeling doubly morose, I opened the door quietly and walked into her home. The area around the coffee table had grown even messier. More empty bottles. More wrappers. A few wadded-up sheets of paper.

She didn't glance up, her eyes on the monitor. Light reflected off her glasses, and she looked serious as she typed away, key clicks the only sound inside the room. She tucked a wayward tendril behind an ear with an impatient gesture, then immediately placed the hand back on the keyboard.

I stood for a moment, taking her in. Although she wasn't dressed any better—and her hair was a freakin' *mess*—she was beautiful in her creative process. She seemed to shine, as though something was lit within her—likely the fire I didn't have anymore. I wondered if I'd be able to rekindle the flame if I watched her long enough.

Doubtful, I decided. It wasn't that easy.

Since she didn't want to be bothered—and I was loath to pull her out of her work anyway—I left the bag of food in the kitchen and went upstairs for a quick shower. When I came down topless—since I refused to admit I'd made up the need to air-dry my chest hair to annoy and fluster her on the first day—she was still hunched in the same position, her fingers moving methodically.

"No, you can't do that," she said suddenly.

Huh? What did I do?

"What are you talking about? How could you think I did that?" she said. "You *knew*..."

I crossed my arms and watched, finally understanding. Maybe her hero didn't perform well enough. The heroine didn't lose count of the number of orgasms.

"Oh, shut up, Molly. You knew this was coming."

I leaned my shoulder against the wall and watched Emily. She was cute when she got emotional over her characters and started talking like they were real people.

"Yeah, yeah, bite me. Write your own book, Ryan." Suddenly, she jumped to her feet. "Ah-ha! I knew it!" Fist pumping in the air, she jumped around in a circle like she'd just won history's biggest jackpot.

My lips twitched with amusement. She must've had a breakthrough.

She stopped abruptly and blinked at me. "*You*." The word vibrated with shock and embarrassment.

"Yep." I smiled, my amusement intensifying at the flush coloring her pretty face. "Me."

"How long have you been there?"

I shrugged. "I don't know. Five minutes?"

Her cheeks turned pinker. "You should've *said* something."

"Why? It was great watching you. Besides, you told me to be quiet."

"I did not."

"The note outside...?"

"I meant for you not to interrupt my flow. I didn't mean to spy on me."

"*Spy* on you?" I laughed. "To what end? You were on your computer the whole time."

"I know." Her lips pursed. "Did you, um, notice anything else?"

"You mean like you muttering to yourself?"

She rolled her eyes, but from the way she fidgeted, she was slightly embarrassed. "Don't act like it's weird. It helps me think."

"You think with your mouth?" I said, highly entertained. Being with her took my mind off the failed ice cream shopping and the fact that I couldn't come up with anything for the band's next album. She made me focus on the present.

"I think with my brain *and* mouth. You should try it. Might work better than doing it with your big head"—she pointed at my skull—"and the small one down there." She gestured at my crotch. Then she frowned a little, like she was slightly annoyed.

Probably because she'd realized how wrong she was. I cocked an eyebrow. "I'll have you know it's quite large."

Her gaze stayed on my eyes. "Not as large as your brain."

I pretended to consider, setting my features into an expression I'd seen on a neurologist in London who was studying my MRI. Emily kept staring at me like I was being nonsensical. Maybe she shouldn't have said what she said about my dick. "Large enough, and it has never failed to rise to the occasion. Unlike my brain, which faltered a few times in trig class."

That got a laugh. I smiled too. As I took her in, in her work environment with her laptop, I grew a little wistful about not being able to drum away. But since she'd gotten a ton of writing done, maybe she'd take mercy on me now. "But you know, I obviously don't want to overwork my dick. So I usually think with my brain, and drumming really helps."

She narrowed her eyes. "Don't even think about backing out on our deal. I can't write if you're going to be a noise polluter again." She put her hands on her hips and leaned forward, a dark scowl forming on her face. "Did the plumber guy call and tell you he could come replace your water heater tomorrow or something?"

Ha. I wish. Not having hot water was a pain in the ass, even if showering wasn't an issue.

She continued without giving me a chance to answer. "You said you wouldn't drum for four weeks."

"I remember. So I'll take the 'thinking with my mouth' method under advisement." I was mildly disappointed that she didn't want to give me a break. On the other hand, it had been a long shot. Women, in my experience, were grabby creatures who liked to hang on to things, even if they didn't need them anymore.

Emily gave me a long look and then finally said, "Okay," like she was torn between fighting and settling into peace and satisfaction. Probably too much adrenaline. The woman seemed to be full of it.

But I understood. She was in the middle of creating something. She'd slept on the couch and gotten up early because her muse wouldn't leave her alone. Restless energy and ideas must be swirling in her head like a tornado. You had to be prepared to grab them and get them down on paper, or they vanished as quickly as they'd come.

I envied her for it.

She glanced at her monitor, then looked up suddenly. "Hey, can you help me with something?"

The bright sparks in her eyes lightened her entire demeanor, and I stared at her, mesmerized. She looked like a mischievous pixie.

"With what?" Pixie or not, I was a little wary. She looked entirely too pleased with herself, and that couldn't be good, could it?

"I'm trying to see if a particular scenario is possible."

"Sure. Shoot." I was willing to give her an opinion. Ideally, she'd have a question about sexual positions.

"Awesome." She smiled happily. "So Molly is sitting here, perched like so." Emily moved to the back of the couch and leaned her hip on the top, then squirmed around a bit until she seemed satisfied.

I knew Molly was Emily's book character, but hearing it was still a little jarring. My brain kept bringing up Molly Patterson. And she'd never "perch" on anything. The woman preferred to sit, her butt parked firmly on a flat surface.

"And then she tips over backward. And Ryan has to catch her. Just so you know how it's set up, he's about three steps away from her."

Must. Not. Think about Ryan Johnson. He'd throw his geriatric back out attempting this maneuver.

"Why?" I asked. "You're going to fall on the sofa." Which looked incredibly soft and more than capable of keeping her uninjured. Actually, it might be more comfortable and safer for her to fall on it than to rely on some guy catching her.

Emily wagged her index finger. "Because Molly's not going to fall on the sofa in the book! She's perched on a wall, trying to escape, and loses her balance when a dog barks and startles her. I want to see if it's realistic for me to end up on top of you if you catch me and roll over or whatever to keep me safe and all that, like the hero you're supposed to be, you know?"

Ohh... Her on top of me. If I were a romance hero, how would I have this go?

Would she be straddling me? Most likely. Better balance that way. On my belly...? No, that wouldn't be comfortable. She should straddle me lower. Nestle against my dick. After all, where else should she be flush against except my cock?

Yeah, that was perfect. And sexy as hell. I looked at her curves. Mmm, definitely hot. My blood started flowing faster. I shifted to hide my dick's eager reaction to my imagination.

"If Ryan's as smooth as me? Sure, it could happen," I said, as though stuff like that happened to me all the time. "Hell, I'd *make* it happen."

She tapped her chin with her index finger thoughtfully. "But I write contemporary romance. So it can't have Hollywood-esque special effects action."

"There won't be any special effects involved." A real man didn't need Hollywood to have a hot woman straddle him properly.

Her lips tightened. "Let's block out the scene. I want to make sure. Skye said it wasn't physically possible, but I think she's wrong."

"Who's Skye?"

"My writing friend. I asked her to act it out with her husband because her house has a fence she could use to set the scene, but he's apparently out of town on business. She said it was more likely that Ryan falls on Molly while trying to catch her, but that won't work because it isn't romantic. Anyway, we bet two shots of tequila at a book signing we're going to in San Francisco, so come on." She beckoned me closer. "I have to prove her wrong."

The gleam in her eyes reminded me of a stubborn goat. But far be it from me to leave a woman in distress.

"Anyway, I'm going to tip over," she said, rubbing her hands eagerly.

"Well, the couch is too low to be a wall," I pointed out.

She straightened. "You think?" She stepped away from it and looked around. "You're right. Now what? Is there an appropriate fence around here?"

I thought for a moment. "Got a ladder?" I asked.

"A small one. Why?"

"We can set that up and you can get to the right height and then pretend to fall."

"Ooh, that's smart." She grinned. "We can even do this in the living room."

She ran to a closet between the living room and the foyer and pulled out a ladder. It was so small that I wasn't even sure why she'd bought it. It might be useful if she wanted to clean the ceiling fans in the living room, but given the general condition of the place, I doubted dusting them was high on her priority list.

While she set up the ladder and climbed a few steps, I placed cushions from the couch on the area where she was supposed to fall.

She ended up with her butt about six feet off the ground, which was eye level for me and kinda nice. "Is that about the right height?" I said.

"I think so. How high can a wall be?" She looked down at the cushions on the floor, then frowned a little. "I thought you said you could catch me."

"Of course I can. But these are just in case. Backup. For me, really." I added the last bit so she didn't get too anxious.

Her lips pulled together. "I'm not going to break your back."

"It's my hands I'm worried about." But I was actually concerned about her. There was a small chance that things might not work out the way we envisioned. I'd rather not risk her getting hurt.

"You should've insured your hands," she said. "You can insure anything, you know."

"I'll make sure to call my agent and add my hands to the policy," I said. "Ready?" I got into position and waited for her to signal.

"Yeah."

I pictured how this would go and tensed up, ready to spring into action.

"You can't half-ass it to make Skye win."

"I don't even know Skye. But you owe me a beer if I help you win. If you lose, I'll settle for a kiss." I gave her a playful grin so she could tell herself I wasn't super serious about the kiss. I didn't want to force it out of her...but I wanted her thinking about it.

Her tongue flicked over her lip, which heated my blood further. I really hoped she was out of beer.

"Fine," she rasped, then cleared her throat. "Okay, here goes."

The moment slowed as adrenaline spread through me. She started to tip over. I moved, extending my arms to catch her. Our bodies slammed into each other, which I hadn't counted on, and my breath whooshed out. I ended up landing on the cushions on my back, then almost immediately, she fell on me, straddling my stomach, but too far above to cradle my dick. Her hands flexed on my shoulders, and all the blood in my body started to rush south. Her hair fell forward, tickling my cheeks and chin. It felt as soft as feathers and smelled like mint and lime. Her glasses sat crooked on her face. Her green eyes were wide and her pink lips were parted as she looked down at me.

I stared up at her as electrifying excitement sparked through me. Was it my imagination, or did her skin seem soft and glowing? Actually, her entire being seemed to glow, like an angel. My pulse went into overdrive as something unfamiliar lanced through me. And my lower body felt uncomfortably tight.

What the hell was with this reaction? We hadn't even kissed.

At least she wouldn't notice anything, since she had no reason to wriggle downward. I stayed still, waiting for her to get off. Then had an immediate fantasy triggered by her "getting off"...

She got up, pushing against my chest. Normally I'd consider it an obvious ploy to cop a feel, but Emily wasn't looking at me that way. She just looked mildly confused as she nibbled on her lower lip. I wanted to put my finger on it to make her stop.

You just want an excuse to put a finger on her lip...maybe even accidentally *push inside her mouth—*

Okay, time to rein myself in before I did something really stupid. Like slide her body down then let her rock against me. I wasn't a horny teenager, and I had more finesse than that.

"It worked," I said, needing something to cover up the weirdly loud heartbeat in my ears.

"Yup. It did."

She climbed off, careful not to knee me in the process.

"Thanks," she said, then cleared her throat and slapped her cheeks a bit. They were red, but I couldn't tell if it was from the slapping or something else. "I need to wrap up this scene before I forget...um...things. So the kitchen's all yours."

Without looking at me, she tossed all the cushions back on the couch and dove straight for her laptop. Which worked for me, since I didn't want her to see that I was I-beam rigid over that little PG-rated bit of playacting. I was most certainly not disappointed that she didn't want to lean down and brush her lips across mine. Or wriggle her body lower...

She sat in front of her computer and started typing away, keys clicking furiously, so I put away the ladder and went to the kitchen with a deliberately measured step. I took my time, so my body could calm the hell down, and my heart could find its equilibrium again. I hadn't been with a woman in a while. My dick just wanted to spurt because it was primitive like that.

But I hadn't reacted like this to women in skimpy bikinis in Bora Bora. Actually, I hadn't reacted like this to any woman, period, including Caitlyn.

On the other hand, I'd never been around anybody like Emily. It must be the novelty. She was interesting and unique. And pretty. And smart. Contradictory at times, and unpredictable, too.

That was it. Nothing special.

Feeling much better after getting my thoughts in order, I made breakfast, then placed two plates on the table and set out utensils and syrup. "All ready," I called out.

She sat up and snapped her fingers. "Missed it," she muttered as she joined me.

"Missed what?" I asked. I parked my butt in my seat.

"You cooking..." She shook her head. "Never mind. I can't say it."

"Why not?"

"Because you'd have to rip a bigger neck hole in your shirt."

I laughed, pleased she was thinking about me in that way. "I don't mind tearing up a shirt. Go ahead, compliment me."

"Absolutely not." She looked over the food, then let out an appreciative sigh. Fluffy pancakes, scrambled eggs and bacon. It never failed.

"Fine. I'm going to use my imagination, then. 'Oh, Killian, you are so big and stupendous!'" I said, breathing hard and fanning myself dramatically. "'I take back what I said earlier. You can do anything with your dick.'"

"There's a difference between imagination and delusion," she said with a sniff. But her eyes were twinkling.

I winked. "It's not a delusion if it's true."

"Ha ha." She took a bite. "This is really good. Since you went above and beyond, you can take two tubs of Bouncy Bare Monkeys with you when you leave."

My fork hit the table with a clatter. "You're giving me ice cream?"

"Yeah. You're cooking for me, buying the ingredients and all... so I figured I should give something back."

"I think I'm touched. Wow. Thanks. Not even my own sister would give me a tub of that."

"Well, I got six, so..." She shrugged.

"*Six*? Did you buy every last tub again?"

"What do you mean *again*?"

"You bought it all last time."

"They had *one* last time. Buying any was buying it all. Anyway, I happened to see them when I went shopping yesterday. But since there's more than one, I decided to be generous." Then she added meaningfully, "With you."

"Generous, my ass!" I said, even though technically she was being much nicer than my own sister. But I was a little put out that I'd gone to Sunny's for nothing. "You're giving me two and keeping four. True generosity would be splitting it fifty-fifty."

"Or you could simply not take any," she said. "There's no 'us' in 'ice cream.' Why? Because it isn't meant to be shared."

"That's the most ridiculous thing I've ever heard."

"If you learn how to spell 'ice cream,' you'll understand what I mean."

"There's no 'us' in 'breakfast,' either."

"Which is why I'm sharing my ice cream with you. It's an even trade."

This must be some weird female logic. Like how women never order fries because they're on a diet or some bullshit, but always filch one—or half the carton—from their men, as though theft makes them calorie-free. "You're illogical and unreasonable."

"The possibility exists. But I'm also the person with the hot water and the ice cream." She smirked smugly.

"Which you negotiated for."

"I just didn't want any noise pollution. It was a public service to the town."

"You really have no clue who I am, do you?" It was kind of stunning. It'd been years since I met somebody who didn't know who I was. Hell, I'd started to wear sunglasses and a pulled-down cap when I was out in public. In a lot of cases I'd been forced to hire security to keep the weirdos away. Emily had to have been living under a rock to be this oblivious, although...somebody in town *had* to have told her about me. Maybe a cashier at Sunny's. Or maybe one of the local radio stations had done a piece on me, like they often did.

She paused and studied me, her gaze traveling up and down. "Are you a model?" she asked finally. "Maybe do photoshoots for romance novels? If so, I'll buy a few photos for my next book."

My jaw slackened. "Where did you get *that*?"

She shrugged. "Just a guess. You keep talking like you're somebody I should recognize...and you have a pretty face. But I haven't seen you on any covers, in case you're wondering."

"Nope. Totally off."

"Then what are you? Obviously you think you're some hot shot. The mayor's nephew, maybe? Not the good one who went to Harvard, but, you know, the tat-having, cigarette-smoking troublemaker who likes to visit from time to time from Maryland? I heard he rides a Harley." She gazed at me thoughtfully. "I can picture you straddling one on the road."

"Uh, do you know what Mayor Cruise looks like?"

"Short, with dark hair? A pug nose?"

"Yeah. What does that say about your guess?"

She shrugged. "You could've been adopted."

I shook my head. This was even worse than her thinking I might be a romance cover model. "Where the hell do you get all these ideas?"

"I'm a creative person." She didn't actually say *duh* at the end, but it was clearly implied.

"Here." I pulled out my phone and tapped the screen a few

times. The band's number one hit from last year flowed from the speakers. It was one of our best, and I was proud of it. It connected deeply with our fans, which was the main purpose of the music the band created.

Now Emily would finally put things together. Damn it, I knew her work, and I wanted her to know mine too. And like it. For some reason, it was important she enjoy my music, just like I enjoyed her writing.

"Is that you pounding the drums in the opening?" she asked hesitantly after a moment.

"No, that's Dev. I'm the lead vocalist."

"Oh."

Oh? That was it? Just a mildly surprised *oh*? She hadn't heard this song anywhere? But I wasn't seeing any sign of recognition in her eyes, and I didn't think she was messing with me. I couldn't tell if she liked the song, either, although she was nodding slightly to the beat. My mouth felt parched all of sudden. This was worse than my first audition.

"So why were you playing the drums?" she asked.

"Well, I also play drums."

"So why is this Dev guy playing them in the song?" she asked, obviously obsessed with the damned drums.

"Because he's better than me," I said, starting to get annoyed that this was what she was focusing on while listening to this song. She might as well have stabbed my ego with a rusty knife.

"Ah. Division of labor. You should keep that up. Let him do that, while you focus on singing. Even if all the windows are open in your house and mine, I won't be able to hear you sing, unless you got yourself a mic." She gave me a look. "Don't get a mic."

Nobody had ever told me they didn't want to hear me sing live. The *no "us" in "ice cream"* section of her brain must still be in charge. "So...that's it? That's all you have to say?"

She pulled her lips in for a second, then cleared her throat. Her eyes were clear and bright. "What were you expecting?"

"That's our biggest hit from last year."

She looked confused. "Okay..."

"You don't recognize it?"

"Should I?"

Was she kidding? Disbelief flashed through me. This must be revenge for when I told her I'd never heard of her writerly alter ego. "Well...yeah. I mean, it was everywhere."

She shrugged. "Sorry if you're disappointed, but I don't listen to music."

"You don't..." What was this blasphemy? I'd never met somebody who didn't listen to music. It was like, like...somebody claiming they hated cake. Only the devil's spawn hated cake. "What do you listen to when you drive?"

"Audio books. Maybe a podcast. Or nothing, depending on my mood."

"How about when you write?"

"Nothing."

Wow. So devil's spawn did exist in the world. "That's sad. A life without music is like a body without a soul."

"I have a *soul*," she said, slightly put out. "I write romance, remember? I couldn't have more soul if I tried."

Maybe. But personally, I just couldn't picture a life without music. Music was everywhere. It was one of those things that made life more pleasurable and exciting.

"Music is distracting," Emily explained.

"No wonder you had no clue who I am." And I had a lot of work to do if I wanted everyone in the world to hear my music, just like everyone knew about the Beatles. I was aiming high, but what was the point of aiming low?

"You didn't exactly give me your stage name."

"Everyone knows me as Killian from Axelrod."

"Maybe you should make a T-shirt that says so and wear it everywhere," she said.

"Do you have a T-shirt that says, *I'm Emma Grant, and I write romance*?"

"No. But that's a great idea. I love what I'm writing, and I'm proud of my work."

She wasn't being sarcastic. And it pained me. Not because I expected everyone to love my work, but because *she* wasn't even giving my music a chance. And it felt personal.

"So am I," I said, keeping my voice even.

She sighed. "I didn't mean you weren't proud of your music. I don't think that came out well. I'm just...not very eloquent at the moment."

"What does that even mean?"

"I've been up since four, writing. I just poured out over five thousand words."

I was impressed. "So you're out of good words?"

She smiled. "That's a good way to put it. I've used up all my good words for the moment on my story. They're *so* good that I expect most will remain after revision. But right now I'm brain-dead, and all I have left is garbage. I need to nap and recharge."

"Your creative process is very different from mine." But then, our songs didn't require hundreds of pages of words. It was about the melody, the mood, the feel—capturing the most emotionally intense moment in a specific yet universal experience with the right beat.

"Well, yeah. I'm not a musician."

"Yeah, but you still do creative work." I leaned a little closer. Maybe learning about her process would shed some light on how I could break through my current idealess drought. "Do you always get good words after you nap?"

"Not all the time," she answered. "It depends."

"I see." So naps weren't the cure-all I was hoping for. "What's the difference between the time you get good words and the times you don't?"

She pursed her mouth. "Probably just fatigue? Or maybe I need a change of scene or have something else on my mind...like some chore I should be doing but have been putting off for one reason or another. Like cleaning up my work area."

My eyes slid over to the mess there. All the empty Hop Hop Hooray bottles. Candy wrappers. Empty cracker bags. Wadded-up sheets from notebooks. She should definitely clean it up. Or get a housekeeper.

Somehow, though, she was still getting the creative juices running, while I was drier than the Gobi Desert. But I did have something I needed to do, something I'd been procrastinating about for months and months. "Makes sense. Thanks, Emily."

"Sure," she said. But of course she had no clue what I was thanking her for.

CHAPTER 15

Killian

Talking to Emily turned out to be useful, maybe even insightful, for figuring out why I'd been so blocked. I'd been putting a bunch of things off.

Like going through Grandma's stuff in the house.

I let out a long breath, as though it could expel the months-old sadness and ease the hole in my heart.

Although I'd had "go through Grandma's things" on my to-do list for almost half a year now, what with the tour and all, I hadn't even started. Mir would've done it for me if I asked, but she had the beach cottage Grandma had left her to deal with. It wouldn't have been fair.

But as I stopped in front of the basement with all the things Grandma had collected over the years, I couldn't make myself go past the threshold. Everything in it held a memory, each one good and treasured. It felt like burying her all over again.

I didn't know if I wanted to do that. If I could face it again.

Because Grandma Donna hadn't been just any grandmother. She'd taken us in after our parents' deaths almost twenty years ago. She'd raised me and Mir, guided us, encouraged us. She'd done everything in her power to ensure we wouldn't continue to feel the lingering pain of losing our parents.

I resented the heart attack that had taken her, even though I understood she'd been old and none of us live forever.

After a few deep breaths, I turned back to the living room and picked up the next one of Emily's books, then lay on the sofa. I didn't have to go through Grandma's things right now. I might rush, throw out things I shouldn't. And then where would I be?

Besides, I wasn't planning to rent or sell this place, unlike Mir, who'd rented the beach cottage. And I'd been performing and touring fine before, even with Grandma's things still in the basement and attic and a few closets. Going through them wasn't an urgent matter, and it wasn't the problem.

What I should be focusing on was finishing Emily's entire backlist and resting so my muse would return. Then my creativity would flow again. I was sure of it.

Emily

After Killian had left with the two tubs of Bouncy Bare Monkeys, I sat down to work. But I couldn't seem to focus. My skin felt too...sensitive. And the flesh between my legs... It was tight and tingly. Probably from having my thigh muscles stretched, I told myself. I'd ended up straddling Killian, and he was a large guy. And I hadn't even warmed up for the little stunt.

Because there was no way this was sexual attraction. The guy was... Okay, so he was hot, but I didn't get all tingly and slick over somebody I didn't know well. And who would likely be a disappointment in the end. I should know. I'd dated pretty guys before, albeit none of them as hot as Killian. They'd all ended badly. I needed to look at what was inside, not the packaging.

I'll bet his package is impressive.

Okay, I had to pull my mind out of the absolute gutter it was in. The gleam of my phone on the table caught my eye and reminded me of the bet I had with Skye. Woohoo, a distraction from thinking about Killian and being on top of him!

Doing my best to push aside how my blood still seemed warm from that, I texted Skye the result with a taunting emoji.

–Skye: No. Way.

–Me: Way. You owe me two tequila shots.

–Skye: How do you know? Who did you try it with?

–Me: My next-door neighbor.

–Skye: The one who's using your shower? Give me more details.

–Me: Yes. He came by to make me breakfast again.

I added the last bit for an extra friendly taunt and to steer Skye from asking for more information about how the catch-the-girl experiment had gone. She had a thing about men cooking breakfast.

–Skye: Why can't I have that too?

–Me: You have a husband.

–Skye: He doesn't make me breakfast, though.

–Me: Make him borrow some hot water, then.

I smiled as I sent that last message. Skye often complained her husband didn't always understand romance or what she wanted. But I'd met her husband, and the man was solid. A good, salt-of-the-earth American man with a heart of gold who was blind to every woman except Skye.

That was worth more than anything. Ask my mom, and she'd say the same. Or not, I thought with a scowl. If Mom agreed with me, she would've dumped Dad years ago. Probably when I was in junior high—or even earlier.

I shook off the annoyance and exasperated resignation over my parents' marriage and started to work. I didn't stop until I'd wrapped up four more chapters. I needed maybe two or three more chapters to finish Molly and Ryan's story. It was amazing how fast the writing went. Normally, I would have needed the two whole weeks.

It probably meant the book was either smoking hot or a complete mess. I'd know when I sent it off to my editor for feedback. It wasn't possible for me to go over what I'd written so far and tinker to make sure the story was as good as I hoped, as I didn't have the luxury of time. Also, I hadn't given myself enough distance from the work to be able to judge my writing objectively.

Since I was way ahead, I decided to take a break and look up Killian's band. Although he'd played me that supposed hit from last year, I was distracted by his nearness and hadn't paid as much attention as I should have.

But now that I knew more about what he did, I was curious about his career. He'd asked me twice if I knew who he was, and that meant he was somebody well known, whether I recognized him or not.

Let's see... I typed in "Killian Axelrod," and Google came back with over a quarter of a *billion* articles and photos.

Okay, so he really was famous. His band, Axelrod, had sold tens of millions of albums. And he was rich, too. Net worth estimated to be north of five billion. Damn. Did music pay *that* well? His band had taken off five years ago. That was a billion or so dollars per year. It almost made me wish I sang better.

Interestingly, though, his band mates didn't seem to be as wealthy. Did he get all the profit because he was the lead vocalist? Or maybe it was something else. I couldn't imagine them giving Killian billions while they took comparative peanuts. I took a quick look at the profiles of the other three members, including that Dev guy Killian had mentioned. It turned out to be short for Devlin. The band also had a guitarist named Max and a bassist named Cole. Hmm. What the heck was a bassist? The picture showed Cole holding a guitar, just like Max. Ugh, bands were so confusing.

Google also gave links to Axelrod's music videos on YouTube. I clicked on one of them and recognized the opening immediately. It was the one Killian played during breakfast. Chin in hand, I let the music flow over me. The vocals were hauntingly sweet, with a hint of masculine rasp that tickled my senses. A tingle ran down my back as he sang, and I listened to the whole thing, mesmerized. I closed my eyes to better immerse myself in the sound.

YouTube automatically played the next song, "Eat Your Heart Out, Baby." Here, his voice was edgier—sharp enough to cut—as it sang of stark anger and pain due to infidelity. Shivers went down my back, and I nodded to the lyrics. Yeah, I totally felt this, deep in my soul. Not just because of my parents, but because one of my exes from college had cheated on me. He'd been dating two other girls at the same time, and actually thought he'd be smooth enough to get away with it. Asshole.

As YouTube played more and more of Axelrod's music, I realized none of the songs felt recycled or the same. But they all had one thing in common—the most amazing vocals with good color to it. I was certain "color" wasn't the right term, but I couldn't think of any other way to put it. It was what made Killian's voice husky in one song and mellow in another. Depending on the lyrics and mood, he sounded different. At the same time, there was something distinctive about it that said it was *him*. Like the way I recognized an author's writing, whether she was writing romantic suspense or romantic comedy. Even when he spoke, it was there—a sexy resonance that made my mouth dry.

As the songs continued, I opened a new tab and looked through his pictures. Some were staged for promotional photoshoots or magazine covers. Photographers generally emphasized his piercing blue eyes and chiseled looks. Many of them also had him in a shirt with buttons undone, showing off his spectacular chest and abs. My fingertips prickled as I remembered how hot and hard his muscles had felt when I laid my hands on him. I put my fingertips over my mouth, as though that would help me taste him.

You are a sad, sad woman...

Ignoring the judgmental voice in my head, I scrolled and noticed many pictures of him with a mic or guitar. Other shots were candid and likely snapped with somebody's phone—at parties and tours. Many of the latter showed him with at least two or three hot young women hanging on him like jungle vines. Something sour and bitter rose within me. The pictures reminded me of my dad—and his women. Dad was more discreet—he was married, after all—but if he were single, he would've flaunted his popularity. As a matter of fact, he was probably sad and morose that he couldn't show off all the women he'd been cheating on my mom with. Just thinking about it made me want to puke. Ideally on his face.

I looked back at the pictures of Killian surrounded by fawning women. A seed spewer and his farm. Men had an innate urge to spurt their seed everywhere. There was a reason porn often had men ejaculate all over the women, ruining the sole purpose of seed spreading. It was like a farmer who threw all the seeds into a stream next to his land, missing the fertile field ready to accept and nurture and grow those little kernels.

For some reason, the image was beyond irritating.

I closed the laptop, not wanting to see the photos anymore. The living room plunged into an abrupt and heavy silence as the music cut off, and I let out a tight breath. Why did I care who Killian was seen with? A handsome, young, single man with fame and fortune was bound to wrap his arms around every female shoulder he could. Then if the vaginas attached to said females were in a consenting mood, he'd also stick his dick into them. It was par for the course.

You don't have to be so crude about it, though.

When did honest observation become crude? It was what everyone did.

True love happened in romance novels. That was why I wrote romance. But I'd never dated with the expectation that the relationship would last. And my attitude had served me well. For me, dating was something fun to do with guys I didn't mind not seeing again if I became too busy or distracted.

Obviously, Killian was of the same persuasion, so I shouldn't be annoyed. As a matter of fact, I was certain I wasn't annoyed. Probably just surprised he shared my philosophy.

I'd spent enough time thinking about him. It was time I threw myself back into finishing the manuscript, to give Molly and Ryan the kind of everlasting love they deserved.

CHAPTER 16

Killian

When I showed up the next day, Emily had the same sign on the door she'd had from yesterday. It could be that she'd just forgotten to remove it. Or she could've left it there for a reason.

So I walked inside silently, trying not to disturb her, since she was working on her computer. I showered quietly too, then left my shirt on the back of a dining chair and made eggs Benedict.

Emily typed away on her laptop until I was finished cooking, then joined me at the table, but something felt a bit off. She didn't say anything except "Good morning. This looks good." She also didn't hold my eyes.

Not that she was overtly avoiding eye contact. She was too smooth for that. But every time our eyes met, she'd turn her head just an inch further to focus on something beyond my shoulder. It was like she'd discovered her favorite candy taped to the wall behind me.

The back of my neck bristled unpleasantly. Mir also did something similar when she was upset with me for some reason, but didn't want to say anything because she was hoping I'd broach it first.

For some bizarre female reason, Mir thought if she broached the topic, she was giving me some kind of advantage. But I couldn't imagine Emily was doing this for the same reason. I went over what had happened yesterday, and... Nope. Couldn't recall anything that would elicit this kind of reaction.

I took a bite of the food, thinking while I chewed. As I swallowed, it hit me. She was embarrassed about how she'd treated me because she'd finally realized who I was. She'd probably looked me up, just like I'd looked her up after reading her book for the first time. There was tons of information about me and the band all over the Internet.

But she shouldn't let that bug her. She'd said she didn't listen to music, in which case she probably hadn't heard any of Axelrod's songs. I wouldn't hold that against her, any more than she would begrudge me not recognizing her pen name.

"How's the food? As tasty as it looks?" I asked, trying to start a conversation to let her know I was fine, so she should let go of whatever weirdness she was harboring.

"Yeah, it's good."

"Thanks." I beamed, pleased at the compliment. And she would've seen my smile if she'd just glanced up. I tried not to let my frustration show. I was trying to smooth things over, which isn't easy when the other person won't look at you. "It's my first time making eggs Benedict, so I didn't know how they'd turn out."

She looked impressed, her gaze still on the damned eggs. "First time, huh?"

"My grandmother's recipe," I explained, pretending I hadn't noticed her singular determination to stare at the eggs. Did she think there was an ant or something on the yolk? "I found it in the kitchen last night while I was rummaging around trying to find some dried pepper flakes. So I knew it'd be pretty good as long as I didn't mess up."

"How can you mess it up when you're following a recipe?" she asked, finally giving me a glance.

Ah ha! My "act normal" plan was working! "Because it didn't specify exactly how much to put in. Just, you know...a pinch of this, a dash of that, an appropriate amount of blah blah blah. Which is so much like Grandma." I sighed with affection...and longing. I missed her terribly. "So I had to wing it a little."

"Your grandmother would be proud." Emily gave me a small smile.

"Thanks," I said. "She was a fantastic cook."

She cleared her throat. "I ran into her a few times. She seemed like a really nice lady."

"Yeah, she was. She was a hoot. I wish she were still here."

Emily gave me the small, comforting smile that people give when they want to console someone but aren't sure how because they didn't know the deceased very well. As friendly as my grandma had been, Emily was too much of a hermit.

We ate in silence. Emily polished off her food, then licked her fork clean and took a sip of her coffee.

"I listened to some of your music yesterday during my break, by the way," she said. "You sing pretty well."

"Thanks." I acted like I was happy with her assessment, although part of me was disappointed her reaction was so ho-hum. "Pretty well" wasn't much of a compliment, especially when spoken in the tone Emily had just used.

It bugged the hell out of me that she didn't absolutely love my music. Granted, it wasn't for everyone. Some critics had given us shitty reviews, and it wasn't like I hadn't seen nasty comments online. But Emily's assessment got to me anyway. It felt personal. I wanted her to *like* our music, at least, even if she couldn't outright love it the way I loved her writing. It seemed only fair.

Except that too was an outlandish expectation. I didn't enjoy her books in the hopes that she'd do the same with my music. I just...

I wanted to give her pleasure with my music, the way she'd given it to me.

"What?" Emily said when I continued to gaze at her. "Do I have yolk on my face?" She licked her lips.

The gesture was quick, her pink tongue darting in and out. But somehow it mesmerized me, made my skin tight and hot, like it were a particularly arousing segment in a porn movie. And my body reacted.

Shit.

I shifted in my seat, annoyed with my lack of control. A woman had let me use her shower, let me feed her, then given me a half-assed compliment on my music, and I was hard. Okay, so there was the tongue thing, too, but that didn't count. I'd seen far more seductive moves from women in skintight dresses with plunging necklines. Emily was in a T-shirt that read *Virginia Is for Lovers* that didn't show any cleavage, and stretchy black pants that covered her legs from the ankles up. And unlike the day she'd confronted me to get me to stop drumming, she *was* wearing a bra. Compared to the groupies at parties and tours, she might as well have been wearing a nun's habit.

And not a porno nun's habit. The real deal. Like what you see in churches and...well, wherever authentic nuns hang out.

But Emily had been making me feel something I shouldn't since the moment we met in Sunny's Mart. That spark was there, even though she'd been in hole-y clothes rather than holy clothes. That crackling sensation when she'd come to my place to demand I stop drumming. And the sizzle when I'd acted out the scene with her yesterday.

"Why are you looking at me like that?" Emily squinted at me. "You didn't like the book you took yesterday and you aren't sure how to tell me?"

I frowned in confusion. How in hell was her mind going in that direction?

"Don't worry about it. It isn't my most beloved work," she said in a small whisper, her cheeks pink, like she was confessing to something embarrassing. "I mean, some people liked it, but not everyone."

I sat frozen for a moment, unsure how to tell her my mood had nothing to do with her book, because then she'd want to know why I was acting weird, and I didn't want to tell her the truth. I couldn't think of a good way to tell her without sounding like I was fishing for a compliment about me or the band. I didn't want Emily to think I was desperate for a good word from her. That was pathetic, the kind of thing that could make her lose respect.

And her respect and good will mattered in a bizarre way.

"But I wonder why you keep reading romance. Don't you have better things to do?" she asked finally. "I can't believe it's really your kind of thing."

What did she think I read? "It's not the first thing I'd typically pick up...but I wouldn't be reading them if I didn't like them."

"Weird. There's a reason romance is a genre for women, written by women. And you don't seem like the type to like romance."

I raised my eyebrows. What made her think that of all things? Her stories generally had nice guys, so... What was she implying? "Are you stereotyping me?"

"Nope. Just looked you up on Google." Her voice cooled a little.

"And...?" I didn't remember mentioning dissing romance in any of my interviews. Actually, books had never come up because people don't get close to a rock star to talk about reading.

"You were surrounded by a lot of half-naked women. So why would you be into stories about everlasting love with one person?"

"That was the conclusion you came to after seeing those pictures?" That was totally unfair. Did she think I could control how women dressed around me? Or that other people's choice of clothing would affect what I wanted in life? A possibility flashed through my mind. "Were you jealous?" Emily could be, and she was letting me know by being meh about Axelrod's music and saying romance wasn't for me.

The notion improved my mood for some reason. It wasn't like me, since when women grew clingy and territorial, I got annoyed. But with Emily, I wanted her to act possessive.

Emily scoffed. "Don't be absurd."

"I don't believe you."

"You're no naked Chris Hemsworth in a Thor costume. Now, that's somebody I could be jealous over. He has the nicest pecs and ass." She gave me a superior smirk.

"It's Chris *Evans* who has America's Ass," I said, ignoring her attempt to scratch my ego. She was definitely jealous. *And* trying to cover it up by dragging another man into the conversation, even though the chances of her, me and Chris Hemsworth hanging out naked or otherwise were pretty slim.

"Chris Hemsworth has Asgard's Ass," she countered. "And Asgard is bigger than America! It's in outer space."

"Well, he can't be naked if he's in the Thor costume."

"It's a figure of speech."

I shrugged. "A bad one."

"Are you always this argumentative?"

"Don't have to be, generally speaking. Since I'm always correct."

"Ohhh, I see. I guess if you're constantly surrounded by sycophants and groupies, you would be." She stood up with the empty coffee cup. "I need more. You?"

"No thanks."

I followed her to the kitchen to put the dirty plates in the sink. Normally I wouldn't feel the need to defend myself against her ridiculous accusations, but I was going to see Emily every morning for a while, and I didn't want her in a snit over nothing. It had nothing to do with me caring about what Emily thought of me.

"I'm not surrounded by sycophants and groupies all the time," I said. Security kept most of the people away, since I wasn't interested in getting entangled with those women. The ones who got close enough knew my band mates, especially Dev, who hadn't met a woman he couldn't fall in love with since his breakup with Ashley. That breakup had inspired the song "Eat Your Heart Out, Baby." Thankfully, he fell out of love just as easily. Otherwise, he'd be on trial for polygamy.

Without grabbing another coffee, she turned around to face me. "You should get your head checked, then. Because your judgment sucks."

"My judgment is perfectly fine." How was it my fault people shouted and flung themselves at me? That kind of crap was the price of fame the band had to put up with, but it didn't define me.

I stared at her flat mouth, the challenging arcs of her eyebrows. Fire sparked in her eyes, and everything about her screamed "dare"—*I dare you to prove you're more than what was in those photos, more than your public reputation. I dare you to prove you're a person with thoughts, dreams and needs that are your own.*

And it reignited something deep inside that had gone cool and dormant since my collapse, making it burn so hot and bright that I couldn't ignore it anymore. Moving purely on instinct, I cupped the back of her head and kissed her. Felt her soft inhale of surprise, her breath feathering my skin.

Her mouth was softer than anything I could've imagined. Sweeter than cotton candy.

She stood still for a moment, then raised her arms, letting them hover in the air as though she didn't know what to do.

I licked across her lips, silently seeking an invitation into her mouth for more. She opened up, stroking her tongue against mine. Every nerve cell in my body came to attention, like she'd sent a shock of electricity through me. And I craved more of that sensation. I hadn't felt that in...forever. It made me feel so *alive*, so anchored in the present.

Her hands came to rest on my shoulders, fingers flexing against the muscle. I held her warm, pretty cheeks in my palms and plundered her mouth. She tasted like spice and honey. She smelled like clean forest and citrus. She felt like life, vibrant and full of energy.

She kissed me back aggressively, stoking the scorching need inside my gut with her heat. Her breathing grew rougher and uneven, just like mine. Every little sigh, every lick was unbearably erotic and precious.

I pulled her closer, felt her breasts crush against my hard, bare chest. I wanted to take her to bed, lick, kiss and taste the rest of her, explore her and feast on her. Watch as pleasure broke over her, hear her sob my name as she came while wrapped in my arms.

Suddenly, she pulled back and put a hand over her mouth like a shield. For a fraction of the second, I wondered if I'd gone too far or misread the cues and she didn't really want it. But her gorgeous eyes were large, dark and glazed with lust as she looked at me.

What was this about? "Emily...?"

She put up the other hand. "That was nice, but—"

Did she just say "nice" to describe the best fucking kiss of my life?

"—I have to finish the rest of my book."

What the fuck? She had to finish it *now*? "Can't you do it later?" I blurted.

"No. Unless *you* can finish in under ten minutes." She immediately scowled. That probably wasn't what she'd meant to say.

And I'd be damned if I rushed through our first time. *Under ten minutes.* What the hell kind of guy did she think I was? "Then I'll leave you to your work." It came out more tersely than I intended, but I didn't try to soften it. "I'm going to need a lot more of your time than that. Like two hours. At least."

Then I snapped my shirt over a shoulder and stalked out.

CHAPTER 17

Emily

Damn it.

I scowled at the laptop screen. Not even two thousand words since Killian had left. I'd been typing away furiously, but I'd also had to hit backspace a lot because my mind had been elsewhere. The kiss with Killian, to be precise.

The man had kissed like...

What was important wasn't how he'd kissed. It was how I'd felt. Molten lust had struck me from head to toe like lightning, the liquid heat pouring through me, making me wet. And needy. And greedy.

I hadn't been able to remember why I was annoyed about the pictures. Or why it was a terrible idea to kiss him back. The only thing that mattered had been my desire to have him continue.

Holy shit.

If I hadn't stopped just then, I would've dragged him down on the floor. And I wouldn't have settled for just straddling him like I'd done the day before. I would've stripped both of us naked and let him push into me. The intensity of that need had scared the hell out of me. Thinking about having him inside me made my skin tight and prickly.

So thinking about a prick makes you prickly, har har har.

With a groan, I buried my face in my hands. I was being pathetic. A nympho.

You haven't had sex with a man since you moved to Kingstree.

That was why I had sex toys. Since I wasn't going to get romance from men in real life, I didn't need them for orgasms, either. But somehow I wanted to have some with Killian rather than my toys. What the hell was wrong with me?

My phone buzzed, pulling me out of my humiliatingly horny thoughts. I picked it up because that would be more productive than glaring at the poor, helpless Word doc or fantasizing about Killian. I'd have to change my underwear at the rate things were going.

–Skye: Somebody please! I think I'm going to murder Tiffany's band director!

–Me: Why?

–Lucy: Don't. There is no perfect murder!

–Skye: It's a freakin' fundraiser. Again! We did that, like, two months ago, but apparently they didn't sell enough stupid candy or something. I swear, we pay through the nose in property taxes for school, but they never have enough money for anything!

I sighed with sympathy. This was Skye's constant gripe with her kid's school, and I didn't blame her. I'd hated fundraisers in high school. Thankfully, Mom had sold the stuff for me, since she was an extrovert.

–Me: I'm Paypaling you $100 for some candy.

–Skye: You don't have to. You bought some last time.

–Me: Please. If I can't do this for you and Tiffany, who can I do it for?

–Lucy: Same for me! Save me $100s' worth of candy, too. Anything with chocolate is fine.

–Me: You can give mine away or eat it yourself. I don't care.

I was particular about my junk food. And I didn't care enough to leaf through candy options from Tiffany's band.

–Skye: You're the best, girls! Thank you!

–Me: It's nothing.

–Lucy: Less than nothing.

–Skye: Well, I appreciate it anyway. So how's writing going? Almost done?

–Me: Should've been done this morning, but I'm not even close.

–Lucy: How come? You're an hour ahead of me, and I'm already done with my daily quota.

I sighed. I envied Lucy her focus and prolificity.

–Me: I'm distracted.

–Skye: Stuck? Need to brainstorm?

I smiled at Skye's ready offer. She was the font of ideas in our trio.

–Me: Thanks, girlfriend, but I already know exactly what needs to happen.

–Lucy: So what's the problem?

I sighed, then decided I might as well tell them. They might have some ideas as to how I could get my head back into the story.

Speaking of getting head...

No, stop*!*

–Me: It's my neighbor.

–Lucy: Didn't he promise to be quiet?

–Me: Yes, but we kissed.

There. That got the important point across, without revealing who Killian was. I still didn't know how I felt about him being a rock star, and I didn't want to derail the girls' focus with that factoid, because Lucy and Skye both loved music.

–Skye: Whoa! Wait, wait, back up a little.

–Lucy: Was it good?

I paused, thinking back on the kiss in the kitchen. How should I describe it? Among all the adjectives I could come up with, my mind kept wandering back to the first one. It was too dramatic a word choice, but I couldn't think of anything better and more apt. So I typed it out.

–Me: Soul-destroying.

–Skye: Wow. So did you seal the deal for real?

–Lucy: Don't leave us hanging!

Their excitement amused me a little, making me feel like a teenager discussing her first crush with her friends. Except Killian wasn't such an innocent crush. The man was too hot, too popular, too...surrounded by women. Well, maybe not in Kingstree. But I'd bet a year's income that as soon as he left town, women would converge on him like moths around a searchlight.

–Me: We were arguing, and I was kind of egging him on, and then...bam, he kissed me.

Okay, that wasn't exactly how that had gone, but I didn't want to give all the details, especially the part about him deciding I was jealous. I'd wanted him to lose his cool for that arrogance. I'd been annoyed about his pictures for reasons unknown, but I hadn't been jealous—I'd never felt that way about a guy, ever—and I had no reason to start.

–Lucy: Woo, a hate kiss!

–Skye: Was it good? I've never had a hate kiss before.

I ran my tongue over my lips. The kiss was long over, but I swore my mouth was still feeling an echo.

–Me: It was good.

Might as well be honest, I told myself. It was only fair to share —it could be inspirational...or used as research. Skye wrote wholesome contemporary, but she could always write something edgier. As for Lucy... Maybe she could write about a serial killer antihero.

–Me: And he was yummy.

There. An extra detail. I didn't add that he had been as delicious as Bouncy Bare Monkeys, all that rich, textured flavor of male and lust and "take no prisoners" aggression. I'd wanted to devour him on the spot, consequences be damned.

That seemed a bit too private. Weird that I felt that way. I hadn't minded giving away details about the few dates I'd had in the past.

–Lucy: And then what?

–Skye: There's more to this, right?

–Me: No. He went home, and I started working. I have a deadline. The bet, remember?

I wasn't going to tell my friends I'd pulled back from that logic-vaporizing kiss because the intensity of my need had scared the hell out of me. Sex was supposed to be pleasant and generally pleasurable. But feeling like I'd die if I didn't have him? That wasn't normal. It only happened in romance novels, between the heroes and heroines.

Then there was Killian's parting shot.

Two hours.

Actually, he'd said *at least* two hours.

What could a guy do with two hours? Stuff like that only happened in romance novels. In my experience, a girl was lucky to get thirty minutes.

Still, part of me wanted to know what Killian was imagining that would take so long.

Stop thinking about that! He probably said it because he read your books. All your heroes do it like they're getting a Cialis IV while they're fucking.

I frowned at the possibility, displeased that I'd forgotten that critical detail. Men lied about their prowess all the time in order to get laid. The prime exhibit—my dad. Ugh. Now I needed to throw up.

–Lucy: Aren't you ahead of schedule? You could've taken a little time to explore the attraction some more. Especially if he was yummy.

–Skye: Exactly. I love my husband, but I need to hear those first attraction spark stories. Keeps me revved up for books.

–Me: Work comes before play.

That had always been my motto. It'd made me good at my career, and I wasn't going to change that for a fling.

–Lucy: Yeah, but YOU could come before work!

–Skye: Beat me to it.

I loved my friends. But I needed to explain.

–Me: Sleeping with him would be a terrible idea. The worst. He's a neighbor, but he isn't type to stick around.

That was the least of my objections, but it sounded pretty good.

–Lucy: How come?

Because he's a rock star? But I hesitated to share that detail. I hadn't seen any crazy tabloid people out here yet, and I was certain that had something to do with people of Kingstree being discreet about Killian's whereabouts. I didn't think Lucy or Skye would shout it to the world, but it seemed prudent to keep the fact under wraps, especially since Skye had a gossipy daughter.

–Me: He's only here to take care of his grandmother's estate or something. I'm sure he'll leave as soon as it's done because he has a career elsewhere.

–Skye: That sucks.

–Lucy: Don't let that stop you. If you decide that he's The One after getting to know him better, you could go with him. It's not like you absolutely have to be in that town to write.

–Me: No, thank you. Kingstree is perfect for an introvert like me. I'm not giving up my little hermit haven for any man.

Especially not a rock star who was used to the spotlight and being surrounded by pretty young things. I could make myself presentable when I was attending a conference or book signing, but I generally didn't bother to do much. A shower and brushing my hair were about the extent of my daily self-beautification routine. I didn't want to change that for what was essentially a fling, and I also didn't want to be compared to younger, prettier women who probably worked out all the time to maintain their firm and toned size-two bodies.

My idea of exercise was typing, occasional stretching and going to the kitchen to grab more water or beer. I sometimes ran, but only when I was blocked. The torture worked wonders, because if I forced a choice between running or writing, my mind always chose the latter.

–Me: Anyway, I gotta get back to the manuscript. I'm sending it off to my editor today, even if it kills me.

And Killian wasn't getting in the way.

–Lucy: Okay then. Ciao.

–Skye: I need to start writing too. Talk to you later, girls.

After placing the phone back on the table, I took the last sip of the beer, then reached over for some crackers. But all the bags were empty. Sighing, I forced myself off the couch and started toward the kitchen.

Something moved in my peripheral vision. I turned to look and—

A snake!

I screamed and scrambled back, almost falling on my butt as my heart started pounding a billion beats per second. Cold sweat beaded on my back, and the temperature in the house seemed to plunge.

The snake lifted its head in my direction. It flicked its forked tongue. Its beady eyes shot messages in evil telepathy: *I'm going to eat you, bitch!*

It reared back a bit, getting ready to launch itself at me and attack. I could envision its jaw unhinging and swallowing me whole. I heard they could eat things ten times bigger than them, no problem.

My mind empty of everything except for an instinctive and blind drive for self-preservation, I ran out into the yard. Without the snake in view, my heart slowed to a mere two million beats per second. I placed my sweaty palms on my knees and thought about my options. *Call 911.* Or should I go to the police station?

Then I realized I was outside without anything—no keys or phone! Freakin' great! I put both hands over my mouth and a few moments later almost blacked out, because blocking one's airflow isn't a good idea while hyperventilating. I started wringing them instead, which worked better. There was no way I was going back in there when a giant snake was waiting to bite my head off. That was what snakes did—I'd seen it in a B-movie once with Lucy and Skye while on a writing retreat. And the one inside had definitely made its deadly intent clear.

Since the only savior I could think of was Killian, I ran over to his house. He'd been borrowing my shower for days now. Surely I could get one phone call.

I knocked on his door and started to bite my nails as the seconds ticked by. What if he wasn't home? A car was parked in the driveway, but he was a rock star. He might have other cars—or a Harley. What would I do if he wasn't home?

What if the snake followed me? It could smell me, right—

I whirled around, expecting to see serpentine jaws of doom expanding to engulf me. But apparently the snake was contenting itself with taking over my house.

I turned back to the door. Now I almost wished I'd let Killian play his obnoxious drums. Then I would've known he was home for sure without this nauseating anxiety twisting around in my gut. I felt like throwing up.

He could be ignoring me because of the kiss. Maybe he'd been insulted that I jumped back and told him I needed to work.

Most women probably melted and magically incinerated their clothes when he kissed them.

Argh. I banged on the door with all my might, as though if just I hit it hard enough, he'd appear.

"Killian!" I yelled. "Killian! Come on!"

"Okay, okay!" came a grumbly voice from the other side.

My knees shook, almost buckling with relief. I propped my hand against the wall for support.

He stuck his head out, his eyes flinty. "Yeah?" Then he took a closer look at me and straightened, concern softening his gaze. "Whoa, Emily, are you okay? You need to sit down?" He put a hand on my forehead. "You feel clammy."

"Oh my G-G-God, I..." My teeth were chattering. Thank heavens I wasn't alone in my fight against the snake that had taken over my home. "There's this, this..."

"Okay, you need to sit down."

"I need to go home." No, that came out wrong, because I couldn't go home on my own. "*We* need go home. Over there. To my house."

He gave me a look. "Why?"

"There's a snake inside! And I need your help."

His eyebrows quirked briefly, then settled into a serious V. He pressed his lips together. "A snake?" he said finally.

I nodded. "A huge one. Vicious."

"I see." His eyebrows pulled tighter until the V was narrower and even more solemn.

Shit. He was realizing the gravity of the situation, and didn't want to risk his life. Well...should've expected that. Why would he, after what had happened in the morning? Maybe I should've pretended to swoon at his feet, my arm wrapped around his thigh, imitating one of those clinch poses from an old-school historical romance.

"If you don't want to go, can I borrow your phone to call 911? Maybe the cops could come and shoot it."

The muscles in Killian's jaw flexed. He was probably insulted again, guessing—correctly—that I'd figured out that he was too scared to risk his masculine neck. "That won't be necessary. I'll take care of the snake for you."

My whole body went slack with shock and gratitude. "You will?"

"Of course. If I don't do it, who will?" He shrugged, like rescuing women from man-eating snakes was something he did every day.

"You aren't going to sue if you get hurt, right?" I asked just to make sure. It would be an expensive lawsuit. "You called your insurance agent to expand your policy to cover your whole body?"

He looked at me like I was some kind of alien. "I have enough insurance to cover my bases. Come on." He gestured at me to follow as he started moving toward my house.

"Me?" I squeaked.

"Yeah. Somebody's gotta show me where the vicious snake was last seen."

CHAPTER 18

Killian

Emily stayed close behind me as I made way over to her place, which was good. I didn't know how much longer I could maintain a straight face. It'd taken all my willpower to not burst out laughing back in my house.

Kingstree had a few varieties of harmless, non-venomous snakes. They usually only ate bugs, or maybe frogs or field mice—sometimes baby birds if they were quick enough. But from Emily's reaction, I wouldn't be surprised to find a thirty-foot, man-eating anaconda in her home.

Call the cops so they could come and shoot it dead. Ha ha ha. I could just picture Sheriff Claymoore's face. His thick gray mustache would quiver in sync with his bushy eyebrows. Then he'd laugh that wheezing laugh of his until he doubled over. They might end up having to defibrillate him.

I bit my lip hard. I'd been feeling pretty irritated and upset about how the breakfast ended. I hadn't believed my ears when I heard Emily bang on my door and scream my name.

She undoubtedly hadn't changed her mind about the ten minutes. But at least she thought I was good for disposing of scary wildlife. I'd settle for that...for now.

The door to her house had been left completely open. Good thing we lived in a town as safe as Kingstree.

I stepped inside. Emily stuck to my back close enough that I could feel her body heat through our shirts, and it felt damn good. My body perked up, ready for a continuation of our kiss earlier, because it didn't know nothing was going to happen until I took care of the scary snake.

"So. Where'd you see it?" I asked, my voice slightly huskier than normal.

"Over there." She gestured without sticking her head out from my back.

"There...where?" I asked again, all innocent.

"In the dining room. I was walking toward the kitchen, and it just leaped out of the blue to attack me."

"Leaped, huh? Must've been traumatizing." For that poor little garter snake. I'd have to gently pick it up and let it out. It deserved no less after the ordeal it'd been through.

"It was. I thought I was having a heart attack."

I pressed a knuckle to my lips because Emily would murder me if I laughed. I managed to produce a sympathetic growl, then walked further into the house.

She followed me as though that would keep her safe. Which was an encouraging sign. At least she felt secure around me. A big step in the right direction.

Although her reaction to the snake was overblown, I understood. Most women couldn't stand snakes. When Mir had first seen one, she sprained an ankle in her rush to get away. At least Emily hadn't hurt herself.

And there was part of me that was pleased she was sticking so close. It was as though she understood I could keep her safe from the super-evil viper of doom that had been threatening her. I bit back a smile of satisfaction. God had obviously created snakes to make men look good.

Then I spotted it—a green and mustard-yellow reptile. It wasn't even two feet long. Barely big enough to overpower a fat mouse. It was on the floor underneath the dining table. Probably cowering in fear, since it had no real defense mechanism against predators. Or somebody as big as Emily or me.

Mischief sparked in my mind. I made a slow half-circle. Emily did the same, her hands on my sides. They felt soft and warm, and her fingers kept moving like they couldn't decide on how to touch me. Or maybe she was copping a feel, which I was totally okay with. Hmm. I wondered if she'd feel me up like this when we rolled around in bed, naked.

But first...

I turned my head to look at her over my shoulder. "So, what color was the snake?"

"Green and brown, I think?" She wrinkled her nose. "It was mottled."

I flicked my gaze beyond her head. "Oh shit! Is that it?"

Before I could point, she jumped on me, screaming like a spooked banshee. She wrapped her arms around my neck, cutting off my air, and clamped her legs around my waist. I gripped her forearms and pulled them down so I could breathe, then tried to enjoy the feel of having her wrapped around me for a moment. But it was hard to appreciate how feminine she felt when she was shrieking. "Shh! Stop screaming. It's going to come at us if you do that! They don't like it when you're loud. Noise pollution, remember?"

The high-pitched yelling cut off abruptly. Her body was so tense that it was almost shaking.

"Snakes don't like it." *Do not laugh,* I thought. That would ruin everything.

"Really?" she whispered.

I nodded, doing my best to set my face into my most serious expression. Just in case there was a mirror in the room somewhere I didn't know about. "Yeah."

Her voice grew quieter. "Aren't you talking too loud? You should whisper."

"I'm a guy. Vocal register is too low to bother snakes." Totally making shit up, but it sounded scientific enough. And how was she going to know? She had no access to Google. She had to rely on Killianpedia.

"Damn sexist snakes." Emily shifted, still clinging to me. I could feel all of her—the lean, strong muscles of her legs, the softness of her breasts crushed against my back. She seemed solid and real, and I appreciated that after being surrounded by women who were mostly stick figures with some silicone chest stuffing. The spots where Emily's tits were pressed seemed to tingle, making my blood rush to my dick. Jesus. Was the back an erogenous zone for men?

I could feel her swiveling her head as she looked around. "Can you do something about the snake if you find it?" She was so close that her lips brushed my neck as she whispered, her breath ticklish.

I almost didn't want to move, just so she would continue to say stuff. I didn't care what came out of her mouth as long as she stayed in this position.

But I wouldn't be much of a hero if I didn't eventually get rid of the snake. So I said, "Of course," trying to infuse my voice with as much casual, manly confidence as possible.

With Emily still clinging to my back like a koala, I walked into the kitchen and grabbed a pair of barbecue tongs. Then I went back to the dining room, squatted down and grabbed the snake with them. The snake wasn't quick enough to escape. Emily let out a small squeak and buried her face in my neck. I almost groaned as she tightened her hold on me because my mind went to sex...and I wondered if she'd cling like this when she came.

I put the snake down out in the backyard. It fled immediately, parting the grass as it moved away. I watched it go, then went back inside. Emily stayed glued to my back the whole time.

"Is it dead?" she asked in a small voice, probably to avoid attracting the snake's attention.

I made a vague noise in my throat, enjoying the feel of her. "It's been dealt with."

"But it's alive?" she whispered against my neck. Jesus, this was erotic.

"Yeah," I said.

"Won't it come back?"

"I doubt it." The weather was too warm for it to want to hide inside a house.

"You're not *sure*? I can't have it come back."

"The problem isn't it coming back," I said, not wanting Emily to climb down my back.

"It isn't?"

"No. You know how snakes are cold-blooded?"

"Yeah..."

"That means they need a way to keep warm." I let it sink in.

"Okay. So it's going to be back."

"Not *it*. *They*."

"*They*?" Emily squealed.

"Not so loud."

"Oh my God! What do you mean, *they*?"

"Snakes live in dens. With other snakes. They ball up to help stay warm. People do it, too. You know, in the wild when you're stuck in a blizzard or something. You huddle together, and it helps you survive."

"So...what? You think there are *more* in here?"

"Could be. You never know."

A shudder ran through her. It wasn't exactly like a sexual climax, but it felt good anyway. "What do I do? Can I stay with you until we make sure they're all gone?"

Normally, I'd say yes. But lust was raging in my body, and the petty part of my mind brought up how she'd said I was only worth ten minutes of her time. Therefore, I shouldn't give in easily.

"What's in it for me?" I asked.

"Um." She squirmed some more against my back.

Jesus. My dick said, *Man up. She might offer to sleep with you. Women sleep with guys who perform heroic deeds.*

Don't count on it, I shot back at my one-track cock. Women also offered to sleep with rock stars, but Emily wasn't even close to interested.

"How about dinner?" she said finally. "You like pizza?"

Was she serious? She could do better. "I can buy myself a pizza."

"Okay. How about shrimp scampi? I make a great scampi."

Well, then. I liked Italian. And having dinner together was a good next step. Like a date. Besides, based on how she ate crackers and junk food all the time, I could see how cooking for someone would be a big deal to her. "I accept."

"Hey, can you grab my laptop and phone on the way?" she said, still on my back.

"Why?"

"I have to work. I'm about to wrap up Molly and Ryan's story."

"Molly and Ryan's story" still sounded weird. But I picked up her electronics without arguing. "Anything else?"

"No, that's it. Now carry me out of this nest of serpents!"

CHAPTER 19

Emily

After calling the local pest control and animal removal company for some emergency service, I spent the rest of the day at Killian's house working on my manuscript. Although Killian gave me full use of his dining table and took himself into the living room, I was braced for endless interruptions I couldn't do anything about.

Sad to say, most people didn't respect my time because I was *home*. Which to them meant I wasn't doing anything worthwhile. That was the biggest reason I no longer bothered to date. None of the three men I'd been involved with before moving to Kingstree had learned the art of entertaining themselves while I was working. In addition, since I was "just on my computer," they'd thought they had every right to bother me, no matter how many times I explained I was working. They hadn't respected the fact that every time they tapped my shoulder or talked to me, I was pulled out of my flow, and it would take me at least half an hour to reimmerse myself in the story.

However, I couldn't dump Killian because we weren't dating. I needed him more than he needed me, and I owed him dinner for taking care of that awful snake.

But—amazingly—Killian stayed quiet. He put on a headset and read one of the books he'd borrowed the day before. The peace and quiet lasted the entire afternoon, and I had to admit I was impressed. *Or maybe my book is just that damned good,* I thought with satisfaction.

Finally, I typed the long-awaited *The End*, emailed it to my editor and jumped to my feet, closing my laptop. "Yes!"

It was done, done, *done*! I was sure I'd get hundreds of comments to review later, but for now, the thrill of having the basic manuscript finished was sizzling through me. It was the best thing I'd written, and if it didn't resonate with my readers, I didn't know what would. I couldn't *wait* to see Dad eat his words!

Killian looked over from the couch, raising his eyebrows. I gave him both thumbs up, and he pulled the headset off. "All done?"

I grinned. "Yup. This baby's off to my editor." I put my hands up in the air triumphantly and did the "my book's finished" celebratory butt-wriggle dance. "Ooh yeah."

He laughed. "No wonder you write romantic comedy. You're cracking me up."

"Don't let the dance fool you. I've considered writing dark, angsty romance, too."

"So why don't you?"

"Because my first book was funny, and it took off. Lucy told me I should stick to what works." Then I added, "Lucy's one of my closest friends. She writes romantic thrillers, and she's brilliant."

He smiled, genuine pleasure lighting his eyes. "Does this mean you're ready to head out to grab whatever you need to make us dinner?"

"Is it already time to start thinking about dinner?" I asked, looking around for a clock.

"It's a little after four."

The scampi itself wouldn't take too long, but the shopping... Well, that was another matter. I picked up my phone and checked to see if there was a message from the pest and animal removal company. Nothing yet. "Let me see what you have in your fridge. I don't want to assume anything."

"We're gonna need at least the shrimp. But I'll go to Sunny's with you, to help carry everything." He flexed his arm muscles ostentatiously.

I laughed. "Okay."

His offer ended up working in my favor because I suddenly realized I didn't have my keys. I'd left them in the house. And I wasn't setting foot back in there until I knew it was safe to do so.

So Killian drove us in his SUV. The inside was surprisingly clean and tidy, and the radio played some music I didn't recognize, not that I'd expected to. Some woman was singing, so it wasn't his band. I snuck a peek at Killian from time to time, just moving my eyes sideways so he wouldn't know. His long, lean fingers were wrapped around the wheel, the index finger drumming steadily to the beat of the song. My mind went back to what happened between us that morning. It had felt amazing, his hand wrapped in my hair, trapping me, while his mouth moved coaxingly over mine. Like he couldn't bear to let go... Like he'd wanted me to want him with the same intensity.

My lips tingled. I placed three fingers over them, as though that would stop the sensation. But it only intensified the throbbing, and I pulled out my phone to pretend I wasn't still affected by that kiss.

You know, if that kiss and the snake rescue had happened in your book, your heroine would be totally doing the hero by now, an unhelpful voice pointed out.

Yeah, but this wasn't one of my books. In real life, women didn't just sleep with men for that, especially when the man was a neighbor she had to see every morning. Things could get awkward real fast.

He'd said he'd need at least two hours. But what if he didn't get to use up all one hundred and twenty minutes? What if the sex was just okay? Not that I wanted to make assumptions, but he was a rock star, and his groupies had undoubtedly told him he was a sex god no matter how he performed.

Although, based on how my body had throbbed every time we touched... Maybe he was better than average. But experience had taught me that there was no such thing as "mind-blowing" sex in real life. Just some nice orgasms here and there.

The air in the car seemed to grow thinner, and I squirmed. Must stop thinking about sex and orgasms with Killian.

"What are you doing?" he asked.

I almost dropped my phone. "Writing out what I need," I said, busily tapping the cool surface and pretending to be all nonchalant. Then I glanced up and saw his long, lean fingers again.

Bet they'd feel really nice between the legs, too.

I almost choked. *Okay, hormones.* I knew I hadn't been laid in a while, but really? This was not the right place or time.

"I hate having to go back because I forgot something," I added in an extra-smooth voice, as though my mind had never conjured up anything dirty. I stole a quick look at his face, wondering if he'd had any X-rated thoughts. But he looked entirely too calm.

Well, he probably kissed women all the time. *I bet he's forgotten about the kiss already.*

The possibility peeved me. If I was thinking about it, he should be too. But since that didn't seem to be the case, I decided to act like I wasn't either.

"It's been a while since I cooked, so I'll have to pay more attention than normal." Before he wondered if I could produce something edible, I said, "I'm good, but I might not remember to grab the parsley, for one. Cooking is almost like riding a bicycle. You never forget it, even if you might get a bit rusty and out of practice."

"So why don't you cook more often?"

I shrugged. "Too much hassle when it's just me."

"You can't live on crackers and beer."

Oh geez. He sounded like my mom. "I also eat ice cream for protein and fat."

"And candy for carbs. I've seen the wrappers."

"Are you judging me?"

"Just making an observation."

I rolled my eyes. "I also eat TV dinners. They're healthy."

"Full of sodium and preservatives."

"It isn't like you're some paragon of a healthy male specimen," I said, then immediately shut my mouth. That was a dumb rebuttal because Killian looked so healthy that he practically glowed.

Instead of mocking me for being wrong, he merely nodded. "Exactly. I'm not as healthy as I could be because I didn't take care of myself. It's no fun getting wheeled off to a hospital and having a couple bags of IV pumped into your arm."

I glanced at him. I hadn't seen anything about that when I looked him up. But then, I'd been too focused on his basic information, his music and the women and everything that I could easily have overlooked other stuff.

"Did you...um...OD?" I asked, keeping my voice low and calm. I didn't want to give the impression that I was digging for some lurid celebrity gossip. Artistic types often suffered from less-than-stellar mental health—depression, anxiety, insomnia... And lots of them tried to self-medicate.

He made a choking noise. "No, I didn't *OD*. Despite the stereotypes out there about rock musicians, I don't do drugs or indulge in other risky behavior."

"You have to admit, it's not just a stereotype, though. Rock music is littered with corpses. Even I know that."

"Yeah, that's true. But not me. What would I do if I screwed up my voice?"

That was a good point. And it relieved me that he didn't indulge in risky behavior. "So...can I ask why you were in the hospital?"

"Just pushed myself too hard. Skipped one too many meals, had one too many shots of espresso to stay awake. My body kept going, then one day, it decided, 'Fuck it, I'm done,' and bam, I hit the ground. That was almost two months ago."

I gaped at him. I would never have known, based on how strong he was now. But I could understand the need to drive oneself hard. I'd done that too when I first started to write, and had to take a couple of weeks off to recover after my body rebelled. "Did anybody catch you?"

"Dev did, which was the only reason I didn't get a concussion." We reached Sunny's Mart, and Killian killed the engine. "Anyway, you should consider taking care of yourself better unless you want to collapse like me. What if you don't have anyone to catch you?"

He climbed out of the car before I could reply. But he had a point. I was usually alone. I could theoretically crack my head open on the hardwood floor. My skull probably wasn't harder than the oak.

He came around and opened my door while I was still fumbling with the belt.

"What?" he asked.

"I didn't know rock stars opened doors."

"This one does. I was taught to be a gentleman."

Right. A gentleman surrounded by groupies. I swallowed that thought, though. I was here to pay him back for saving me from the giant snake, not obsess about his sexual history.

We headed into the store, where Killian grabbed a cart. As we walked by the produce section, I snapped up two bulbs of garlic and some parsley and dumped them in the cart, careful not to brush by him.

"Butter? Olive oil?" I asked.

"I have both."

"Good. We need some good-sized shrimp, too. Ideally fresh." I didn't cook scampi with small specimens. What was the point?

"I don't see any fresh ones," he said, looking around the seafood section, which was composed of several feet of refrigerated area.

"Okay, then frozen."

I led the way to the freezer, familiar with this part of the store because it had ice cream. But there was no Bouncy Bare Monkeys this time. I would've been shocked if the store had gotten another delivery so soon.

I grabbed a bag of deveined and shelled frozen jumbo shrimps and tossed it in the cart. "We also need some pasta. What kind do you like?" I looked around, wondering where all the employees were. I had no idea where Sunny's Mart kept noodles.

"Pasta's over here." Killian turned the cart to our right. "Linguini good, or you want something else?"

"That's fine," I said, relieved he'd made the choice. Otherwise, I'd have debated for a while wondering what he liked. "Need some wine and bread now. I know where the wine is, but where are all the workers? I don't want to look through all the aisles."

The store usually had at least one or two clerks around stocking shelves, but now that I really needed them...

Killian sighed. "The bread's right there with the wine." He gestured to the open area.

Oh yeah. I noticed the bakery in the open area with all the wines and liquors. I probably didn't know because I never bothered to eat bread. Crackers had plenty of carbs.

"Grab me one good French bread, will you?" I moved over to the wine racks. Since scampi wouldn't be as good with some decent wine, I picked out a nice Sauvignon Blanc from Napa. It'd be about thirty bucks with tax. And a bottle of Pinot Grigio to share over the meal. Might as well splurge a little, I thought with a small smile. This wasn't just a "thank you for saving me" dinner. It was also a small, personal celebration for finally finishing the book.

I turned around, a bottle clutched in each hand, and ran smack into Killian's chest. I lost my balance, falling back, and he caught me, one strong arm looping around my waist. The breath whooshed out of me, and I stared up at him, feeling his hand on my back like a brand. A weirdest thrill sizzled over my skin, goosebumps breaking out.

"Sorry about that. You okay?" Killian asked.

"My fault. I'm fine," I said, my mouth dry. I righted myself, then inhaled, trying to be all cool.

He made a general sort of gesture, indicating the store. "Anything else?"

"Nope. We're all good."

He took the Pinot Grigio from me and studied it. "This is an excellent choice."

I smiled, relieved he wanted to discuss something as innocuous as wine. "I know. If we were having cheeseburgers, I might've offered the beer, but it's Italian."

"You do burgers, too?" he asked, raising both eyebrows.

"Yeah, but shrimp scampi is faster."

CHAPTER 20

Killian

Emily tried to pay for the groceries, but I was faster. I swiped my card before she could.

"Hey!" she said.

"Too slow."

Her mouth pursed. "I don't want you telling me I owe you something else because you paid."

"I won't. You said you'd make me dinner, not pay for the groceries."

"Okay." She shrugged.

Besides, contrary to what I'd told her, I couldn't have her pay for all this. Technically, I'd lied about the snake nest. Thankfully, Emily hadn't realized that because she hadn't Googled the truth yet. My guess was she probably didn't want to see any photos of snakes on her computer. Mir refused to look up anything whose image she didn't want to see on the Internet. She'd also called me an "unforgivable asshole bastard" when I sent her an article about cockroaches' ability to live without their heads for a week.

At the same time, I didn't feel guilty enough to fess up. I wanted to spend more time with Emily, especially now that she was done with her book, and figured she'd set aside a few days to take a break. If the weather was nice, we could have a picnic. Or go to the lake. It was an hour away, but the view was spectacular. It was prettier in the fall when the leaves were red and gold, but it was nice in spring, too. Best to avoid places with lots of crowds, since she seemed to hate that. Better for me, too.

When we arrived home, I carried the groceries in and set them on the kitchen counter.

"Need help with anything?" I asked, hoping she'd say yes. A kitchen was a great place for a couple to get closer. All that innocent accidental brushing of bodies as you grabbed one thing or another for the other person. We could even start drinking while we cooked.

"Nope. You just go chill over there and stay out of the way. It'll go faster that way."

I arched a skeptical eyebrow, slightly disappointed that she wasn't thinking about all the kitchen touching. But she ignored me and started to take things out of the paper bags, putting the Pinot Grigio in the fridge to keep it chilled.

"You want some music?" Nothing set the mood like a good piece of music, and this was the second-best option, since she didn't want me in the kitchen with her. Since she wasn't writing, it shouldn't bother her.

She looked up from turning the oven on. "You want to bang those drums *now*?"

"No," I said, laughing at her expression. She could be unexpectedly adorable. "I meant we should listen to something."

"Why?"

I searched her face. She was genuinely perplexed. She'd told me she didn't listen to music, but...how could she not listen to something while she was making dinner? "Because it's relaxing?" And it would be fun and sexy and...

She shrugged. "If it makes you happy. Whatever you want is fine."

I put on something jazzy and smooth on the Bluetooth speakers.

"How come you aren't playing *your* music?" She minced garlic using a knife, with an expertise and precision that surprised me, then tossed it into a pan of olive oil. Contrary to what she'd claimed, I didn't expect her to be good at it. She'd said she rarely cooked, so when would she have practiced?

"It isn't really, you know, dinner prep music."

"I want to listen to it anyway." She slathered warm butter and the lightly cooked garlic and olive oil inside the French bread.

I was flattered, but also wondered why she was insisting on it. "I thought you wanted me to decide."

She rolled her eyes. "Because I assumed you'd play yours. What rock star wouldn't?" She wrapped the bread in aluminum foil and put it in the oven, which was now hot.

"One who understands time and place?" Also, as much as I loved my band, we didn't exactly put out date music. We had maybe three songs that could be termed romantic, but I didn't want to just loop those three forever.

She smiled. "Yeah, but I want to listen to it. I was going to check out more of your music, but...got a little distracted." Something flashed through her gaze, but it was gone when she blinked.

"Okay." I swapped out the playlist to one I'd created for Axelrod. Our debut hit split the air, the fancy guitar solo by Max kicking off the song. "So. About work and sound."

"Yeah?"

"If you're done with your writing, is it such a big deal if I drum again?" I'd been pretty good about taking care of myself. I wanted to try to see if anything would pop into my head. An inspiration. A word. A note.

"Hmm. That depends."

"On...?" I asked, hoping she wasn't going to ask for a kidney.

"Your keeping windows closed and not doing it for hours on end." She put a bowl of frozen jumbo shrimps under running water to defrost them and glanced at me. "You're a vocalist, and your band has a drummer. Do you really need to practice for that long?"

"It helps me think. And I want to see if I got my creative mojo back," I said, since it wasn't like she was going to tell everyone on streets.

"What's wrong with your mojo?"

"It's been sort of MIA since my health incident. The one I told you about in the car."

She looked me over, her eyes going soft. A warmth that had nothing to do with physical attraction unfurled. It was like...she actually cared about me as a human being, not as some hot celeb dude she could take selfies with to post on social media for likes and comments.

And I liked her. A lot. Not just for her body, not just because the kiss had been hot, but because she made me feel like a person. Somebody worthy of something genuine.

"Aren't you completely recovered now?" she asked finally.

"Physically, yeah. But I have to be creative, too. It's what I do. I don't know what I'd be without it." I didn't want to be a parasite who didn't do anything except live off a trust fund. Grandma had always felt that that was a despicable way to live, and I agreed one hundred percent.

"But your band has other people, like your drummer friend. Devlin. And the guitar guys. Max and Cole, right?"

I nodded, surprised she knew who they were. "We all contribute creatively. Not just to songs, but the direction of our next album, where we want to go musically... All that stuff."

She tapped her chin. "So maybe you shouldn't think about it."

"What?" I let out a stunned laugh. She probably didn't get it. She was a writer, not a performer. "I can't do that. My career's important."

"I didn't say it wasn't. But thinking about it hasn't been working, right? Did you have any inspiration when you were drumming?" she asked. "Like you had this amazing creation going on in your head and I ruined it when I knocked on your door?"

I wish. "No."

"Well, there you go."

"But you think about your stories all the time. You write all the time," I pointed out, annoyed that she was telling me to do the opposite of what she did.

"I don't, actually. You just saw the tail end of my flailing." She looked around. "Paper towels?"

"Here." I walked over, tore a few sheets from under the shelf and handed them to her. Our fingers brushed. My fingertips prickled, a small electric current running all the way up my arm, down my spine and gathering somewhere south.

Did she feel it too?

Emily stilled for a second, her teeth digging into her lip. Her gaze darted from my hand to my face, then to the paper towels she was holding, and her shoulders sagged just a tad. With a small sigh, she turned away and started to pat the shrimp dry.

I didn't understand her reluctance. The women I usually hung out with didn't play *I didn't notice any spark between us* games. Fine, Emily could pretend she hadn't felt it. But I wasn't going to go with that, because I didn't share her reluctance.

I started to move closer, but a soft clearing of her throat stopped me.

"As I was saying," she began, "I was seriously blocked for two weeks with this book, and I was freaking out because I *really* had to hit my deadline. So I read, I watched TV and movies and I slept. Oh, and had a nightly bubble bath."

Okay, so she wanted to talk about my block. I crossed my arms and leaned against the counter space next to her, since figuring out why I was blocked was just as important as getting Emily to admit there was a spark between us.

"Did it work?" Bubble baths weren't my thing, but...

"Nope," she said. "That's why I had to go run. It works wonders. You should try it."

"I do run. As a matter of fact, I have a morning run at least three times a week. It doesn't work. At least, not for me." My mind usually stayed blank when I ran.

She turned around and stared at me in awe...or maybe terror. "What are you?"

"Uh... Is this a trick question?"

"Doesn't the torture of exercise *force* you into creativity? I mean, so you can quit the self-abuse and go back to writing?"

I laughed. "Is that your motivation? Exercise is so bad that your mind has no choice but to come up with something so you can quit?"

"Yeah. It's the nuclear option because it's my absolute last resort...but it works. Just leaves me really tired and shaky. And definitely in need of a lot of sugar and fat. But sometimes I just have to accept that I need to let my mind work on something subconsciously. Trust the process even if I can't feel it working."

She tossed the garlic, butter and oil into the pan and started to stir everything around. The kitchen filled with the most amazing aroma. She then threw in all the shrimp, only using her wrist to flip and turn them.

"Did you ever work in a restaurant?" I asked as she drained the pasta and put it on plates in a swift motion. It was sexy as hell to watch her dominate the kitchen with such confidence. She could win one of those cooking competition shows that Cole and his fiancée loved so much.

"I waited tables in college. It was okay. College kids are usually too poor to tip well. Actually, they never spend enough in the first place." She expertly put the shrimp and sauce on the pasta.

"Ever done a stint in a kitchen? I still haven't mastered the art of flipping things in a flying pan like you just did."

"Oh, that?" Emily flashed a smile, but it couldn't quite hide a tinge of sadness underneath. "It isn't hard. You just need a lot of practice."

"Yeah, but you said you rarely cooked."

She might've done it all the time for one of her exes. The notion sat with me as well as rancid almond butter. Based on her reaction, the bastard—or bastards—hadn't appreciated her effort. If she cooked for me like this all the time I'd handle the cleanup, then draw her one of the bubble baths she seemed to like so much, lick her all over until...

Shrugging, Emily sprinkled chopped parsley over the shrimp scampi and took the plates to the dining room. I grabbed some utensils and helped her set the table, and she immediately returned to the kitchen to take the garlic bread out of the oven.

"Get the wine for me, would you?" she said.

I took out the bottle of Pinot Grigio from the fridge, uncorked it and handed it to her. While she placed it on the table, I grabbed two wine glasses.

"Perfect." She smiled. "We have everything."

I smiled too. It was such a sweetly domestic scene. I hadn't experienced this much. My exes had been too busy to bother, and I realized I liked it a lot more than I'd expected.

I pulled out a chair for Emily, and she sat down.

"No salad or veggies?" I asked, half curious and half teasing, as I settled in my seat. I started to pour wine.

"We have plenty of greens."

"Where?"

"Here." She pointed at some parsley bits with her fork. "See how green that is? And garlic is considered a vegetable, I'm sure. Some kind of vegan thing, anyway. It doesn't come from dead animals."

I laughed. "You eat like a kid."

"Don't knock it. This is a tasty way to eat, and tasty food reduces stress, which is good for you."

Food wasn't the only thing good for me. The company was pretty fine, too. Her pleased smile, the way she said what was on her mind...

We clinked our glasses. "To a neighbor who lets me borrow her hot water."

"To a neighbor who heroically took care of a dastardly snake monster."

The wine was delicious, and the food was even better. I knew it'd be good, but not this good. "Damn."

"Told ya. I'm awesome."

"Did you secretly mock my breakfast because you could do better?"

She laughed. "No. I totally appreciated that because I don't like to cook breakfast." She took a small bite of her bread, then sighed softly. "Dad always left too early, and I was rushed in the morning too. But in the evening, I cooked." She sounded wistful.

"Lucky him," I said.

The soft look in her face vanished and was replaced with the hint of a sneer. "Yeah. Lucky him." From the way she gazed at her pasta, I wasn't sure if she realized the change in her expression. "He sure is a lucky guy."

There was a story there, but I didn't probe. It probably wasn't a happy one. We all had things we didn't want to think about, much less talk about. Now I wished I'd agreed to have her buy me dinner. Then maybe her eyes wouldn't have been so narrow because of old, unpleasant memories.

An impulse to kiss her and make her think about something

other than the past tugged at me. Shockingly, it was less sexual and more on the caring side. Yes, I was attracted to her, but the need to make her smile was the primary driver and motivation. The realization startled me because I'd never had such desire, not even for Caitlyn.

Time to change the subject. "Well, I'm lucky too. Because I'm here in my favorite place in the world with a clever romance writer with a secret talent for cooking."

The unhappiness in her eyes dissipated. "Kingstree is your favorite place?"

I nodded.

"Not the Maldives or whatever super-secret, ultra-luxurious resorts the rich and famous go to for their media-free vacation?"

"What do you know about those places?" I asked. My money and fame opened doors to all that I wanted, things I hadn't even known existed.

"I've written about billionaires, and I do my research. Those places looked nice. Very exclusive."

"I've been to a few," I said, making a mental note to find out if she planned to feature one of them in her next book. Later, of course, since she probably wanted a break from even thinking writing at the moment. But if she wanted to do some in-person research, I'd take her there. Flying absolutely sucked, but I'd put up with it for her. "They're nice, but they're more like a dream you can only stay in for a little while. Everyone has to return to reality. Kingstree is reality for me—and it's fantastic."

She sipped her wine. "How is Kingstree so wonderful for you?"

"I grew up here. My grandmother raised me and my sister here after our parents died, and people know me. I mean the *real* me, not the magazine cover version. They treat me like a person, not a celebrity, and they don't try to use me to their advantage."

"Do people often try? Use you, that is." She regarded me. "You seem too smart to be used."

"Thanks, but they do often try. Lots of women approach me for exactly that."

She shot me a skeptical look as she had another bite of pasta.

"But you like it, right? I mean, you're getting all the sex you want in exchange for hanging out with them. Isn't that how it works?"

"Yeah, but I don't want just sex. I mean, okay, sure, I won't lie. At first it was fun. Like, a *lot* of fun. And it's still fun. But I want somebody I can be friends with, too."

And Caitlyn would never be a friend. Or any of the others, either, now that I thought about it. A "girlfriend" I'd had early on after Axelrod broke out only stuck around because she thought she could use her connection to me to break into the music business. Remembering her reminded me of the reason I'd assumed Caitlyn would work out—she wasn't an aspiring musician.

An old resentment fleeted through me. I should never have assumed anything.

"Don't feel too bad about it," Emily said softly. "I'm not friends with my exes."

"How come?" I asked, part of me happy that she wasn't close to her exes. The latest story by Emily I'd been reading was a reunion romance, where two lovers were getting a second shot. I thought she believed in stuff like that.

"Because they were bastards. I'm not the type to think about what-ifs with some douche who wasn't good enough for me in the first place."

A woman who knew her value. That was hot. "What if one came back for another chance?"

She scoffed. "No way. He could beg on his knees, lick my boots, and I'd still say no. You know what I learned over the years?" She guzzled down half her wine. "People do not change. They can say they did. They can say they're capable. They can make promises. But they don't fundamentally change who they are. Cheaters cheat, liars lie and assholes asshole." She wagged her finger. "And before you say anything, 'asshole' is totally a verb."

"You're pretty cynical for a romance writer. Don't you believe in true, everlasting love?"

She laughed like I'd said the funniest thing ever. "What gave you the idea that something like that is real?"

"My parents. And grandparents. They were together forever and made the best lives possible." And I remembered how much they'd cared for each other, tried to create warm, laughter-filled homes. It was something I'd always imagined I would have at some point in my own life, when I met the right woman.

"My parents have been married forever too, but that doesn't mean there's true love, Killian. It only exists in books and songs, which is why people will pay to read about it. It's a beautiful, fleeting dream, like your super-secret vacations. But like you said, it isn't reality."

If she'd said it with nothing but cynicism and mockery, I might've argued. But there was such calm acceptance and wistfulness to her that I couldn't bring myself to say anything over the odd fist of emotions lodged in my throat. Maybe she'd been too badly burned by some asshole. I found myself hoping that he was impotent, too.

She gave me a small smile. "Don't look so shocked. Here. Have more wine." She poured some Pinot Grigio for me, as though alcohol would be enough to soothe the burning ache her words had left in my chest.

But I didn't want the wine. As soon as she set the bottle down, I held her hand, then kissed the knuckles. "I'm not shocked. Just sad that you think it can only happen for your imaginary couples, but not for you."

Emily

I went still as the impact of his words hit me. It wasn't even that he was saying anything super enlightening. I'd thought the same in the past. But no other man had ever voiced it. And no other man had looked at me like he wanted a chance to change my mind.

Longing shot through me, because yeah, it would be amazing to have a happy ending like my couples. But then fear followed, chilling me from the inside out. Even my heart seemed to beat unevenly at the idea. If I hadn't been able to find anything close to a romance-novel happy ending, what made me think I could find it now, especially with a rock star who had hot young things chasing after him all the time?

Because he isn't chasing them back. Because he's with you right now.

And I wanted to listen to that voice, let him show me what was possible. But the walls around my heart remained. The suspicions and the old scars didn't just vanish.

Suddenly I couldn't draw in enough air, like the day I'd published my book for the first time. I stood up. "I have to go. I forgot to...uh...do something."

Smooth, Emily. So smooth.

I looked down at my plate. I'd eaten all the shrimp, left some pasta. It wasn't a big deal. If I got hungry later, I'd munch on Animal Crackers. "You mind taking care of the cleanup? Actually, if you want, I'll do it tomorrow."

"I'll take care of it." Killian rose, peering at me. "You okay?"

"Yeah, fine. I just, you know, forgot something, and I have to take care of it right now. Otherwise...er...my editor can't start working on my book." It was a terrible lie, but he wasn't a writer. He wouldn't know.

I rushed home...then stopped in front of the door. Shit. *The snake nest.* I pulled out my phone to call the pest control and animal removal company, and spotted a text from them an hour earlier informing me my house was clear. My phone must've gone off while I was cooking.

I went inside my house. Now that I was away from Killian, my heart was beating more steadily, my skin wasn't prickling and my chest didn't feel funny.

I trudged to the fridge, keeping an eye out for random serpents, and grabbed a beer. I wished I hadn't said anything about my faith in real love—or lack thereof. It wasn't something I'd ever told anybody. As a romance author, it was expected of me to believe in the power of love, just like Killian was supposed to believe in the power of rock and roll.

It was just that my guard came down every time I was around him. He made it easy for me to bypass my safeguards—even my all-time favorite: keep my mouth shut so nobody would have anything to lob back at me. My dad had taught me the value of silence by using his cross-examination skills over and over again to corner me into saying or admitting things I didn't believe in.

I put my feet up on the table, slowly sipped my beer and thought back on the day so I'd be better prepared next time I saw Killian. I wondered what it was like to believe in love the way he did. He'd seemed genuine when he told me. On the other hand, my exes had seemed pretty genuine too until things started to get hard for them. As in I'd started to pay more attention to my career than their needs.

It was most likely that Killian loved the *idea* of love—having somebody who'd put him above all else. Didn't rock stars have egos? He was successful, too. And hot. It only made sense.

I cued up Netflix to watch some movies until I fell asleep, even as my mind whispered that Killian might be different.

CHAPTER 21

Killian

The morning after the dinner with Emily, Billy's Plumbing and All Things Water called. They had a cancelation, and could come out if I was okay.

Was the sky blue? Hell yeah, I was okay. I wanted hot water for my dishwasher and laundry. Grandma had always said the whites never looked right without a hot-water cycle, and my recent loads had proven her right.

So I put some music on and waited for their work van to show up while reading one of Emily's books. But I kept drifting, thinking about Emily's reaction toward the end of the dinner. The wide, uncomfortable look in her eyes. The squirming. The slight trembling of her fingers. I didn't think she'd realized how transparent she was. An unfamiliar ache wrapped around me, because she was obviously freaked out about making what we had between us something more.

My phone—the personal one—buzzed on the table, interrupting my train of thought. I picked it up to see who it was, since it wasn't playing Darth Vader's theme.

Group video call with the guys. I hadn't talked to them in a while. Smiling, I answered it.

"Hey."

"Yo, yo, yo, yo! How's life?" Dev said with a wide grin. Mischief and good humor lit his eyes, his black hair slicked back. The man hadn't shaved in at least two days, but that undoubtedly hadn't stopped him from scoring. It looked like he was in a hotel suite.

"I'm good. How's Fiji?" I asked. He'd been wanting to go since forever, and had split for the archipelago as soon as the tour was over and the doctors said I was okay.

"Wasn't bad. But I'm in Spain now. Lots of hot chicks, man. *Lots* of hot chicks."

I almost laughed. Dev lived for women. He didn't believe in "limiting his horizons," and he was the biggest reason the band always had a swarm of women buzzing around. They knew he welcomed them all, even if I didn't. And that was okay. It was a big improvement over the dark phase of his life immediately after his relationship with Ashley imploded. She'd been cheating on him, and he basically quit believing in commitment.

"You should join me," Dev said. "I know you hate flying, but man, it's awesome. I kept a box of chocolate-flavored condoms for you."

"Thanks, but I haven't even opened the one you snuck into my bag." It had been his not-so-subtle way of telling me to get laid. There was no problem a vagina couldn't fix.

Max rolled his eyes. He also enjoyed women, but didn't pursue them the way Dev did.

Cole merely shook his head. He was engaged, so he kept his dick on the straight and narrow.

"How you feeling, K? Better?" Max said.

"Yup," I replied, smiling a little. Max never called me Killian. Mainly because he didn't want to say more syllables than absolutely necessary. He preferred nonverbal communication when possible, grunting when some kind of sound was required.

But that didn't mean he didn't say what needed to be said. Max was the one who'd suggested taking time off and doing our own thing after my hospitalization. We'd lived and breathed in each other's space for a decade. He thought it'd do us good to do our separate thing for some time. Everyone had agreed, and we generally looked more energetic and rested now, the break and time away obviously having done everyone some good.

Did I look better too? I was still bothered by the fact that my brain wasn't creating music yet, but I didn't bring it up. I didn't want to cause any unnecessary concerns when I hadn't given Emily's method a try yet. Not the bath idea, but trusting the process. I hadn't done that before because I'd never had to. Ideas had always come to me in a fire-hydrant gush, more than I could ever possibly use. But things were different now, and I was a firm believer in trying pretty much anything at least once to see if it works.

"You're always welcome to come hang with me and Teri if you're tired of small-town living," Cole said.

"Thanks, man, but it's okay. Kingstree's treating me well." Besides, as nice as his repeated offer was, I didn't want to intrude. Time on the road could be hard on a couple, and I wanted Cole and Teri to have as much privacy and time together as they needed.

"Or you can join me," Dev said. "Nothing recharges you like a country full of willing women."

"Women aren't vitamins," I said.

"Dude, they're like vitamin *coffee.* They wake you up. Make you think better. Make you feel young and studly."

"Still no thanks." I had no reason to fly thousands of miles for that when I had Emily next door. She made me laugh and put me off my guard, and I liked her. And she made me want to shield her from the world, even though the urge was ridiculous. But when she had that sad, resigned look in her eyes yesterday, I'd felt the need anyway.

"Bro, you still sore about Caitlyn?" Dev asked.

Cole tightened his mouth. "She's a bitch." He knew how I felt about people violating my privacy—and trying to profit off me. "She recently posted that she had to leave you because you were impotent."

I let out a hollow laugh. *Of course she did.* Caitlyn would say or do anything for attention. She probably didn't know I'd blocked everything—all her social media and email accounts, phone numbers, everything—so I couldn't see any of her shit.

"Don't worry. I commented and reminded her that she didn't leave you, but you threw her out like month-old trash because she was frigid and fourth-rate in bed," Dev said, his eyes flinty. "I also added that no self-respecting man wants to stick his dick in a bag of icy sand."

Damn. I *almost* felt sorry for Caitlyn, although she'd kind of asked for it. Dev had a thing about women who betrayed their men, and he had a very sharp tongue.

Max grunted. "Total bitch." Three syllables meant he had my back one thousand percent, no questions asked.

"She sure is, but just so you know, she has nothing to do with my life anymore. I've completely blocked her." I put the book down and shifted on the couch to get more comfortable. Emily was the one who occupied my thoughts.

Devlin's eyes grew large. "*The Very Bossy Engagement*?" He laughed. "What the hell are you reading?"

"Chick book," Max said. He sounded like he was in shock.

Cole frowned like he was trying to remember something. "I think Teri liked that one..."

"She likes Emma Grant?" What a coincidence. My baby sister, and now Cole's fiancée. Emily must have been more famous than I'd realized.

Or maybe not, because Cole looked confused.

"Who's Emma Grant?" Dev said. "Your new girl?"

"Hot?" Max grunted.

"Is she a rebound? Hotter than Caitlyn?" Cole said.

I considered that. Emily was nothing like Caitlyn, and I didn't think of my ex when I was around Emily. She wasn't hot in the flashy, overtly sexual sense. Not like Caitlyn or the women who swarmed around us—or around Dev in particular. Emily was beautiful in a quiet and almost nerdy way, seemingly unaware of her feminine appeal. Or maybe she simply didn't care about people who only wanted her when she had perfect makeup and a thousand-dollar dress on.

But no matter how messy her hair was, whether she wore glasses or not, or what crazy shirts and pants she put on, she made me feel alive. Interested. *Engaged*. She was one of a few women who didn't make me feel like I had to be "on"...being the rock star

Killian Axelrod. I could just be a guy, who happened to live next to her house, and she treated me that way, even though she now knew who I was.

It was liberating and sexy as hell.

And she tasted like heaven, too, my dick reminded me as it swelled.

"Of course she's hot. Why would you date an unhot chick?" Dev said before I could answer.

"*Unhot* isn't a word," I said.

"It is when you're discussing people." Dev grinned. "Got a pic?"

"No," I said, not wanting to share even her official author photo. I didn't want Dev checking her out when she and I hadn't cemented anything yet. We'd had that one kiss...and the dinner. I wanted us to be an official couple before Dev met her. That way, he wouldn't scare the shit out of her by wanting to know if she was a faithful type or some bullshit like that. "She's a writer, and my next-door neighbor."

"But... *The Very Bossy Engagement*? That's a thick book. She worth all that effort?" Dev asked, growing more serious.

"It's a *good* book." I defended Emily's creation, feeling like she would've done the same for my music. I hoped.

"I watch chick flicks with Teri," Cole said. "They aren't that bad. I mean, as long as you don't mind watching something dull that your woman thinks is funny."

"Obviously they weren't her books adapted into movies," I pointed out.

"You have a fucking crush on her," Dev said.

Max grunted his agreement.

"Shut it," I said. I liked Emily and all, but a crush? That sounded so...junior high.

"Your face is getting red," Dev said.

"He's right." Cole grinned, the traitor.

"He hasn't slept with her yet." Dev said.

"Uh, guys? Hello? I'm, like, right here with you."

"Yeah, right there blushing," said Cole.

"It's the lighting. Sunset." I gestured in the direction of the windows.

Cole guffawed. "Does the sun set at three sixteen p.m. in Virginia?"

"Fuck off," I said, since I couldn't come up with a better comeback.

"Just do her and you won't have to read about bossy engagements anymore," Dev said. "Besides, it isn't like you can stay in Virginia indefinitely. Do her before June. It'd be a bitch driving back and forth between Virginia and Dallas."

I paused. June wasn't even two months away. But that was when our vacation was over, and we were supposed to get back together and start working. We'd be in Dallas, and Emily would be here. In Kingstree.

The idea of being away from her clenched around my chest and squeezed until it hurt. For some bizarre reason, I couldn't imagine not having breakfast together. Or just hanging out, reading her books and talking with her.

Loud knocks on the door came, pulling me out of the sudden funk.

"Billy's!" the man at the door boomed.

"Gotta go. It's my plumber."

"Is that what you call her?" Dev laughed harder.

Even Max and Cole sniggered.

"It's *the plumber*. For my water heater." I gave the gang the Vulcan salute. "Fuck off and prosper."

I hung up and opened the door to a couple of burly-looking men who looked like they could play extras in a prison yard scene. Then I prayed they knew what they were doing with water heaters.

CHAPTER 22

Killian

The next day I got up early and went for a hard run. I kept thinking about what my band mates had said.

June First.

Then no more Emily.

Despite the sweat pouring down my body, I felt a cold shiver along my spine. It made my teeth clench.

Cole and Teri stayed together despite a lot of time apart and all the bullshit that came with him being in a rock band because they'd known each other since forever. Emily and I had barely exchanged a kiss.

If I left Kingstree in June, she'd move on. Probably find some other guy who didn't play the drums or guitar or sing. The fucker might have heard of Emma Grant before meeting her. Might even be a fan and consider it his duty and privilege to cook for her. If gods loved me, he'd be terrible in bed. Otherwise, Emily would let him stay for more than ten minutes.

It was a predictable outcome. And unreasonable of me to expect she'd pine away for me or swear off other men forever. But her with some other guy sat in my belly like a lump of cold, congealed fat. I wanted to barf, even as my legs moved faster, my strides long and furious.

My jaw ached. I forced the muscles to relax. My dentist would be unhappy if I cracked a molar.

After looping around the trail three times, I headed home. Billy's Plumbing had replaced my water heater, and it was producing plentiful hot water.

But I'd be damned if I'd take advantage of that.

I grabbed my stuff—and breakfast ingredients—and went over to Emily's house. It was after eight, so she was probably up. Or maybe she'd be sleeping in after finishing her project.

I knocked extra quietly just in case. If she was sleeping in her room, she wouldn't hear me. But if she was in the living room, she would.

She opened the door with a confused look, squinting at me through her glasses. She'd told me she wore them when her eyes felt too dry for contact lenses or if she'd stayed up too late. I hoped she'd been up all night thinking about me. But it was more likely she'd been thinking about her next book.

"What are you doing here?" she asked, sweeping her gaze over my sweaty body.

I watched her mouth move as she spoke. Everything inside me tightened, blood pumping hotter and faster, even though I should have been cooling down after the run. "Here for a shower, like always."

"Isn't your water heater fixed? I saw the contractor's van outside your house yesterday."

"Oh...you did? Yeah, uh, the water heater they brought over was DOI." Dev would be proud. He believed white lies were perfectly ethical, if done in the service of getting a girl you wanted. I wasn't a fan of lying in general, but I had kept my promise not to play the drums, so I felt like I'd earned the right to use her shower.

"DOI?"

"Dead on installation."

Her frown grew deeper. "Seriously? Didn't they test it before bringing it over?"

"Probably not. If they'd installed it in somebody's house, it wouldn't look new. People don't want to pay new equipment prices for stuff that looks used," I said, certain she wouldn't know anything about contractors or how they worked. Most people didn't. Hell, *I* didn't. The crew that had come yesterday probably tested the water heater before leaving their office to make sure they wouldn't have to come out a second time.

"Oh. Well, okay." She let me in and went to her tablet on the coffee table.

I followed her inside, thanking my lucky stars Emily bought my story. The house looked tidier. No empty beer bottles or candy wrappers.

Since I was sweaty, I put the pancake mix and bacon on the counter and went upstairs for a quick shower. I still didn't have a plan for what to do about leaving in June and Emily being in Kingstree. I couldn't exactly ask her to come with me. We weren't anything yet.

But I felt like I couldn't leave her behind, either.

The thing was that I didn't know how to move us to the next stage soon enough that when I broached the topic of going to Dallas, she wouldn't look at me like I'd lost my mind. If it had been any woman but Emily, things might've gone smoother and easier. I could've dazzled her with my fame or songs or whatever. But then, if Emily were the type to drool over all that, I wouldn't like her.

Catch-22s were a bitch.

I should let my subconscious work it out. A perfect plan would probably bubble up from *somewhere*. Running hadn't produced anything, but maybe sticking my finger into a live socket would. Self-torture might work, the way Emily had claimed.

When I was back down in the kitchen, Emily was tapping at her tablet, her eyebrows pinched. I made pancakes and fried up the bacon—feeding her could never hurt whatever plan I'd come up with later—then served everything on the dining table.

"Breakfast is ready," I said.

"So soon?" She sniffed. "Mmm, bacon..."

Her smile made my chest puff out like a peacock. She came over and we sat down to fill our stomachs.

"Hey, which do you like better?" she asked, showing me a picture of a book cover on the tablet. After a moment, she flipped to another image. The model was the same, but the lettering was different. One had a swirly font in hot pink and baby blue, and the other had a blockier one in red and white.

"Is that your cover?"

She nodded. "I didn't get to finalize it earlier because my cover artist was sick."

"I like the pink and blue." My sister would like that one, and Emily was selling to women.

"Really?" Her eyebrows went up. "Not the block font?"

"Women like pink."

"Hmm. True." She looked at the pink and blue version again. "You're probably right." She grinned. "The model's hot no matter what font you put around him."

Was he? I wasn't paying attention to the guy at all, but I should've known that would be Emily's focus. "Lemme see that again."

She gave me the tablet. Yeah, he was a handsome bastard. Smirking, his eyes on the potential reader. The suit worked for him, too. But I bet he didn't look nearly as good out of his clothes. Most men didn't, I decided, ignoring the small bit of acidic burn in my belly. "You like guys in suits?" The last time I'd put on a suit was Grandma's funeral.

"Oh yeah. Nothing says billionaire like a man in a suit. And I like 'em pretty. Real pretty. As long as they're pretty, they don't have to be in suits." She gave me a long, speculative look, opened her mouth like she wanted to say something, then cleared her throat. "So. When are they coming back to replace your defective heater?"

No way that was what she wanted to ask. And she didn't have to sound so eager to get rid of me. I'd been a pretty decent hot-water borrower. "They weren't sure. Next month, maybe?" It was the first thing that popped into my head. So I added in mumble, "Something like that."

She dropped her jaw. "*Next month*? Who are they again? I'm going to blacklist them."

Sorry, Billy. But I'll leave a fair review on Yelp. Which actually wouldn't be all that complimentary, especially given how uncaring and uninterested their phone person had been when I contacted them. "They weren't very specific."

"You didn't pay them for the nonworking heater, did you?"

"Uh, no. Not yet." Oh look: my nose seemed to have grown two inches. "I'll pay them when they replace it."

"Next month, geez. Are they mining the iron to make the heater with?"

"Probably." I laughed as her eyebrows moved up and down in outrage. I didn't think she was aware of the tic, and it reminded me of an angry marmot I'd seen on a documentary once.

"So, does this mean you'll be coming over to use my shower for the foreseeable future?" she asked, a little too casually. And I swore there was something hopeful in her gaze. Whether she was just interested in my breakfast or the bare chest display, she wanted me to stick around.

That put me in a much better mood. "I doubt I'll be for *too* long." I used the same casual tone she had, trying to see how she'd react to what I was about to say. "If nothing else, I'll be going to Dallas in June."

She studied the three strips of bacon on her plate, then finally picked one. "For what?"

"That's where our studio is." Dallas was a good choice because Teri lived there. It gave Cole a chance to be with his fiancée as much as possible. "Gotta get back to work sometime."

Emily looked up. Surprise crossed her eyes, even though her features were set in neutral line. "So you'll be gone?"

"Yeah." Then I casually added, "You going to miss me?"

I wanted her to say yes. I wanted her to realize maybe she liked me a lot more than she'd expected and decide to move our relationship further. Not limited to a kiss or ten minutes in bed, but much, much more.

She swallowed her water. "I'll certainly miss your breakfasts."

Disappointment tugged at me, hard. Then stung pride wrapped around me like armor. "I can teach you how to make it before I go." It'd give us more time to spend together.

"No, thank you. I prefer that you cook." She cleared her throat. "Besides, I don't normally eat breakfast like this anyway. You've been spoiling me." She focused her gaze on me. Her eyes were as clear as the pond on the outskirts of the town. They were the kind of eyes that could pull a man in and make him forget his own name.

"I like you, Emily." The words tumbled down from my lips before I could regain my better judgment.

She inhaled sharply, the tip of one eyebrow tilting up. "Even when I take all the Bouncy Bare Monkeys and Hop Hop Hooray?"

"Even then."

Her soft lips parted. "Killian, I—"

Darth Vader's theme blared from my phone and shattered the moment. *Shit.*

Emily straightened and pulled back a bit. "You should answer that."

I hit the red button. "It can wait. I want to know what you have to say."

CHAPTER 23

Emily

I bit my lip, my mind blank. It was ridiculously ironic that I, a writer, couldn't think of anything clever to say.

But when I wrote, I got a chance to revise. I couldn't travel back in time and emend a real-time conversation. And that was why I hadn't been able to say any of the things that had been flashing through my head since Killian said he'd be gone in June.

Weird. Why hadn't I thought of that possibility before? He might be from Kingstree, but he'd left. He had his own career and things to do. Tours and interviews. Maybe professional conferences. Did musicians have music conferences?

I didn't want him to teach me how to make breakfast like him. I wanted him to be here and make the breakfast every day. Or at least stop by every morning.

When had I become so dependent and needy? The realization was scary, but there was nothing I could do to change how I felt. It was as though Killian had somehow managed to slip through my shell and lodged himself inside me. Like a grain of sand that later became a pearl.

I was going to *miss* him. Even if he'd said he liked me, it didn't change the fact that he was going to be gone in June. Being one of hundreds of notches on his bedpost wasn't my idea of a nice spring fling.

His phone rang again. He swore.

"You should definitely answer that. Nobody ignores Darth Vader and lives," I said, relieved at the interruption. Whoever was calling must have been ultra-scary for him to assign that ring tone.

Sighing with irritation, he answered it. "Yes, Mir?"

I started eating again, trying not to listen to his call in case it was private. That wasn't like me, either. I listened to phone conversations all the time. I liked to guess what the other person was saying and what the speakers' relationship was. Sometimes I got story ideas that way.

But Killian was a celebrity. He wouldn't like people using details from his life in a book—even if it was fiction—when it might be recognizable to oodles of music listeners around the world. I wouldn't want to use him that way. He'd earned his spotlight, his fame. Nobody had the right to leech off it.

He hung up, looking annoyed. "Sorry. That was my sister."

Darth Vader was his sister? "Is she okay?" I asked even though what I really wanted to ask was: *Are you okay?* Whatever she wanted couldn't be good, especially if she was the evil Sith. And I understood better than anybody how complicated and dysfunctional a family could be...and how you couldn't ignore it, no matter what. Just look at the way I'd been dealing with my parents' marriage.

"No. She's on her way here. To visit me...supposedly."

Supposedly? Weren't they close? Or maybe they'd fought recently?

"Surprise visit, my ass," he muttered.

Yup, definitely annoyed. "Do you need to get going?" I wished there was something I could do for him. Except what could I do? I wasn't his family or girlfriend or anything. I was just a neighbor.

Three firm knocks came from the door. I glared, wondering about the interruption. I hadn't ordered anything.

Killian got up and opened the door. "Hey, Mir," he said.

His sister was *here*? Like, at my house? But why?

I craned my neck to get a look at the person who merited supervillain music, but Killian was blocking my view.

"Oh my God, you didn't tell me you were having breakfast with Emma Grant!" Killian's sister squealed.

That didn't sound like somebody who deserved Darth Vader's theme. Actually, she sounded like...a fan.

And I wasn't sure what to make of that. I'd heard from friends that they had weird, stalkerish fans show up at their house, but I'd never had it happen to me. Besides, this was Killian's sister. Did she count as a stalker fan or a standard fan?

On the other hand, would your everyday fan show up at your doorstep?

"You didn't ask," Killian said.

"Wha—?" his sister said. "Because you never even gave me a hint that—"

"I don't *hint*. I *state*. I'm a man."

"Can I see her? Please?" She started hopping, the top of her head appearing intermittently over his shoulder. "She's my *favorite* author!"

I sighed, wishing I were somewhere else. I was not ready to meet a fan, no matter how much she liked me, especially when it was Killian's sister.

"She might not want to," he said. "You can't just barge in."

"I'm here to visit *you*. And it isn't my fault that instead of being home, you're over here with my favorite author."

"Oh, so it's my fault?" Killian said.

"Okay, fine! I'm only about ten percent here to see you, and ninety percent hoping I'd run into Emma Grant. I just didn't want to sound like a freak. Now come on! I missed her book signing in D.C.!"

Since I didn't want any bloodshed, verbal or otherwise, I stepped forward and gently tapped Killian's shoulder, all the while thanking my lucky stars that I'd picked up the trash the night before, and that I was in a T-shirt that was only four or five years old and my yoga pants had been freshly laundered this week. "It's okay. I don't mind."

Then I looked at the petite woman. She had a sleek brown bob, warm with a hint of golden highlights, but her eyes were the same intense blue as Killian's. The bridge of her small, narrow nose was freckled, and unlike her brother, her complexion was milky white, typical of somebody who worked in an office all the time. The Axelrod T-shirt she wore had autographs from all the band members, and her black denim shorts were neat and looked new. She even had her nails done in pink. There was nothing remotely dark or evil about her, but I reminded myself not to judge a book by its cover. My dad was clean-cut and suave, with the kind of smile that put you at ease, but he was a complete dick.

Killian's sister stared at me like I'd just saved her from Genghis Khan's Mongol horde. Meanwhile, I was trying to remember whether I'd brushed my hair. And I wished I were wearing something other than a black T-shirt that said *Short Your Innocence and Long Your Pain*. I'd custom-ordered it the day I became disillusioned with my old corporate job and drank like my liver was made of titanium.

"Wow. You're *Emma Grant*," she whispered.

"And who are you?"

"I'm Miriam, but please call me Mir. All my friends do."

Were we...*friends*?

"I absolutely *adore* your books," she said.

My cheeks heated. I could never get used to this. I was still stunned and ridiculously blessed that people not only read my books, but really liked them. Mainly because every time *I* reread my old books, I wanted to rephrase things, work in new character motivations and tweak descriptions and dialogue. It was an oddly contradictory feeling, because I was generally proud of my writing.

"Hi. Thank you," I said with a smile, hoping she was too star-struck to notice anything except the fact that she was meeting her favorite author. Then I remembered her brother was a big freakin' celebrity. She wouldn't stay impressed for long.

Sure enough, her gaze dropped to my shirt. "That's such a cool saying."

"Yeah," I said vaguely.

"I don't think you've written anything angsty, though. Are you going to?" Mir asked me, half curious, half anxious. "I really love your rom-coms."

"It's a shirt I bought on a whim. I'm still writing rom-com," I said with a smile that would hopefully reassure this woman.

"Oh, awesome. Angsty books make me cry, which makes my eyes swell up like dinner rolls, you know? Not a good look when I have to go to work."

"I'm sure," I said, waiting for her to reveal her dark side or go wherever she needed to go to. But she just stood there, her eyes bright and expectant. "Do you want to come in?"

"You don't have to," Killian said.

"Shut *up*," Mir muttered, then turned to me. "Can I?" she said in her regular voice. Then she nodded to herself. "Yeah, of course. I'd love to. Thank you."

She was flustered. It was cute. And it made me wonder what she'd done to deserve that ringtone.

She came in and Killian shut the door. He caught my eye and mouthed, *Sorry*.

I shook my head with a small smile. It seemed like Mir had ambushed him with the visit, like my mom did with me when she needed somebody to sob to about Dad's infidelity. I wasn't going to hold it against him.

"Have you had breakfast yet?" I asked.

"Yeah, I ate on the way. An Egg McMuffin."

"You eat like a kid," Killian muttered, staying close to his sister.

"Breakfast of champions."

I raised my eyebrows. He must have something against quick and tasty food. He'd said something similar over the shrimp scampi, too. As far as I was concerned, anything not ready to eat right out of a box or a bag was adult food.

"He disapproves, but I like food that I don't have to slave over." Mir noticed the notes on the coffee table. "Wow. Are those for the next book?"

"Yes, for the May release." I started to move forward to stop her when she began to approach the table. They were my promo ideas and tasks to complete. I didn't let anybody look at them except my mom and the PR company I'd hired.

"Hey, hey, hey," Killian said before I could. "Stay away from her inspiration. You're going to jinx it."

"Oh, that's right." Mir stepped back, her gaze still on the notes. But she was too far away to read anything. Not to mention she'd have to decipher my shorthand. She turned to me. "I'm so glad to meet you. I worked extra hard to take time off."

"Oh. Well...I hope it's worth it." I didn't know what else to say.

"Totally." Mir was gazing at me, her eyes shining. A moment of silence stretched.

"Um... Want something to drink?"

"I'm okay," she said. "Thank you."

Killian looked like he needed something strong, but he didn't ask. And I didn't offer. He knew where the alcohol was kept, and that he was welcome to it.

I gestured at Mir to sit with me at the dining table then flipped my notebook shut so she couldn't see anything. Killian joined us, positioning himself between me and Mir.

"So what do you do?" I asked. Mir had spoken of taking time off like it was some sort of feat.

"I'm an accountant. I audit, though, which is the only reason I could take two days off. Otherwise, my manager would've fired me for even asking. I wanted more, but I have to drive back tomorrow after lunch. There's a meeting I really can't miss."

I nodded. That was so corporate. And I didn't miss that lifestyle. But I also felt guiltily grateful that she would be leaving tomorrow afternoon. I couldn't deal with people in close proximity for much longer than that.

"By the way, are those for a book about Miriam Young?" Mir asked, gesturing at the papers.

"No."

"Who's Miriam Young?" Killian looked confused.

"One of my secondary characters," I said. "A popular one."

"Are you going to write about her?" Mir asked.

"Maybe at some point. I can't say for sure." Just because a character was popular didn't mean my brain came up with suitable ideas for a book. Actually, it was harder to come up with something for an established character because I had to work within specific parameters.

"I hope you do. I *love* Miriam Young, and it's extra cool

because we have the same first name. It got me so psyched, you know? The story felt more real to me. And if you write one about her, it'll be like *I'm* inside the story when the hero whispers my name."

Killian made a choking noise next to me. He was probably vowing never to read any book with a Miriam as the heroine.

Mir went on like she hadn't noticed Killian's reaction. "And..."

I sighed, resigned. I wasn't going to get any work done today.

"We should get going," Killian said. "Emily has stuff to do."

"Really?" Mir looked surprised. She'd probably assumed, just like Molly Patterson, that I wouldn't have a set work schedule because I worked from home.

I didn't have a schedule I had to stick to, per se, but that didn't mean I could just, on a whim, dedicate a bunch of hours in my day to something else. Like hanging out with an unexpected guest.

"But I thought you'd have to work on your next album," Mir said in a small voice, sending a glance in my direction.

"Well, yeah, but I'm not drumming or playing the guitar."

Although he didn't say it like he was upset—after all, it'd been a fair deal—I suddenly realized just how long I'd made him stay away from his music. If somebody forced me to stop writing for four weeks, I didn't know how I'd react.

And he had to leave in less than two months. I had no clue how rock bands worked, but as Axelrod's frontman, Killian would probably have to bring some ideas.

"Why don't you go do what you need to do for your next album?" I suggested.

"But..."

I inhaled deeply and waved him away, firming up my resolve. Otherwise I might have chickened out of spending time with Mir, who seemed like one of those exhausting super-extroverts. "I'll hang out with your sister while you work, if that'll make you feel better."

Killian looked at me, as anxious as if he were leaving an unsupervised child near a pool. "Are you *sure*?" he said.

"Very. Go on. Go do your...drum thing or whatever. I'm not writing today, so it won't bother me."

"You should listen to her. She knows everything," Mir said with a smug smile.

Killian looked torn, but I made a shooing motion with my hand. He started walking backward, his eyes on Mir. "Behave," he warned her.

"You know I will." She stuck her tongue out, then grinned.

"Don't bother Emily too much. She has a lot of work to do even if she's not writing today," he said before shutting the door behind him.

Mir turned to me, an apprehensive look on her face. "Are you really busy? I mean, I can just go hang out at a café or something so you can get stuff done."

I smiled. At least, unlike some people, Mir recognized when she might be wrong about my workload and was willing to adjust her expectations. "It's okay. I just turned in a book. So I can afford to take some time off while waiting for editorial feedback. And besides, it's only one day."

Her eyes lit up. "Your editor is *sooooo* lucky. She gets to read your book before it gets released."

"I'm sure she doesn't feel that way." Especially given that I had never gotten an editorial letter shorter than ten pages from her. The woman was thorough, but then, I paid her to be thorough. I would've fired her otherwise.

"We should celebrate," Mir said, clapping her hands together like an excited child.

"Celebrate what?"

"You finishing your book! Don't you do that after each book?"

"Um... Not really." I did once, when I finished my first book, but never since. There were always things to do after I turned in a manuscript, and the more I wrote, the more of a routine it became. I blinked at her flushed face. Was it going to destroy her illusions about me and my career?

"But it's such a *huge* achievement! If you don't celebrate, I mean..." She trailed off, clearly at a loss. "What do you do when you've accomplished something awesome?"

My idea of celebration usually involved some beer, ice cream and a good movie or a book. Possibly, if I felt extra indulgent, sleeping in for the following day or two. But I was pretty sure that wasn't what Mir had in mind.

"We should go out!" Mir said. "Sam's Brew has karaoke night today, which means Hop Hop Hooray beer specials. It's an awesome bar, and everyone loves it. I'm sure Killian would be happy to come along, too," Mir added, probably as a final convincing.

I looked at her awkwardly. I'd never been to Sam's Brew—hadn't been planning to go—and karaoke wasn't my idea of fun. But didn't seem possible to say no to that expectant face. She looked like a puppy waiting for a walk. "Yeah, sure. It sounds... great." *As long as you don't expect me to sing.*

"Yay!" She clasped her hands together. "Do you have anything to wear?"

I looked down at myself. "T-shirts and jeans okay?" I should have something respectable. And my vanity had some makeup I used for signings and conferences.

Mir gasped, scandalized. "Sam's Brew has dress code. We'd be kicked out in T-shirts and jeans."

"A place in this town has a dress code?" *You've got to be kidding.* "What am I supposed to wear, then?"

"Something sexy, of course."

I mentally reviewed my closet's contents. There was nothing that could be labeled *sexy.* Now I was already beginning to regret agreeing to this so-called celebration, because I realized I'd have to do more than just eat ice cream or watch something on Netflix with a huge bucket of popcorn. I contained a sigh. This was too high maintenance.

She studied me, her eyes narrowed. "We need to go shopping."

CHAPTER 24

Emily

After I tied my hair into a ponytail, Mir pulled me into her car and drove us to the small strip mall where Sunny's Mart was located. A boutique with a colorful blue and purple sign that read "Fashionista's Dream" stood at the opposite end. I stared at it in shock. I hadn't realized clothing stores existed in this town for some reason. But of course Kingstree would have at least one. It wasn't like the people here were walking around naked.

Mir led me into the store. Actually, herded might be a better word, since she was behind me, blocking my exit should I change my mind. Thin gray industrial-grade carpet muffled our footsteps. The store had multiple sections—clothes, shoes and accessories for babies, children and adults. It even sold underwear in one corner. The fluorescent lights cast bright but harsh illumination. The place looked a bit claustrophobic, due to the low ceiling. But at least that meant everything was within my reach. I hated asking for help from clerks, because that meant interacting with people.

A middle-aged lady with reddish hair and murky green eyes came toward us waving both hands. Her colorful, loose tunic sleeves fluttered to the movements of her arms. "Well, hello, Mir!"

"Hey, Val!"

"You visiting with a friend?"

Mir laughed, her cheeks red. "This is Killian's next-door neighbor, Emily."

"Oh my goodness." Val put a hand over her generous chest. "I never thought I'd run in to you. Thought you were a legend, like the yetis!"

"Not a legend," I murmured. I just preferred to keep to myself, which didn't make me a yeti. But if I had it my way, I'd have remained a legend. A hermit legend.

"Apparently not." She stared at me with an uncomfortably bright gleam in her eyes. "Heard from Jo Anne that you wanted to have Killian arrested for playing the drums. Is that true?"

My jaw slackened. What was she talking about?

"You did?" Mir said.

"No. Who is Jo Anne and why would she say that?" I demanded, annoyed by the gossip. "And why would anyone believe it?"

"She's one of the 911 dispatchers here," Mir said. "Knows everything about everyone."

Then it clicked. That woman who'd told me to be happy about the "free" concert. Ugh. I resisted an urge to pinch the bridge of my nose, since I was wearing glasses. But my head was hurting, and I was embarrassed. I hadn't realized this Jo Anne person would tell everyone. Shouldn't she keep things confidential? 911 dispatchers should sign NDAs.

"Well, she's wrong. I never tried to have him arrested. Just called in one complaint about noise pollution," I said. "Anyway, we're here to shop," I added before Val started to share more ludicrous tales.

Mir snapped her fingers. "Oh, right."

"You need a basket?" Val gestured at a stack of plastic black baskets. "Or we have carts, if you prefer."

"I'm good, thanks," I said before Mir could respond, then marched deeper into the store where a sign that read WOMEN was located.

"A basket might be nice," Mir said, following me.

"I only need one outfit, not a basketful."

"Yeah, but you might want more for later."

"Later...what?" I asked. Wasn't Mir leaving after tomorrow?

"When you go out again? You can't wear the same stuff all the time."

"'All the time' would be a big exaggeration. I'm a reclusive yeti, remember?"

Mir cringed. "Sorry. Val can be a little gossipy and obtuse, but she doesn't mean anything."

Easier for her to say, since she wasn't the one being labeled a big, hairy—and undoubtedly *smelly*—monster. On the other hand, I shouldn't take it out on Mir. It wasn't her fault.

"I'm sure. I'm just a little introverted, so interacting with strangers can be a strain," I said with a smile, not wanting Mir to be upset. She was a fan and Killian's sister. I could be gracious.

"Oh, sure. Totally get it. I just thought you'd be a little more comfortable with the whole social thing." Mir looked through some dresses hanging from a rack.

"You did? Why?"

"Because your bio said you worked a corporate job and got an MBA. I figured you wouldn't get that degree if you preferred to work alone at home. I mean, didn't your old job required you to interact with other people in an office and so on?"

"You can be an introvert and still do that," I said, not wanting to get into all the reasons I got that degree, which I'd never wanted in the first place. But Dad had insisted. I'd wanted to quit my soul-killing position and do something more fulfilling. I just hadn't been sure what that was back then. He'd been so certain that if I got an MBA, I wouldn't want to waste my amazing Ivy League education doing "stupid shit," as he called whatever I might decide to do with my life. He'd assumed wrong, because after I graduated, I set my sights on becoming a romance novelist. That had been why he and I started the bet on my career, and he refused to be proven wrong and lose the bet.

Mir looked thoughtful. Probably mulling it over. *She* was obviously an extrovert. Just look how bubbly she was. But then, she'd had loving parents. And I was certain Killian was a good brother to her. I just couldn't picture him being rude or nasty to anybody.

She pulled a dress from a rack. "How about this one? Looks like it's your size, too."

I checked the label. "Yeah, it is." Then I looked at the item she was holding out.

A bright red dress. The skirt seemed a bit short, the neckline low. If I put that on, I'd look like one of the barely legal groupies who'd surrounded Killian in pictures, except older and fatter. And unless he was blind or suffering from amnesia, he'd know and compare. It was definitely a huge no.

I opened my mouth to say it was a terrible choice, but Mir was wearing the most hopeful, happy expression. "I don't know. It's really...loud," I said instead.

"Well, yeah. But it's *totally* hot." She held the dress in front of me to see. "Red is a good color for you, and we should look hot when we go out."

Maybe if I were barely legal and wanted to hook up, I'd consider the dress she was holding. But the only person I might want to impress was Killian, and the effort would be wasted on him, the way a bottle of decent wine would be wasted on a man used to drinking Dom Pérignon.

"Let's look around some more," I said. "There might be something better."

"Okay." Mir draped the dress over an arm and started looking through the rest of the offerings, her fingers shifting the hangers as she gave each outfit a critical once-over.

I spotted a cute and modest white maxi dress and pulled it out. I could probably pair it with the pink sandals in my closet. And it could be repurposed for signings and conferences. The red one was too sexy for either.

Mir picked out a flashy strapless silver number. Oh dear.

"I just can't believe Kingstree has a new celebrity," she said, admiring the metallic outfit. "And this will make you sparkle like—"

"What celebrity?" Was there an actor hiding out in town? If so, I hadn't seen him. Or her. On the other hand, I didn't go out except to grab groceries or—very occasionally—run.

Mir looked at me like there was a purple lizard growing between my eyes. "*You*. You're the new celebrity."

"*I*'m the celebrity?" *Since when?*

"Of course! I've read every single one of your interviews, and try to go to every book signing you go to as long as I can get away from work. But so many interviewers ask similar questions. I wish they'd get more creative so you could share more about yourself."

"There isn't much to say." My life was pretty ordinary. Minus the embarrassing Dad thing, which wasn't for public consumption. "I bet you and Killian have a much more interesting history. He said you two were raised by your grandmother."

"Yeah. Our parents passed away in a plane crash when we were young." Mir gave me a small smile that people used when they didn't want pity over something that had happened a long time ago. "They were in a small private plane, and it had a mechanical failure. No survivors."

Killian had told me he'd lost his parents, but not the details. It must've been devastating, especially since they sounded like great people. "I'm sorry to hear that."

Mir nodded. "Me too. But my parents had a great life together. Did everything on their bucket list, too. A safari, scuba diving in the Maldives, seeing the pyramids, canoeing up the Amazon...all that stuff."

"Wow." That was a great list, and what was more amazing was that their parents had wanted to do everything *together*. That explained a lot about Killian's attitude about true love. I tried to imagine my parents traveling together like that...and failed. They would tour separately. How else was my dad going to screw around?

"And they did it in style." Mir smiled. "Pretty amazing for an electrician and a DMV clerk, huh?"

"I had no idea electricians did so well," I said, shocked. I didn't know exactly what Mir meant by "in style," but it probably didn't include budget travel options.

Mir laughed. "The magic of the lottery."

"Really? They won?"

"Yeah."

"Huh. I've never met a lottery winner."

Mir laughed. "You still haven't."

"Or someone related to them. You know what I mean."

"They won when I was three. It was for something like three hundred million dollars."

"Holy cow! That must've been amazing. Did they retire?" If I had that kind of money, I'd retire. And buy myself a huge plot of land and build a house that had everything I needed. I'd write one or two books a year and spend the rest of my time reading. Although a love of reading was the genesis of my becoming a writer, ever since I'd started to write seriously, I hadn't had time to read as much as I wanted. The situation was ironic, but I wasn't the only writer with the problem.

"No. They continued to work. It's just that they started to travel more. But what made them the real fortune is that they put the winnings into Amazon stock."

The *real* fortune? "All three hundred million?"

That was the most terrible investment strategy ever, even though in retrospect it was a jackpot move. But in general, when somebody had that kind of money, they usually looked to diversify their portfolio.

"Almost all of it. They bought some Apple and Disney shares, too." Mir shook her head like she still couldn't believe it either. "The reason was that Dad just liked the name Amazon because he'd always wanted to visit the river. Plus apples were his favorite fruit, and Mom's favorite cartoon growing up was Disney's *Cinderella*. So they figured, why not? Dad had a good feeling about them, just like he had a good feeling when he picked those winning numbers."

Damn. "They must've showered with fairy dust. That is the weirdest reason to invest in something, but I'm glad it worked out."

"They lived modestly, too." Affection softened her voice, her eyes. She paused, then flipped through more dresses. "Left us all the money when they passed away. We still haven't touched most of it."

That was unusual. Most people would've gone hog wild when they came into that kind of money. Hell, that was why so many lottery winners went bankrupt. "Why not?"

"Grandma didn't want us to. She thought we ought to be contributing to society, not sponging off the trust. But even then, knowing that we have such a huge cushion provides a lot of peace of mind. And for that, I'll always be grateful."

That explained why some of the articles had said Killian was worth over five billion. It wasn't all from his music. I'd wondered if music was important partially because it gave him financial success. But what was driving him was his passion—the need to create.

Now I was doubly glad I'd left him alone to work on his next album. And pound those damn drums to his heart's content. I shouldn't ask him to stay quiet all the time, either. My deadline had passed, and I didn't want to get in the way of his creative work.

Then something else occurred to me, about the specifics of what Mir was revealing.

"Should you be saying all this stuff about his money to me?" I asked, curious why Mir was oversharing. Most people didn't talk so openly about finances, and I didn't have a face that invited people to tell me all their secrets.

She blinked slowly. "It's all public, except for what I said about my parents' bucket list. Some magazine did a huge article about Killian, and it's all in there. Didn't you read it?"

"No. I skimmed the Wikipedia entry, but that's about it." Then, because I felt a tad guilty about not knowing more about him, I added, "I didn't want to pry too much."

"Oh." She frowned. It couldn't be she was sorry she'd told me if it wasn't secret. "Huh. I figured you'd look more into his background."

"I was on a deadline," I explained as my writer brain started to get that tingly feeling. "Don't you ever worry that a guy you're with just wants your money?" I asked in a low voice. "If the stuff about Killian's inheritance is out there, people must know you have money, too."

"Sometimes, but that's why God created prenups, right?"

I didn't think it was God who'd said, "Let there be prenups." It had to have been overpriced lawyers who wanted an innovative way to bill a couple before they even filed for divorce. But I kept that to myself. Mir looked entirely too pleased. And I wondered if Killian would have a similar expression if he proposed to a woman with a ring and a prenup. Then I asked myself why I wanted to know what Killian would do when he proposed. It wasn't like he was going to propose to *me*. I wasn't even sure I wanted to get married, prenup or not. I couldn't even manage a long-term boyfriend.

"And that's why I read romance," Mir said with a big smile.

"For prenups?" I asked, utterly lost.

"No, for true love. Nothing else matters when you love somebody." She looked at me expectantly.

This was the moment I was supposed to nod and say, "Of course," even though I didn't agree. Mom loved Dad in her own warped way, but love *wasn't* enough. Not when the other person didn't respect you. But I put on a smile. "Of course. True love trumps all."

"And we really should get this gold dress," Mir said, pulling out another risqué item from a rack. "It'll bring out your..." She stopped. "It's just so *golden*."

"Let's see first." I laid out the maxi dress, and she laid out the other three she'd picked out on a T-shirt table.

"You should get them all," Mir said.

"I don't think so. But I'll try them all on."

CHAPTER 25

Killian

Mir's impromptu visit wasn't like her, and it worried me. She didn't just eat like a kid; she had the boundless energy of a kid as well. And a substandard filter between her brain and mouth. I still marveled that she was an accountant. She definitely didn't fit the stereotype.

She was going to pour out all sorts of thoughts and stories, whatever flitted through her mind, to Emily. I prayed she didn't say anything embarrassing, or overwhelm Emily by trying to do everything she'd ever wanted to do with her favorite author in one afternoon.

When my phone buzzed, I picked it up immediately. It was probably an SOS from Emily. Then I realized she didn't have my number. I should've given it to her before I left.

–Mir: Hey, Emily and I are going to Sam's Brew to celebrate her new book. You should come.

Was that even Emily's idea?

–Me: Are you dragging her out to the bar?

–Mir: No. She finished her book! She deserves some fun, don't you think?

I wasn't sure if that was Emily's idea of "fun," and wondered if I should've stayed around to rescue her from Mir. Since it was too late to stop the outing without looking like a weirdo, I decided to do the next best thing.

–Me: OK. What time?

–Mir: Don't know yet. When we're done shopping and getting ready. How about we meet at seven at her place?

It was barely four. Unease sat in my belly.

–Me: How long does it take to shop and get some clothes on?

–Mir: No judging. Us girls are entitled to spend our time as we see fit.

Yeah, but did Emily think this was a good use of her time?

On the other hand, I recalled the way she'd told me—in no uncertain terms—to stop drumming the second time we saw each other. She could handle my bulldozer sister.

Probably.

After putting the phone down, I picked up the sticks again and started to drum the beat of our first major hit, "Sweet Nothings," and sing. The song was five years old, but still a fan favorite. It also had a special spot in my heart, not to mention the rest of the guys'. No one ever forgets their first. I thought my heart would burst when I heard somebody request it on the radio for the first time. And still got a thrill when people wanted to hear Axelrod's music.

My mind started to wander. The beats changed into something different. The melody coming out from my throat was altered, too. The sound was fresh—a little sweet, a little edgy. Too new to be anything definite yet, like a wildflower sprout coming up in a field, but it had potential.

Snippets of possible lyrics started to coalesce in my mind. Flashes of images. I closed my eyes, joy welling inside. The dam that had blocked my flow wasn't there anymore. Inspiration was just trickling in, but I knew it was only the beginning. My gut told me there was more to come. Torrents of music, and I had to be ready and quick enough to catch every drop of the words and tunes before they vanished. Because inspiration was that fleeting.

Then suddenly it all poured out, the beats, the lyrics and the song. Shivers rushed through me as I sang my heart out in the living room with nobody to listen.

When the Darth Vader theme went off, I stopped, my body

drenched in sweat. I realized it was dim in the living room, the sunlight a weak orange. *Shit.* I picked up the phone.

"Yeah?"

"Hey, you coming or not? It's seven," Mir said, her voice hushed. From the way she sounded, I wouldn't be surprised if she was cupping her mouth like she was telling me a secret.

"Already?" I lifted my gaze to the clock on the wall—7:03.

"I texted you half an hour ago so you could come wait, but you didn't answer."

I hadn't heard my phone ping. I was still high off the new music. "Why would you want me to wait half an hour?"

"That way you look like a gentleman. Gentlemen always come early and wait."

I rolled my eyes. Mir had the weirdest ideas sometimes. Emily was too practical to want somebody hanging around for half an hour for no reason. "Okay, sorry. Look, I need to grab a quick shower here."

"Fine. Make it fast. Emily's almost ready. I'll leave the door open so you can slip in quietly and pretend like you've been waiting like a good man."

I hung up. So *technically* I wasn't late, because Emily wasn't ready yet either. But from the way Mir had spoken, I might as well have missed the last flight to heaven.

I bounded up the stairs to take the fastest shower in history. Emily might still have some prep to do, but it would be embarrassing to have her wait because of me.

Excitement ran through me as I got ready. Although my sister was tagging along, this felt like a real date, with me and Emily going out.

I finger-combed my still-damp hair and put on a dark blue V-neck shirt with black jeans. Then, on a whim, I put on a necklace with the band's logo: a stylized *A* done in sterling silver. I no longer felt like an imposter whose music had gone dry, so I felt worthy to wear it again.

Then I went over to Emily's, and sure enough, the door had been left ajar.

"Come on in," my sister said. She was in a tight black dress with a low neckline and a super-short skirt. A dark plum color coated her lips, and her lashes were heavy with mascara.

"Should you be wearing that?" I asked, not liking her outfit. Although she was a big girl now, I remembered some of the assholes in town who'd had crushes on her. Men were all fucking dogs, and my sister should be more covered up.

"Why? It barely shows anything. Besides, God gave me these legs. They're too pretty to remain hidden."

She did indeed have a pair of nice, long legs. I could admit that—grudgingly—but that didn't mean I wanted every guy in town staring at them. "Still. That dress is way short."

"It's only three inches above the knees. Nobody can see my underwear when I bend down. Now stop being medieval. Your groupies wear a lot less than this. And for God's sake, don't criticize Emily's outfit."

I gave her a sidelong glance, wondering if Emily was going to wear something similar to what Mir had on. I wanted to see Emily's body, but at the same time I didn't want her parading around in so little material, for all the assholes in the town to drool over. "Did you pick it out for her?"

"Of course. That's why we went shopping." Mir beamed, looking proud.

I tried not to cringe. Mir was a firm believer in showing off one's assets. Sometimes it seemed like she was applying for Dev-groupie status. And I didn't want Emily to dress like a groupie. I wanted Emily to dress like how she'd normally dress when she went out to a bar.

"Hey," came Emily's voice from the staircase.

I turned my head. Air caught in my lungs as I took her in. Her hair was down, flowing over her shoulders in gentle golden waves. Pink lipstick and blush added a lovely flush to her face, and the scarlet dress she had on covered everything it needed to, but also fitted over the soft curves of her breasts, the sexy double dip of her waist and flare of her hips. Her feet were in a pair of pale silver sandals with thin heels. The entire ensemble was hot as hell, and made me want to unwrap her like a Christmas present.

My heart pumped faster, my blood heating up.

She stepped down the stairs, running her fingers along her hair, and gave me a small smile. "Do I look all right?"

Finally, air came back into my lungs. "Wow," I said. "Yes. Better than all right."

Her smile widened. "You look pretty neat yourself."

"I didn't realize we had to be this fancy."

"Mir said the bar has a dress code," Emily said.

"She did?" *That lying little...*

My sister stuck her tongue out behind Emily.

Impudent, too. But then I got to see Emily decked out. She was pretty anyway, even with her hair messy, glasses skewed and in an old T-shirt and ratty yoga pants. But I didn't know until now how much more beautiful she could be. I couldn't believe I'd thought she was a vagrant when we first met. Now I wished I'd brought flowers, because a woman this stunning deserved them.

Emily deserved the best.

Making a mental note to get some later, I extended an arm. "Ready?"

"Yup." She placed a hand in the crook of my elbow. "Let's go."

CHAPTER 26

Emily

Although I'd spent close to two hours fussing over my hair and makeup, all the while arguing with Mir, the end result was worth it. The look on Killian's face was the perfect reward for the effort —the darkening of his blue eyes and the soft exhale of breath when he'd said, "Wow."

Mir was sitting in the back of the SUV, and she was chattering about stuff I wasn't paying much attention to as Killian drove, but it almost felt like a date. I couldn't remember the last time I'd been out on one. Maybe early last year? Nor could I remember a time when there had been this many butterflies in my belly. I didn't think I was this excited when I went out with the first-string quarterback from my high school.

The drive to Sam's Brew was short. Killian jumped out and opened my door for me. Mir knocked on the window and said, "Hey, what about me?"

"You have arms," he said, then reached over and opened it for her anyway.

My smile widened a bit. You could figure out what kind of man you were dealing with by looking at how he treated his mother and sister. And I liked what I was seeing between Killian and Mir.

The sign outside the squat wooden building read: SAM'S KARAOKE NIGHT! SING, DRINK AND BE MERRY! $4 HOP HOP HOORAY! Judging by the noise coming from inside, there were a lot of people there already. But then, it was a little after seven thirty now.

I took a deep breath. It was inevitable that I'd have to deal with the people in Kingstree at some point. At least I wasn't facing them all by myself. If I got lucky, they'd be too busy interacting with Killian to notice me much. And at least the rumors about me being a yeti would disappear after this outing.

Killian held the door open; Mir walked in, and I followed. Killian put his hand at my back, the touch warm, and moved inside with me, matching my pace half a step behind.

The interior was dimly lit, with lots of small tables. Three giant TVs hung from walls, each one showing a different sport, although the sound was muted. A pool table occupied one corner, along with a dartboard and a jukebox. In the area opposite the main entrance was a raised stage, big enough for about four to five people to stand and sing, with a drum set in the back.

A middle-aged man in an unbuttoned flannel shirt over a white undershirt and jeans was belting out "We Are the Champions." Given the accompaniment from the speakers, he was butchering the melody, but nobody seemed to care, since a lot of the patrons were singing along with him.

People in the bar were dressed just as casually as the singer, so that made me overdressed. So was Mir. I should've known better than to believe her. Sam's Brew was a bar in a small town with casual folks.

I leaned over to her. "Dress code?"

"Maybe things have changed since last time I was here." She shot me a shameless grin.

I snorted, then decided it didn't matter. She'd probably just wanted to dress up with me, and that was fine. I could use dressing like a normal, responsible adult once in a while. Besides, it had been worth it to knock Killian's socks off. That was an ego booster.

"Hey, Killian! And Mir! I didn't think you'd come!" someone said in a loud, growly voice.

"Here to have fun with a friend." Killian tilted his head my way.

"Oh?" The man's eyes widened as he checked me out thoroughly. "Who's this?"

"Emily. My next-door neighbor."

The man looked like he'd just gotten sucker-punched. "No way. I mean... Yeah. I just... Huh."

I almost laughed. If he'd seen me around town before, no wonder he couldn't recognize me. "Nice to meet you," I said, extending a hand.

"Yeah. I'm Bob. Pleasure." He held my hand like it was made of glass, then let go slowly.

"So, Eric's in a great mood today?" Mir said, glancing toward the singer.

"Yeah." Bob grunted. "His team is playing, and this is his good-luck song. He said they win every time he sings it." He looked at the stage ruminatively. "Practice ain't made him any better, though."

"It's an improvement from what I remember," Mir said, then went to get a table as its occupants left.

"There's no waiting list or anything?" I asked.

"Nope. First grabbed, first served," Killian said, leading me over.

Eric struck a triumphant pose, one fist in the air, as he sang the last note. "To victory!"

Everyone clapped as we sat down. A waitress came by and cleared the table. "Hey, guys. Want something to drink?" she asked.

"Hop Hop Hooray raspberry, if you have it," I said.

"Two," Killian said.

"Three. And Sue, you know I want one of each appetizer."

"Smart," Sue said with a grin. "You always know how to have fun, Mir."

Mir laughed. "What's life without fun?"

After Sue left, I turned to Mir. "You know everybody."

"Kingstree's a small town. Killian knows everyone, too." That made me pause for a second, but it made sense. He'd said he grew up here, and when he heard my characters' names, he'd made connections to actual people in town.

I saw Sunny get on stage and grab the mike, which was a little weird. The supermarket owner always seemed so proper. On the other hand, I guessed this was how she had fun and blew off steam.

"You know, it's downright unfair of me to sing when we have our own homegrown rock star here. I didn't know he'd be out on the town tonight," Sunny said with a small laugh.

I gave her a look of sympathy even though she probably didn't see it from the stage. I imagined that vocals were touched up in the studio to make them sound better than in real life. But if Killian sang live even half as well as his recordings, it was going to be a tough comparison for Sunny.

"Nobody cares. It's not an audition," somebody called out.

"Then why don't you come up here with me, Calvin?" Sunny said.

"You know I flunked music."

"Flunked? You didn't even take the class!"

"What were you gonna sing?" Mir called out.

"'Bohemian Rhapsody.'"

"Two Queen songs back to back?" Mir said.

"I sing better than Eric," Sunny said with a wink. "But I don't sing better than Killian."

"Let's get our rock star up on stage."

As though in agreement, the people started to chant Killian's name. I clapped to the beat of their chant, smiling at the crowd's eager reaction. It was inevitable they wanted him on the stage. What was that 911 dispatcher had said? Right. Free concert. And given how small the town was, they didn't often have a big star show for a concert, free or otherwise.

Killian took a sip of his water. "You wanna go up there with me?" he asked me.

"Ha! And embarrass myself? I don't know this song well enough to sing. Besides, I don't do music, remember?"

He pursed his lips. Before he could find a way to drag me up there with him anyway, I quickly added, "But I won't mind it if you go up there and wow me."

"Well. If you insist." He stood with an easy grin, his eyes on mine.

And for some reason, it felt like he was doing this for me—to wow me like I'd asked him to. My cheeks warmed.

The people hooted and shouted encouragement.

Killian held up his arms. "All right, *all right*, you cattle wranglers! Let's be civilized here," he said, then hopped on stage.

Sunny gave him the mike, her shoulders relaxed now. "Good. I would've hated it if I had to sing in front of you."

"Do 'Nowhere'!" somebody said from behind me.

"The machine won't let you cancel a song about to start," the bartender said. "But you can erase the rest of the entry and put that one in for next." Then he turned to Killian. "You ready?"

"Yup."

Sue came back with three beers. "Hot damn. We're in for a treat," she said, her eyes on the stage.

I took my drink and watched Killian get ready. I'd never been to a concert—or a karaoke night—so I had no idea what to expect. But even I could tell Killian somehow already owned not only the stage but the whole bar. He just *commanded* attention, his bright blue gaze shining on everyone there to see him perform.

He began singing, his voice slightly husky. Unlike Eric, who'd been loud but not necessarily good, Killian was hitting the notes, and there was a charge to the way he sang—a power that made your nerve endings come alive and your blood to pulse a little faster in your veins.

When he reached the chorus, everyone was singing with him. He even pointed the mike at the crowd, which had gone crazy. Since I didn't know the words, I merely clapped and enjoyed the show.

The last note died, and the crowd erupted. "'Nowhere'! 'Nowhere'!" they shouted in unison.

I laughed at their reaction. I'd expected "bravo" or "encore," not "'Nowhere.'" They must be eager for more. And to be honest, I was too. I wanted to see him sing his own song.

"Come on, Killian! 'Nowhere'!" the bartender shouted.

Killian laughed, his eyes bright and full of joy, then he nodded.

An elaborate guitar and drum started, and he belted out the song I'd heard only a couple of times on YouTube.

Hearing the recording—even with the music video—was nothing like watching him sing live. There was a raw power and charge to his voice that no recording equipment could capture. And it flowed out over the crowd—over me—unrestrained. He was a musician, a hypnotist, and I couldn't look away. He shone like a supernova as he performed for the small crowd in a small bar in small town, Virginia. It felt like he was singing only for me, his eyes only on me, and I finally understood why rock stars were called rock *stars*.

Everyone, including me, got to their feet and swayed to the music. It was as though in this moment, nothing else existed. My heart pounded, my body hot. All thought seemed to have vanished except for the joy his music was pouring into me at the moment.

Our eyes met, and an electric jolt went through me. And with that came an understanding and admiration—he was taking people away from their mundane life and making them feel alive. People were listening to him for *this,* this experience, just like people bought my books to escape for a while.

Something hot and sweet and unfamiliar welled in my chest. I almost couldn't draw in enough air, sweat misting over my skin even though all I was doing was standing and immersing myself in his mesmerizing voice.

When the song ended, the crowd erupted again. Killian grinned at them, then at me, his eyes bright.

The excitement from his performance still sizzled through me. I smiled at him, wanting him to see how his music affected me.

Somebody handed Killian a glass of water and a piece of paper. He took a sip, then read it. His eyebrows quirked up, and I wondered what it said. Better not be a phone number.

Whoa, wait. *Where did that hot, angry thought come from?* We weren't dating, were we? Just because we'd spent a lot of time together recently and he'd helped me with a snake didn't mean...

But that searing, ugly feeling was definitely jealousy.

Before I could think about my reaction, Killian said, "Okay, so apparently today is Sam and Fiona's anniversary."

"Yeah, Sam and Fiona!" came a shout.

"Congrats!"

One person started clapping, and everyone joined in.

Mir leaned over and indicated a beaming couple sitting a few tables away. They waved to the crowd.

"And he'd like to dedicate a song to his wife," Killian added when the crowd quieted down some. "Now this is the last song I'm doing, 'cause I'm starting to get hungry."

Everyone laughed.

We sat down. And a mellow melody I didn't recognize started. I tapped Mir's shoulder. "What's this one?"

She looked at me like I'd come from Mars. "How can you not know this? It's 'Wonderful Tonight.'"

"I don't do music that much," I said.

"Ever hear of Eric Clapton?"

I thought. "The name kind of does ring a bell, but..."

Mir continued to stare, but then Killian began singing a slow love song. It surprised me that he handled it so well, because he was in a rock band, and I assumed a rocker wouldn't be able to sing something like this. But his voice was so full of intimate longing that it sent the same kind of longing through me. Okay, now I totally understood why women fell for rock stars and dressed as skimpily as possible and exercised nine hundred hours a day while eating two leaves of lettuce.

Because if I had a chance with a man who sang like Killian and made me feel like this, I would do the same.

When the song ended, the cheering and clapping were deafening. Killian took a bow and blew kisses, basking in the moment.

Suddenly, he turned and looked directly at me, a boyish grin on his lips. In the midst of the tumult, my heart galloped harder and I swore I could hear it thudding, even over the crowd. If I were more fanciful, I might've thought it was the sound of myself tumbling into a major crush.

CHAPTER 27

Killian

I jumped off the stage and made my way back to the table, the performance high still rushing through me. Being on the stage and having a crowd go wild was always a rush. During that moment we were one, connected to each other through the magic of music.

The appetizers Mir ordered had just come out—Sue probably delayed them a little out of consideration for me.

Mir high-fived me. "Still got the power, bro!" she said.

"Thanks." Sitting down, I glanced at Emily. She'd said she didn't do music, but it looked like she was having fun. I'd been able to see her smile from the stage, but she could've done that to be polite. She was the only woman I knew who considered my drumming "noise pollution."

"So. Did you have fun?" I asked, trying to sound careless.

She lifted her chin and gazed at me. "Amazing," she said. "You were a*maz*ing."

The light in her green eyes was electric. My mind got wiped clean of every thought except one—*she is so beautiful*. Beautiful wasn't enough—she was brilliant. I wanted to freeze the moment, etch her like this in my memory forever.

I wanted to kiss her and see her look at me with that same

shining light. And dance with her all night, our hands linked, fingers threading fingers until our hearts galloped in unison and we were both breathless, our blood rushing fast and hot.

Emily flushed, but didn't look away.

"Oh my gosh, it's Yve! I gotta go say hi," Mir squealed. The smile on Emily's face shifted to a curious look, and the moment broke.

Thanks, Mir. That was twice she'd broken the mood.

My sister jumped up and ran to see her best friend from high school. They hugged and hopped around like overexcited teenagers, looking like they were planning a sleepover. Which might work out better, since that'd leave me and Emily alone until at least tomorrow.

I pushed the chicken wings toward Emily. "This isn't much of a dinner. If you want, I can whip up something more substantial." *Say yes. Come over.*

"Thanks, but I don't want to trouble you. This is fine." She picked up a piece and delicately bit into it. "Mmm...good. I can't believe I've never come here. Not bad for a quick meal." She took a French fry.

I guzzled down my now lukewarm beer, thirsty after singing three songs. Her rejection was disappointing, but then I should've known whatever moment we'd had wasn't coming back. Next time I should bring Emily here without my baby sister to squeal like amp feedback.

The stage stayed empty and the bartender put on some music. I munched on a few things, most of them fried. This was what happened when Mir took charge of the order. I couldn't taste much, though. Adrenaline from the performance, no matter how short, was still sizzling in my veins, making me jittery, my senses extra sharp. And right now, everything was focused on Emily. Her presence. Her nearness. The way her hair moved when she tilted her head.

"You know, I didn't realize how good music could be until now," Emily said. "I can see why you're famous."

"You can hear me sing any time you want," I said, my voice raspier than usual. I'd never sung for any of my exes privately before. They'd never asked, and I'd never offered. But for

Emily, I would love to so I could watch her reaction beat by beat.

"I wouldn't know what to request." She gave me a small, light smile.

"No problem. You tell me what kind of mood you're in, and I can pick something and sing it."

She wiped her fingers and dabbed at her mouth. Her gaze skimmed the area next to us where some couples were dancing. "Do you dance as well as you sing?"

"You kidding?" I grinned, surprised and pleased. "Wanna dance?" *I want to hold you.*

"Yeah. But don't laugh at me. I'm out of practice."

"Just follow my lead."

I wiped my fingers, then took her hand as I led her to the open space where people were moving to the music, then took her into my arms. My pulse throbbed, like a kid on his first date with the girl he'd had a crush on since forever. Somehow everything was new and different with Emily. The feel of her body against mine was like nothing I'd ever experienced.

The song was sweetly romantic and slow, probably in honor of Sam and Fiona's anniversary. We held each other and swayed. Emily smelled like citrus and mint and something warm and sweet, like honey. My heart was pounding so hard that I wondered if she could hear it over the music. She looked up at me despite her heels. Her usually sharp eyes seemed gentler somehow, without their customary edge. Leaning over, I crooned the lyrics into her ear. The heat from her body burned me. My mouth was close enough to her ear to graze the delicate shell, and she shivered. She angled her head, and her lips brushed mine.

Everything except the song and her seemed to melt away. We kissed each other softly, just a cushioning of lips. The touch was so erotic that it left me dizzy, my senses spinning. She tasted like the beer and spices and all Emily. That smart mouth. That *take no prisoners* attitude. I wanted to take her to bed, make her feel great. Show her I could give her the kind of night she deserved.

We continued to sway to the music, brushing our lips and sharing the air between us. She licked my mouth, then blinked, pulling back a little. "Can we tell Mir we're leaving early?" Then she flushed. "Tell her I have a headache."

For a second, I froze, trying to process what she'd just said. Then lust shot through me like lightning, obliterating everything but the need I had for Emily. Although my dick was painfully hard, I almost laughed. That was what women usually said when they *didn't* want to have sex. "Right now?"

"Yes. And see if she can get a ride with somebody. No point in cutting her evening short."

"You got it."

CHAPTER 28

Emily

"Your place or mine?" I said when Killian pulled into the cul-de-sac. Then I smacked myself mentally. What was I thinking? I wasn't thinking at all. I couldn't. "Actually, mine. We don't need Mir walking in."

"She's spending the night with Yve." They actually *had* been planning a sleepover. "You have condoms?"

"No."

"Then mine."

"Okay." I hadn't thought as far as condoms, and it would've been disastrous to start and then have to stop because of a lack of latex.

My blood had been simmering the entire short drive. If Killian had put on music, I didn't notice. All I knew was that I actually ached between my legs.

I'd never felt that before. I thought it was something that only happened in romance novels. Hell, I'd written it into my books, because I figured it would hurt to want so much but not have it, even though I'd never experienced anything like that.

Killian's car screeched to a stop in front of his house. I stepped out immediately, not wanting him to waste time trying to be a gentleman and open my door. He fumbled with the key to unlock the door to his place. I stood behind him and touched him, needing the contact, then ran my mouth along his bulging triceps. We needed to be inside for what I had in mind. It wasn't my idea of fun to get arrested for indecent exposure and whatever obscure decency laws were still on the books in the state of Virginia. Although this area was secluded, it wasn't gated, and you never knew who might be around to call in a complaint.

The key turned and he went in, reaching back to grab my hand and pull me along behind him. Once we were inside, he turned around. I looped my arms around his neck and claimed his mouth, all aggression and lust.

He tasted so damn good. Felt so damn good. All those lean muscles I'd been secretly eye-fucking every morning pressed against my torso, crushing my breasts. Damned bra. It was in the way.

Actually, everything we had on was in the way.

Killian kissed harder, his tongue gliding into my mouth. I met it with my own. His erection pushed against my belly, and I groaned. I needed it if I wanted the aching emptiness between my legs to go away.

"Upstairs. To the bedroom," I said. Not necessarily because I needed to be in bed for this, but because I felt like a bed would more appropriate than the living room floor for our first time. Besides, I knew I'd insulted him with my "ten minutes" comment. I didn't want anything to remind him of that and ruin what could be something amazing.

"Okay." Killian picked me up, his muscles tightening around me. I wasn't a tiny waif, and the strength I felt in his body stoked my desire. I wrapped my legs around his waist, and he carried me up the stairs to his bedroom. With every step my pubic bone rubbed against him, and I was going out of my mind before we even got naked. The notion was unsettling but also too exciting. This must be what the prelude to "earth-shattering sex" felt like. And I knew Killian would give it to me, because he could and because he wanted to make both of us feel amazing.

We fell on his bed. He put his hands on both sides of my head so he didn't crush me, then fused our mouths in a lush kiss. I clung to him, my fingers fumbling and pushing his shirt up. He yanked it over his head and tossed it away before kissing me again. His hands skimmed across my dress, his fingers exploring and making my body tingle everywhere. I reached over to the side and pulled the zipper down, so I could get out of the obstructive thing.

He undressed me, pushing the dress down, past my hips, then tugged at my thong and took everything all the way down my legs and let it drop by the bed. His eyes took me in, and for a second, I felt awkward and exposed. Was he disappointed that I didn't have a perfectly toned body? Clothes cover up a lot of flaws. I wondered if I shouldn't have eaten or drunk anything at the bar so my belly would look flatter. But then he let out a soft groan like he was looking at the sexiest damned thing in the world and couldn't bear it, and my reservations melted away faster than a snowflake in Singapore. He unhooked my bra; I shrugged out of it, letting it fall on the floor. Heat flushed my skin, pooling between my legs as his eyes darkened.

"Take off your pants," I demanded, my breathing uneven. My chest rose and fell, and his gaze went to the tips of my breasts. "*Now,*" I said before he got even more distracted.

His eyes on me, he disposed of the rest of his clothes and shoes, and then he was on me. His mouth, his tongue, his hands. He kissed me everywhere, touched me everywhere, leaving trails of fire on my body, making me weak and needy and desperate. I clung to him, my legs wrapped around him, as hot streaks of pleasure sizzled through me, leaving me dizzy and wet.

He touched me like he'd die without me, and he devoured my lips like I was the only one who could satisfy his hunger. It made me hot for him. But it wasn't just lust I was feeling. There was a softer and sweeter edge to everything that made what we were doing more than just a rush to mutually satisfying orgasms.

He massaged one breast, and I arched my back. "More," I said, panting.

A low, wickedly masculine chuckle tore from his throat as he took my breast into his mouth and sucked. Oh my *God.* I threaded my fingers through his hair, holding him there. He nipped me, and my pussy clenched so hard that it almost hurt.

"Now, Killian. Inside me now," I begged, but he merely

moved further down, his tongue laving my belly, leaving wet trails along my breasts and below. He was driving me crazy. Why didn't he want to plunge into me? Any of my exes would've done that by now, but not Killian. It was as though he had a destination in mind that would require a different route.

He reached for my hands and linked our fingers. Our palms pressed together and seemed to throb.

My thighs went over his wide shoulders, seemingly of their own accord, and his mouth closed over the flesh between my legs. *Holy...!* Heat blossomed in my gut, and the ache I'd been feeling since the moment he sang on the stage was more like sharp pain now. I'd felt how hard he was, and he must want to be inside me, but he took his time, bringing me to a climax with his mouth.

I sobbed softly, his name on my lips. I wasn't used to this kind of tender but hot sex. Or the care and attention he lavished on me, making my heart flutter for reasons that had nothing to do with the orgasm I'd just had. He pushed me again, but it didn't take much effort for another orgasm to shatter over me, my spine bending, my arms taut, and my fingers tightening between his.

But I wanted more—to feel him inside me. I wanted to be as intimately connected as possible, to see pleasure break over his face as he moved inside me, making both of us feel incredible.

He shifted. I heard a something tear, and then he was back, settling between my legs. I cupped his cheeks then pulled his face down for a kiss. His mouth was slick against mine, tasted intimately like me and him.

He drove all the way in with one smooth stroke. I shivered, my moan caught between our lips. He felt so good, so solid, so hot. He was aggressive, slightly out of control, and I loved watching him lose himself in me, pleasure playing over his face, sweat beading on our skin as lust heated our bodies.

"You feel so fucking tight. Shit," he said between clenched teeth.

I laughed breathlessly. "And you feel *huge*. I love it."

He cursed, then thrust faster and more roughly. The added stimulation flung me into another climax, and I came hard around him, my inner muscles spasming. He plunged in and out, his jaw bunched tightly. I put a hand over the tense muscles, then dragged my fingers all the way down to his chest, where his heart raced. I pulled him down to kiss him deeply, to show how much I loved this moment with him...how much I'd like to see him let go. When I came again, his entire body clenched, a shudder going through him as he joined me in orgasm.

I held on to him, waiting for our breathing to even out, our hearts to stop galloping. He kissed me tenderly, his lips on my forehead, the corners of my eyes and the tip of my nose and my chin. "You're so beautiful," he whispered as he licked my ear.

Something sweet and languid swelled in my chest, stealing my breath. He said the words like they were the truest thing in the world, and I felt like the most beautiful person on Earth.

"I know," I said, feeling too happy to be modest or argue. "So are you."

With a small laugh, he kissed me. "And we're going to make beautiful love all night long."

CHAPTER 29

Killian

I stretched, still slightly bleary, sleep clinging like cobwebs. It was still early, just a sliver of light coming in between the bedroom curtains. Emily was sleeping, curled up, hugging one of my pillows, her face buried in it.

Should I wake her?

The bedside clock said it wasn't even eight. And she could use some extra sleep, because I'd kept her up late. We'd used up a lot of condoms. *Yeah, no Mr. Ten Minutes here,* I thought. *Ahh heh heh heh.*

I put on a pair of boxers, brushed my teeth and went downstairs to get some water. My mouth felt dry and dehydrated. I made it a habit to have at least two bottles of water after I sang, but last night I'd skipped that. I'd had a more pressing matter, namely, having Emily.

I took a few sips and sighed. It was already almost mid-April. Not even seven weeks remained before I had to go to Dallas, and I didn't want to leave Emily behind. Would it be too early to ask her to consider coming with me? I hadn't seen her hang out with anybody or mention any close friends in town. So maybe she'd be okay with it.

On the other hand, what if she had a specific reason for being in Kingstree and couldn't go to Dallas?

Long distance was an option, but not a great one. We'd be too busy, and I didn't want to waste time traveling back and forth between Dallas and Kingstree when we could just be in the same city.

And...Emily could write in Dallas just as well as she could in Kingstree, couldn't she? If the logistics or cost were a problem, I'd pay for all the expenses and arrange for movers. All she'd have to do is grab her laptop. I'd make sure it'd be as easy and seamless as possible.

The door to the house opened with a quiet creak. Mir walked in, still in her dress. Her face was cleaned of makeup, her hair messy and uncombed. *Shit,* I thought with a small sigh. I was hoping Mir would stay with Yve a little longer. Until lunchtime at least, catching up and doing what best friends did when they had a sleepover.

"Hey," she said, walking in. "Got some coffee?"

"Not yet."

She gave me a weird look. "What happened to you? No coffee in the morning?"

"I just got up."

"Wow. You slept in."

Mir and I were both early risers.

"It was a late night," I said, feeling slightly pleased about the reason.

Grunting, she went over to grab the TV remote.

"Hey, don't turn on the TV," I said.

"Why not?"

"Emily's sleeping."

She blinked slowly once, then put both hands over her mouth. "You *slept* with her?"

I gave her a look reserved for a particularly dim child. "Yesss. Both of us consenting adults consented to sex."

Mir covered her eyes. "Oh my God. I so do not want to hear about your sex life."

"Hey, now it's your favorite author's sex life, too."

Her face scrunched even worse. "That doesn't make it better!

But wait... Does this mean I get to read her books before other people?"

"I make no promises. She hasn't let me read her latest book either," I said, not wanting Mir to bug Emily about that. I honestly had no idea what Emily's process was, but she shouldn't have to show her stories to anybody until she was ready. And part of me wanted to be the first to read her new books, except maybe for her editor.

"Oh. Well. I'll figure out an angle. I got time..." Mir suddenly studied me, her gaze flinty. "Did you tell her you don't live here? That you have to leave soon? You have both of your expectations about this relationship clear, right?"

"Jesus, Mir. It's not a job position."

"I'm pretty sure I know what kind of position it is."

I had to laugh. "You're acting like I took advantage of some high school girl or something. Emily's a romance author, for God's sake! She knows what we're doing."

"But you figured out how not to break her heart, right? I mean, she isn't one of your groupies."

"Thanks for the vote of confidence." And for making me sound like an asshole. Breaking hearts was what Dev did, not me. I resented Mir's narrow-eyed gaze. Just whose sister was she? She wasn't getting any more backstage passes, damn it.

"It's important. One of my favorite romance writers never finished her series because her husband left her. I don't want that to happen to Emma Grant. I mean, Emily."

I paused for a second. I hadn't considered what a breakup might do to Emily's mindset or her career. Dev had been out of control after the things went south with Ashley. On the other hand, Ashley cheated on him, and I had no intention of cheating on Emily or doing anything to hurt her.

I always went into a relationship with a positive outlook. What was the point, otherwise? So I hoped that things worked out between me and Emily, but if they didn't... Well, we could end it amicably. We were both adults.

But why was Mir acting like it was inevitable I would screw something up? Didn't she know me better than that?

"First of all, I'm not her husband. Second, she isn't writing a series. So you won't be left hanging," I pointed out sarcastically, too annoyed to let Mir know about my decision to ask Emily to come with me to Dallas. Besides, Mir didn't get to hear about it before Emily.

"Didn't you see her shirt from yesterday? I don't want her to write angsty stuff. I already have my favorite angst romance authors."

"Mir, not everything's about you and what you like to read. It's about who I want to be with, and who Emily wants to be with. And she's been with other men before, okay? She kept writing her books when they broke up, so I'm sure she isn't going to quit writing, regardless of what happens. She'll be fine." But even as I said it, I was vaguely annoyed. I didn't want to think about Emily's previous boyfriends. I also didn't want to think about what would happen if Emily and I broke up... And I most certainly didn't want to imagine how incredibly fine she was going to be on her own again.

For some bizarre reason, I wanted her to feel a little sad. At least wistful. Regretful. Realize she'd never have a better stud in the sack again.

It was immature as hell, but I couldn't will myself *not* to feel those things. Damn it.

"Fine," Mir said. "I'm just going to have some ice cream," she groused, walking past me to the freezer and opening the door violently, like she was taking it out on the poor appliance. "You don't have a single tub of Bouncy Bare Monkeys?"

Because Emily has all of them. And I had already eaten the two tubs she'd given me, which were extra delicious. But I didn't to tell Mir that. "Why don't you go to Sunny's and see?"

"Fine, fine," she said, and left with her key.

Knowing her, it'd take at least an hour or two to finish the ice cream run because she'd want to say hello and gossip with everyone. She was one of the most social people I knew.

I drank some water, then stared out the windows over the kitchen sink. I didn't like what Mir had insinuated—that I would break Emily's heart or that I'd hurt her so badly that she wouldn't be able to write. My sister should know me better than that.

But my gut twisted with something that felt like anxiety, as I wondered what Emily thought of me...and if she shared the same opinion as Mir.

CHAPTER 30

Emily

I blinked, then slowly turned and stared at the unfamiliar pale green ceiling. The walls were the same color. And the sheets were soft cream. The other side of the bed was cool to the touch. Killian must've gotten up. He was such a morning person. Cheery, too. Those weren't huge pluses in my book. People should hate getting up in the morning and be grouchy until they'd had at least two coffees.

But he made a great breakfast. And he was fabulous in bed. On balance, that more than made up for the cheery early-riser thingy.

Since my bladder was declaring a state of emergency, I used the bathroom, then rinsed my mouth with some minty mouthwash that was on the counter. The mirror showed a slightly reddish mark on my collarbone, where Killian had bitten me last night. My cheeks flushed. *Holy shit. I had sex with a rock star.*

Dazed, I went back to bed and plopped down. My face fell on the pillow I'd hugged last night. It smelled like Killian. I couldn't believe how hot I'd been for him, how madly I'd craved his body. But I didn't regret any of it.

For the first time in my life, I'd experienced the kind of sex I'd only read and written about in romance novels. The kind that lasted literally all night long with a guy whose stamina put me in awe. And the orgasms...

No way I could remember them all. All I knew was that I'd come *a lot,* and all of them had been good—so, so good.

No wonder Killian had been annoyed when I said *ten minutes.*

I sighed, shivering with a languid soreness and remembered pleasure, but my head said I needed to snap out of that and think about what was next. After all, I couldn't stay in bed forever, and Killian and I did have a life outside of the bedroom.

We hadn't talked much the night before. Maybe we should, over breakfast or lunch if Mir wasn't around, since it wasn't the kind of conversation I wanted to have with his sister listening. This didn't feel like a nice but meaningless one-night stand. If all he wanted was a fuck buddy while he was in town, he could've slept with anyone. And he certainly wouldn't have had to wait until last night.

He had to leave Kingstree in June, but I could offer to go to Dallas with him, see where things went from there. As nice and quiet my home here was, I could write anywhere, so long as I had my laptop. I could even join him when he toured, assuming he was okay with me coming with him while he traveled.

Feeling much better, I looked around for a clock and spotted a box of condoms on the bedside table. I squinted at it. *Chocolate-flavored?*

I picked it up, then shoved my nose inside the box and sniffed, wondering if the condoms smelled like chocolate too. I'd never thought Killian would be the type to use flavored condoms. He seemed like a plain, standard condom kind of guy. But then, what did I know about rock stars? But if he really wanted a sex partner to enjoy chocolate flavor, wouldn't it be more effective to buy chocolate syrup instead? Latex didn't have the right tex—

"Why are you sniffing the condoms?"

I almost dropped the box. "Geez, you scared me."

Killian walked closer with an expression that was halfway between amusement and confusion. A teasing gleam shone in his bright blue eyes. "Yeah, because you were too busy sniffing rubbers to notice someone coming in."

My face heated. He didn't have to make me sound like a perv. "I was trying to see if they smelled like chocolate."

His nose wrinkled. "Do they?"

"I don't know."

He raised an eyebrow. "Seriously?"

"I'm not sniffing them again." I put the box back on the table. "Do they taste like chocolate?"

He laughed. "I have no idea. Not that flexible."

"What do you mean—" Then it hit me. "Oh for..."

He laughed again. "Dev stuck that box in my bag after our last tour."

"Why?"

"Because he's a weirdo? But they came in handy last night." He smiled, then started to move onto the bed, on his knees and hands, his eyes gleaming.

My gaze flicked between his legs. I could tell even with boxers that he was hard as hell. I was growing wet in response.

He stripped and sheathed himself in one of the so-called chocolate-flavored condoms. I watched the whole quick process, anticipation pooling.

"Don't worry. I'm not going to make you eat the rubber," he joked. "I have a much better idea."

He kissed me. It was slow and leisurely, a kiss of a man savoring the final bite of a delicious dessert. And I matched it, a liquid heat spreading through me.

He moved his mouth slowly down my body, layering sweet, gentle kisses on my neck, my chest. He licked my nipple, then watched the glistening tip with a wicked satisfaction. "I knew you had great tits the day you came over to tell me to be quiet."

I looked at him curiously.

"You didn't have a bra on, and your nipples were pointed right at me. I'll never forget how hot that was."

Oops. I had no idea. I'd thought I had everything that needed to be on. My cheeks grew warm as I thought back on the scene and the sight I must've made. It was a miracle that Killian remembered I was angry about his drums that day.

But the embarrassment dissipated when he pulled the nipple into his mouth then used his tongue and teeth to make me cry out in bliss. Patient torture seemed to be the theme of the morning as he moved to the other nipple and subjected it to the same exquisite torment. My breathing went ragged as pleasure pulled me deeper into the magic he was creating. He was careful to take me with him into its warm center, and I'd never felt this close to another person before.

He moved his hands under me, cupping my ass then squeezing. He buried himself deep inside, pushing easily into my wet flesh. I let out a soft sigh. He was moving so slowly that I could feel everything—every inch, every little change of the angle, every little twitch of his cock.

A plateau of pleasure shimmered, just out of reach, as he continued to drive into me lazily, like he had all the time and patience in the world, while my heart cantered endlessly, driving toward him, and desire pulsed and grew steadily within me. With supreme focus, he tilted my pelvis, and each thrust sent a jolt through me. But it wasn't enough to push me over. I needed more speed. And him touching my clit. I'd never been able to come with just vaginal stimulation.

"Killian," I said, my voice low and needy. "I wouldn't mind too bad if you want to go faster."

"Do you want to come?" He somehow sounded taut, amused and affectionate all at once.

"Don't you?"

"I can wait."

I debated for a moment. He'd drive me crazy like this all morning if I didn't tell him exactly what I wanted, but I wasn't used to giving orders in bed. Mainly because my previous partners had pouted—*are you saying I'm not doing it right?*—or had some creative interpretation and failed to give me what I wanted. Or it could be that they'd been physically incapable.

But Killian's dark blue eyes invited me to tell him what I needed, and he moved his body in a tantalizing way, as though trying to tell me he could give me whatever I wanted.

"I want to come," I said finally, a breath shuddering out of me.

The smile he bestowed on me was blinding. "Your wish..."

He pushed my legs up and over his shoulders, opening me wide for him. He drove inside me, harder and faster. Sharp pleasure shot through me with each thrust, and I moaned. I wanted to tell him to touch my clit, but couldn't, not when all my throat could produce was moans and sighs and ragged cries. My senses were out of control, and the tension in my belly grew tighter—almost painful.

Then it broke—a scalding-hot climax. I screamed, my fingers digging into his sweat-slick muscles. Fireworks seemed to go off inside me, and I shuddered and clung to him helplessly while he continued to have his way with me, driving me crazy and weak with pleasure.

He grasped my hair and kissed me hard before he gave one final thrust and came inside me. Then he held me tightly in his arms as though I was the most priceless treasure in the world.

CHAPTER 31

Emily

By the time we showered and came downstairs, it was too late for breakfast and too early for lunch.

"Looks like a day for brunch," said Killian.

"Where's Mir?" I asked, resting my hip against the kitchen counter. I was in one of his T-shirts and a pair of his boxer shorts. They were both too large, but with a safety pin, the shorts stayed put around my waist.

"She went to Sunny's, but it'll be a while. What are you in the mood for?"

"Coffee. And anything you want to eat is fine..." I trailed off as I spotted a juicer on the counter. I hadn't seen that while making the scampi. An unpleasant possibility went through my mind. My mom had bought a juicer last year and told me I should too so I could just "drink" my vegetables, since I didn't like eating them like a good, responsible adult.

"Kale's so good for you," she'd claimed, but it seemed to me that kale was a slow-acting poison, one of those silent killers. There was no other explanation for its vile taste, and you'd never know until it was too late.

I cleared my throat. "Well... 'Anything' as long as it's not kale or Brussels sprout juice or something gross like that."

"Why would I feed you something so terrible?" Killian said.

I indicated the juicer. "Because you have one of these torture machines."

He laughed. "Ah. I made some carrot and apple juice and forgot to put it away. Want some?"

I pulled back, my body stiff. "No thanks. Like I said, I don't do veggies before noon." Actually, I preferred not to do veggies at all.

"Aye, milady."

He stowed the juicer and pulled out a couple of presliced bagels. As he put them into the toaster, knocks came from the door.

Probably Mir coming back from the market. "I got it," I said, since he was busy in the kitchen.

When I opened the door, a tall, dark-haired guy with a pretty, sun-kissed face was standing there. He looked really familiar, but I couldn't quite place him. He wasn't from Kingstree—I would've remembered somebody this good-looking if I'd run into him in town.

There were several women hovering behind him. They had a rainbow of different hair colors: golden, brown, apple red, black, pink and purple. Gorgeously tanned, the six were dressed in skintight dresses with perfect hair and makeup, their feet in hooker heels that made my feet ache just from looking. The six had such huge breasts and tiny waists that they looked like a collection of living, breathing Barbies.

And they all had their phones out and were snapping selfies in different poses.

I stared, unable to process the scene. Kingstree was a nice, normal small town. It didn't have people like the women in front of me. Otherwise I would've heard about them from some gossip-loving resident. Or one of the cashiers at Sunny's Mart.

Actually, now that I thought about it, the women reminded me of the groupies I'd seen in some of Killian's photos on the Internet...

The man was looking at me with puzzlement. "Isn't this Killian's house?" He turned to the Barbie Sextet. "Babe, can you check the address?"

All of them moved to do his bidding. "Two-five-zero," the blonde said, snapping a picture of the numbers. She had a slight accent.

"Huh. Should be it," he said. "And hey, delete that pic. I told you, no personal info on the net." The blonde pouted but did as he asked.

Okay, time to get to the bottom of this. "Who are you?"

He didn't look like a weirdo stalker fan—or a reporter—but it wasn't as if weirdos always looked like weirdos. But given how many pictures his sextet had taken, the whole tableau was creepy. Maybe he looked familiar because I'd seen his mug shot on the news. Now I wished I was carrying the gun Mom had given me for self-protection. I didn't know if Killian had anything for home defense.

The stranger stared at me like he couldn't believe what he was hearing. "What did you say?"

"I said, who are you?" I spoke more slowly in case he was dim-witted on top of being hard of hearing.

He put a hand over his chest. A silver skull ring flashed on his middle finger. "You gotta be kidding! You don't know who I am?"

Definitely dim-witted. "Obviously. Otherwise I wouldn't have asked."

Now he seemed even more confused. "I'm Devlin Marsh."

Devlin Marsh? *The drummer guy from Killian's band.* He looked very different without black eyeliner and wax in his hair.

"Who are *you*?" he demanded.

"Emily," I said.

He frowned. "Emily? There's an Emily now?"

Weird. Why was he acting like he expected somebody other than me to be here? If Devlin hadn't been behaving oddly, I might've thought Killian was cheating, but right now, I was giving Killian all the benefit of the doubt.

"Has to be the wrong address. Or maybe I'm still drunk. Or... he's having trouble scoring properly." Devlin smirked.

Scoring properly?

Before I could respond, he bellowed, "*Killian!* Come out, you bastard. If I can travel halfway around the world to visit you, you can drag your ass out of your house."

"Dev?" Killian appeared from the kitchen. "What are you doing here? I thought you were in Spain."

Devlin took Killian's hand and did the man hug, bumping shoulders and slapping Killian's back. "I was," he said, "but since you weren't going to come out to Spain to hang with the babes, I figured I'd bring the babes to you."

Wow. I let the information trickle through my mind, trying to come up with multiple acceptable scenarios. But no matter how much processing I did, I couldn't think of a single case where I was okay with the "babes" Devlin had brought from Spain, especially after what had happened last night and this morning between me and Killian.

Besides, seeing the kind of women Killian had been around in pictures and seeing them in person was very different. The pictures hadn't felt real. And I could rationalize that they were in his past. After all, it'd be unreasonable for me to expect Killian to have lived like a monk. Fame and fortune gave men access to lots of hot, willing women. And if the man happened to be as young and sexy as Killian, the world was full of consenting vaginas.

"And you know what's more inspiring and restorative than a threesome? A *four*some," Devlin said with a grin. "You can have all of them except for two, because I hate sleeping alone."

How generous of him. And why did he need two women? One would be enough to keep him from sleeping alone. Besides, he hadn't brought the right number of women for one foursome and one threesome. And I needed to stop thinking about his inability to count, because otherwise I was going to hurl.

On the other hand, seeing him covered in puke would be oh-so satisfying. Was it possible to projectile vomit forcefully enough to hit him in the head on an empty stomach?

I *so* wanted to find out.

From the way Devlin was talking to Killian, I wasn't even a bed partner worth considering. I wasn't the right size or shape. And I was much older than the six he'd brought. None of them seemed a day past twenty, if that. And I was in my *late* twenties. Ancient to this type of man. I knew from years of watching my dad.

My earlier thoughts about going to Dallas withered away. It

wasn't an option if I was going to have perfect late-teen bodies rubbed in my face twenty-four seven.

Killian just stared at Devlin, his eyes slightly narrowed as he processed the scene.

Devlin leaned closer. "Looks like I made the right move, since you aren't having any luck with that Emma chick."

He was trying to whisper, but I could hear him anyway. Then I wondered who "that Emma chick" was. Emma was my pen name, of course, but how would Devlin know that? And if he'd heard about me through Killian, wouldn't he have recognized me when I introduced myself as Emily?

The women squealed and moved toward Killian, sighing and fawning. They paid as much attention to me as one might a piece of grass. It made me feel small, like when Dad's girlfriends had patted my head and cooed at me because I was too young to realize what he was doing with them was wrong. Then it reminded me of the times when I'd cook a special meal like lobster pasta or fancy beef stir-fries to get Dad to come home and have dinner with me and Mom, and I'd even tell him it was okay to bring "those nice ladies" because I was just that naïve and stupid. I clenched my fists at the sudden pang that pierced my heart. I was letting Killian's groupies jog the humiliating childhood memories and making me feel the same hurt and shame.

Because I'd looked too far ahead. Shit. I should've never considered going to Dallas with him in June when he hadn't even asked. Thank God Devlin and the women's arrival stopped me from bringing it up and embarrassing myself.

"Killian..." the girls sighed in unison. Must've spent hours practicing that.

Raising his hands, Killian pulled away from them. "Whoa, don't come any closer. I'm not interested."

The embarrassment stopped welling. Actually...it started to deflate.

"What?" Red tossed her perfectly curled scarlet hair over a shoulder. "But I have plans for us. My followers expect me to post something amazing. I promised and received over a thousand likes in two hours."

Did she track how many likes she got on that post by the hour? That was sad. Dedicated...but sad.

"Take it up with Dev." Killian's tone was hard enough to scratch glass.

His unexpected reaction made me blink. He wasn't interested in these women. Not even a little. He hadn't taken a single peek at their breasts or other butts. In fact, from the set of his mouth, I'd say their presence actually irritated him.

Pleasure and relief started to unfurl. Maybe, just maybe, Killian was okay. He wasn't like my dad—he seemed to have all the qualities I'd give my own romance heroes.

"Hey, don't drag me into this," Dev said. "I was trying to help you out of your funk, since you were reading junk like *The Very Bossy Engagement* and shit."

I inhaled sharply. Based on how immersed he got in my stories, Killian would never call my books junk, but Devlin's attitude was typical of people who knew nothing about romance. It grated badly, especially given the fact that he'd brought those women for Killian.

"Shut up, Dev," Killian said, clearly annoyed.

"What? It's not like I'm saying something that isn't true." Devlin rolled his eyes.

I should've puked on him. "Yeah, well, even if you believe that, you probably shouldn't say it."

He spared me a glance, a hint of stubbornness fleeting across his face. It was the same look that my dad got when he knew he was wrong but would rather die than admit it. "It isn't like you wrote it."

Killian closed his eyes briefly. "Actually, she did."

"No, she didn't. She said her name was Emily. Didn't you say the author was Emma something?"

"Emily *is* Emma," Killian said. "It's her pen name."

"Ohh..." Devlin's eyes widened. It was comical how eloquently his expression said, *Oh shit*. "You should've told me that before." He said it like it was one hundred percent Killian's fault that he'd shoved his giant foot into his mouth.

"Well. At least now I know what you really think," I said coolly, in my most evil corporate tone, the kind I'd used when I needed to let somebody know they were being terminated for poor job performance.

"Ah, don't be mad," Devlin said, all the chest-puffing bravado gone. "Killian, uh, forgot to mention he was doing you. Otherwise, I would've been much more polite."

"Shut *up*, Devlin," Killian said, trying to put a hand over the drummer's mouth.

Devlin leaned away. "It's true, man. You didn't say you were banging *Emily*. I thought you wanted to bang *Emma* the chick-lit writer!"

I crossed my arms over my chest. It didn't surprise me that Devlin knew Killian and I had had sex. He'd have to be braindead to miss the fact that I was wearing Killian's shirt and boxers this time of the morning, and what that meant. Devlin might be prone to saying stuff he shouldn't, but he seemed quick enough about things like sex and getting laid.

Killian stepped between me and Devlin. "I'm really sorry, Emily."

"It's okay," I said, out of reflex, then stopped. Why was I saying that? To smooth things over? To make them feel better? To hang around with them and their Barbie Sextet?

"Actually, it's not. I don't feel okay at all. I think I'm going to get my things and go home now." I waved in the general direction of the people. "Hope you have a great time together. We can talk later, Killian."

CHAPTER 32

Killian

Ah, fuck. Emily walked right past me to grab her purse, then marched out. She wasn't bothering to get her dress and underwear, which were still in the bedroom. From the stiff way she was marching to her house, she had to be fantasizing about murdering me. Then Dev and the girls. What woman would be okay with this kind of mess thrown at her right after the first night together?

I should've known Dev would pull something like this. To him, women were nice, fun distractions, a great way to relax and rejuvenate. He didn't understand why I liked Kingstree when it didn't have a thousand fawning females rubbing their tits all over me everywhere I went. He'd said it was fine for when I was settled down with a wife, but until then, I shouldn't be wasting my youth.

I jogged after Emily. Dev called out, "Hey, where you going?" but I ignored him.

"Emily, I'm sorry," I said, slowing down to a walk next to her.

She didn't respond.

"I didn't think he'd show up like this. Or bring all those women. I certainly didn't *ask* him to bring them. I also didn't say your books were junk. He's just being a dick. You know how much I love your writing."

She kept marching, her eyes straight ahead. Every taut line of her body said she was too irritated to talk.

Shit. Anxiety like I'd never felt ran through me. It was worse than my first audition. Now Emily was never going to give our relationship a shot. I'd be lucky if she didn't point and laugh when I asked her to consider coming to Dallas with me.

Damn it, Dev!

"I'll kick his ass. Would that help? I'm faster and stronger than him. And then I can pack him and those girls up and send them back to Spain."

When we reached her driveway, she stopped. "I know you didn't have him come here with those women. And I've heard worse about what I write and my career, so I shouldn't be this upset. But I am. I hate it that somebody as close to you as a band mate would say that about me. Or bring those women and be that insensitive when he had to know why I was at your place at this hour, dressed like this." Her lips were pressed tight, and I hated the unblinking gaze—or the fact that she wasn't looking at me. She was trying so hard to appear calm, but I could sense the tightly suppressed hurt.

Fuck. Emily took such pride in her work. I'd seen how hard she worked, and you only did that with things you cared about.

And the girls... Contrary to what Dev thought, they weren't my type. People generally put too much stock in women's cup size and hip-to-waist ratio. I also happened to care about brain size because I needed somebody I could talk to and laugh with.

Although I understood that Emily's reaction to the women wasn't completely out of bounds, I was vaguely disappointed that she considered me shallow enough to go stupid over a collection of silicone tits. Didn't she know me better than that?

On the other hand... If her close friend had shown up with a group of aspiring male strippers the morning after we had sex for the first time, I might not have been taken it too well either.

"He doesn't understand the situation," I said. "And he's probably still half-drunk. Just ignore him. You're so my type, those women don't even register."

She finally lifted her gaze to make eye contact. There was

uncertainty and pain, and I hated it that they had replaced the light and lazy satisfaction from earlier.

"I saw you step back from them, but..." She sighed, her shoulders sagging a little. "I have issues, Killian."

"I'd have issues if I were in your place," I said. "And unlike you, I would've broken Dev's nose."

Her lips were pressed nearly white, but they twitched. Just a little. Hopefully she wouldn't get more upset about Devlin's stunt.

"Um. Why are they filming this?" Emily said, her gaze flicking beyond my shoulder.

Filming? My body stiff, I spun around and saw the six women with their phones out, Dev watching them.

"What the hell, man?" I shouted, and then at the women, "Are you livestreaming this?" I was going to murder them all if they were. Then I'd murder Dev again just because I could. He knew how much I hated having my private life broadcast everywhere. The public got to see the slices *I* chose to share, not everything.

And I'd be damned if those women were going to use me and my life for their agenda. To get more likes. To get more followers. To get more publicity and adoration from strangers on the Internet. So they could somehow turn them into profit and even more spotlight.

"I wish," the black-haired one said. "We're just recording it. In case you want to let us post it later."

The pink-haired girl pursed her lips. "Now I have to edit the video, though. I don't like you turning around and yelling at us. It doesn't make for a good sharable experience. People are going to think we aren't friends."

"We *aren't* friends, and you absolutely can*not* put that up!" My blood pressure shot up with anxiety and fury that their thoughtlessness might ruin the peace and quiet—the *normalcy*—I was enjoying in Kingstree. "Nobody gets to put stuff about me on social media!"

"But don't you want people to see the real you? Do you know how many likes I'm going to get?" the brunette said. "And new followers. I'm close to a quarter million."

"I don't give a fuck!" I shot back. "If you want to be famous, go do it yourself and keep me out of it."

"Come on, Killian," Dev said. "Calm down. I already told them they couldn't post stuff without talking to me first. Their phones don't even have GPS on. I made sure before coming here."

It made me feel better. But only a little. "Delete the damned video. And the pictures," I said tightly. "Everything. Or you'll hear from my lawyer." I paid a shit-ton in retainer fees. He could think of some reason to sue.

"You're no fun!" The purple head pouted.

"Make sure of it, Dev," I said, dead serious.

Devlin grew sober. He knew how much I hated people using me, and that had been the main reason I not only broke up with Caitlyn but quit trying to date or hang out with people who weren't at my level of fame and popularity for a while. He held up a hand, indicating surrender. "No problem. Got it, man."

I turned to Emily, who was watching the ridiculous drama unfold. "Don't worry about it. Nothing about what happened here will be on social media," I said soothingly, confident now that Dev would take care of it. Nobody liked to have their privacy violated. And thank God we lived in an empty cul-de-sac with just our two houses. No neighbors secretly watching us with a bucket of popcor—

What the...?

A silver Mercedes swerved in, its engine roaring. The car got on the one-way loop serving the cul-de-sac, but was going the wrong way. For an instant I wondered if it was another of Devlin's surprises, but he was staring at the car with his mouth slightly parted. So it wasn't him.

The Mercedes veered sharply toward Emily's house without reducing speed. She stayed on the spot, frozen with her eyes wide.

"Shit." I grabbed Emily's shoulders and pulled her back, out of the driveway, as the silver vehicle screeched to halt. If I hadn't, it would've hit her. Heart racing, I put Emily aside and stepped toward the car. "*Are you fucking crazy?*"

The door opened, and a driver in a white jumpsuit spilled

out, holding on to the door for support and tears streaming down her face.

Uh... Whatever I'd been expecting, this wasn't it. I felt a little bad about yelling. Okay, maybe not the yelling, per se, but yelling "fucking."

"Emily!" The woman sobbed, one hand outstretched.

Emily closed her eyes for a second, then gave a resigned sigh. "Hi, Mom. What's wrong?"

This was her mom? I looked at the woman more closely. She had the same golden hair as Emily, the same build. I couldn't see her eyes because they were so swollen from crying.

"It's your father. He *admitted* it. He *is* having another affair, this time with his new assistant!"

CHAPTER 33

Emily

I stood there, my palms slick and my face cold, then hot. I should be used to this. After all, every time Dad admitted to screwing somebody, Mom came over crying. It was how she coped. And after a day or two she'd calm down and drive back to McLean, where she and Dad would go back to their lives like the affair had never happened.

But it was one thing for me to go through it in private. Quite another to have an audience, especially Killian. Not to mention the Barbie Sextet, who were still recording this. At least they wouldn't upload it to every social media and video site out there without Devlin's permission.

Why didn't she go to a hotel like I told her? That would've been better than driving all the way to Kingstree from McLean, crying her eyes out the entire time. I'd made the suggestion partly because I didn't have the time to deal with her while on a deadline, but mostly because I didn't have the mental and emotional energy anymore. At some point after twenty-plus years, I'd started to question the madness of continuing the toxic cycle. And why I was playing a role in it.

Suddenly, it was all too much. I shrugged away from Killian and pressed the heels of my hands against my temples, praying my head didn't explode. Or maybe that wouldn't be such a bad outcome. At least that way I wouldn't have to see the mess.

I couldn't think of a single thing to say to Mom. This was such a familiar routine, but I never seemed to know the right words to offer. Although it wasn't what Mom wanted to hear, I wanted to tell her, once again, to divorce Dad because he was never, ever going to change. He didn't love her enough to bother. Surely she didn't love him either by now.

But it wasn't the kind of thing I could say in front of everyone. And what would be the point, anyway? Would she respond differently? She always told me how her place was by Dad's side and how love was too wonderful to give up on. She refused to accept love wasn't some kind of chastity belt that could keep Dad's dick from touching other women.

"Oh my God, you poor woman!" someone said from behind me.

The Barbie Sextet was coming toward Mom, clopping precariously along in their heels and putting holes in the lawn. They surrounded her, the expressions on their faces eager and sympathetic. At least they weren't filming this particular spectacle for likes.

"Did you slap his face? That is what he deserves!" Brown said.

"No, no. Punch." Pink made a fist. "You *punch* a man who screws his assistant."

"Kicking hurts more, yeah?" Purple said.

"But you have to put on boots for that. Otherwise, your pedicure!" Blondie said.

Purple looked at her feet. "Too much work, then. Just punching's good."

Mom stared at them, mouth parted and tears no longer flowing. She was probably too bewildered by their presence and the words coming out of their perfectly lipsticked mouths. She also had no idea who they were. They looked nothing like the writers I'd been hanging out with over the last few years.

"Run him over with your Mercedes," Pink said. "Insurance can fix it."

"No, no." Brown waved her hand. "Insurance doesn't fix broken penises. She needs to get a new husband."

I put a hand over my mouth at the absurdity of it all as hysterical laughter started to bubble up. Maybe the Barbies weren't so bad after all. *I* wanted to punch my dad and run him over every now and then. And if it made him impotent, so much the better. At least that'd force him to be faithful.

Mom let out a small, shaky chuckle. "Yeah. Maybe."

"Don't let a cheating man make you feel bad," Red said.

"Look at your eyes. So swollen." Blondie peered into my mom's eyes. "No false lashes until you get the swelling down. They're going to look fake."

"False lashes *are* fake," Mom said with a sniff.

"Yeah, but not too fake. It's not good. You want them to look only a little bit fake," Blondie said with a practiced head toss that made her look like she was starring in a shampoo commercial. The breeze caught her hair and moved it sinuously.

Mom nodded, then dried her cheeks. "I'll take that under advisement."

I squinted, scrutinizing my mother. *No more tears.* No more wailing over what Dad had done...and how he'd betrayed her. She was *never* mollified this fast. It usually took me at least a day to get her to stop crying.

Relief started to ripple through me, and along with it came a reluctant gratitude to the girls. They didn't have to rush to console a stranger like that. Maybe I'd been too harsh and quick in deciding to dislike them.

"Hey, are you..." Killian stopped, running a hand through his hair. He looked lost and unsure. "Never mind. I'll just take the girls and let you talk with your mom."

There's no way I'm letting you take the girls away from Mom. She'd never looked this soothed before. But then, I didn't coo or fawn. I didn't want to take Mom's pacifiers and handle infidelity crisis number ten billion on my own.

"Um, no need. I think they're very good at dealing with her." I didn't add that there was no point in talking with her privately because this wasn't the first time Mom had come to me to complain about Dad's infidelity. I'd already known this would happen at some point. Dad had been "working late" when I called to confront him about the One-Star Hit Squad. Mom complained she'd smelled unfamiliar perfume on his clothes. The next step was him saying he was screwing another woman and Mom reacting dramatically to that and coming straight to me to unload the same ol', same ol'. It was practically preordained.

And I was terrible at consoling her. Mainly because I kept telling her to leave him. But she always refused, and my resentment bubbled the entire time until my chest felt like it was rotting from the inside out.

I'd never said it out loud because it would be too hurtful for Mom to hear, but I suspected Dad kept on cheating just to see how far he could push her and still get away with it. He seemed proud of the fact that he could do whatever he wanted and still keep his wife.

Dickhead.

"Honey," Mom said. "I'm hungry."

Holy crap. That was a signal that she was feeling a *lot* better. I looked at the Barbies in amazement. In less than ten minutes, they'd accomplished what would have taken me a full day and copious amounts of alcohol.

"I have some cereal, but no milk," I said. "But it'd probably be okay with some rosé." Mom deserved a drink or two.

She made a face. "That sounds disgusting."

"Plus too much carbs," Brown said with a sneer.

"I like carbs," I said. Carbs were so misunderstood and unloved, but without them the world would be a sad place. No crackers, bread, pasta or cookies? Just kill me now.

"They make you fat," Blondie said, glancing at my belly.

Bitch. I looked down. I wasn't skinny like her, but it wasn't like I had a huge potbelly, either. Besides, women were supposed to be rounded! Otherwise, God wouldn't have given us breasts!

"And *old*." Red shuddered like that was the worst thing in the world.

I was retracting the good opinion I'd formed just seconds ago. "Carbs are life."

Killian stepped forward. "If you don't mind, I'd love to treat you to breakfast," he said.

Mom finally looked at him, then her eyes went completely round in shock. Not surprising, since she'd been surrounded by the Barbie Sextet. She probably hadn't really noticed him until he spoke.

"Oh my *God*! You're Killian Axelrod!" she squealed in an unfamiliar, high-pitched voice. Her face turned red, and for once, it had nothing to do with Dad.

I cringed inwardly, but I should've expected this. She loved music, and she was never shy about hiding how she felt about her favorite celebrities. And I was certain her adoration wasn't all that over-the-top compared to teenage fans Killian had dealt with. I'd heard complaints from Skye, who told me her teenaged daughter considered fangirling a matter of life or death.

"I'm your biggest fan," Mom gushed. She lunged forward, grabbed his hand in both of hers and stared up at him like he was a rain cloud she'd found after days of wandering in the desert.

Killian smiled. "Thank you, Mrs. Breckenridge."

"Oh, *no*! Call me Abby." She laughed and looped an arm through his. "I had *no idea* you lived in Kingstree."

"Just visiting," he said. "And...could this be our little secret? I don't want any reporters or paparazzi showing up."

"Of *course*. Like I said, I'm your biggest fan. I only want what's best for you," she said breathlessly.

It was awkward to watch my mom cling to a man I'd clung to just hours ago...even if the context was totally different. But at least she wasn't so desolate over Dad anymore. That was a good thing, even if her fawning over Killian gave me an uncomfortable urge to look away.

"Are we going to have something other than carbs?" one of the Barbie Sextet said.

"He always has a lot of food options," Devlin said, finally walking up to the rest of us. "Let's go, babes."

CHAPTER 34

Emily

The brunch turned into a madhouse. Killian's place wasn't big enough for so many people. Or so many egos and pouts and endless snapping of photos.

Mir walked in soon after and stared at the group like she couldn't believe it. "Where did they come from?" she demanded. "I only got one tub of ice cream!"

"We don't do ice cream," Red said with a sniff. "It always turns into hips."

"And belly," Purple added.

"Hey, I can eat it," Devlin said with a grin.

Mir shot him a look frigid enough to freeze water. "I said only one tub."

"We can share, babe." He grinned harder, but she ignored him, shoved Bouncy Bare Monkeys in the freezer and shut the door. Maybe he'd insulted her before. Probably called her work junk.

The number of people didn't seem to bug Killian, who whipped up bacon, eggs and bagels for everyone. He ended up sitting between me and Mom, which was good, because it made her forget why she'd been crying on her way to Kingstree. Mir ended up directly opposite me and next to Devlin. She scowled and looked like she wanted to move, but all the other seats were occupied by the women.

The Sextet didn't eat much. Just two strips of bacon each, like they'd already agreed on a menu beforehand. Then they took lots and lots of selfies with the bacon. I didn't understand the obsession, but maybe with the right hashtags—#keto, #JustSayNoToHips, #NoCarb—they'd get a million likes on the pictures. Who could possibly hate bacon?

"I'm so stuffed!" Brown announced, patting the concave wall that passed for her stomach.

"Me too! So much food!" Pink said.

Mir gave them a look. I inwardly agreed with her sentiment, then took a large bite of a bagel, laden with lots and lots of cream cheese, since I'd already polished off four strips of bacon.

"I think I overate." Purple finger-combed her hair. "I feel a little sick. I should probably get up and walk." She went into the living room and started walking in a large square, elbows high.

"I'm going to do some cardio later," Red said, then sipped her coffee, which she had taken black.

Blondie nodded.

Amazing. If I ate like them, I'd weigh, like, two pounds. I couldn't decide if they went on about how much food they ate because it was some kind of weird bragging competition. After all, they were trying to stay skinny and young.

"That's a lot of carbs," Blondie said to me as I bit into my bagel again. "I'm serious. Carbs will make you old."

I'd rather look old than eat only six bites of food a day. Life was too short.

"Not to mention the bloating. Gluten does that," Red added.

"Do you have a degree in nutrition or something?" I asked, wondering what made them decide to give me unsolicited advice on my food choices. Weirdly enough, they didn't sound judgmental. Just really concerned, which was bizarre and awkward. I couldn't even get angry with them, even though I had every intention of ignoring their advice.

Pink made a small *I can't believe this* sound in her throat. "You don't need to go to college to know. It's common sense."

"I like women with hearty appetites," Killian cut in before

more unasked-for comments could come my way. "And I love eating carbs with Emily. She makes the best shrimp scampi."

I smiled. The remaining five girls looked at Killian and me as though we'd just announced we performed sacrifices of jelly-filled human biscuits and ate the remains afterward every full moon.

Purple returned to the table with a book in her hand. It was mine—*The Very Bossy Engagement* that I'd let Killian borrow. "I didn't know you read, Killian," she said, sitting down with the book with a small frown.

"In fact, I can," he said dryly. "Count pretty well, too."

I smothered a laugh, as it hadn't been that long since he'd equated watching TV shows and movies based on books to reading. He'd come a long way. He actually changed in order to read my stuff. Thinking about that sent a curl of warmth around my heart. No other boyfriend had expressed enough interest to read my stories until Killian.

"Is it good?" She flipped through a bit. "It has a *lot* of words."

"It's amazing." If Killian were a peacock, his chest would be puffed out and tail feathers fully fanned. "I loved it. Emily wrote it. She's an amazing writer. A bestseller."

"How many do you have to sell to make it?" Blondie said.

"A lot," Killian said before I could. "Readers love her work. The only way her books could be better was if they were longer."

I patted his hand. A lot of my readers said that, but if my books were actually longer, the stories would drag with filler.

Red frowned like she couldn't understand him, then turned to me. "You should turn them into books with fancy photos. You'll sell more. People love visuals. And they like to show off books like that on coffee tables."

I almost laughed. *One of my novels as a giant coffee table book.* I could just imagine the kind of photos required for the sex scenes.

"She doesn't write that kind of book. Besides, you're supposed to use your imagination," Mir cut in, her tone snotty.

"Pictures help," Red said. "Nobody wants to read this much text."

"Her books are perfect the way they are," Killian said, putting a hand on my shoulder. "If you disagree, you're wrong, and that's that."

Mom beamed.

I finished my coffee, heart fluttering, and used the mug to hide a smile I couldn't suppress. I loved it that Killian was defending my writing—and praising my career. Not to mention it was sexy as hell. The modern-day equivalent of a knight defending his lady's honor.

Killian stole a quick look at me, and I grinned. He smiled back, his blue eyes shining with something I couldn't quite decipher. But it didn't matter because, oh God, he was gorgeous.

As our gazes fused and the moment lengthened, I sensed a new emotion welling up inside. It was so sweet and warm that I wanted to hold on to it. And share it with Killian, because I knew he was the reason I was feeling this...this...whatever it was. The people around us receded into the background, and I reached over and brushed my fingertips along the corner of his mouth. His eyes followed the movement, then lifted back to mine. He looked at me like I was the only person on the planet who mattered, like I was the sun in his life.

He held my hand, his thumb stroking my pulse. My mouth dried, the air in my lungs hot.

"Stop it!" Red screeched.

I started, and the moment was broken. But that didn't lessen the impact of what I'd felt.

The Sextet squabbled, then started to take selfies with my book. If their followers were curious enough to check the book out, I hoped their heads didn't implode from the excessive number of words between the covers.

Mom watched Killian, her eyes bright with celebrity love, and got up to help him clean up afterward. I let her have some time with her favorite rock star, since that was an order of magnitude better than her thinking about Dad and the new assistant he was banging. I stayed in the dining room, while the babes from Spain and Mir argued over what to watch on TV. The Sextet had wanted to go into the kitchen with Killian, but he'd told them, rather firmly, that they should stay out for everyone's safety.

Devlin, who'd been four seats away, moved over and sat right next to me, taking Killian's chair. "Hey. Is it okay if we start over?"

"Do you want to, for real?" I asked, surprised.

"I might be an idiot from time to time, but I'm not blind. I can see K's crazy about you."

He noticed that? So that moment at the table wasn't just me? The fact that Devlin noticed made me feel good. It made it seem less like something I might've imagined.

He continued, "I don't want any bad feelings between us. Really sorry for what happened earlier." His voice was steady, and he didn't try to avoid eye contact or shoot me a pretty smile to get me to forgive him.

"Apology accepted." Devlin and Killian were band mates, and ultimately, they had to work together. I didn't want to be the reason they had a falling out, especially when Devlin was apologizing.

"You aren't going to hold it against me for the rest of my life, are you?" He gave me a slightly suspicious look. "You're saying it in a tone that says you might."

"Maybe you shouldn't do or say things that require an apology."

He shrugged. "Wouldn't have been necessary if Killian had just flown out to Spain like I told him to."

"Why didn't he?" Kingstree wasn't bad, but Spain had to be gorgeous. If I'd been burned out and had a lot of money like Killian, I would've gone to a beach in Spain to recover.

"He gets really anxious every time he has to fly. Absolutely hates it. I mean, it isn't like we fly crammed next to a toilet or anything. But no matter what cabin we're in, or even if we fly private, he acts like we're about to die. I sent him some studies on airline safety." He laughed. "Didn't help."

Devlin's explanation made sense. Sympathy stirred. I remembered what Mir had told me about their parents' death. It must've been traumatizing, enough to make Killian avoid flying if he could.

"You should've just left him alone," I said. "Then none of this would've happened."

Devlin frowned, then looked at me like he didn't understand

what I'd just said. Maybe he couldn't compute why he'd have to take responsibility for anything.

Then he shrugged again and grinned. "You're different than I thought."

"Why? Are you sad I'm not the type to fall to my feet at the fame and good looks of Killian and you?"

He leaned closer. "You think I'm good-looking?"

I almost rolled my eyes. Should've known he'd latch on to that. "You're missing the point."

"No, I'm not. You think I'm hot." He sat back, all smug and self-satisfied.

"Careful. If your head gets too big to fit into an airline cabin, you might have to check it."

"It's not bragging if it's true."

"No, it's still bragging. You're just bragging about something true."

He laughed. "Okay. So only Killian's worth banging?" I almost choked. He continued, "Don't be shocked. Pretty much every woman in the world thinks it's her life's goal to bang him."

This was such a weird conversation, but maybe he was trying to shield Killian, in case I was a gold digger. Killian was filthy rich and handsome and young, and hadn't he said that women had tried to take advantage?

My gaze darted briefly to the Sextet, who were busy channel-surfing. If Killian and I had never met, they'd be banging him, as Devlin had put it.

I looked back at Devlin. "Banging someone isn't a life goal," I said. "It's a bonus, frosting on the cake at the most."

"Huh. Figured you'd be more sentimental about it." He propped his chin in one hand. "You're a romance writer."

"I'm surprised you haven't snorted any coke yet." When he raised his eyebrows, I added in my extra-sweet voice, "You're a rock star."

He laughed. "Okay, you have a point. And I like you. So I'll make it up to you."

"How? I'm not interested in your body or anything else you could offer."

He shrugged. "I don't want your body either. I don't bang my buddies' girls, and I don't like women who *don't* look at me like I'm on their bucket list. But I'll think of something, 'cause I'm awesome like that."

CHAPTER 35

Killian

My gut tightened as I watched Dev move next to Emily and start talking with her. What was he saying? Probably nothing about the orgy he'd invited every band mate to last year. That had been embarrassing. And resulted in over a hundred thousand dollars in damage at the hotel because some of the girls who'd attended got out of control. Devlin was totally over Ashley, but he'd been hooking up with more and more unsuitable women even though he could do a lot better. It was as though he was purposely trying to avoid a situation where he might fall for a woman he was with.

The urge to quit cleaning up and evict him and his harem swelled. I hadn't wanted to invite him or the girls in for breakfast. If Abby hadn't shown up, I would've told them to go feed themselves somewhere else, because I was still annoyed about the way my morning with Emily had been ruined.

But Abby smiled at the girls like they were wondrous, mythical creatures, and I hadn't had the heart to kick them out. And if I asked them to get out now, that would make me look like a dick. I was experienced enough to know that pissing off the mother of a woman I liked was a terrible idea.

"I can't believe Emily's dating a rock star!" Abby's voice shook, her eyes still wide and bright. "She never even hinted."

"Really?" Emily had thought I was a pest trying to steal her ice cream and shatter her peace and quiet, but wouldn't she have had a chance to tell her mom about me? Or tell everyone, for that matter? Every woman I'd dated since the band's breakout hit had bragged everywhere about dating me.

My reactions used to range from mild irritation to outright hate, depending on the result of such bragging. But now I was annoyed Emily hadn't said anything about me to somebody as important as her mother.

Inconsistent, but there it was.

"She didn't know who I was when we first met," I said, as I took the plate she handed to me and loaded it into the dishwasher. For some bizarre reason, I didn't want Abby to think Emily hadn't mentioned me because I wasn't important enough.

"She didn't?" Abby straightened. "Well, she isn't into music."

"Yeah, she told me."

A soft sigh. "It's Brandon's fault."

Brandon? Some ex-boyfriend, or...?

Abby saw my expression. "Her father. My husband."

"Oh, okay. He doesn't like music either?" I asked cautiously, not wanting to trigger another bout of crying. Consoling a woman who was sobbing over a cheating husband was beyond my experience.

"Oh, he loves music. That's why she stopped listening to it. That's also why she eats junk food rather than cooking for herself."

I remembered how competent Emily had been in the kitchen when she made me the scampi. And how much she'd enjoyed herself at karaoke night. She'd never said anything about her dad, but I already hated the man for being a cheater and the cause of Emily giving up things she liked. When a man had a family, he had responsibilities—to nurture, to provide and to protect. Emily's dad apparently hadn't done any of that.

"He isn't a great husband...or father, frankly." Abby sounded a little sad. "He only supports Emily when she does what he wants her to, what makes him look good. He was so proud when she got into Harvard. Then he was furious when she graduated and told him she was going to be a romance writer. Apparently he'd told all his buddies she was going to work for Goldman Sachs."

My mind conjured up Emily working. Her hair a little messy. An old T-shirt. Yoga pants. Candy wrappers and cracker bags everywhere. Muttering to herself more often than not.

Probably not a Goldman Sachs look.

"But he should be happy with how she's doing," I said. "She's a *Wall Street Journal* bestselling author. That's a big deal. A huge accomplishment."

Abby laughed, then shook her head. "That's not success in his view. He loves to brag that Emily is successful because of him, and her writing 'mommy porn' isn't what he had in mind. He's determined to ensure she fails, so he can say, 'I told you so.' Emily and Brandon made a bet. She's supposed to hit number one on Amazon within four years or she's going to take out full-page ads in the *Wall Street Journal, New York Times, USA Today* and *L.A. Times*."

"Ads? Saying what?" I asked, my mouth dry with something that felt like dread for Emily and loathing for her dad.

"She has to admit that her dad's right—that romance is stupid and its readers are silly and she should've listened to him."

What the hell? "That would ruin her career!" And she worked too damn hard to set fire to it like that.

"That's the point," Abby said, like it was par for the course. "He believes that it'll make her rethink her career choice and force her into doing something more ego-boosting. For him, that is."

What a dick. My hatred for Emily's dad doubled. "But she doesn't have to take out the ads for real, does she? Who's going to make her?"

"There's a lawyer with an escrow account with sufficient funds to cover the ads. She's going to make sure."

I ran a hand across my mouth. This was freakin' serious. "So what happens if Emily does hit number one?"

"Then Brandon has to take ads out in those papers and admit that she's right—that romance is a lovely genre, its readers are smart and so on."

A much better scenario. Besides, I thought romance was pretty damned cool, and I considered myself smart.

"Can she do it?" I asked. She hadn't beaten her dad yet despite the fact that she'd been on bestseller lists before.

"Oh yes. We have lots of fabulous plans for her next book, and we're going all out because it's her last shot. Emily has been building her fan base, and they're wonderfully supportive. I'm sure she'll succeed this time. I can't wait to see Brandon's face when he loses. I've already designed custom frames for each of the ads. I'm going to print them out, blow them up and hang them in the bedroom, where he can see them every day." Her smile was mean, her teeth gleaming.

"Does she need help with publicity?" I asked, willing to lend Emily my team. They were amazing at creating buzz.

"She already has a publicity company she's working with. Thank you, though. We're doing whatever it takes to win."

"I hope she does. I'm on Team Emily one hundred percent." I wanted to see her succeed. If she happened to kick her dad's ass along the way, so much the better. But most importantly, I wanted her to be happy, and she wouldn't be happy if she had to put out those garbage ads and insult the genre and readers she loved so much.

Abby smiled. "I know. I heard you talk about her work. You're a gem, Killian. I'm glad Emily got to meet you."

CHAPTER 36

Emily

After brunch, Mir drove back to Alexandria to attend her meeting. Then Devlin and the Barbie Sextet left. Actually, it was more like Killian evicting them. But Devlin was laughing, so it didn't seem like there were any hard feelings between the two. I couldn't say the same about the girls, who pouted the entire time that they didn't get to post anything.

Mom also decided she ought to leave me and Killian alone.

"You don't have to go," I said, following her to her car. She was in a vulnerable place emotionally, and she might need my support. I also didn't want her to go back home either, because that meant Dad won too easily. He needed to sweat a little more. And attempt his usual routine to get Mom to come back.

"I know, but I'm not going to bother you two love birds."

My face grew hot. "We aren't love anythings."

"Oh please. I've seen the way Killian looks at you. And he's so handsome! Even better than Neil Diamond!"

"Who?"

"Never mind. He cares about you, Emily." She patted my arm. "You should recognize that. You're a romance writer."

"Romance happens in books, Mom. Not in real life."

Yeah, but Killian gave you romance-novel sex. So maybe he can give you other stuff, too.

Shut up, libido-addled brain. I wasn't talking to you.

"You shouldn't be so cynical, dear," Mom said.

"What I am is realistic." Even if I weren't, seeing Mom and Dad's marriage would have soured any starry-eyed expectations about relationships. "And I don't want you going home so soon. Dad needs to suffer some more. He hasn't sent you a single flower."

He always sent her gifts to get her to come back. Mainly chocolates and flowers. He even gave her apologies, which were empty, since he was going to cheat on her again.

But she always caved after he showered her with enough presents and enough *sorrys*. What was it about him that she couldn't ditch him?

"Don't worry. I'm going to Charlotte to stay with your aunt."

"Okay, then." I let out a soft sigh of relief. If my mom was a butterfly, easily won over by flowers and sweets, Aunt Gail was a dragon. She'd make sure Dad groveled enough.

"I'll call, sweetie. We need to talk about finalizing the ads and graphics," she said, giving me a hug.

"I know." I hugged her back and made a mental note to text Aunt Gail asking her to be extra nasty to my dad when he tried to get in touch. "Drive safe."

"I will. And keep in touch with those girls."

"You have to be kidding."

"But they're so friendly! I'm following them on Instagram. And I got their numbers in case you need them."

They exchanged numbers? It was a little creepy. Besides, I didn't want to socialize with Killian's exes or wannabe groupies.

On the other hand, it was my mom, the textbook extrovert. That was why she handled my social media for me. Because if I were in charge, I'd never post anything except once in a while when I had a new book coming out.

Mom drove off. I watched the Mercedes turn onto the main road and then went back to the house, dragging my feet and feeling like a dishrag after a Thanksgiving feast. I hadn't dealt with this many people in a while, and my introvert brain wanted to shut down and take some time to recover. Process what had happened. It was a bit too overwhelming, especially when the visits had happened so unexpectedly.

Killian was standing by the door.

"Hey," I said.

"Hey." He shoved his hands into his jeans pockets. "Can we talk a little? It won't take long."

I was torn because I wanted to plop down and think about nothing. But he had a stubborn look, the same one he'd had when we first met with our hands on the same ice cream. Except this time he looked more determined. Claiming there was a cockroach on his foot wasn't going to cut it.

"Okay," I said, slipping into my home and motioning for him to come inside.

He followed me in, shutting the door behind us. I threw myself on the couch, leaving him just enough room to sit. He did and waited until I arranged myself comfortably, with my feet up on the table in front of us.

"Okay. Number one, Dev won't bring girls over like that again," he said. "And whatever he told you is bullshit, so delete it from your memory."

"Which part? He said a lot of things," I said. "Besides, you don't know what he told me while you were in the kitchen with my mom."

"Pretty sure I do. He's kind of predictable."

"You mean that he's highly concerned about women who aren't a size two and don't think a life goal is banging you because they're unnatural?" I teased.

Apparently he missed the teasing, because he dropped his head into a palm with a groan. "Yeah. Some crap like that."

"Killian, I'm not going to hold his opinion against you. That wouldn't be fair. And he isn't wrong about me not being a size two or not thinking my life exists solely to have sex with you." I shrugged to let Killian know I wasn't that affected. Seriously, I'd heard worse from my dad, who should've been on my side.

"No, you don't get it. The reason I *like* you is that you aren't size two, don't want to post every minute of our time together online and don't look at my cock like you're going to take it with you if we break up."

I choked, then laughed.

"I'm serious. I don't want a woman who only eats salad or is too, too"—he searched for a word—"*vacuous* to do anything but take a bunch of pictures and upload them to every account she has. I've dated more than a few like that, and trust me, it's no fun."

I could imagine how annoying that would be. The Sextet's antics with selfies drove me insane. And they couldn't have been clearer that their sole goal was to get attention. Even spending time with Killian hadn't been about being with him, but how it could help *them*.

Relationships shouldn't be so cold and calculating. I felt terrible that Killian had to put up with people like that, and I was glad he knew I'd never be with him for anything other than the sheer enjoyment of his company.

Killian leaned forward, his gorgeous blue eyes on mine. "I know the timing's not the best. Fuckin' Dev." He huffed out a breath. "Anyway, I told you I'd have to leave in June to go to Dallas, and... Well, look. Long-distance relationships suck. I want to avoid that as much as possible. This is sudden and all, but I don't know how much time you're going to need to think about it."

It was a very long intro. "What's sudden?"

He let out a breath in a rush. "I was wondering if you want to come with me. I mean, at least consider it. I'm not saying you have to sell your house here or anything, but come to Dallas for a few months. Be with me. Let's see how it works."

Shock shot through me. Had he read my mind earlier this morning?

If we'd had this conversation without Devlin's visit, I would've smiled and said yes. It wasn't like I had any ties to the small town, and I definitely wanted to be with Killian more than I wanted to stay in Kingstree. Or at least if Mom hadn't visited, crying, because of Dad's infidelity for the nth time. But both of those things happened, and I couldn't just smile and say okay.

But maybe we should talk about this more openly and rationally, and perhaps even bring up the practical aspects of cohabitating. Although we'd spent some time together, we certainly hadn't done anything close to living together. And since I didn't want to sound like I was being accusatory, I decided to bring up my flaws first.

"I'm messy." I gestured around us, at the empty bottles and notes strewn everywhere.

"We can hire a housekeeper."

"I don't really like strangers in my home."

"Then we'll clean up together when we have the time."

I narrowed my eyes at his ready answers. This was too easy. "I will likely ignore you when I'm busy working or have a book launch coming up."

"No problem," he said. "I know you have a career you enjoy. I don't want you to give that up."

Pleasure rippled over the surprise and mild unease at what he said. But I wondered if he really knew what me not giving up my career would look like. Quite a few of my relationships had broken up because of my work. Even before I became a writer, I'd left guys because they hadn't understood why I worked so much. To them I should work from nine to five and spend the rest of the day with them, instead of billing over eighty hours a week to clients like I'd been expected to, or fly to wherever my client company happened to be located.

And being a writer didn't mean I worked less. I actually worked even more and kept irregular hours. Plus I had other needs for my workspace.

"You might not be able to drum when I'm working, which is almost all the time," I said.

"So? I'm not the drummer in the band, and that's what studios are for. Look, I like it that you aren't perfect, because God knows I'm not. I like it that you have dreams and goals that aren't tied to me and my career. I hate being around women who just want to, you know, hitch a ride on my coattails."

Resentment had slipped into his tone. Somebody—or maybe everybody since he'd hit the big time—had tried to take advantage of him. And I knew how nasty a taste that could leave in your mouth. I had peers who'd treated me like garbage when I was coming up suddenly become nice once I began hitting the best-seller lists.

"Like the girls who wanted to use you to get more followers and likes?" I said, stroking the frown lines between his eyebrows.

"Exactly. Or women who wanted to get introductions to people in the music industry. You don't care about any of that. When you're with me, you're with *me,* one hundred percent."

He was saying all the right things, the kind of lines I'd give my romance heroes. My head said I should be more cautious. But my heart boomed, *Yes, yes, yes.* He wouldn't be doing this if he didn't really like me.

And I liked him, too. He'd defended my career and my place in his life. He was kind to my mom. His actions had shown that he was serious about what we had, that he wasn't just some asshole like my dad.

Hadn't I thought that he might be able to give me more than just romance-novel sex? Hadn't I thought that we could have an entire romance novel *relationship?*

The nerves in my belly shivered and prickled. My mouth was dry, half with fear and half with excitement. It was a huge step, but I should take it, rather than letting my prejudices color everything. Because despite my upbringing, my head understood—at least logically—that not every man was like my father. If so, the divorce rate would be stratospheric.

"Okay," I said. "Dallas sounds like a great place to spend the summer months."

A smile broke out on his face. We sealed our agreement with a kiss...and then much more.

CHAPTER 37

Killian

The next day, Emily worked at the dining table while I reviewed email and some reports from my financial manager. He sent them every quarter to let me know how rapidly my money was multiplying. And it was, which was great... But every time I thought about the money, I missed my parents. Almost everything—all those billions—had come from them. And it had provided the initial funding the band needed to buy our first instruments and equipment, get studio time, pay the sound mixers and all that. It was as though they'd known what I would need to pursue my dream, even before I was old enough to know what it was myself.

My phone buzzed with a text from Dev.

–Devlin: Hey, wanted to catch up because we didn't get to talk yesterday. The girls are finally gone now. Sorry about what happened. I would've never done that if I'd known.

I sighed. It was hard to stay mad at him for long. He always knew when he screwed up and wasn't too proud to say he was sorry. Besides, he'd genuinely thought he was doing me a favor by bringing those girls.

–Me: It's okay. But next time, ask before you decide to bring women over. Not having that again with Emily.

–Devlin: I will. I was just trying to help. I thought maybe you were spiraling into some kind of abyss to be reading romance novels. So I'm gonna be good in Dallas. Shit, I guess that means I need to start being good now. I also owe a favor or two to your girl, too.

I frowned as I tried to process his text. He could be a bit unclear, especially when he had more than two things on his mind.

–Me: You there already? Not hitting a nude beach in Europe before June?

–Devlin: Trying to get my head back into the music. And the girls in Dallas are hot, too. Gotta diversify my diet. I've eaten enough European.

I shook my head. Discussing women like they were food groups. Don't just eat veggies—gotta have some meat, too.

–Devlin: And since I'm here, I'll get the house cleaned up.

We had a huge gated mansion in the city. Paid about two million for it three years ago. There was tons of space, but it was a bachelor pad with video games, an indoor basketball hoop (Max's idea, not mine), a pinball machine, bowling alleys, a hot tub big enough for an orgy (Dev's contribution) and a gigantic, in-progress pyramid of empty Red Bull cans. That was why Cole spent more time in his fiancée's modest apartment than at the mansion. And I couldn't envision Emily working in a space like that. She couldn't even tolerate drums. I definitely needed to figure something out for her.

–Devlin: Got any requests? Any new toys you want?

–Me: Nah, I'm good. But I need to look for a new place.

–Devlin: Dude... You still mad at me?

–Me: No. Just can't have Emily live there.

–Devlin: She's moving here with you?

I wanted more than just to move in with her. I could see myself with her long-term. Live and be together, like Mom and Dad. Emily seemed a bit skeptical about romance in general, which was understandable given what I'd heard about her parents' marriage. But I could make up for that. I could show her how it could be.

–Me: Yeah. I asked real nice, like a gentleman.

–Devlin: Gentleman, my ass. You're a rock star.

–Me: A gentleman rock star. It's a new category.

I could almost hear Dev grunt and laugh at the same time.

–Devlin: Want me to look at some places for you?

I started to type *yes*, then stopped. This was Dev. His idea of *good* was probably going to be an orgy pad. As though he'd read my mind, Devlin texted again.

–Devlin: I have excellent taste and judgment. Just ask anybody.

–Me: Is that what your girls said, or your lawyer?

–Devlin: I'm not having a lawyer pick out a place for you and Emily.

–Me: Don't bother. I'll have Felicia handle it.

–Devlin: You trust your assistant more than me?

–Me: Yep. Nothing personal.

–Devlin: That's what people always say when it's personal. Anyway, I gotta go. I'm meeting an interior designer.

An alarm rang in my head.

–Me: Why? Are you going to redo the house?

There was a big difference between *cleaning* and *interior decoration*. The band didn't need a brothel-themed home away from home. What if Emily wanted to see it? It'd be too embarrassing.

–Devlin: No. But I'm going to say that I am. Gives me a reason to meet her. She's hot.

I relaxed in my seat. Should have known.

Then I felt sorry for the poor interior designer, who might be counting on the potential contract.

–Me: You shouldn't lie and waste her time.

–Devlin: Lie? She wears a push-up bra, heels and a ton of makeup.

–Me: You have a point.

–Devlin: It's called dating, not lying. Birds always fluff up their best feathers to get the chicks. It's the same thing. If she gets mad because she found your ugly feathers, oh well. She should've inspected the merchandise better.

Spoken like a true player with lots of nonsensical mixed metaphors thrown in. I ignored his advice and texted Felicia to work up a list of a few decent places for me and Emily.

CHAPTER 38

Emily

I rolled my shoulders to unkink the knots. Staring at all the teasers, graphics and posts for the book launch made my eyes ready to fall out. The manuscript was edited, proofread and formatted in record time...but the process had still taken three weeks. Less than a day remained before the release date. It felt like nausea had been roiling in my gut forever, and had now gotten to the point that it just felt *buzzy*—like a million angry bees were trapped inside. Sweat slickened my palms, and I wiped them on my pants.

This was it. *My Fair Molly* was the best book I'd written, and had the most extensive publicity and promotion campaigns to push it out into the world. If it failed, I didn't know what I'd do.

Probably throw up. Then cry. Then consider fleeing the country so I could avoid seeing the ads.

My gaze landed on the lavender flowers Killian had brought yesterday. The purple bouquet smelled amazing. He said I needed to relax, and since it wasn't easy with so much riding on this book, he decided to bring me something to soothe my nerves.

He was just too damned thoughtful, like he knew exactly what I needed before I even said it. And that made me more optimistic about the decision to go with him to Dallas.

"How come you know how I'm feeling?" I'd asked him.

"Because I feel the same way when we have a new song or album coming out."

I'd never understood what "my heart melted" meant until then. My exes hadn't understood. They'd considered me neurotic and paranoid. But not Killian. If

I were writing a perfect boyfriend for myself, Killian would be it.

You have it bad.

Yeah, I did. It was almost enough to make me believe in true love, because true love wasn't about grand gestures, but everyday things someone did for the person they loved.

My phone pinged.

–Skye: Don't forget to send me your cover, blurb and links for My Fair Molly. I'm going to post them in my reader group and feature the book in my newsletter.

–Lucy: Ditto.

I smiled with gratitude and affection. Although Skye, Lucy and I didn't write the exact same type of romance, some of our readers overlapped. And asking them to help me promote the book had been on my to-do list.

–Me: Thank you! I'm just so nervous.

–Skye: Prerelease jitters. You'll kill it.

–Lucy: Seriously. I used to puke before every soccer match in high school, but I did fine.

That was true. She'd received an athletic scholarship to college. And they both understood what it was like to launch a book themselves, although they'd never had the kind of stakes that I did with this one.

–Skye: Don't forget to eat and sleep.

–Lucy: Right. We don't need you nearly passing out again from a lack of sleep like you did with the last release. We have a signing to attend.

Right! I'd almost forgotten in my pre-launch frenzy. We were all going to the signing in San Francisco this weekend. Which would be amazing, since I hadn't seen Skye and Lucy in months. There was something so exciting and energizing about spending time with like-minded friends who understood everything about the author world. And I loved meeting fans who liked my work enough to take the time to come see me. I knew there were people reading my stuff, but seeing them in person made it feel all so much realer. And when they told me how much my work made them laugh or brightened their day, it made me realize once again why I'd chosen to be a writer—to allow people to escape into a book world I'd created and feel happy.

–Lucy: Blue's coming. It's going to be so much fun.

–Skye: So is Zack! The hubs can hang out and amuse each other, while we sign, sign, sign.

I'd known Skye was bringing her husband because her parents-in-law wanted to take the kids for the weekend. But I didn't realize Lucy was going to bring hers.

Should I ask Killian if he wanted to go? He could see photos of authors and their significant others at the signing, and might feel excluded if I didn't even ask. But at the same time, I didn't want to make it seem as though he had to now that I knew how much he disliked flying. It was one of those situations that required a delicate touch.

Then there was the matter of him being a rock star. Unlike other husbands, people would recognize him. Which would then cause a stir and take some of the spotlight away from the authors who showed up. And that would be unfair to them. I didn't want to do that to my fellow writers.

Maybe there was no point in even bringing it up when I couldn't really have him come with me anyway. Shit. I should just tell him I was going to San Francisco for a signing and leave it at that.

–Lucy: Blue has a few friends in the Bay Area, so we're going to spend some time with them, too. Emily, you can join us. Some of them are single.

Lucy the matchmaker. She believed everyone had a soul mate out there, just waiting to be discovered. Unlike me, who thought the whole soul mate thing was an overrated fantasy. But then... Killian shared the same belief as Lucy. He'd told me he believed in everlasting love, like what his parents had shared.

–Skye: Ooh. Are they cute?

–Lucy: Unless the pictures are photoshopped, some of them

are totally cute. Blue said they're great dancers too. You know dancers have good moves in bed. I can vouch for that from experience.

I thought of Killian—the way he'd shone on stage and electrified the crowd. The way he kissed me and set me on fire that night and every night since. My heart throbbed at the memory, my breathing growing slightly shallow. No man had mesmerized me the way he did, and I doubted anybody would again.

I should let my friends know I was unavailable before Lucy wasted energy trying to set me up with someone. And withhold as much info as possible about Killian.

–Me: No, thanks. I'm seeing someone now.

–Lucy: WHAT?

–Skye: Since when? How come you never told us?

–Me: It's sort of recent. And I've been busy.

That was a terrible partial lie. I just hadn't been able to figure out how to say I was dating, because then they'd want to know every detail, and I knew I couldn't tell them everything, especially when Killian had made it clear he wanted his privacy. But Lucy and Skye were persistent—you couldn't make it in the writing business if you weren't—and I didn't want to deal with an inquisition. I didn't think they'd sell the info to some trashy tabloid, but they might let something slip. And Skye's daughter was totally into music, so she would recognize Killian for sure.

–Skye: You are NEVER too busy to talk about a new man in your life!

–Lucy: Details!

–Skye: Hold on. I'm calling. This requires a real convo, not just texting. Gimme a sec.

Torn between amusement and a pinch of dread, I waited. Skye always claimed she and technology didn't get along. But when she needed to gossip, suddenly she became a tech magician.

And there it was. A three-way video call from her. Since her kids were in school right at the moment, she was doing it all on her own.

Skye's wide brown eyes filled the screen. "Okay, you have to tell us everything. I can't believe you found the time to write, edit, plan a release and find a man, all at the same time!"

Lucy nodded, tendrils escaping her messy topknot. "Seriously."

"It's my neighbor," I said, trying not to give too much information.

"The one who drummed?" Skye said.

"And borrowed your hot water?" Lucy asked.

"I guess he didn't poison you..."

"Yes, yes, yes," I said. "Yes to everything."

"Are we going to meet him soon? Like...in the next week?" Skye asked.

"I...doubt it."

Lucy's face fell. "He couldn't take time off?"

"It's not about taking time off. He doesn't like flying. And it's a long way to San Francisco."

"That's true, but..." Skye sighed. "That's too bad."

"Is it not serious enough that he wants to ignore his flying phobia to support you in San Francisco?" Lucy asked.

Crap. "No, it isn't like that. We're pretty serious. I'm planning to go to Dallas to be with him."

"For real?" Skye said, her jaw slack.

"About ninety-nine percent certain." I reserved one percent just in case.

Skye and Lucy both formed perfect Os with their mouths.

Skye laughed first. "Oh my God! You're in love!"

"Am not," I said quickly, even as my belly started cartwheeling inside me. Love sounded way too serious and much, *much* too soon. "It's just a trial. I'm not selling my place in Virginia."

"Yeah, but you're thinking about moving to another state for him!" Lucy said, her eyes bright. "I think it's amazing. Like a romance novel. Instalove with an irritating but super-hot next-door neighbor."

"And it's perfect because you don't have to give up your job or anything. The best happy ending," Skye added.

"This is real life, not a book. It's a lot more complicated," I said, because it *had* to be more complicated. Otherwise nobody would be cheating on their spouse or getting divorced or crying their heart out over a broken relationship.

"How complicated can it be? He sounds like a decent guy," Skye said.

"What do you mean, 'sounds like'? I haven't told you anything about him."

"He cooks." In her mind, any guy who cooked for a woman was a great catch.

"Well...yeah. He does cook. He also reads my books," I said.

"Does he enjoy them?" Lucy asked.

"I think so."

"Total winner! Is he better than Scott in bed?" Skye demanded.

"Scott who?" I didn't have any ex named Scott. Neither did Skye or Lucy as far as I knew.

"Your hero from *That Hot Night*. His book has the best sex you've ever written," she said. "And the hero was hung like a stallion, with endless stamina."

Lucy nodded. "That's true. In one romance group I'm in, he got voted 'hero I'd most want to bone' last year."

I knew which one she was talking about. I'd been so flattered when the group admin emailed me a banner to put on my social media and website. And I put it up proudly.

"So. Better or worse?" Skye of the one-track mind asked.

"Better," I said immediately. Scott was my imagination. Killian was not. And he was incredibly enthusiastic in bed. With great technique and raw power. And endurance.

Skye and Lucy let out loud squeals.

Lucy fanned herself. "You *have* to bring him to the signing!"

"Totally! I'll pay for his airfare! And enough Xanax to chill him out!"

"A man who can give you better-than-Scott sex is totally worth going to Dallas for," Lucy said. "He might even give you better-than-Scott romance, too!"

I laughed softly. I'd had similar thoughts about Killian. Optimism began to bloom.

I could totally give the relationship a few months. And if it was still good, then... Well, then it'd be love.

The door opened.

"I'm home!" Killian said brightly.

I perked up, but the need to end the call surged. I didn't want Skye or Lucy to catch Killian in the background accidentally. Or recognize his voice. "Gotta go," I said. "Dinner's here."

"Isn't it a little early?" Skye said.

"Skipped lunch. See ya!"

"Don't skip! Eat. Enjoy!" Lucy said.

"Happy early release day!" Skye said.

We hung up. Killian dropped something off in the kitchen, then came to the table with a cheese pizza and a bottle of Riesling. "Still in that shirt?"

He looked at the loose Axelrod shirt I'd filched from his closet a couple of days earlier. It was so large that I wore it like a mini dress.

"Didn't get a chance to change," I said with a shrug. Then I gave him a long, assessing look. "Want me to get out of it?"

"Yeah, totally. We shouldn't wear clothes at home. Can we make that our relationship rule, like what the hero and heroine did in *The Dating Rules*?"

I laughed at his hopeful expression. Of course he'd remember that from the book and bring it up at the first opportunity. But it was partially my fault for not phrasing things correctly. My brain was foggy with the lack of sleep and food, but I was too wired to sleep. "I meant do you want me to put something else on?"

"Of course not. If I can't have you naked, I'd rather have you in my shirt. Gets me super excited, like you're all mine."

Warm, tingling sensations moved through me and made me smile.

He kissed me. "Ready to rock and roll tomorrow?"

I nodded, then stretched my neck to relieve the tension. "Yeah. I checked off everything on my list."

"Awesome." He grinned. "And I brought us an early dinner, since you worked through lunch." He frowned. "You shouldn't do that."

"I just lost track of time, *Mom*."

"Hey, somebody's gotta take care of you. Otherwise you'd eat nothing but crackers all day long."

No point arguing that. Animal crackers and Hop Hop Hooray had sustained me last time I had a book out. Actually, they generally kept me going most of the time. But not for this book, because Killian was determined to make me eat like a responsible adult.

He set everything on the table, including two wine glasses, then sat down and opened the box. I stared at the steaming pizza. My brain said I needed the fuel, but my stomach said no. Not because I didn't like pizza—I was a well-adjusted, normal human being—but because my belly felt tight and slightly acidic from not having eaten since breakfast.

"Come on," he said, handing me a slice on a paper plate.

I took it, but instead of biting into it, I sipped some of the crisp wine. Killian took a piece and finished it in five big bites. I finally started nibbling on mine.

"Not in the mood for pizza?" he asked.

"No, it's fine. I'm just... My stomach feels a little weird."

"You need something?"

I shook my head. "It's just stress. I shouldn't be feeling it. I checked my to-do list three times. I've already scheduled everything, so my newsletters and social media updates should go out automatically over the next seven days."

He nodded and squeezed my hand warmly. "There you go. So now it's time to sit back and give yourself a break."

I managed to chew and swallow a few more mouthfuls for his benefit, then had more wine, although I knew alcohol wouldn't help much. It never did.

He watched me, his eyes dark with concern. Then, wiping his hands on a napkin, he got up and moved behind me. He slowly rubbed my neck and shoulders. I sighed as his fingers dug into my muscles, loosening kinks that were now a couple of days old.

"That feels really good," I said after a moment.

"You're really tense."

"I'm always like this. Well, this time more so."

"You have a lot riding on this one. I heard about the bet from your mother."

"She told you?"

"Yeah."

I sighed, wishing Mom hadn't said anything. The wager was mortifying. Hell, the entire drama with my dad was humiliating.

It was awful enough that Killian knew the situation with my dad's affairs, but now he had to know what a bad father Dad was, too?

"He's not going to win, Emily. Karma's going to come bite him in the ass sooner or later."

"I hope it's sooner, for my sake," I grumbled.

A moment of hesitation. "Is there anything I can do to help? I could mention it on my profile or something."

I turned around, surprised at the offer. He'd made it clear he hated people using him, and honestly, the idea of asking him to promote my book on his social media accounts had never crossed my mind.

"No, thank you." I added a smile to let him know I appreciated the offer. "You're already doing enough to help. Just keep rubbing."

Killian laughed and continued to massage me, and I closed my eyes to enjoy it. But my mind wouldn't relax. Now the stakes felt bigger, especially with Killian knowing about the bet. Losing with him watching would be extra humiliating. Should I re-check the images Mom and I had selected for the promotion? What if I rewrote the newsletter?

"You're the only person I know who can tense up more while getting a massage," Killian said.

"Sorry. I'm just...distracted." I patted his arm, feeling like a failure for not responding to the nice rub like a regular human being. Just ask anybody what they'd do if a hot rock star brought home an early dinner and rubbed their back. It wouldn't be "think about marketing."

A determined gleam lit his gaze as he looked into my eyes. "You're such a challenge at times."

"Does that bother you?"

"Nope. Makes me like you more."

He turned the chair around and kissed me, wrapping his hand around my neck. I kissed him back, our mouths fusing, our tongues stroking each other. He tasted like wine and lust. My blood rushed through my head, slowly drowning out the *shouldn't you try to do...* voice screaming to be heard. The man knew exactly how I liked to have my mouth ravished, how I wanted to be touched.

His other hand traveled lower...cupping a breast through the shirt. He groaned. "I love it when you work braless."

I let out a breathless laugh. "It's cumbersome when I'm just home alone."

"When *you*'re alone?" he murmured. "You know how much it gets in *my* way?"

He rubbed his thumb over the hard tip. Sparks of excitement shot through me, heating me inside out. He continued to tease my nipple, then bent to nip it, the shirt blunting the sharp edge of his teeth.

God. I didn't want to feel him through the cloth. I wanted his mouth on my bare skin. I pulled the shirt up greedily, and he laughed, the sound wicked and satisfied. He closed his mouth around my nipple, directly this time. I arched my back, gripping the edge of the seat as he sucked, sending streaks of white-hot pleasure through me.

He moved to the other breast. I watched him lick my other nipple while he pulled my hips until I was perched on the edge of the chair, his shoulders between my spread thighs.

He touched me through my thong, and I hissed out a breath. I was already so wet there. My clit was pulsing with need. Could he feel it?

He pulled the thong aside, his mouth still on my breast, then pushed two fingers inside. I arched into him, moaning and wanting more. He didn't hesitate as he lowered his face between my legs.

Every lick, suck and gentle nip sent hot shivers through me. Lust and desire entwined tightly until I felt like I'd die from pleasure. Killian was ruthless with his tongue, and it was all I could do to not fall off the chair as bliss overpowered me, pushing me further until I climaxed.

I tried to regain control of my breathing, my vision orgasm-hazy. He carried me to bed, kissing me hard. He tasted like me, and I shivered at the raw desire shooting through me.

He laid me on the bed and got rid of all of our clothes in a few impatient movements. After sheathing himself in a condom, he spooned me, his hard cock pressing against my backside. Kisses rained down on my neck and shoulders, and I bit my lip at the intimacy of the moment. This didn't feel like just sex. It felt like more. But all I could do was immerse myself in the lavish attention Killian showered on me.

He gripped my breast and teased it, while his cock drove into my slick depths, filling me and making my breath shudder.

"Fuck, you're so wet and hot," he said, his breath fanning against the nape of my neck.

A moan tore from my throat. I'd never been this turned on or in tune with another person before.

Killian moved. And I gripped him, moving my pelvis to match his rhythm as pleasure as thick and sweet as honey flowed through me.

I cried out his name as his hand slipped between my legs and rubbed against my clit. My toes curled, and my mind went empty of everything but the ecstasy shattering through me.

"Emily. My Emily," Killian said against me as he came.

Every muscle in my body went limp, and I started to slip into sleep. I blinked, tried to resist, but Killian ran his large, hot hand along my arm and kissed behind my ear. "Get some sleep. You've been up late for days."

"But..." Sleep sounded so good. I couldn't remember why I wanted to resist his suggestion. But something in the back of my mind said I should get up.

"I'm going to hold you. We're both going to sleep."

Getting up meant giving up the warm space between his arms. An unbearable thought. I snuggled closer, ignoring the part of my mind that wanted me to go back downstairs.

CHAPTER 39

Emily

I opened my eyes. The bedroom was fairly bright.

Too bright. Mild panic shot through me, but I told myself it couldn't be that late. The sun was up earlier and earlier these days. I checked the time.

A little after eleven—

Oh shit!

I jumped out of bed. Killian was already gone. Eek! Why didn't he wake me up?

He came into the room, carrying two mugs. "Morning, sleepyhead."

The aroma of coffee managed to penetrate the alarms going off in my head. "Okay, you're forgiven," I said, taking the proffered mug. Getting upset with him wouldn't do a thing, and if I was mad at him, it would be weird to accept the coffee.

"Forgiven...?"

"You let me sleep in! It's late in the day." I needed to watch the Amazon Kindle chart. Not because staring at it would make a difference. But that was all I could do right now, and I had to do *something.* It was like a football fan watching his favorite team play in the Super Bowl—staring at each second, wide-eyed and sweaty-fisted, even though he couldn't do anything about the outcome of the game.

But unlike the fan, I *could* do something. Dump more money into ads or something, although it'd take at least two or three days before I could see the result.

"You needed the rest," Killian said. "Don't you feel a lot better now?"

Why did he have to be right? "Yeah..."

"Besides, what would you have done if you'd gotten up early? You said everything was scheduled to go out automatically."

I took a sip of coffee. He'd already had at least one cup, so it seemed unfair for me to talk about this without caffeine, even though I did feel much better after a good night's sleep. "Sit in front of my computer and refresh the screen to see how my book's doing," I mumbled. And my fingers were itching to do exactly that, even as I was trying to take in the caffeine I needed to function.

"I'm sure your mom's doing that. And I did too."

My mouth dried as nerves jittered. Actually, everything inside me jittered, unsteady and fragile. He didn't say I'd won the bet. But then, this was just the first day. I should relax for the next two hours—at least—for the Amazon rankings to be updated. And he was right about Mom. She checked how my book was doing even more obsessively than me, so she could have her revenge against Dad vicariously.

"If you need help relaxing, I can always rise to the occasion," Killian said.

I laughed, appreciating his attempt to distract me. "You did enough of that yesterday." I kissed his cheek. "Thank you."

"My pleasure," he said. "Literally."

"I should be used to this, but I never can just relax."

And it wasn't just about the bet. I'd never been able to just sit back and chill when I had a new book coming out. But this time, the stakes were so much higher. The bet weighed heavily. Holly Stein was waiting for a text from either me or Dad so she could go ahead and have the ads published. And if I lost and the full-page ads went out as Dad wanted, they'd be the ultimate slap in the face to my readers and all hardworking romance authors. I'd have to get a new identity to hide from all the hate I'd get.

Or tell everyone the truth about the bet.

But that seemed stupid on its own. It was ridiculous to make a bet like that, especially when you weren't a hundred percent certain you could win. I'd done it out of anger and stubborn pride, but those were dumb, dumb reasons. And not everyone would see my post about the story behind the ads. So I'd still end up being the most hated romance author ever.

But *My Fair Molly* had just become available in the Amazon store. I was being much too impatient thinking that it should be number one right this moment.

"Hey, you care," Killian said. "I know the bet is part of it, but I also think you care a lot about how your fans receive your work."

"Yeah, I do."

I set the pillows so I could lean against the headboard comfortably. Killian settled down next to me with his coffee.

"I just want them to laugh and have fun with the book, you know?" I said. "Nothing brightens my day like getting an email from a fan telling me my books made her laugh or made her feel better after a long, hard day."

"They'll love your new book, too."

I leaned my head on his shoulder. It was lovely and comforting to be able to share the moment with somebody who respected my work. "Do you feel this nervous when you release a new album?"

"Of course." He held my hand in his, running his thumb gently along my fingers. "We think it's great stuff. We want everyone to love it. But tastes can change, or the timing isn't right... Lots of things can make or break how the songs are received. It's hard to put a piece of ourselves out there because we're vulnerable."

Yeah, I thought. *That's it.* I finished my coffee. Killian got a call and went downstairs to take it. So I went to the bathroom to brush my teeth and take a quick shower.

Afterward, trying to breathe slowly, I went to the living room to check my laptop. I told myself I'd be okay as long as I was in the top ten at the moment, although a small part of me knew that was a lie. Nothing less than number one would do.

Before I could open my laptop, my phone started ringing. It was Mom.

Oh shit. She didn't usually call me on the day of the launch unless something was wrong.

Please don't let it be another Dad's Cheating on Mom drama, please please please...

On the other hand, it might be something worse. Like all my ads were rejected or my newsletter service server went down.

My stomach in an ugly knot that made me want to vomit, I hit the green button.

"Hi, Mom." My voice quavered a little.

"Oh my God!" She let out a squeal loud enough to fry my phone's speaker. "Oh my *God!*"

"What happened?" My heart started to beat faster. My mouth dried until it felt like it was full of dust. It was either really good news or bad. She had to tell me which before I lost my mind. "*What?*"

"It's number one! I just checked! It's number one!"

The words trickled into my brain, but my mental gears got stuck for a second. All thought vanished, and I couldn't feel anything.

"I screencapped it! I sent it to you and your dad! You need to email Holly and have her put out the ads!" Mom laughed. "I can't *wait*! I can't even sit still."

"Oh my God!" I said finally, repeating what Mom had said in lieu of greeting. "*Oh my God!*"

"I know, right?"

"Thank you, Mom! I gotta go!"

"Of course. Celebrate! Woohoo!"

The phone slipped from my shaking hand and fell on the table next to the laptop. Then I started jumping, my fists up in the air. I screamed, "Yes, yes, yes!"

Killian came into the room, looking at me curiously. I ran and jumped on him, my heart swelling until it felt like it'd explode with joy and triumph. I laughed, breathless, my face hot.

"I did it! Mom just said I topped the chart!"

A huge grin split his gorgeous face, his eyes bright as the corners crinkled. "I *knew* it! Congratulations!"

He wrapped his arms around me. Our mouths met in a kiss that ended in a laugh.

"You're shaking," Killian said.

"I'm just in shock." It was one thing to dream of making it, but something else to have it happen for real. All the hard work, all the anxiety and insomnia—and that damned *running*!—had paid off. And I got to celebrate my victory with everyone when Dad paid for the ads, admitting that he was wrong and romance freakin' *rocked.*

"I thought you had everything in place to make it happen."

"Yeah, but I wasn't sure. You never know how a book is going to do. And I was certain Dad would do whatever he could to sabotage me."

"Sabotage?" Killian tilted his head. "Seriously?"

I nodded. "Oh yeah. More times than I can count. But it doesn't matter now."

"You're right, it doesn't. We have to celebrate. And I"—he turned and indicated the kitchen—"just *happen* to have a bottle of Dom chilling in the fridge."

I stared at him. "When did you get it?"

"Yesterday. I had a feeling."

Air clogged in my throat. I couldn't believe how he could be so certain when I hadn't been. And it sent a warmth through me that spread everywhere in my body and ended in my heart. "You're awesome," I said, my voice thick.

"Hey, you're the one who's number one." He kissed my forehead. "Let me pour the champagne."

He pulled the blue-green bottle out from the fridge and two flutes from the cabinet, then brought them to the dining table. He expertly uncorked the bubbly wine, muscles flexing under those forearm tattoos, and as I watched him, my entire torso fluttered with something that felt like anticipation, surprise and maybe even love. He poured two flutes and handed me one.

"To my *very* successful girlfriend," he said.

My cheeks and neck warm, I clinked my glass with his. I liked the way he called me his girlfriend. A *lot*. It made our relationship feel that much more concrete and real. The obvious and logical next step toward making this more than a fling. Something worth moving to Dallas for.

"How do you want to celebrate?" he asked.

"Other than the champagne?" I sipped it, let the bubbles fizzle in my mouth and throat, coat my tongue with mellow flavor. Dom tasted like gold, and it was worth every penny of its exorbitant price.

He nodded. "This is sort of...anemic."

Spoken like a true rock star. I took a moment to consider. I'd never really celebrated big writer career wins. My writer friends lived too far away, and nobody else really understood why it mattered, especially my exes. As for other types of milestones... The ones my dad had thought worthwhile had been celebrated, at his discretion, the way he saw fit. My preferences hadn't been much of a factor.

I looked at Killian. He was gazing at me like he'd do anything I wanted—like I was the center of his universe, the reason for his existence. Something sweet and effervescent fluttering in my belly, I said, "I want to hear you sing...and dance with you."

"I thought you didn't really like music," he said, surprised.

"But I like it when you sing. You were super-hot on that karaoke night."

He finished the rest of his champagne in a couple of big gulps. "Well, if you *insist*..."

Rising, he extended a hand. I laid mine on it and felt his strong fingers close.

He sang a song I didn't recognize, but I didn't care. The husky timbre of his voice stroked my spine, sending shivers running up it. He wrapped his arm around my waist, and we moved to the sweet melody like we'd danced to his singing a thousand times before.

He'd been incandescent on the stage, the crowd going crazy for him. Now, with only me as an audience, his performance was intimate. He was singing only for me, his body against mine, his breath fanning the side of my neck as he crooned one love song after another, making my heart throb, my insides hot and liquid.

And I finally realized—and accepted—that I was in love with this rock star.

CHAPTER 40

Emily

My phone pinged and buzzed nonstop. I ignored it while we had our champagne and danced. But eventually I had to take a look at what all those messages were about. They might be just a bunch of "congrats," but they might be "Oh shit, something went wrong."

Besides, I needed to contact Holly with the screencap Mom sent as proof. Since it was easiest, I texted her.

–Me: I won the bet against my dad. Here's a screencap of me being number one on Amazon. Please have the ads go out this weekend. Thanks.

I then sat in front of the coffee table and checked my messages and email, responding to them as quickly as possible. The phone rang with a call from Dad. I smirked. Should I bother or not? Well...maybe I should answer. And gloat. It could be part of the celebration.

"Yeah?" I said, my tone all smug. But he deserved that.

"Welp, looks like you finally hit number one."

I frowned. He didn't sound angry. More like...self-satisfied. What the hell? "Yeah, you lost," I said, in case he'd forgotten about the bet. Or thought he could wriggle his way out of honoring it.

"No, not really."

"Oh yes you did. I'm number one, which you said I'd never achieve. So Holly's going to use your money to put out those ads." And Killian and I would be dancing with the ads spread out around us.

"I didn't lose anything. I'm the one who made sure you could be the best you could be."

What the hell? "How? With your fake nasty review team? Or with your very real nasty attitude?"

"Without me to motivate you, you would've been just a mediocre writer. Most novelists are lucky to make twenty grand a year. But thanks to me, you're already a bestseller. Because I lit a fire under your butt and made you work hard!"

For a moment, I couldn't even react. It was that ridiculous. But then, I should've expected he'd find a way to twist this so that no matter what happened he was still the winner. "So if I hadn't hit number one, that's when you would've lost?"

"No, because I would've won the bet."

Heads I win, tails you lose. It pissed me off, but I knew the longer I argued with him, the angrier I'd get. And he would never realize or accept he was wrong. It was best to cut this short, because my inbox was exploding. They mattered more than him, which was sad but true. "You know what? I never needed you to be successful. So screw you and your idiotic justifications."

He *tsk*ed. "Come on, now," he said. "Credit where credit's due."

Of course. It was all him. All through my life, everything I'd accomplished was due to him, not due to my hard work. Suddenly, I was too furious. Just sick of his trying to steal the spotlight from every good moment in my life. "Fuck you," I said between clenched teeth. "Don't ever contact me again, because I don't need your brand of motivation. And you know what? I'd be a lot happier and more successful without you and your toxicity in my life!" I hung up, a growl stuck in my throat.

My phone pinged again, jerking my attention from my rage. A text from Holly popped up.

–Holly: Congratulations, and thank you for the screenshot. I will have the ads go out as agreed.

I stared at the text, then let my lips twist with bitter triumph. It didn't matter how Dad had tried to spin this. This weekend would be extra delicious, since I'd be at the signing to celebrate this with my friends. And Killian and I would have delicious, mind-blowing sex—again—on Sunday when I got back to Kingstree.

Killian

While Emily made sure nothing urgent required her attention, I propped my feet on a chair and picked up my phone off the dining table to look at her social media profile. Her team had to have posted about her topping the chart for the first time. I had a secret private profile that I used online, and I wanted to like the post and congratulate her there, although I'd already celebrated with her in person.

The graphic thanking her fans for their support in helping her hit number one was the first thing I saw. I liked it, then put "Congrats!" And because I couldn't resist, I added three hearts and five stars as well.

I scrolled down to look at the pictures her team had been posting to promote *My Fair Molly*. I should probably buy a copy to support her, even though I wasn't sure if I'd ever read it. No matter how much I told myself it was fiction, I couldn't help picturing the real-life Molly and Ryan, people I knew, in the roles. And that wasn't going to be good—

I went still. The next photo was of me and Emily at the dining table in my home. It was taken while Dev and his harem were in town, that meal when I'd said Emily's books were perfect the way they were. The moment was etched into my brain because it felt that special. I was looking at Emily, and she was smiling, her fingers brushing a corner of my mouth. When I'd looked into her eyes, I'd felt a connection so deep, so intimate that the people around us didn't matter anymore. Maybe that was why I hadn't noticed anyone taking the picture. It also had her book

The Very Bossy Engagement. Although it was in the corner of the shot, you couldn't miss it.

I stared, then read the caption.

Be a rock star. Read Emma Grant.

A cold feeling started in my gut, tendrils spreading cancer. My fingers grew stiff and numb. I gripped my phone tighter, staring at the photo and the caption, willing them to vanish from the screen. The comment right below the pictures caught my eyes.

Oh my God! Killian Axelrod! I had no idea he read your books or that you guys knew each other! This is so awesome! He's my favorite, and so are you!!!!

Emily had responded: *Thank you so much! I hope you like my new book coming on May 5! Don't forget to let your friends know!*

The commenter had written: *Don't worry! I'm sharing this in his fan group and all my friends!*

What the hell was this about? And if Emily was going to use me to promote her book anyway, why had she declined my offer yesterday?

My exes flashed through my mind.

I only wanted an introduction, is it such a big deal?

Smile! I want to put this on my Instagram!

What's the problem, Killian? I just wanted everyone to share in our happy moment.

The last bitter argument had come from Caitlyn. She hadn't understood why it wasn't okay to use me—and our intimate moments—to increase her following and popularity. Why I didn't want to livestream the proposal so that everyone in the world could be part of something that should've remained private.

Emily had made it sound like she didn't want or need me for that. Like she wanted to build a career on her own. But maybe she was just too slick to be that blatant. Or maybe she was just like others, who hoped to get away with it... Or at least milk our relationship until they got caught.

But unlike my exes, Emily had a team that took care of publicity for her. What if somebody there had used the picture without getting her approval? It was possible.

Give her a chance to explain. It might be nothing. You could be overreacting.

Emily made a growling sound in her throat, then checked something on the screen.

"Emily," I said, gripping my phone and getting up to move to the couch where she was working. "Who does your social media?"

"Umm..." She hit a few more buttons on her laptop, then looked up. "My mother does almost all of it, but my PR company also helps out."

"Does she do it independently?"

She looked at me oddly. "No. We talk about what we're going to say and what pictures we're going to use—or need to make. I trust Mom, but ultimately I'm the one in charge of my brand."

So Emily had known what Abby was going to post...and approved it. It felt like a huge betrayal, especially after she'd declined my offer of help. I didn't understand why she'd done it—or hadn't come clean about using the picture from the breakfast—and I didn't trust people whose motives I couldn't comprehend. And I especially didn't like people who acted nonchalant about it, like she was doing right now.

"You should've asked me before using my picture to promote your book." The words came out in an ugly, seething tone, but I didn't care.

"What are you talking about?" Emily said. "You aren't mentioned in any of the promotions."

I held the phone up to her face. "What do you call this?"

"What?" She squinted at the screen, then turned red. "I didn't know anything about that. But I can check and see who posted it."

"It's on your page, Emily. And you just said you review what people post there for you! You wanted to use it to sell your book! No wonder it hit number one!"

She went pale. "Are you saying I wouldn't have if it weren't for that picture?"

"Yes." No. Maybe. I honestly didn't know. But I'd be damned if I gave in. She didn't get to act all outraged after getting caught. Shouldn't "sorry" be the first word out of her mouth?

"So you're saying what happened is all due to you?" she demanded, her eyes flashing.

"Obviously!" A small voice in my head warned me I shouldn't behave like I was taking credit for her success, but I ignored it. I was too pissed off. I hated that she'd acted like she didn't need me to help with publicity—something I'd never offered to anybody else. Then she had gone behind my back and posted my picture anyway to promote herself. Maybe she'd demurred because she didn't want to look like she was using me. She knew I despised that. But doing it behind my back wasn't any better.

Her face crumpled for a moment, but I hardened myself. Tears, recrimination and accusations. I knew all the weapons in a woman's arsenal.

"You're such an asshole," she said.

"*Me?*"

She opened a browser and navigated to the page in question. She deleted the post. "There. It's gone. Happy now?"

But I wasn't. I was too angry, too worked up because what she'd done brought back memories of other girlfriends. The unpleasant doubt—especially when I'd been so high and happy—tasted of ashes. And deleting the picture didn't undo the fact that she'd used it. Used *me*. It stung. It was disappointing. And I felt like an idiot for believing what she'd said.

And I hated feeling like an idiot.

When I didn't respond, she clenched her hands. "What do you want? Do you expect me to give you credit for everything I've done? My writing has nothing to do with you. I was a writer before you popped into my life, and I'll continue to be a writer after. My accomplishments aren't about *you*! You have nothing to do with it!"

"I don't want *credit*," I shot back, furious she was trying to reduce the reason for my anger to something so petty. "I just don't want you to lie to me."

"If you think I'm such a liar, why are you here? Get out!" She pointed at the door.

The exact same fucking repertoire. Caitlyn had done the same. The only difference between Caitlyn and Emily was that the latter wasn't crying prettily.

I left, slamming the door behind me. But that didn't do a thing to improve my mood. The bang as the door closed felt like a shot to my heart instead.

Emily

I stood in front of my laptop, shaking, my eyes glued to the door. I couldn't believe Killian had yelled at me like that. Accused me of lying and using him.

All because of that picture.

Okay, so it looked bad. I didn't know it had been posted. I hadn't seen or heard about it, but I'd noticed that it was Mom who'd done it, since the account owner could see who had posted on their behalf. And I honestly didn't know why she felt the need to post it, except... Well, she was a huge fan—of Killian, that was—and might've wanted to brag or something. Which wasn't the smartest move.

But I was incredibly frustrated with Killian's reaction. If he'd just asked me about it without being so nasty, I would've apologized. And talked to Mom and told her not to do it again. But when he got angry and then made it as though without that photo, my book would've languished, my temper had flared.

Because he was acting just like Dad.

I'd worked too hard to let a man make it about him. One lousy picture didn't trump all the things I'd done—writing the book, and arranging and paying for promotion and publicity.

Bitter disappointment sat in my gut. Why had I thought he'd be different? Because Killian had kept saying the right things, done the right things and made me feel the right things?

Why hadn't I learned they didn't mean anything?

A hand over my forehead, I breathed out, muttering to myself. Then spotted the Dom that Killian had uncorked.

More than half the bottle remained, but I'd be damned if I was going to drink it. I'd taken it as a symbol of his faith in my ability, but that had been an illusion. He'd only wanted to buy it so he could look good. Like Dad had always done when he wanted to feign generosity.

I poured the rest of the champagne down the drain, washed the flutes and put them away. Through the kitchen window and trees, I could see his house. Another wave of anger surged.

This was supposed to be my day to bask and glow. Instead, all I had left was disappointment, anger, resentment and self-hatred for thinking that he could ever be a real-life romance hero. He was just an asshole. A villain. The worst kind, too, because he wasn't evil from the beginning. He made me think he could be different from all the rest...then showed his true colors when I realized I was in love with him.

Dick.

I couldn't stay here where I could see his house. It was just too close. I dashed to my bedroom and pulled out my suitcase. I needed to be in Northern Virginia to catch a flight to San Francisco. I was going to tell him about that today, then depart the day after tomorrow, but there was nothing stopping me from taking off now...and everything to make me want to leave.

CHAPTER 41

Killian

Emily didn't come by that evening or the next day. But then, I expected her to be stubborn. None of the women who'd tried to use me ever apologized. To them, what they'd done wasn't anything bad—just something they were entitled to in exchange for sleeping with me. Bitterness unfurled in my mouth, leaving a nasty tang. Their actions reduced everything between us to a transaction—intimacy for profit. I might as well have slept with a prostitute.

And I hated that Emily's behavior had made me feel like that again, when I really, really...

Fuck. I loved her. That was the problem. I thought what we had was real, that we could be happy together...and then this had to happen. Watching the sky turn dark blue in the predawn, I pulled a pillow closer. It smelled like Emily. I missed her now, even after what had happened.

There are literally three billion other women out there, my rational side pointed out. *Surely you can find another one good enough to fall in love.*

Emily is one in three billion. Should have been nicer to her. Maybe there really was an explanation for the picture. And you know perfectly well that one lousy picture of you couldn't have been the sole reason she beat her dad in the bet, my heart whispered.

But she really wanted to win that bet. Her mom said so. People will do anything to win.

This is why people don't fall in love. You use your head too much, rather than listen with your heart.

If people used their head more, they wouldn't divorce so much, because they wouldn't have gotten married in the first place.

I put the pillow over my head, wanting to drown out the pointless argument I was having with myself. My phone buzzed on the table, and I grabbed it, hoping it was Emily calling to apologize. I'd be magnanimous and say it was forgiven because... Shit, the things I felt for her were deeper than anything I'd ever felt for any other woman.

"Hey, maaan..." It was Dev. He sounded drunk.

The letdown was so abrupt that it hurt. "You out partying?" I asked, trying to decide if I wanted to talk to him if he was intoxicated. Normally I wouldn't mind, but I was out of patience at the moment.

"No. Wass thinkin'."

God save us all. "About what?" *Don't say an orgy.* It was too damn early in the morning to talk orgies with Dev, even if it would provide a much-needed distraction from my shitty situation with Emily.

"Found the bess place for you'n Emily," Dev said. "Betcha not even Felicia got anythin' better. You may thank me now."

The muscles in my jaw tightened. I wished he hadn't bothered, because now I was going to think about things I couldn't have. The mornings with her when she grumbled and hugged a pillow and wrinkled her nose, trying not to wake up. Or the days when she pounded away at the keyboard, murmuring to herself and lost in creation. Or the smiles she gave me, her eyes bright and beautiful. Every moment with her had been as precious and perfect as a sunny, breezy summer day with an endless blue sky. "Sorry, man. Don't need it."

"Wha—? How come?" His confusion was palpable. Then outrage followed. "Felicia foun' somethin' first?"

"Emily and I aren't moving in together." Because there was

no way we could after that ugly argument. And I said it like I wasn't affected at all, even though my heart felt like it was full of broken glass.

"What happened? Thought you guys were screwin' like bunnies 'n' had mad chemissry. Izzn that why you said no to the girls?"

Sighing, I told him everything. Might as well. I might regret it later, but at this point, nothing really seemed to matter. By the time I finished, he'd sobered up.

"Why does every woman have to be like Caitlyn?" I said.

"It's easier to change yourself than change the world, bro. World wants to use you, so you use the world back. That's why I screw everything. It works."

"I don't want it to be just sex." But he probably had a point. Depression started to weigh heavily on me. Was Emily going to do to me what Ashley did to Dev?

"Didn't look like it was just sex with her to me, either, which is the only reason I told her I was sorry. I had my assistant help me make it up to her by buying a print copy of the book. I'm going to take a selfie and post it. It might help promote the book, although I don't know how many of our fans read chick books. Emily seems like a nice girl."

Coming from Dev, that meant she was a saint. The kind of woman you took home to meet your parents. Apprehension ran its chilly fingers down my spine. Had I fucked up?

"I know you're in denial about this, but fame is part of us now," he said. "I grew up with it."

His mom had been a supermodel, and given him his pretty face.

He continued, "It's like a nuke. With the right handling, it can be used for good, but if you're stupid about it, boom, we're all fucked. Look, she might've just wanted to let her readers know you guys are together. You don't want her to hide the fact that she's with you, do you? Hell, some asshole might hit on her, thinking she's available."

"No, I don't." Just the idea of another guy made my blood boil.

"And you like her books, right? I mean, you were reading 'em.

So what's the problem? She didn't say anything that wasn't true. If some reporter asks you if you liked her writing, what are you going to say? 'No comment'?"

"Of course not," I said, starting to feel like the scummy crud on the bottom of my hiking boots. When did Dev become so... rational? At the moment, he seemed more centered than me. "I'd say I liked them."

"So let it go. She might not have thought it would be a problem. And she might not have thought you'd care. People knowing that you liked her books isn't a violation of your privacy. Trust me. Coulda been worse. I had a dick shot posted once. And the bitch didn't even have the courtesy to take it while I was hard. Took the damned picture while I was sleeping."

I put a hand over my face. It had been outright horrifying and ridiculous, especially since the girl had also tagged the band in the picture and sworn she'd get the rest of our dicks as well.

Dev yawned. "So anyway, man, just enjoy what you got. And chicks. And let the chips fall wherever. You can be uptight about stuff." Another yawn. "Okay, I gotta get some sleep now. Tell your girl I'm going to post the pic later today. And go kiss and make up. Otherwise Bianca's gonna get mad."

"Who's Bianca?"

"The blonde from Spain. She's hot, and we're going to hook up again when we're in the same town." Then he mumbled something I couldn't catch and hung up.

I put the phone down and stared at the ceiling. Dev might be right. I could've been overthinking everything. And after he'd given his sleep-deprived analysis, I wondered if I'd gone overboard. He was right—I didn't want to hide our relationship, or that I read her books.

I thought back on our interaction. Emily hadn't recognized me. She didn't check her social media profiles first thing in the morning to see how many likes and new followers she'd gotten the previous night. She didn't post endless selfies, or obsess about every like and comment and share. What she was concerned about was writing, eating like a kid and having fun with me.

To her, I was just a person—Killian the guy next door, not

Killian the rock star. She'd still be with me if I didn't have the trust fund from my parents or fame from the band.

And wasn't that what I'd been looking for? Somebody who loved me for *who* I was, not *what* I was?

Dread curdled in my belly like milk gone bad. I'd broken something that a lot of people spent a lifetime looking for. All because I'd been so busy thinking about all the ways Emily could be like my exes. How could I have been so stupid? I wasn't a fucking rock star. I was a fucking rock. IQ of granite.

I recalled the angry words from yesterday. I'd actually been more upset about her turning down my offer of help than seeing that picture on her account. If she'd asked, I would've likely said yes. If I was really honest with myself, I might not have thought much about it at all if she hadn't turned me down two days earlier.

Yeah, I had definitely let my past color my interaction with her.

An image of Emily's furious face flashed through my mind. She'd accused me of trying to take credit for her accomplishment —and beating her dad. Abby had said he liked to boast that Emily would be nothing without him. Did my behavior remind her of her shitty father?

I needed to explain that wasn't what I meant at all. Then convince her to give me another chance. And not just to move to Dallas. But be mine forever. I'd be damned if I was going to lose her. I'd do whatever it took to win her back.

Decision made, I showered and had a coffee. I was going to talk to Emily as a well-caffeinated, civilized person.

I'd apologize first. Tell her I'd been an idiot. Then I'd ask her to give us another go, because what we had was too precious to leave broken. It was fixable. It totally was. I'd grovel, too. I'd never done that, but how hard could it be? My coffee-pumped brain would think of something.

But when I went over to her house, the door was locked and she didn't answer. Was she too pissed off to talk to me? I looked around and saw her car was gone.

I pulled out my phone, then paused. *I don't know her number.*

It stopped me cold. We'd never exchanged numbers. What an idiot move. But it just never seemed necessary, and gave me a reason to come by when I wanted to talk to her. Seeing her pretty face was a bonus.

But now, it was terrifying I couldn't call or text. I couldn't figure out where she was so I could fix things.

I squinted through a window. Her furniture was still in the living room, so she probably hadn't moved out. She might've gone to Sunny's to grab some stuff. I just needed to be patient.

I went back home and wrote a note: *Can you come by when you see this? Or call me.* I added my number—the one I gave out to my family and close friends—and scowled. I should've written it on a sticky note. Except I didn't have any, because how often did I have to write someone a note?

Did I have any tape? Rummaging through the drawers only yielded a roll of duct tape. Better than nothing.

I returned to her house. The driveway was still empty. I taped the note to the door, then stepped back. There. No way she'd miss it.

When she called me, I'd come over. And do the apology. Might actually work out better, because it'd give me time to compose a good "I'm sorry" speech.

I went back home, sat at the dining table, pulled out a piece of paper and started to write out what I should say.

Emily, I'm so sorry. I didn't mean what I said.

No. I wadded that up and tossed it over my shoulder. I pulled out another sheet.

Emily, I've been a dick and I'm sorry. I just

Nope. Too blasé.

Half an hour passed and there was enough wadded-up paper on the floor to carpet half the Amazonian jungle. Nothing seemed good enough.

I checked the time. *Noon now, and still no contact from Emily.* She was probably too angry to call. I ran a hand across my mouth, feeling like an idiot for not thinking about that. I should be the bigger person and go over again. It wasn't like it was a long way. Maybe my brain would come up with a good apology while I walked. Like Emily, sometimes I had the best inspiration when I moved around.

I strode to her house. Her car was still gone, the note still on the door. Where was she? She couldn't have been out shopping this long, could she? Kingstree wasn't big enough for that.

Unease settling around me like a fog, I walked around and looked inside again. Nobody was home.

For once, I resented that the cul-de-sac didn't have any other houses. Otherwise some nosy neighbors might've noticed something.

When she still hadn't come back after three, my unease started turning into alarm. Had Emily's car broken down? No... If so, she would've called for help, and she should've been home by now. An accident? I quickly searched for news about car accidents in the area. Nothing came up.

Had she been kidnapped? Held for ransom? Kingstree was safe, but no place was completely crime-free. News sites didn't say anything about crime, but of course it would take a while for something like this to get reported.

Shit.

I stared at the phone, then remembered Emily and Mir had hung out together. Maybe they'd exchanged their numbers. A slim chance, but I called Mir.

"Hey, Killian," she said, her tone brisk. "Can't talk for long. Only got ten before my next meeting."

"That's okay. It won't take long. Do you know Emily's number?"

"Huh? Why are you asking me? Don't you have it?"

"No. She's not home and I'm worried about her."

A short pause. "What's going on?" she asked, no longer distracted.

"She's been gone since this morning."

"She didn't tell you where she was going or when she'd be back?" I could practically hear my sister's eyebrows arch.

"If she had, I wouldn't be calling you, now would I?"

Mir sighed. "What did you do?"

"What do you mean?" I said, not wanting to admit to my sister how much I'd screwed up. Damn it, I wanted to talk to

Emily *now*. And time was of the essence. She could be lying in a ditch even as we were speaking.

"You and Emily were like...*this*. And she left without saying a word. You don't even know her number. So what did you do?"

"We had an argument yesterday," I said with a sigh.

"Jesus, Killian. Women don't just leave for hours over an argument. Did you do something stupid?"

"It's fixable."

"*Fixable*? Remember what I said about not taking my favorite author away?" Mir said, growing agitated. "I knew it. I knew it!"

"I'm trying to talk to her, okay? Are you going to help or not?" If she wasn't, I'd have to find some other way.

"Depends on what you did."

"Fine." So I told her in a quick summary, because Mir was more stubborn than century-old rust. But laying it out made me sound like America's National Asshole.

"You *shit*," she whispered, probably not able to yell like she wanted to because she was at work. "I can't believe you said that! If she was a debut author, maybe I could see how she might think of using you. But she's already a bestseller! She honestly doesn't need you for anything. And it isn't like your groupies can read! What did that girl said at the breakfast? Oh yeah, something about how *The Very Bossy Engagement* has no pictures! Do you think that's the kind of person who likes Emily's books?"

Now that Mir put it that way, my reaction from yesterday seemed even worse. I wasn't just America's Asshole. I was Asgard's Asshole, too.

Mir continued, "I can't help you because I don't know her number. And you can't message her through Facebook either, because she told me she didn't manage that stuff. She said she has too many weirdos sending her dick pics and 'wanting to get to know her.'"

"Fine," I said, still staring at the empty driveway. I should just drive around until I found her. Hit the likely spots she could be visiting.

"Oh, wait. I think I know where she might've gone...although it's a little early."

"Where?"

"There's a book signing this weekend in San Francisco."

There was? In San Francisco? Confusion and disappointment mixed together. How come Emily hadn't said anything about it?

On the other hand, she'd been super stressed and busy with *My Fair Molly,* so maybe it had slipped her mind. And even if she wanted to tell me yesterday, I'd blown up on her. She definitely wouldn't have been in the mood.

Mir continued, "I wanted to go, but can't. Too much work. Anyway, I'm pretty sure she's going to be there because her name was on the list of authors. Oh, and I'm extra sad about missing it because a lot of hot cover models are supposed to be there, too. Maybe she'll find somebody to hook up with and continue to write. I mean, it isn't like you're the only guy in the world. And romance cover models are super sexy. Most of them are nice, too, I heard. Hotel rooms. Bars. Drinks. Voilà! And you know what happens when a pretty and successful woman is accused of using her guy's fame to further her career. She tends to get angry and rebound. Hell, I would."

Just imagining Emily hooking up with another guy... And why the hell did Mir sound so smug and happy about it anyway? "Whose side are you on?"

"Mine. 'Cause I love reading her books. Anyway, the next meeting's about to start. Bye!" She hung up before I could say anything else.

I stared at the phone, then recalled Emily's book covers. They all featured topless men in incredible shape. And if I absolutely *had* to be honest with myself, they could be considered good-looking.

And *those* guys were going to the signing? For what? It was a signing, not a concert that required backup dancers. Wasn't a romance conference supposed to be more, like...dignified? Basically just a gathering of bookworms?

Acid was starting to gurgle in my stomach. I called Felicia to launch Project Get Emily Back.

CHAPTER 42

Emily

I flew out of Dulles Airport on Thursday, after informing the hotel I was coming a day early. The clerk had sounded a bit confused, but the check-in went smoothly. I texted Lucy after unpacking my suitcase. It was about a quarter before six, and she should've already landed. Skye wasn't coming until tomorrow.

–Me: You in SF yet?

–Lucy: I just dropped off my bag. Why?

–Me: Because I'm here too.

–Lucy: What? Already?

–Me: Change of plans.

–Lucy: Woohoo! Let's hang out. Dinner and drinks! Just us girls!

–Me: What about Blue?

–Lucy: He's out with some friends. Boys' night out.

Perfect. I didn't want to be in my hotel room alone. Being alone made me think about Killian. And I didn't want to think about him. It wasn't good for my blood pressure. Or appetite. Or sleep.

–Me: Okay. Meet you downstairs in ten.

I went to the lobby bar a few minutes later and found Lucy there. Her purple hair was tied back into a simple ponytail, showing her pretty, friendly face. The dye job was new, so I figured she'd done it for the signing. She looked fabulous. And totally happy, as she should be.

I waved and rushed over to her, pleasure unfurling inside. "Lucy!"

A huge grin split her face. "Hey, girl." She hugged me.

I hugged her back. "So good to see you."

"You too!" She looked around. "Your man seriously didn't come with you? Or is he having a guys' night too?"

"He's..." I shrugged like it didn't matter—that I didn't care. "We had a fight."

"Oh no." Her face fell. "How come?"

"Long story. Let's grab a drink first."

She and I went into the bar, and were quickly shown to a table. I ordered a rum and Coke, she got a Long Island iced tea, and I started to unload everything. But trying to explain without letting her know Killian's identity was tricky. So I fumbled a bit, then settled on labeling him "somebody famous."

"Wait." She lowered her voice, but the light in her eyes betrayed her excitement. "So you really are dating *Killian Axelrod*?"

How on earth did she know? I tried to play it off. "What makes you say that?"

"I saw the picture on your page, silly. But I thought maybe it was somebody who looked like him that your mom found."

Well, if she already knows... "No, it really is him. And you can't tell *anybody*, because he's really particular about his privacy."

"Okay." Lucy nodded, but her lips twitched as though she could barely contain her excitement. But I knew her. She'd keep it a secret.

As I went on with the rest of what had happened between me and Killian, Lucy, God bless her, made all the right noises of sympathy and outrage. "What a dick. So you're through with him? There's no second chance?"

"None," I said, then took a gulp of my drink so I could continue to pretend I was fine. It wasn't as though I'd never broken up with someone before, but with Killian it was a million times worse. It was all my stupid heart's fault! It had said that Killian could not only give me the romance-novel sex, but romance-novel everything. And my head was partially to blame, too. If I'd just stuck to *true love doesn't exist in real life*, I wouldn't be so down. "Men just aren't worth it, Luce. The only thing that matters in life is what you can actually hold."

"You can hold a man. It's even nice, if it's the right guy."

"No, I mean like money and things, not a guy. And I don't like the whole process of finding the right guy. Kissing all these frogs sucks. Not to mention it's gross." I knocked back the rest of my drink to wash away the imaginary amphibian taste from my mouth. Lucy didn't get my unhappiness—or how nasty it was to deal with subpar men—because she'd gotten lucky with Blue. They'd been together since high school. So it made sense she'd believe in true love. "I'm going to go become a nun and write in some quiet, reclusive abbey." I'd make sure to pick a place so remote that no groupies could ever visit. Or stalkers. Or celebrities, especially rock stars. "Somewhere in the Alps," I added.

"Can nuns write about premarital sex?" Lucy asked.

"I don't know. Probably. And I'm sure nobody would care very much so long as I paid..." I snapped my fingers, trying to think of the word and failing. "You know, the ten percent church tax."

"The tithe," Lucy said, laughing softly.

"Yes. That."

"I know a better revenge." She leaned forward. "Write him into your next book. He can be the villain. And not even a sexy villain, but a dumb, bumbling villain with a small and permanently limp penis."

I chuckled weakly. Yeah, that was the most logical and realistic revenge. I'd done that to my dad in all my books, even though he didn't know because he didn't read my books and I never told him. So it hadn't felt all that satisfying. And winning the bet hadn't seemed to improve my satisfaction quotient either.

Killian could star in my next book as the horrible ex-husband of my heroine. Who was short, ugly, smelly and impotent. Coming up with a revenge character usually cheered me up. But right then, it didn't make me feel any better.

CHAPTER 43

Emily

When I got up the next morning, I dashed to the door and opened it. The hotel had left a bag with four papers. This was the day Holly should have had the ads appear. I needed my trophies.

After all, I didn't have much else to look forward to. Other than meeting my readers at the signing in three hours, that was.

My heart pounded as anticipation rushed through me. I flipped through the first paper, looking for the ad. Articles...more articles...some pictures... Ah ha!

To Emma Grant,

You are right. Romance is the most wonderful genre. It celebrates love and an optimistic future. Its readers are intelligent, interesting and lead fulfilling lives. And most importantly, they are amazing women who deserve to be as happy and beloved as the women in the romance novels they read.

I'm sorry I didn't accept that sooner. I'm glad you taught me better.

–Brandon Breckenridge

Bitterness and triumph hit me at the same time, two hard fists from opposite directions, stealing my breath and leaving me dizzy and shaky. At least he sounded humble in writing, even if he'd been a total asshole when we talked on the phone. My hands slightly unsteady, I took a snapshot of the ad with my phone, then posted it on all my social media profiles. I made sure to tag my dad so all his friends could see it, too. As the shakiness faded, gleeful pleasure started to bubble up within me, and I laughed, imagining the expression on Dad's face when he saw what I'd done.

Then I blocked him from my phone. I was done with him.

No matter how he tried to spin it, I'd won. I'd done it on my own. It had nothing to do with him, and he didn't get to take any credit. And I was proud of the fact that I accomplished what I'd set out to do.

I wish Killian were here to see the ads with me.

I scowled. *Shouldn't be thinking about him.* He didn't get to be part of the celebration, not after what he'd said and how he'd made me feel.

Not after breaking my old cynicism about love and making me think that he was the one.

I flipped through the rest of the papers so I could take pictures of them all before grabbing coffee and heading to the signing. Then stopped short.

There was another full-page ad:

Dear Emily,

I'm sorry. Can you forgive me?

–Killian Axelrod

P.S. You are absolutely awesome and amazing.

What the...? My mind went blank, then my pulse started to race as confusion and exasperation at myself surged. I had to be seeing things, because there was no way this was the same Killian

Axelrod who'd broken my heart. I must've just been really hung up on full-page ad apologies. I blinked a few times to clear my vision. The ad remained right next to Dad's. Was this really Killian?

Okay, so maybe it really was him, because how many Emily and Killian Axelrod pairings did we have in the world, and how many of those Killians had done something bad enough to warrant a huge apology? But a full-page ad? That was over the top, wasn't it?

I thought about it, running my teeth over my lower lip, uncertain what to make of this move. Why not just call if he wanted to talk? Why do this? He was always freaked out about his privacy and people posting stuff online. Although this was print media, it was still too public for his taste, wasn't it? If he wanted to apologize, why didn't he just ca—

We never exchanged phone numbers! But still... Wasn't this just over-the-top crazy?

My phone rang with a call from Mom.

"Did you see that ad?" she squealed. "That rat bastard's one I expected, but the one with Emily and Killian... That's you and him, right?"

"Yeah," I said, happy she called Dad something appropriate for once but not too thrilled she'd seen the other ad.

"Did something happen between you and Killian?" She sounded concerned and mildly curious, without a hint of judgment. Like that time I'd told her I was going to be a romance writer.

"We...had an argument."

"You should call him. He apologized. Publicly. It's like a fire signal that everyone can see."

That was true... Given how particular he was about privacy, this was a huge first move on his part. And just like that, my heart turned as gooey as warm chocolate. "I don't have his number."

"But he's going to fret. I always do when people don't respond to my texts."

I almost laughed. She was the one who was worried. "He didn't text, so he won't be fretting."

"But you're going to forgive him, right?"

"I'll see him when I get back to Kingstree." I wanted to talk with Killian first. After all, he deserved to know before my mom that I forgave him. "Gotta go. I need to get ready."

I hung up over her protests and suggestions about what to say when I forgave him, and felt my lips twitch into a smile.

CHAPTER 44

Killian

I checked for new texts as I stepped into the room where the signing was taking place.

–Devlin: Good luck.

–Cole: Ditto, bro.

–Max: Yup.

I nodded and inhaled deeply, clutching a print copy of *My Fair Molly* in my hand. I was wearing sunglasses, but people around me were whispering and staring anyway.

A lot of them had recognized me. They were pointing, making me feel like some kind of exotic animal. I was never going to point at an animal in a zoo again.

I ignored the stares and whispers and discreet raising of phones. These people didn't matter as long as they didn't get in my way. I held the book proudly, making sure the cover showed. Emily deserved my support, and this was the least I could do to show her I was sorry.

My body braced for a fight, I scanned the crowd for anybody who looked like a cover model. No buff men in sight, shirtless or otherwise. Mir had probably gotten confused. Emily was a classy girl who did classy signings. She wouldn't be throwing herself at a model, no matter how muscular or pretty he was. Those guys probably couldn't last more than ten minutes anyway. Where else would she have gotten the notion?

The authors were arranged in alphabetical order. It wasn't difficult to spot Emily at her table. There was a pile of books laid out on it, as well as a few boxes underneath, near her feet.

I took a moment to gaze at her. My heart twanged with longing and nerves, like when I'd gone on stage in front of a crowd for the first time. It was because I was gazing at my dream, a future I wanted more than anything else, personified by the woman in front of me. Emily looked so pretty, sitting there with a smile on her face, greeting each of her readers. She wasn't wearing glasses and she'd let her hair down, reminding me of the way she looked on our karaoke night. It was as though the fight we'd had wasn't weighing on her mind, and the only thing that mattered was making sure each one of her fans felt special.

She was a fucking pro. And I still couldn't believe I'd been so stupid.

I went and stood at the end of the long line. Somebody glanced at me, then did a double take. "Hey..." She squinted. "Are you...Killian Axelrod?"

"Nah, 'fraid not," I said, pitching my voice a little higher than usual. I didn't want to make this event about me. This was Emily's moment to shine.

"Wow. You look just like him," she said.

"Yeah, I get that a lot."

"I'll bet. It's eerie." She poked her friend. "Don't you think he looks like Killian Axelrod?"

The friend turned around. "Oh my God. I saw Axelrod in concert once. You could be his twin."

"Maybe we were separated at birth." They both laughed, but now I wished I'd worn a disguise. If I'd shown up in a professor-like outfit and a pair of nerdy glasses... Hey, it worked for Superman.

More people noticed me and whispered, but I ignored them, pretending people always mistook me for a rock star. I even ignored a few bold ladies surreptitiously taking my photos, gripping *My Fair Molly* more tightly even though it felt like ants were crawling inside my belly.

When I finally reached Emily, she looked up and went still, her mouth parted slightly.

My mouth dried, and my throat felt closed up, like I had a tie around my neck. I cleared it. "Hi. I'm your biggest fan."

"Um. What are you doing here?"

"Did you see the ad?" I couldn't call, so that had been the only thing I could think of to make sure she knew how sorry I was. Since her dad's ads were going out this weekend, I had mine go out on both Saturday and Sunday, just to make sure. She had to know how sorry I was. And how much I wanted to fix what I'd broken. If she wanted, I'd buy every copy of *My Fair Molly* in print right now. Or instantly compose an "I'm sorry" song and perform it.

"Which one?" she asked blankly.

Shit. She didn't see it, even though I'd put it in the four papers Abby had mentioned. If that was the case, she might not like what I was about to do, but it was too late now. I couldn't slink away like some spineless loser.

"Can you sign this?" I put down *My Fair Molly* in front of her.

"Sure," she said automatically, and flipped the cover open.

Then paused.

My heart went still. I forced myself to not squirm as tension wound through me. A fist tightened around my chest, making it hard to breathe.

She stared at the page for a long moment, then finally scribbled something and signed it. Closing the cover, she handed me the book. "Here you go."

No smile. No hint that she'd read or seen what was on the page. The ground underneath my feet seemed unstable, like a field in the middle of an earthquake or landslide. "Emily." Despite myself, my voice came out too tight.

"People are waiting," she said, then looked directly into my eyes and held them. "See me afterward."

I left the huge space in a daze and tried to breathe. Blacking out from a lack of oxygen wouldn't go over well. Then, remembering she'd written something inside the cover, I flipped the book open.

Emily,

I love you. Marry me.

–Killian

My grandmother's ring was taped to the page. It was the ring Grandpa had used to propose all those decades ago when he realized she was the only one for him. They'd been together all their lives...and so, so happy. And I wanted to use it to ask for Emily's hand in marriage because I wanted us to have the same amazing, loving life together.

Emily had written:

Don't want to do this in front of the crowd. See me after.

–Emily

My shoulders sagged. I rubbed my hand over my jaw. She didn't want to say no in front of everyone. She was too nice to upset and humiliate me like that, because of course then they really *would* know who I was. Maybe I should cling to the fact that she was nice enough to care about my feelings. Maybe there was still a chance that I could convince her to say yes when I saw her later.

Dream on, the cynic in me whispered. *If she was going to say yes, she would've said so when she opened the book.*

My phone buzzed.

–Cole: How'd it go?

–Devlin: When's the date?

–Max: We all gonna be groomsmen?

–Me: She didn't say yes.

–Cole: She said no?

–Devlin: Did you tell her you've never proposed before? She's the special one.

–Max: Why'd she said no?

–Me: She didn't say no. She said "See me after."

That sounded pathetic, even to myself.

–Cole: Oh man. I'm sorry.

–Devlin: Tell me what I need to do to make you feel better. Girls, booze, you name it.

–Max: Sorry.

I didn't text back. Even my band mates thought her response was a rejection. And my gut agreed. There were only two types of answers to a proposal: yes and not-yes.

But she said she wanted to see you after the signing. If you mope and don't come up with a plan, you're screwed. But if you get your shit together, maybe you'll get to change her mind, the determined part of me whispered. *Grab the opportunity. Take it!*

I inhaled. That was true. I still had a chance. No matter how slim it was, I shouldn't waste it.

I rushed to the concierge in the lobby.

"How can I help you, sir?" a middle-aged man in a dark suit said with a courteous smile. Then his eyes widened. "Mr. ...*Axelrod*?"

I started to tell him he was mistaken, then changed my mind. Dev had said that fame was part of who I was now, and that it was a nuke that could be used for good or bad. "You know who I am?"

"Know who...? Of course! I love your songs. 'The Danger Zone' is my wife's and my favorite."

I smiled. "Awesome. Would you like an autograph to take to your wife?"

He lit up. "That would be spectacular. Thank you, sir. Shirley's not going to believe this!"

"Not a problem. And your name is Piers, right?" I said, reading his tag.

"That's correct, sir."

I signed a stiff piece of paper he brought out. As I gave it back to him, I said, "Listen, Piers, I'm in a little bit of a bind. Think you could help me out?"

"Of course, sir." He drew himself up, the Axelrod fan being replaced by the professional concierge. "Of course."

"Great. I need to rent out your best restaurant. The one with the best view. The whole thing. If that isn't possible, then an entire, I don't know, terrace facing a garden or something like that. I need it today, for at least three hours, after the book signing over there ends." I gestured vaguely in the direction of the event. Given the number of people in line, I suspected it'd go on for at least another couple of hours. I wouldn't want to be the organizer having to face the wrath of a female horde, furious it didn't get to see its favorite author.

"I'm sure I can arrange something appropriate."

"Excellent. And the place is going to need flowers. Lots of them." Cole told me he'd arranged for a hundred bouquets to set the mood when he proposed to Teri. I wasn't going to fail because I'd forgotten flowers.

"Anything particular in mind?"

I thought for a moment. Emily had never mentioned her favorite. And I couldn't ask now. "Something that says, 'I'm sorry, I'm a dick, I love you, marry me, I'll make you happy.'"

"I begin to understand the dimensions of the issue. I assume that, ah, budgetary considerations won't be a factor?"

"Not at all. Spend what you need to."

"Very good. What about music? Food? Will there be any specific requirements?"

"My..." What could I call Emily? Not really a girlfriend, not a fiancée... "My lady will order when she's ready, so the kitchen should be prepared to make whatever she wants. As for music..." I paused and considered. She'd said she didn't do music. The only time she'd asked for it... Well, she'd wanted me to sing for her. But I didn't think rock would set the right tone. "Nothing. No music."

"No...?" He frowned. "Begging your pardon, sir, as I'm sure your experience in this area *vastly* outstrips my own, but one can't help thinking that the, ah, proceedings are more likely to succeed with music. I could perhaps make some suggestions on romantic pieces...?"

"Yeah, normally you'd be right. But she just doesn't like it."

"I see." He stood straighter. "Very well. You'll have what you need."

CHAPTER 45

Emily

My mind had been whirring since Killian asked me to sign *My Fair Molly*. I smiled and said all the right things to the fans, operating mainly on autopilot, but I couldn't remember much of anything.

When the signing was finally finished, Lucy and Skye came over, Skye's eyes as wide as the real sky. And they weren't the only ones. Other writers converged to my table, sharks sensing the most delicious food there was: gossip.

"Okay, so that was Killian Axelrod, right? Somebody said he just looks like him, but he's *identical*!" someone said, her voice somewhere between a scream and a squeal.

"I know!" Skye agreed. "It's gotta be him!"

"Or his secret clone," another author said from behind me.

I smiled, but I was sure I looked nervous. Lucy and Skye would be more circumspect, especially since Lucy understood I wanted to keep things discreet, but the other authors? I'd hate to have them track him down and post pictures of him all over the internet.

"Why would a rock star read romance?" Almost immediately after I said it, I realized how silly I was being. Killian had asked me to marry him. It wasn't the kind of thing I could hide forever. "It's a long story."

"We love long stories," Skye said.

"Yes, we do." There was a chorus of voices, everyone's eyes eager.

"Okay, fine. We met. And we spent some time together. You know. Romance takes its course," I said with a shrug.

"There's gotta be more to it than that!" Skye said.

"Just use your imagination," I said, then quirked an eyebrow to let her know I'd talk to her later.

I didn't think she understood my sub-rosa message, because she looked at me like I'd gotten all the bars in town shut down. I then remembered I'd told Killian I'd see him after the signing was over. "I gotta go."

Skye gave Lucy a significant look. "She's gotta go hook up."

"No! I have an appointment I can't miss." I grabbed my purse and started running before they followed me out. I waved. "I'll *call* you," I added, praying they'd get the hint.

When I was out in the hall, I scanned the area for Killian but couldn't spot him anywhere. Was he late? Had he *left*?

No, a man who'd taken out ads like that wouldn't just leave. Maybe he'd gone to the bathroom or something. I wished I'd gotten his number when he asked me to sign the book...except that would've been super weird.

"Ms. Breckenridge?" a man in a suit said. A golden pin with his name—Piers Mathieson—and division—Concierge—shone on the lapel of his suit.

"Yes?" I said, wondering what he wanted me for. Had Lucy and Skye sent a gift to congratulate me for topping the chart? But wouldn't it have been more efficient for this man to leave it in my room instead of tracking me down?

"Mr. Axelrod requested that I relay a message: that he is waiting for you on the rooftop garden terrace."

"Oh." For a second I was disappointed he hadn't come in person, then shook myself mentally. Did I want people staring and asking me if they were seeing *the* Killian Axelrod? No, I did not.

"This way, if you please." The man led me to the elevator, stuck his card key into the security slot and hit the RGT button. "Enjoy your time, Ms. Breckenridge."

"Thank you," I said as the doors closed.

The car moved smoothly to the top floor, not making a single stop along the way. I licked my lips, then clasped my slightly damp hands together. Nerves fluttered in my belly. I still couldn't believe Killian had asked me to marry me at the signing. Actually, I couldn't believe he even attended it. By all accounts, Killian loathed airplanes, and it was a long flight from Virginia to San Francisco.

I wiped my hands on my jeans, not wanting to appear overly nervous or anxious. Even though we'd parted after an ugly fight, the only response that popped into my head when I saw his proposal was a resounding *yes*. It had taken all my willpower to hold back and ask him to talk to me later.

But I wanted to know why he was proposing after saying all those hurtful things. What made him change his mind? I wanted to make sure we were both on the same page before we committed to something as huge as marriage. I might be cynical about romance in real life, but that didn't mean I wanted my relationship with Killian to fail.

Taking a deep breath, I stepped out into the huge garden. The lawn was lush and soft. Pink roses in full bloom twisted around twin arches. But it was the sight of an endless sea of flowers that stunned me. The air was heavy with their sweet fragrance, and I walked into the middle of it, where Killian stood by a table set for two, waiting.

He looked brilliant under the sun, his hair slightly messy, his blue eyes focused and determined. Although he was smiling, his jaw was set in a resolute line.

My knees grew weak, but I managed to remain standing, breathing shallowly. God, I was so nervous. And hopeful.

"Emily." His raspy voice sent shivers down my back.

"Hi," I said, unsure how to start.

"Wanna sit down?" he asked, pulling out a chair.

"No, thanks. I've been sitting for hours."

He nodded, then pushed the chair back. "I bought full-page ads in all those papers."

"Yeah. I saw." My mouth was parched. I felt like I should say something more, but I still wasn't sure what. If I'd run into him immediately after seeing the ads, I might've said, "I forgive you," but I was seeing him after he'd *proposed*.

He frowned a little. "I thought you didn't."

"How could I miss them? They were next to Dad's ads in the papers."

"So... I know they weren't really that eloquent." He frowned a little. "I wanted to say, 'I'm sorry. I acted like an asshole,' but apparently newspapers don't like people using words like *asshole* in their ads."

I let out a small laugh at how serious and annoyed he sounded.

"So I'm going to ask." He cleared his throat. "Can you forgive me for jumping the gun and acting like an idiot?"

I nodded. "Yeah. Thinking back on it... You tried to ask me who was in charge of my accounts, and my answer probably didn't reassure you."

"I overreacted because I thought you were the one." He took a step closer and held my eyes. "And you *are* the one. You make me laugh. You make me feel like a person, not some rock icon. When I saw you again at the signing, I knew I was looking at my future, and if I didn't hold on to you, I'd regret it for the rest of my life." He pulled out the ring he'd taped to the book. "This is my grandmother's ring. The one my grandfather put on her finger when he proposed to her. I want us to live in love and happiness like they did, Emily."

Love for him fisted around my heart, swift and firm, like it was going to be part of me forever. I couldn't breathe, and my eyes grew hot with tears of joy. I looked at the simple diamond solitaire. His explanation made the ring even more special. The vision of our bright future stirred in my head, expanding until all I could think of was us, loving, laughing and growing old together.

Killian dropped to one knee. "I love you, Emily. Will you marry me?"

"Yes. Of course I will."

Smiling, he rose to his feet and put the ring on my finger.

I kissed the man who made me believe real love could exist in real life. "I love you too. We're going to be awesome, Killian."

CHAPTER 46

Emily

September in Virginia was perfect for an outdoor wedding—still warm, but without the oppressive heat of July and August. The sky was high and clear, just white, fluffy clouds dotting the endless azure.

I'd told Killian an outdoor event would attract paparazzi, but he'd said he wanted everyone in the world to know he was marrying me. "You're mine, all mine." I'd smiled, since that was sweet, and I was happy he was becoming less uptight about that kind of publicity.

Since we didn't have a ton of time to prepare, I'd considered wearing my mom's dress, but she categorically refused to even consider the idea. She insisted I needed something new—not a dress tainted with something as terrible as her own marriage. And as of yesterday, that marriage had become a thing of the past. Thanks to the kick-ass lawyer Killian had helped me find for Mom, she got to flip Dad the bird. Legally speaking, of course.

"Give me, like, two seconds. I'm on my last sentence," I said, typing away in the bride's dressing room as Mom fussed with my hair and the small train on my wedding gown. I knew it was ridiculous to still be working on my book, but I didn't want to be wrestling with it on the honeymoon.

"I can't believe you set your wedding date as your deadline!" Mom said.

"I didn't! It was supposed to be done two weeks ago. I just couldn't meet the original deadline because of a certain person."

"Who on earth are you talking about?" She sounded bewildered.

Oh, for God's sake. I typed *The End,* saved the manuscript and sent it to my editor. Then I shut the lid on my laptop and spun around to face my mom. "You! The certain person is you. You've been dragging me around everywhere."

"Because weddings don't plan themselves! You know that!"

"Well, I certainly do now."

"It's the same thing as books not writing themselves."

"Ha! Okay, fine, you have a point. But see, now that I'm done, I don't have to work on it on my honeymoon!" This book was my gift to Killian and Mom, since the bad guys in the story were modeled after Caitlyn and Dad. And it was my revenge as well. Never piss an author off if you didn't want to end up as a bad guy in a book.

"Were you going to?" Skye said. She and Lucy were my bridesmaids. And they were in hot pink dresses—my favorite color.

"Of course she wasn't," Lucy said. "Look at her! She's gorgeous. Very bridal. And brides don't work on honeymoons. It's totally illegal. Now come here," she said to me. "We need to take a picture."

Lucy gestured to Skye and Mom, then took a selfie with the four of us.

"I wish we could have rock star weddings all the time," Skye said. "You wouldn't believe how well the kids behaved after I told them that if they didn't, they weren't coming."

I laughed. "Well. I don't know if there are going to be more weddings." The other three members of the band weren't anywhere close to matrimony. Even Cole, who'd been engaged for a while, hadn't set a date.

"It's time!" Mom said, checking her phone. She handed me a bouquet made with pink and purple roses. "You look amazing. I'm so proud of you."

Since my dad was in a snit about me and Killian helping Mom with the divorce, he had claimed he wasn't coming. But I suspected it had more to do with the fact that Killian had already told him he wasn't welcome at the ceremony the day after I accepted his proposal. So Mom was walking down the aisle with me. Which thrilled me. Unlike Dad, she wanted nothing but the best for me and Killian.

She and I strolled out together onto the huge field. Killian stood in a tux at the altar, his hair falling around his stunning face and his even more beautiful blue eyes shining with love.

As Max and Devlin began a rock version of "Here Comes the Bride," I walked to the man who would show me what true love was every moment of our lives.

CHAPTER 47

Emily

–three months later

I worked on my new book while Killian screwed around on the Internet, feet propped on the table and phone in hand. The band had just finished recording all their new songs, and were chilling until they could figure out the best time to release the singles.

Killian's shoulders started to shake. Since I was typing away, he pressed a hand against his mouth to keep quiet.

I saved the latest chapter, then looked at him. "What's so funny?"

"This." He showed me his phone, then started laughing.

It was a Facebook feed. And it had a live video of Devlin drumming away inside a high school gym. Even through the small screen, the excitement from the high school kids and parents was palpable.

Devlin had promised he'd make it up to me for bringing the Barbie Sextet to Killian's place. So when Skye moaned about the candy selling and additional fundraiser for her daughter's band, I had him volunteer to play at the school, with all proceeds to be donated to the band.

He'd grumbled, but finally caved. Then grumbled some more, but he honored his promise.

"The band director almost shit his pants," Skye had told me over the phone. I'd thought she sounded like *she* was about to shit *her* pants, but I kept that to myself because her enthusiasm was so cute.

Not only did the tickets sell out in a second—mainly because they were only twenty bucks each—but Devlin had also raffled off "a selfie with a rock star" and "a kiss from a rock star." (Not his idea, but mine, ha ha ha.) He'd actually objected to the second one due to worry about whether the winner might be underage. But apparently his lawyer had worked it out so that only people eighteen or older could collect that particular prize.

I had to give Devlin credit, though. Although this was just a high school fundraiser he was forced into, he didn't perform like he was coerced. He played like he wanted to give everyone the concert of their lives.

We must've caught the end of the performance, though, because Devlin soon put his sticks down. The band director came out and pulled out one ticket from each of the two huge bowls they'd set up on the stage.

He said something, which I missed. Somebody screamed close to the phone that was doing the livestream. Something hot pink flashed by. A woman rushed out, her body encased in a tight white top showing her midriff and a pleated pink skirt and silver heels.

Before Devlin could even properly stand up, she grabbed his face between her hands and kissed him.

"Oh my God, is she pushing her tongue into his mouth?" I asked, torn between amusement and horror.

"I think so. Dev looks like somebody's feeding him a hairball."

I laughed. "He doesn't look *that* bad." Okay, his eyes were slightly bugged out, but maybe he was just shocked at the level of enthusiasm coming from the woman who won the kiss.

The kiss went on and on, and Devlin started to get into it. Probably to give the woman her money's worth. The kiss raffle tickets were five bucks apiece. And who knew how many tickets the woman had bought?

Killian smirked. "Devlin's never going to bring his harem around again after this."

"Good. He's welcome to all the women in the world." I'd heard about Devlin's ex, Ashley. She was currently starring in my work in progress as a bad guy because I hated that she'd hurt him, and that he was still acting out. He'd denied his playboy ways had anything to do with her, but I could tell. It was definitely a case of the laddie doth protest too much.

I looped an arm around Killian, snuggling against him. "You're mine."

He kissed my temple. "And I'm always going to be, my pretty novelist wife."

CHAPTER 48

Killian

–two years later

I walked down the frozen foods section in Sunny's. *Come on...* Bouncy Bare Monkeys should be in. I'd bribed Jenny to text me the second they got some.

Ah ha! There! The final tub! I opened the door, then reached inside to grab the prize I'd been seeking...

What the fuck?

A hand with long, manicured red fingernails gripped my ice cream and refused to let go.

"Hey, I put my hand on it first!" I said.

"No you didn't!" Molly Patterson said, her eyes narrowed.

"Wanna check the security footage?"

Her face turned red. "Who do you think you are, Killian?"

"An expectant dad. You?"

"I have a birthday party to plan." Her nostrils flared and she breathed out like a bull ready to charge.

Time for a new tactic. I flicked my gaze to the floor. "Oh shit! Is that a cockroach on your foot?"

"What? Ack!" She jerked back while screeching like she wanted to shatter every piece of glass in the surrounding counties.

"Ah ha!" I took the ice cream and dashed to the cashier.

She quit screaming and started yelling. "Hey, stop!"

"Grabbers keepers, losers weepers." I swiped my plastic, then took the tub and ran to my car.

When I walked into our home—formerly Emily's home—Emily jumped to her feet. "You get it?"

"Of course. I'm the man!" I started to sing the *Rocky* theme, holding the ice cream over my head with two hands like a trophy.

"I love you, honey!" She rushed over with a spoon she'd probably been holding since I'd left.

I gave her the ice cream and watched her dig in like she hadn't eaten in ages.

She was in her first trimester. She couldn't keep anything down except ice cream. And not just any ice cream, but Bouncy Bare Monkeys.

Sitting down on the couch, I pulled her on my lap and kissed the side of her neck. "That good, huh?" I teased.

"Yes." She sounded a little teary. "You don't understand how cravings work."

"It's too bad pregnancy doesn't make women crave more bedroom action."

She snort-laughed. "If I craved any more sex, I'd never leave the bed." Then she looked at the tub...and me...and considered. "Hey..."

"Yeah?"

"Do you, um...want a bite?" she asked.

She was so freakin' adorable. I laughed. "Nah. Let the baby have it."

She relaxed, then grinned at me. "I knew there was a reason I loved you."

"I love you too, Emily." Then, since it was Bouncy Bare Monkeys, I kissed her for a sweet taste.

TITLES BY NADIA LEE

Standalone Titles

Flirting with the Rock Star Next Door

Mister Fake Fiancé

Marrying My Billionaire Hookup

Faking It with the Frenemy

Marrying My Billionaire Boss

Stealing the Bride

The Sins Trilogy

Sins

Secrets

Mercy

The Billionaire's Claim Duet

Obsession

Redemption

Sweet Darlings Inc.

That Man Next Door

That Sexy Stranger

That Wild Player

Billionaires' Brides of Convenience

A Hollywood Deal

A Hollywood Bride

An Improper Deal

An Improper Bride

An Improper Ever After

An Unlikely Deal

An Unlikely Bride

A Final Deal

The Pryce Family

The Billionaire's Counterfeit Girlfriend

The Billionaire's Inconvenient Obsession

The Billionaire's Secret Wife

The Billionaire's Forgotten Fiancée

The Billionaire's Forbidden Desire

The Billionaire's Holiday Bride

Seduced by the Billionaire

Taken by Her Unforgiving Billionaire Boss

Pursued by Her Billionaire Hook-Up

Pregnant with Her Billionaire Ex's Baby

Romanced by Her Illicit Millionaire Crush

Wanted by Her Scandalous Billionaire

Loving Her Best Friend's Billionaire Brother

ABOUT NADIA LEE

New York Times and *USA Today* bestselling author Nadia Lee writes sexy contemporary romance. Born with a love for excellent food, travel and adventure, she has lived in four different countries, kissed stingrays, been bitten by a shark, fed an elephant and petted tigers.

Currently, she shares a condo overlooking a small river and sakura trees in Japan with her husband and son. When she's not writing, she can be found reading books by her favorite authors or planning another trip.

To learn more about Nadia and her projects, please visit http://www.nadialee.net. To receive updates about upcoming works, sneak peeks and bonus epilogues featuring some of your favorite couples from Nadia, please visit http://www.nadialee.net/vip to join her VIP List.